The Quiet Twin

Dan Vyleta

W F HOWES LTD

And I will take a further secret to the grave: that I once observed Mother, how she secretly went into the cellar larder, cut herself a thick slice of ham and ate it downstairs, standing up, with her hands, hurriedly, it didn't even look repulsive, just surprising, I was more touched than appalled. [...] Curiously enough, I like those of whose kind I am: human beings.

Heinrich Böll, *A Clown's Perspectives*

PART I

KILLERS

ONE

When Peter Kürten was but a young boy, he would watch his uncle attend to the slaughter of dogs. The uncle was a dog catcher by profession. This was before the Great War, in the final decade of the nineteenth century. He will have gone about it with a knife, the throat slashed ear to ear, and bled it into a bucket. It is not known whether young Peter was ever asked to eat the meat. At his trial, in 1931, Kürten reminisced how he had taken to torturing dogs not long after: he'd fed them with nails stuffed into sausage, watched them bleed to death from the inside. When asked whether it was this experience that had made him into what he had become, he demurred, and explained that the main responsibility should be seen to rest with the sensational crime reporting of the papers: it was the printed word that served as his inspiration. He also begged the court to keep his crimes in perspective. Compared to the doctors of the Stuttgart hospital who were responsible, he said, for more than five hundred abortions, his nine murders were the work of a mere amateur. Halfway through the trial Kürten changed his plea from innocent to guilty.

He was sentenced to death by guillotine and executed in the correctional facility Klingelpütz, near Cologne. Immediately after the execution, Kürten's head was bisected and his brain removed for scientific scrutiny. The head itself was mummified, and purchased by a collector of crime memorabilia. Today it resides in Ripley's Believe It Or Not! Museum in Wisconsin Dells, Wisconsin.

CHAPTER 1

He had not quite finished dressing when he heard the knock on the door. It was a quarter past eleven, a half-hour earlier than they'd agreed. He opened up quickly, a note of reprimand already on his lips, then grew flustered as soon as he saw it wasn't the party he had expected.

'What is it?' he stammered and sought to soften his rudeness with the ghost of a smile.

'It's the girl, Herr Doktor,' the woman said, eyeing him and the entrance to the apartment that also served as his practice with open curiosity. 'But I see you're dressed to go out.'

Now that his eyes had adjusted to the gloom of the stairwell, he recognised her as Frau Vesalius, the postal clerk's widow, who served as house-keeper in the main apartment on the first floor.

'What girl?' he asked, stepping out on to the landing with her, and drawing the door half shut behind himself. Frau Vesalius did not back away from him, and his movement brought them into uncomfortable proximity. He noted absently that she wore nothing but a dressing gown that was belted over a cotton nightdress; to this she had added a pearl necklace to make herself more presentable. Strands of hair were curling from beneath her hairnet, iron grey. He was struck above all by the coarseness of her features, and the cold, systematic manner in which she embraced her role as petitioner.

'She's sick and cannot sleep. She pants and raves. It is very frightful, Herr Doktor. I fear she has a fever. I tried a poultice, but she shrieked at me and told me to run for the doctor. I fear for her life.'

The woman's eyes sought out his own; he thought them mocking. 'Though if you are going out—'

'You go on ahead. I'll just be a moment,' he said and turned back into his apartment, shutting the door in her face. He considered for a moment taking off his good shirt and waistcoat and slipping into the clothes he had worn during the day, but then simply fetched his doctor's bag and made sure he had all the necessary instruments. His name was Beer. He was thirty-four years of age.

When he reopened the door he found to his annoyance that Frau Vesalius had not moved a step, and had waited him out right there on the landing. There she stood with that same hulking, insolent presence with which she had explained her situation to him, her fake pearls catching the light of the bulb.

'You lead the way,' he said, and she shuffled

down the stairwell ahead of him, slowly and as though rheumatic, though he noticed she did not feel any need to steady herself against the banister.

'So good of you,' she kept on mumbling, like a litany, but devoid of any affect. When she stopped on the landing to theatrically catch her breath, he lost his patience and brushed past her, went on ahead.

'I haven't much time,' he said.

She followed, quicker now, muttering abject 'Thank yous' at his back.

Once inside the flat, the postal clerk's widow refused to turn on the lights.

'The Professor turned in an hour ago,' she explained, in a sort of stage whisper as loud as normal speech, and instead lit a candle that she had ready beside the door. She led him down a gloomy corridor, past the stink of the toilet, and deeper into the flat.

'In here,' she pointed, stopping outside the door as though she were too delicate to enter. She held out the candle on its little metal saucer. He took it from her and ventured in, then turned on the bedside lamp before drawing a chair up to his patient. She was so wrapped into her bedding that only her face was visible, a small, wan face with deep chestnut eyes. Her lids were open but she was staring fixedly ahead, neither moving her head, nor any part of her body. The window was closed and the room was stifling.

'How long has she been like this?' the doctor

asked the widow, who hovered behind, observing his movements with studied servility.

'She's been complaining about headaches for days. And then, last night, she said she couldn't feel her legs and started moaning in her sleep. Tonight she has kept us all up.' And again that empty, jeering phrase of hers: 'I fear for her life.'

'Yes,' he mumbled, not turning his head. 'Leave us alone for a moment.'

He heard her presence shift behind him, then rose to close the door she had left ajar, and opened the little window to the night. Late-summer smells came wafting in, along with the heat of the city. The branches of the courtyard chestnut nearly reached the pane. If he stretched for it, he might be able to pluck a leaf.

'She'll be back,' said the sick girl. She said it so softly that just for a moment he wasn't sure he had heard it at all. It might have been he who spoke.

'I haven't much time,' he told her.

Her face and body showed no reaction. She was eighteen or nineteen years old, not a wrinkle in her pale and pliant skin.

The door opened a crack. It was Frau Vesalius again, leaning through the gap until the whole of her upper body seemed to have entered the room.

'Do you need anything, Herr Doktor? A glass of water perhaps? Or tea?'

'Nothing,' he said. 'Just some peace and quiet to examine the patient.'

'So good of you—'

He crossed the room once more to close the door, then returned to the girl's bedside. Slowly, deliberately, he took a watch from his pocket, opened it, then reached for the girl's wrist. It lay buried beneath her sheet.

'Please,' he said. 'I must take your pulse.'

She did not stir. He changed the watch over to his other hand, took hold of the lip of her sheet and drew it back far enough to expose a naked shoulder, and the sweat-damp ruffles of a nightgown; beneath it, the plump outline of a breast, the areola as big as a cow's eye. He hesitated and surprised himself by his hesitation. The girl did not move. Her eyes remained fixed upon some spot on the ceiling, a dense clot of stucco, painted over one too many times. He searched for some words to reassure her, to tell her she need not be afraid, but the conventional phrases seemed out of place with her. They sat in silence for a moment to the ticking of his watch, the smell of his cologne between them. He watched her nostrils dilate as she breathed, and imagined her sorting through the scent; was conscious of wearing too much of it, and of the incessant chafe where his collar bit into freshly shaven skin.

'I forgot something,' he mumbled all of a sudden, his hand still folded under the lip of her sheet, the backs of his fingers hovering low above her breast. He rose too quickly, stumbled as his foot got caught in the leg of the chair, and for a second he thought that he would fall on top of her.

'I will hardly be a minute.'

This from the door to which he beat a hasty retreat. He was out in the stairwell before he realised that his flight had been met by the faintest, girlish giggle.

Upstairs, Dr Beer took off his tie and threw his collar in one corner. He grabbed a sheet of paper and scribbled a note, then slid it under his door from the outside, making sure only a corner showed. He had already rounded the final turn of the great spiral staircase when he realised that he had not picked up anything he could pretend to have forgotten: no stethoscope or salve that might have covered his embarrassment. He would have turned around again, retraced his steps, but there was the widow, waiting for him outside the apartment door, attentive to his every movement. Her eyes sparkled in triumph.

'So good of you, Herr Doktor,' she started, but he hurried past without so much as a word. The layout of the apartment confused him for just a moment, and he found himself recalled after a step or two, like a lackey, or a dog.

'This way, Herr Doktor.'

In the cluttered hallway, between hatstand and wardrobe, it seemed impossible to squeeze past the widow without brushing against her chest. She stood aside theatrically, then started after him no sooner had he passed.

'We must not be disturbed,' he announced in an attempt to shake her, rushing to his patient's room and stepping inside it with great haste. This time it was the widow's giggle that followed him: a quick snort of a laugh that found him through the gap of the closing door.

Beer was halfway to the bed – his watch already back in his hand, his shirt and jacket sleeves turned up above his wrists – when he noticed she was no longer there, tucked under her cotton sheet, but was standing by the little window, half hidden in shadow. She was a tall girl, creamy; moonlight running through her nightgown and giving volume to her rounded shoulders, her overlong thighs, the narrow hips and boyish buttocks. Another year or two and she might grow into a beauty; first she'd have to learn how to stand, untangle those knock-kneed legs. Her gaze, he noted, was fixed outwards, past the branches of the chestnut tree and across the courtyard. He crossed the room and stood next to her; gauged the angle of her eyes. She seemed to be looking at a window almost straight across, located in the rear wing of the apartment building which had no direct street access, and cheaper rents.

'Do you see her?' she asked at last, the same quiet whisper that had spoken to him before, girlish, but also somehow sure of itself, the voice of someone fond of talking.

'What is it I am looking at?' he asked.

'There,' she said, and as she pointed he saw a

small figure pass behind a set of curtains, and then, for an instant, a little face press itself against the half-open pane before it withdrew again into darkness. The hair of the child was blonde.

'She's shy,' whispered his patient, and for a moment he thought she was speaking about herself.

'Who is she?'

She did not turn with her answer, kept her eyes on the courtyard before them.

'Lieschen. You must have seen her. She's nine years old and lives with her father. Wears a purple dress with a white sailor's collar.'

'The girl with the crooked back?'

'Yes, her. Her mother left her when she was three, and her father, he drinks. I watch him sit at the table sometimes and drink a whole bottle, all by himself. He will sit down at eight o'clock sharp, put a bottle on the tabletop and start drinking. Sometimes he carries on well past midnight. The strange thing is that he always uses a glass, or rather a tumbler. It's small, like a schnapps glass, only it is made out of metal, like something in church. It glows when it catches the light. I imagine if I was drinking like that, I would not use a glass. It puzzles me.'

She stopped, and half turned to look at him. It was the first time they had exchanged glances. It lasted only a moment. Next he knew, she had turned back to the window, moonlight on her breasts, too fleshy for her narrow frame.

'And the girl?' he asked, when the silence grew oppressive.

'We talk sometimes. After nightfall. In gestures, I mean. I will tell her a goodnight story, the one about the fox outwitting the bear. And she – she tells me how lonely she is.'

She smiled as though this, too, was a tale from a story book and, as such, touching.

'All that in a few gestures?'

'You think I'm making it up. There—' She pointed again to where a shimmer of blonde hair pushed through the folds of a curtain, then withdrew. 'She is shyer than usual tonight. It's because I have a visitor.'

He was left with an impression of a thick mop of hair, braided at the sides, a button nose, and a small, pink lip sucked in over the teeth. It was hard to know how he could have made out such details across the distance of the courtyard. It was as though the girl's talking made it so: the rhythms of her speech. She licked her lips between sentences.

Beer had watched her as she had spoken, surreptitiously, from the corner of his eye; had watched her mouth shape the words and her cheeks warm with their telling. Her own eyes had been busy with something else, however: time and again they had darted to another window, further to the left, in the building's side wing, a shabby, narrow structure, boxed in between the front and back, the cheapest living space of all. He was not sure if it was the first or the second floor that she was interested in. There were no lights in any of the windows; in one, on the far side of the narrow row, the tail end of a curtain hung carelessly across the sill, its hem tangled in a row of empty flowerpots.

'And who lives there?' he chanced when he caught her gaze being drawn once again into the darkness on their left.

'Nobody,' she said, and added a smile that let him know he must not believe her.

'You should examine me,' she added. 'You're in a hurry.'

Before he could answer, she had run back into bed and covered herself with the sheet: pulled it all the way up to her chin, like a six-year-old trying to impress her mother. Her grin was playful, dimpled; a bloom of colour on her pasty cheek.

'Are you sure you are sick?'

'Oh yes,' she said, earnestly now. 'I am very sick indeed, Dr Beer.'

'Well then,' he said and reclaimed his chair. His watch, he noticed, had been in his hand all this time.

He took her pulse, then drew back the sheet to listen to her breathing, and to test her lymph nodes for tenderness, beneath the jawbone and in the pits of her arms, then prodded her stomach and abdomen.

'Shouldn't you be asking what is wrong with me?'

Her voice was clear and free of coquetry, and yet he felt as though caught at something illicit. He ceased in his movements, his hands still on her body.

'I had the feeling,' he said after some thought, 'that you did not wish to tell me. Your – housekeeper' (her nose wrinkled at the word) 'she mentioned headaches and fever, spells of paralysis. Does it hurt when I . . . ?' and here he dug two fingers into her flank, just underneath her ribcage. 'Any problems with your menses—?'

She watched him perform his examination with great interest, gave short, precise answers when prompted, and volunteered at one point to slip out of her nightgown if that would make things easier for him. He assured her that this was quite unnecessary. His hands were certain, practised, her skin cool and supple to his touch. He was quite sure now that there was nothing at all the matter with her, but strangely he was not angry about her malingering, and simply persevered with his task. She interrupted him only when he – making a show of his diligence – shone a light into one ear and stood gazing into its depths with a concentration he knew to be studied. His hand lay cradled around his patient's cheek, as it always did when he performed this particular examination: one finger stretched along the line of the jaw, the rest cupped under the chin, and the thumb pointing up, across the soft plain between cheekbone and mouth.

'Does it feel strange,' she asked, her jaw moving under his fingers, 'touching women all day?'

'I touch men, too,' he said, more forcefully than was required, then blushed.

'Yes,' she conceded. And added, 'My uncle. He was a doctor, too.'

'He's dead?'

'No,' she said. 'He lives across the hall.'

It took him a while to take her meaning and he watched her stretch her chin above his palm, pointing towards the door and beyond, into the silence of the apartment.

'Speckstein,' he muttered, and thought he might have done better to add his title.

'Then you have heard of him.'

He shrugged and felt his jacket's shoulders exaggerate the gesture. 'His name is on the bell.'

The girl smiled and nodded, and under the guiding pressure of his hands she turned on to her belly so he could run some knuckles down the long crease of her spine. The examination complete, he buttoned up the back of her nightgown, and made a show of gathering his things. She watched, he noticed, with an air of focused amusement.

'The diagnosis, Dr Beer?' she asked at last, pulling the sheet back up to her chin.

'You know yourself that you are perfectly healthy.'

'You think I have been making it all up? The fever and the fainting spells? The inability to breathe? Pins and needles at the back of my legs?

18

Yesterday, I woke early in the evening and was paralysed from hip to toes.'

'Some form of hysteria, perhaps.'

She frowned, and sucked in her lower lip. For a moment she looked much like the girl he thought he had seen in the window across the yard. It was impossible to tell who might have taught the gesture to whom.

'Can one die from it?' she asked, very serious now. 'This hysteria of yours?'

He looked at her and tried to summon a levity he did not feel.

'I dare say no,' he told her. 'It's a sort of fairy tale one tells oneself. One does not die from the big bad wolf.'

She grimaced at that, then stiffened one hand into a playful claw: emotions running so quickly through her features that he was at a loss to know how to interpret them. All at once he'd had enough of the girl, yearned for a cigarette, and a glass of brandy.

'I really must get going now.'

He gave a bow and turned to leave.

She stopped him at the door. He had expected it, had slowed down his step despite his supposed haste. And yet it caught him unawares, the inflection of it and the topic she chose, as though plucked from the sky at random.

'Somebody has been killing people. With a knife. Have you heard about this, Dr Beer?'

He shook his head and kept his hand on the

doorknob, where it had already half committed to its turning.

'There was nothing in the papers.'

'No,' she agreed, and he pictured her lying there, behind him, the body under its sheet, her eyes fastened on the ceiling. 'But you know about it nonetheless.'

'Well, then everybody knows. A patient must have told me.'

'Four dead in total,' she said. 'All within a few blocks of here. I drew a map.'

'Is that a fact?'

'Yes.'

She paused, and for a moment he thought she was done with him. But still the knob in his hand did not finish its turn.

'My uncle,' she started up again. 'Somebody killed his dog. Also with a knife. Friday week last. You think there is a connection?'

'I don't know,' he said, then took a breath. 'The unhinged mind is a medical mystery. It is capable of—'

'Yes,' she interrupted him. 'I think so, too. But you must go now. You haven't much time.'

It was this taunting phrase that followed him, out into the hallway, where the widow hovered by the light of a candle, wordless now, showing him the door, its locks snapping shut no sooner than he had cleared the threshold. He mounted the stairs in silence, his head tilted, the smile on his lips doing battle with his frown.

20

Upstairs, he unlocked his apartment door and found his note upon the floor. Beer could not tell whether it had been read and returned, or whether his visitor had never called at all. He unbuttoned his waistcoat and stepped out on to the narrow balcony; stared out into the courtyard. A light burned in a kitchen window across and below: a man sitting at a table with a bottle of liquor standing before him. He was in his underwear, a jacket thrown around the shoulders to keep himself warm. He drank methodically. It was impossible to name the colour of his glass: he kept his hand around it always, like a man clutching a rope. The doctor craned his neck to see into the other window Speckstein's niece had studied, but the angle was wrong and the crown of the chestnut tree was in the way. He went to bed at last, having smoked two cigarettes in quick succession, still wondering what had happened to Speckstein's dog.

CHAPTER 2

The girl lay awake through much of the night. A number of times she dozed off, only to come awake with a start: ran to the window then and stood staring out into the dark, or sat on the bed, straining her ears, one palm raised above her head as though to shush the whispers of her breathing. There were few noises to the night. At a quarter past two, Vesalius slipped past her room to use the toilet and sat there coughing, hawking up phlegm into the sink. She stopped on her return, the water tank's gurgle still audible behind her, and stood listening by the door for five, six, seven breaths, before shuffling back to her squalid lodgings behind the kitchen. The girl heard no more from her, and even crept after her to make sure she had gone to bed, the door closed, no light seeping from underneath its crack. At three, she raced to her feet when she was torn from a dream by the bang of the building's door beneath her. She stood, cocked her head, and followed the slow ascent up the main staircase, a drunk man's stumbles, making their way in fits and starts. Within five steps she had lost interest, though she continued to listen until the feet had come to rest, three flights up, and there ensued, upon the landing, a fierce little struggle with lock and key.

'Old Herr Novak,' the girl whispered sullenly into the dark. 'Drunk again. *Pani* Novakova won't be happy.'

When her tiredness threatened to overcome her yet again, she turned her thoughts to the doctor. His hands upon her skin. The memory excited her, and triggered a wheeze in the depth of her lungs. Smiling, she traced with her own hands the places he had touched, then lay stiffly for a moment until all sensation seemed to leave her body and only her face was alive with her joy.

'So I *am* sick,' she thought to herself and wondered when she could send for him again, and how much of herself she would share. Paralysed, smiling, she fell asleep, and did not witness her body unwind itself, burrowing comfort from out her bedding's embrace.

It was near five when she woke again and hurried sleepy to the window. At first she thought she had missed him: that he had returned and drawn the curtains, shut her out from his world. Then his face emerged, greasepainted, out of the darkness of his window: hung wide-eyed, unmoving, at the very centre of its frame, held up by neither noose nor neck nor block of wood. When she had first seen him, disembodied, it had frightened her and made her take him for a ghost. Then he had stripped one night, had peeled off sweater, gloves and tights, and hung them out into the wind, so very black that they cut deep holes into the fabric of the night. But even now, his secret lifted, it was tempting to think him nothing but a face: paper white, with hairline cracks running through its cheeks where the paint had dried and flaked upon his skin.

He was almost perfectly still.

She'd come to love this moment, the perfect stillness of his disembodied face, inhuman in its flatness. It was as though, she thought, someone had sketched some features on a plate of china, or drawn them on a bleached balloon, roughly, that is, with a line of shadow for the mouth, and great white orbs to frame the darkness of his eyes.

It was almost a shock to see the lips move: see them pucker around a crummy wedge of self-rolled cigarette. The glow of the ashes was enough to place something new into the face. She had seen it before and had struggled to put a name to it: had settled on *sorrow* but would not commit to it now, for it seemed too definite to her, and far too human. The face looked sad the way a fish looks sad upon the kitchen table, a bottom feeder, at odds with the sun. There was an absence there where one might have wished for the double line of lips. The cigarette was stuck in him as though through a hole.

That hole opened now, if only a crack, and a tongue emerged, paper-grey and solid at first, then thinning into nothingness as it flicked up across the length of face. On the next puff it stung his eyes, and an invisible hand rose to disperse the smoke: it passed like a bat before his cracked and painted features. Three more drags and the cigarette fell, was flicked in fact, in a flaming arc out into the yard.

She followed its path with her eyes and a sort of passion, curled her own finger into the tension of that flick. How she wished just then that she, too, were allowed to smoke, and to steal such poetry from a starless night.

When she looked up again from cigarette to smoker, the face had turned away from her, was lost in darkness, only to reappear in front of his corner sink and mirror, where he'd turned on a bulb that transformed his room into a stage. He shed the turtle-neck first, threw it over the back of the chair, the body brown against the whiteness of the paint. Then followed his gloves, his socks and tights, and soon he stood naked, scrubbing the face with washcloth and soap, until it came off and ran in gurgles down the plughole (she could almost hear it, across the silence of the yard). Today, there was no blood to join the rivulets of white, nor a knife, that he would dig out of some unseen pocket and stand there scraping with his soap. By increments a man emerged, dark-haired and clean-shaven, with a long scar down one flank.

He was in no hurry to get dressed.

When he was done washing, he bent and dug out a bottle from amongst a pile of clothes and magazines, then shuffled – still naked, naked! – over to the other room. She dreaded it, and revelled in it too, this moment when he stepped off the stage and into the darkness of a space unknown to her. It existed only in her head, in dark pictures of abandon. Here the curtains never opened, and no sounds travelled. Only once, in a rain-storm, a head had peaked out, had been held, it seemed, by a pair of strong hands, and shoved out all the way to the narrow shoulders and the firm rise of breast. This face, too, had been white and unmoving, but here there had been no evidence of paint, just a skin sheathed in its pallor, soon dripping with the rain.

CHAPTER 3

D r Beer rose early the next morning. He dressed in front of the bedroom mirror, then went out to buy a newspaper at the local *Tabak*, and a half-dozen rolls at the corner bakery. Until recently he'd kept a housekeeper who did his laundry and cooked his meals, a woman not yet forty and smelling at all times of the scorched coffee she liked to brew, but he had dismissed her a few weeks after his wife had left, annoyed at the knowing smiles he thought he encountered amongst his neighbours and patients. Besides, there was a pleasure in unwrapping the hot rolls and putting on the water, a homely magic to the spit of percolation. His coffee was no longer burnt. He buttered the rolls and dipped them in his honey jar, the honey flecked now with golden shards of crust; opened the paper and skimmed the headlines. The war was six weeks old, and glorious; Austria a proud part of the Reich. He turned to the obituaries in search of more sombre news, then on to the feuilleton; read a theatre review, a letters page, 'News Around Town'. Vienna was quiet, content. There was no mention of any stabbings, nor of the corpse of a dog.

27

first patient called at a quarter to nine. Soon
group of them sat in the waiting room off
ront hallway, riffling magazines and
exchanging gossip. Beer saw an old man troubled
by gout; a grocer with corns; an ironmonger with
an infected toe. A young widow of twenty-nine
came to complain of breast pain, and shot him
glances a hundred times more suggestive than the
blank stare of the girl, whose name he had omitted
to learn and who troubled him now, one hand
shoved into the woman's open blouse, his own
eyes closed as though in concentration. He
concluded the examination; ignored her banter,
the clumsy assertions that he had such 'gentle,
gentle fingers', wrote out the prescription for a
powder that he thought might purge her if it did
nothing else, and shook off the clammy hand she'd
thrust so boldly in his own. A boy was next, with
a cut on the knee, then an old bachelor itchy with
the clap. Then it was lunchtime and he locked the
door and slipped out of the coat he had donned
for his professional duties; sat down at the kitchen
table and ate a cold sausage with a slice of bread
and a little mustard on the side.

Not long ago, Beer had hoped to establish
himself as a specialist for nervous disorders. He
had worked in the clinic three days a week and
nurtured a growing private practice on the side.
He had resigned two weeks after his wife had left,
and, unable to find a big enough patient base for
himself, had soon drifted into general medicine.

Now he had only a handful of neurological and psychiatric cases: a woman with a phobia of open water who liked to regale him with the details of her boudoir, legs crossed and gazing up into his ceiling cobwebs; and a young man of good family plagued by inexplicable headaches. Those he saw in the afternoons, in the drawing room, where they sprawled upon a red upholstered couch.

It was the woman's turn that day. She came at two, and overstayed the allotted hour; started speaking while he was still busy helping her out of her coat and hardly stopped through the seventy minutes of her visit, though once he startled her by pouring out a glass of water and standing by until she had drunk. He should have been listening but found his mind wandering back to Speckstein's niece and his night-time visitor who had not shown, or else had left without a message. It had been foolish of him to write that note. He saw the woman off, finally, at a quarter past three, and stood in the hallway with his suit coat in his hands, unsure where to take his disquiet.

The doorbell rang, startled him. He was right there, not a foot from door and bell, and it stung him like a slap: that shrill, angry ringing. He jumped and feared arrest, irrationally, implausibly expected a uniform, the waving of a truncheon, neighbours staring through the cracks of their doors. Nonetheless, he opened up almost immediately; checked his breath first, and the knot of his tie, and opened the door, only to find the laundry boy with a basket in his hands: a pile of fresh linen to which was pinned the scrawl of his name. He blushed and bid the boy wait, a man really, gone twenty-five, and a mug like a horse; ran into his bedroom to collect his dirty under-wear, and scoop up a half-dozen shirts he had piled upon a chair.

They stood in the hallway, exchanging the fresh for the soiled. The boy was conscientious in counting off every sock and singlet, and folded the underpants carefully over one outstretched arm, like a waiter piling on napkins. His maths was bad and it took a while, horse-face scrunched under the strain, when, all of a sudden, the fuse burnt out and left them in darkness.

'Not again,' the doctor cursed, and rushed the man into his living room there to finish their trans-action by the light of the window. The oaf had to start over with his count: passed back whatever he had collected, so that Beer stood with linens over his arms and shoulders, and clutched in each hand a crumple of sweaty socks. Then recom-menced that ponderous arithmetic, until accounts could be settled to the lad's satisfaction and he left, basket in hand, a fistful of change jingling in his pocket.

Alone again, the doctor shook his head then smiled about the encounter; lit a cigarette and poured a brandy, found his hand still shaky with the ringing of that bell. Once calmed, he went to the kitchen and bent to one knee to retrieve a box of fuses from under the sink. He lifted it out, hesitated, and then replaced it again, his thoughts running to Speckstein, and the girl. His electricity was out, and he wished for information.

There was a place that could offer a fix to both.

CHAPTER 4

The janitor's flat was on the ground floor. Beer knocked twice before he saw the sign hanging from the doorknob informing him that the man was downstairs, in the cellar, where he had a workshop of sorts and seemed to spend much of his time. The cellar entrance was in the yard, a steep concrete staircase that led down into a low-ceilinged maze. Cold, damp air drifted up, was refreshing for a moment, then fell in a chill around his frame. A curious sound showed him the way, a rhythmic click of wood on wood, like the tapping of drumsticks as they count off the time. He ducked through a doorway built too low for his height, and entered the workshop proper. Empty window frames lined one side of the room, along with some dirty panes of glass, not all of them broken. There were two work-benches and a pile of lumber; a rough bookshelf, laden with tools; a bucket of paint, its glossy surface spotted with flies.

At the centre of the room the janitor had set up a curious sort of table, rectangular in shape and no bigger than the type found at a city café, its surface sanded and polished until it was perfectly smooth. On the edges of the tabletop, travelling the length of the table but leaving open the ends, the man had attached two lengths of board that rose above the table surface and acted as boundaries. It looked as though he had taken a small bookshelf, removed top and bottom and all of the shelving, then mounted it on four sturdy legs.

It was at this structure that the child and her host were standing, each positioned at one of its narrow, open ends; each holding a tool that looked much like a carpenter's plane, a solid wooden block growing into a fist-sized grip, but smaller in size and devoid of blades. Between them, propelled by the push of these wooden paddles, travelled a heavy wooden disc, smooth as the tabletop and gathering astonishing speeds. It was this that he had heard from the stairwell: the sound of wood hitting wood, as paddle bore down on disc and sent it shooting towards the other end. Both child and man kept their eyes on the table as he entered, brows furrowed in profound concentration. Dr Beer stood and watched, trying to fathom the rules of their game.

Its aim, it seemed, was to fire the disc past the opponents' paddle and across the open edge of table while protecting one's own edge from similar infringement. To this purpose they would aim the disc first at one corner, then the other; would shoot it off the wooden boundary at the sides in complicated angles, or slow the pace to a soft, quiet slide only to double it in the next flick of the wrist. There was great speed to the game, and it necessitated strength along with much skill. The doctor should have thought it ill-suited to a crippled girl.

The child stood perched on a crate, for elevation, or so he assumed. She was a skinny little thing with long blonde pigtails, her feet in gym slippers, their canvas uppers as dirty as her legs. He had seen her before, and now recognised her by the crooked run of her shoulders. The bones of her spine were visible through her skin and the buttoned back of her flimsy dress. Its colour was purple. She had placed her sailor's collar on a pile of lumber not far from her, presumably to keep it from getting sweaty.

Her position on the box was awkward, tilted, one shoulder thrust forward and her ribcage wedged into the wood of the table. He watched her play and realised with some surprise that she was very good at the game, with quick hands and a quick eye, her pigtails dancing every time she moved the puck.

Even so, she could not help losing.

Across from her stood the old man, a tall, massive figure, unshaven and dressed down to his shirtsleeves and suspenders, a blond man gone grey with his years, the eyebrows bushy around the blue of his stare. He was big-boned and athletic apart from a paunch that hung from his belt like someone had tied it there, a bulging parcel pert with gristle and booze. An open beer bottle stood by his feet. He, too, was very good at the game, slower of hand, perhaps, but astute in reading the movements of the wooden disc, and with great strength in his bony wrist. He flicked the puck across the table, flicked it harder and harder every time, until, finally, it outraced the girl's defences and shot right across the room into the bare brick of the wall. Then he reached down, picked up the bottle from off the floor, and took a long swig, while the child climbed down from the top of her box, laboriously, and ran to retrieve the wayward disc.

Neither of them so much as glanced at the visitor.

Beer watched them exchange five more points. They were, all of them, won by the janitor, and it made Beer angry, the old man's lack of kindness as he sent the child scrambling into dirty basement corners or hit her squarely, once in the chest and once on the arm, with enough force to raise on her bicep an angry little welt. The doctor had made up his mind to intervene, or in any case interrupt the game and suggest a gentler mode of play, when the girl finally won a point of her own. Frowning, her lips sucked in in concentration, she shot from wrist and elbow and managed to squeeze the puck between paddle and left-side border just as the old man was closing the gap. He touched the disc but could not prevent its slipping over the edge. It fell on the floor and spun like a dropped penny; clipped the glass of the beer bottle, recoiled, and rolled off into the pile of lumber. The point was greeted by the child with a jubilant, misshapen dance: right there, on top of the box, she stuck out a hip and raised both hands above her head, spun and cackled as the janitor got down on his knees and started digging for the disc amongst the narrow planks of wood, cursing underneath his breath. When he finally stood up, his hands and knees were covered with dirt. He picked up the bottle, took another swig, blue eyes sharp under his brows. His hair was cropped like a convict's.

'Twelve-one,' he murmured to the girl, the lips never moving, the words oddly slurred. 'Best take a break and see what the gentleman wants. How can I help you, Dr Beer?'

This sudden shift in attention flustered the doctor, as both man and girl turned to stare at him with great intensity. It took him a moment to recall his answer.

'It's my fuse,' he said at last and took his hat into his hands, though he knew it would have done better remaining on his head. 'The front-corridor light. The fuse keeps blowing. I've had to change it three times over, and today it blew again.'

'I have complained before,' he added when the janitor neither moved nor professed sympathy, the implements of his game still in his hands. 'Something has to be done.'

'I will put it on the list,' said the old man, not

to him but to the space that hung between them, unbridged, unbridgeable, yards of cold air. He produced neither pen nor paper.

'I will deal with it when it's your turn.'

'Very well.'

'Is there anything else you want?'

And yes there was, but he'd forgotten all the phrases he had meant to use, careful little questions that revealed nothing of himself or his interests, they had come to mind quite naturally on his way down the stairs. Now they were nowhere to be found.

Beer stood and thought and turned his hat in his hands.

The girl helped him, unexpectedly. She climbed down from the crate and studied him with great seriousness. Her movements were awkward, shambling, the head fused to her shoulders in a manner that gave to her figure a perpetual lilt. He had heard it said that she'd been dropped as an infant, dropped from a height that is, and spent nine months in a cast.

'You were with Zuzka last night,' she said. 'I saw you. It was quite late. You were standing by the window.'

She said it quite simply, as a statement of fact, but he blushed nonetheless before that name – 'Zuzka' – and the familiarity it implied. He felt the janitor's gaze upon him, curious now, one of his wrists rising to rub at his jawbone, then higher up, along the ear.

'A patient call,' the doctor explained more to him than to the girl, too hastily perhaps, his own voice pedantic in his ears. 'She has been unwell.'

'Speckstein's niece? Aye, I've heard such a thing.' The janitor let go of the paddle he was holding, simply tossed it on the floor, and scratched himself properly now, at the chin and above the ear. The doctor wondered whether it was possible he carried lice.

'She seemed upset about her uncle's dog,' Beer said. 'Apparently it has been killed.'

'Killed? Gutted, more like.'

The little girl heard the old man's answer and followed it with a gesture, oddly assured, as though she had practised it before. She made a spoon of her right hand and scooped deliberately at her midriff, from sternum to pubis, then dumped the contents in a pile by her feet. Standing before him like this, her chin almost on one shoulder, she looked even smaller than during her game, more fragile. Her eyes were turned downwards now, on the invisible offal she had spilled across the floor. Beer felt his own eyes fasten there and removed them with a jerk; straightened up to face the janitor.

'And this happened in his apartment? A burglar?'

'No, no. It was found in the yard across.'

'He kept his dog in the yard?'

'Why don't you go on and have a seat, Herr Doktor.'

And so they sat down. The janitor gestured for

him to draw up one of the wooden folding chairs that stood piled against the far wall, and brought another, more comfortable chair from the back room for himself. They sat face to face across five yards of concrete, the girl kneeling down between them, gathering the dress around her like a tent.

'Here,' the old man grunted and got up again to find a piece of cardboard to slide under her knees. She thanked him very seriously, then resumed her position, spindly arms wrapped across the hollow of her chest. The janitor waited until she had settled herself, then looked up at Beer, those old eyes piercing underneath their brows.

'So what is it you want to know, Herr Doktor?'

'Nothing,' said Beer, 'nothing at all, only it seems strange, does it not, a dead dog in the yard across. Did he keep it there?'

The old man shook his head. 'No, he kept it in the yard right here. For the past few weeks, that is. Before that, he had it up in the flat.'

'Why the change?'

'That's what the police wanted to know.'

'He got the police involved? How extraordinary.'

'Yes. Though really, it was the police that came to him. See, there was some fellow got himself killed, the very same night. Knife in the throat, I heard. Not the first one neither.'

'And so they came to Speckstein.'

'Aye. Some genius down at the *Wachstube* came up with the idea that this was why he put the dog out there, in the empty yard. As bait.' He snorted at the idea, then spat high across one shoulder. Both Beer and the girl watched the lump of phlegm land.

'And what do *you* say?'

'I think it's because the dog started pissing itself wherever it stood. Pissed in the stairwell half the time. I had to scrub the stairs down with bleach.'

'He should have had it put down.'

'Aye, he should've. I told him so myself. But he wouldn't have it. Loved the big brute, past all sense. So he put it in the yard, right there by the tree, on a good length of rope. He would sit with it all through the morning until the sun chased him in. I'm surprised you didn't see him there.'

'I hold surgery till after noon.'

'Well, he was quite a sight. Sitting there in his best suit, on a good chair, too; Frau Vesalius had to carry it up and down for him. A grown man, petting his dog and taking his coffee. Out in the yard! A jacket and tie on him, and cufflinks. It was like he was going to the opera. People would pass and didn't know what to do. Doff their hats and wish him a good day. The Herr *Zellenwart*. Some boys took to yelling abuse at him, but he made a list of their parents' names and that put an end to it.'

'How extraordinary.'

'Yes. And then one morning he comes down and the dog's nowhere to be seen. It was some lad that found him, in the yard across the road. Didn't call the police, mind, just left it there and showed it off to his friends. Took a whole two days till he heard about it. Speckstein, that is. Frau Vesalius says he went white as a sheet when he finally found his dog. Fell right down on his knees and cradled the bloody thing.'

'Cradled it? Down on his knees?'

'Like a babe. Mind, I didn't see it for myself. Happened sure enough, though. I even had a police detective here, looking sheepish. Said he had never investigated a dog killing before.'

'How extraordinary,' Beer said yet again, aware of the repetition, then sat pondering while both the girl and the old man studied him intently. He looked from one to the other, comparing their stares. The girl's was open, and very serious: it was the face he himself tried to assume when he spoke to a patient about his or her ills. He didn't think he had ever managed it as well as this, the very picture of good faith, her thoughts a mystery underneath. The old man's features were less composed. There was amusement there, about the fact that the good doctor seemed so interested in the neighbourhood gossip, as well as wonder, about the ways of the rich; and surliness, too, born of long habit, and resentful now for having been upstaged.

'And they are sure there is a connection to the murders?' Beer asked at last. 'The Fräulein said—'

But at this very moment he was interrupted by a noise behind him and turned to see a man enter

41

the cellar workshop. It was impossible to tell whether the man had just arrived or had been standing outside, in the darkness of the hallway, and chosen this moment to stage his entrance. He was an extraordinary sight, or in any case sick: an emaciated young man, very thin and even somehow physically crumpled, with stringy blond hair and an ill-fitting suit. Beer knew him from his practice. He was a night watchman who lived in one of the garret flats and suffered from chronic bronchitis. Beer had ministered to him twice, both times without accepting payment, and remembered only the man's anxious talk about his duty: he had refused, both times, to be written sick and had dragged his body over to the warehouse where he sat all night waiting for burglars who never came. Now he gestured to the janitor with jerky agitation, and even walked over to him to whisper urgently into his ear.

The janitor nodded and stood.

'I'm afraid I have business to attend to,' he muttered abruptly, then folded up Beer's chair no sooner had he risen and shaken the man's dirty, massive hand. 'A pleasure talking to you, Herr Doktor.'

Beer had no choice then but to walk out, replacing his hat as he climbed the stairs up to the courtyard and the bright October sun.

CHAPTER 5

He was barely out when the girl came running up after him. She had retrieved the sailor's collar and was busy fastening it on, then looked up at him with quiet composure. He'd stopped at the sound of her footsteps behind him and now stood wondering whether she wanted something, a penny or a sweet, and was too shy to ask. Beer went through his coat pockets in search of some money. She followed his movements with open curiosity, then frowned in dismay when he produced his leather wallet. He quickly shoved it back into his pocket and returned his eyes to the misshapen girl in the purple dress.

'Do you want to see?' she asked. 'I know where he was found.'

He looked at her in surprise. 'The dog you mean? You saw it?'

She nodded earnestly, bending her chest along with her head, and reached stealthily for his hand.

'It's right across the road,' she explained, as though she expected him to be skittish. 'It will only take a moment.'

They walked to the front door like that: she leading him by the hand, a half-step ahead. Up close, he could see the tendons of her neck, straining again the oddity of its placement upon her trunk. It must be a great effort for her, he thought, even to walk straight. One of her shoulders hung much lower than the other, and the torso stood oddly twisted on its own axis. Her pigtails bounced with every step.

Outside, the afternoon sun hung low over the city, drew long shadows on the cobbles. It was a hot day, no wind, the smell of baking in the air. The light caught the building's yellow plaster, gave grace and volume to its balconies and decorative mouldings. In the road parallel to theirs, a tram rattled past, announcing itself with the ding of its bell; and as though in response a piano sounded high above them, halting, hamstrung Johann Strauss, soon silenced by a music master's hoarse entreaty to please respect the rhythms of the Waltz. Strauss returned, stuttered, stumbled, found his pace, and a tit dived chirping from some ledge. Beer smiled at all this and thought that he'd not gone out enough, these past weeks and months: that he had avoided the city in daylight, for no good reason, naturally, and only run out on brief errands in the neighbourhood, then taken oddly watchful walks long after dusk. On a day like this it was tempting to think that the city was as it had always been, in love with opera and a cup of *Melange, Kaffeehaus* gossip about the latest scandal

44

on the stage. At the end of the street a chimney sweep tipped his hat to some schoolgirls: they cackled and blushed, then scattered like deer.

'The yard in there?' he asked his little guide, who was dragging him to a squat building somewhat diagonally across from their own. It was some fifty or sixty years older than most other structures in their street, its plaster flaking, the window frames low and plain and rotting with age. At its centre stood a high, narrow gateway – just wide enough to allow passage to a horse-cart or a car – that extended through the depth of the front building and led up to a sheet-metal gate, near six feet high, its dented surface broken only by the square iron grille that surrounded its handle. The girl led him on, from the light of the street into the darkness of this tunnel, its cobbles subtly grooved by the many wheels that had passed. Beyond the gate – visible to Beer on tiptoe – lay a small, rectangular yard, littered with rubbish and enclosed on all sides by two-storey buildings that housed a row of garages and workshops.

'But that's Herr Pollak's auto-repair shop.'

'Herr Pollak has left,' the girl told him as she pressed her face against the grate. 'They've been gone since winter. He and Frau Pollak. She used to give me raisin buns.'

'Left? I didn't know they were –' he started to say, then saw the scrawl of a symbol across the flank of one building, jagged like a scar. It might have been less prominent had the day been overcast;

Beer thought it shameless of the season. All of a sudden he wished to hurry on the sun.

'Things are prettier in the dark,' he mumbled, and the girl looked up at him as though she agreed. They stood in silence while the chimney sweep passed in the street behind them, black-faced under the warm October sky.

'The dog was found right over there.'

She stretched one arm through the bars of the gate, then hooked it into an acute angle and pointed to a pile of rubbish to their right. Beer could not see it from his vantage point and bent down next to the girl to peer through the grating.

'The rain washed away the blood,' she said.

'There was a lot of blood?'

The girl shook her head thoughtfully, made to say something, then sucked in her lip and settled on something else.

'You want to see up close?'

'We haven't a key,' he said, and for a moment he feared she would suggest clambering over the gate. 'Besides, it's private property. We mustn't break the law.'

'There's another way,' she said, and reached up once again to take hold of his hand. 'Come. There's nobody round there this time of day.'

Against his better judgement, he let the girl lead him to a small wooden door set in the side of the short tunnel that connected courtyard and street. To his surprise it was unlocked. Inside, a steep, open staircase led up to the second floor, while

46

the corridor bent ahead of them, turning sharply into the building's wing. There were signs of a recent fire, and a blackened mattress leaned against one wall. Beer remembered no fire but supposed it explained why the yard remained abandoned: its new owners would have to repair the building before business could be resumed.

The girl led him down the corridor, past broken windows and shattered light bulbs, angry slogans scrawled across the floor. Beer wondered for a moment what the neighbours made of this gutted building in their midst, then reminded himself that they were the same people who had witnessed the windows being smashed and the symbols being daubed, and done nothing about it. People like him. Some of them might even have lent a hand. In a month or two, the property would have new tenants, and a new lick of paint. Their name wouldn't be Pollak, but that was all: there'd be another kind of name – no different really, yet somehow better all the same – and a row of motor cars standing polished in the yard.

The girl let go of his hand and cut into a hallway on their right in a lopsided gallop. The corridor was narrow and so cluttered with broken furniture that for a moment Beer lost sight of her. When he caught up with the girl, he found her standing at the top of a staircase of three steps that led up to what must have been a service entrance to the workshop and was now blocked off by two large pieces of plywood, one of them stained by what seemed to be old blood. She stuck a finger into the wood's cracked lower corner, wrinkling her nose at the stains, and lifted the board up like a flap.

'It's loose, see. We can go in here.'

'We really shouldn't,' he protested. 'Besides, I'll get my trousers dirty.'

'I come here all the time.' She ducked through, then turned in the entryway, still holding up the piece of wood. Her body, in this hunched position, seemed intolerably twisted: bent double over the crooked line of her waist, her head and left shoulder fused at the seams. Her little arms were shaking with the strain.

'Here,' he said, 'let me help you.'

Before he knew what he was doing, he had mounted the steps and taken hold of the loose board. He crouched down low to do so, one knee pressed into the dirty floor. The little girl was close now, looking him straight in the eye: he could see the fine web of crystalline ridges that threaded her iris; the pink curve of her lip.

'What's your name?' she asked quickly, her breath sweet in his face.

'Dr Beer.'

'And otherwise?'

'Otherwise? Anton. Anton Beer.'

'Anneliese Grotter,' she said, then turned on her heel and ran ahead into the darkness beyond. He really had very little choice but to follow.

Getting past the plywood wasn't as easy as he had

thought. He tried to duck through as the girl had done, but didn't seem able to make himself fit; straightened up again and began pulling at the board in an effort to widen the gap. It wouldn't budge, then came loose with sudden violence and flew nail-sudden into his arms. He almost lost his footing and slipped off the stairs; threw the board behind himself in a temper, then stood peering about as though to check whether anyone had witnessed the mishap. But the corridor remained as deserted as before, and Beer quickly slid through the narrow doorway he had created, hoping his clothing wouldn't catch on any edges.

The part of the building that lay on the other side seemed unaffected by the fire and the vandalism. Within a few steps, the whitewashed passage Beer had entered opened into a sort of tea kitchen, roughly furnished with shelves laden with cheap plates and mugs and some tin cutlery. The scorched coil of an immersion heater lay not far from an empty metal sink. It struck him that whoever had left this place behind had gone to the trouble of scrubbing the sink clean until it sparkled, and he pictured Frau Pollak standing hunched over its surface, a wad of steel wool in her hand, her suitcase already sitting in the yard. The cutlery was dusty, but none of it soiled.

Beyond the kitchen lay a further corridor, which in turn led to a mechanic's garage, now barren of tools but still alive with the vivid smell of motor oils. On his right, the garage doors stood wide open, blue sky beyond. He stepped out and saw the girl waiting for him by the pile of rubbish she had indicated before, arms thrown high over her head, and rushing her body through a drill of awkward pirouettes that tossed up the hem of her purple dress. The yard was in disuse but not as badly littered as it had seemed from outside. Most of the rubbish was close to the front of the yard, where people had rid themselves of items of household waste by tipping them over the gate. Cabbage stumps and potato peelings lay scattered amongst broken bottles and the carcass of a bicycle, rusted beyond repair. A pulpy bundle of newspapers lay rotting in the sun.

When she saw him coming over, the girl cleared a patch of yard with her dirty canvas shoes, then threw herself down on to the ground as though gripped by a sudden seizure and bent her limbs into a particular shape, one knee tucked up towards her chest, the other stretched behind her, with both arms wrapped tight around her head. The doctor rose on tiptoe to see whether anyone was watching them from the other side of the gate, then crouched down very close to the girl, pulling down her dress a little where it exposed the edge of her dirty knickers.

'You shouldn't do that,' he said mildly. 'You'll get filthy.'

'Just like this,' answered the little girl. 'And the tummy was all slit.'

She gestured to her abdomen, and made a

disgusted face. 'There were rats, you know, but the boys threw stones at them and chased them away.'

'And you really saw it for yourself?'

'Him,' she corrected, then nodded. 'His name was Walter.'

'Walter,' he said. 'It's a funny name for a dog.'

She got up from the ground and dusted off her knees. 'Janitor says it's better this way because he was so very old.'

Her eyes darted up to see what he made of the idea.

'That's probably true,' he said, grudgingly, annoyed with the man for being so open with the girl. 'It's not a nice way to go, though.'

'No,' said the girl, and for a moment he saw in her eyes all the fear and horror that had been engendered by her encounter with Speckstein's cut-open dog.

She reached out to him, and he took her hand again, and together they made their way through the garage and the kitchen, and on through the windings of the corridors beyond. The girl was quiet now, lost in her thoughts. When they came out by the gate once more, she tugged at his hand and stopped him; stood once again with her temples pressed against the grating near its handle.

'I heard the policeman say something,' she murmured quietly, then sucked in her lips. 'He said – he said the dog had *"bled out elsewhere"*. What does that mean?'

'It means there wasn't enough blood on the scene. It must have been killed somewhere else.'

She nodded, then abandoned her stance and turned her back on the gate: a hunchbacked guardsman, turning on her heels, pigtails for a helmet, her lips rolled inwards over the double ridge of teeth.

They were back in front of their own building by the time she spoke again.

'I didn't like the policeman.'

'Why not?'

'Because he said that Father was a drunk,' she explained, patiently, as though to someone younger than herself. 'He is, you know, but it was unkind of him to say so. Don't you think?'

Her eyes had fastened on him yet again, were serious, haunted, playful. He had not thought a child could have eyes such as these.

'How old are you?' he asked, shaking his head in wonder.

'Nine,' she answered. 'Almost ten. Only thirty-eight days.'

'You're a very smart girl,' he said, and she blushed with pleasure and skipped through the open doorway, her body crooked like a broken doll's.

She ran to a letter box, reached up and through the flap to search its contents, pulled out a bent envelope. Each step was a broken dance: was broken, but a dance nonetheless. He was aware that she was showing off for him, and he thought he saw in her smile that she was aware of it, too. She drew closer once again to where he stood on the threshold with the front door still in his hands.

'Do you want to know who did it?' she asked, and curled a finger towards him.

Beer bent forward at the waist.

'The dog?' he asked, surprised. 'You mean you know?'

'Shine-a-man,' she whispered very seriously, shaping the sounds like she was a little unsure of their pitch.

'Shine-a-man?' he asked.

She nodded, raised a finger to each of her eyes and stretched the lids until they formed two narrow slits. 'He plays the trumpet.'

'Shine-a-man plays the trumpet.'

'Maybe,' she said, then turned away, as though no longer certain she should have parted with her secret.

He looked past her into the gloom of the house.

'Coming?' she asked.

'No, Anneliese. There is an errand I want to run.'

'Goodbye then, Anton Beer.'

'Yes, goodbye.'

He watched after her as she ran into the court-yard and across to the back stairwell, the right leg longer than the left.

It was only when she had disappeared from sight that he turned his back and headed for the tram stop up the road.

CHAPTER 6

Smiling, crooked Anneliese Grotter said goodbye to the doctor and raced up to her rooms. The stairs gave her some difficulty, the steps were so high, and she was out of breath when she reached the apartment door and dug around her dress pockets to locate the key. Her father wasn't back yet. He rarely came back before eight, and she had grown used to eating before he got home, then laying his dinner out for him on the kitchen table. She would sit with him and watch him eat: a humped little girl perched on the edge of the counter, her heels drumming against the door of the cupboard underneath. Sometimes, when he was in a good mood, he would tell her stories from work, of the day when the boss's mother had come to visit and told her son off for yelling at the men, or about the fellow worker who'd drunk all the oil from a tin of Polish sardines and minutes later shat his pants. She would laugh then, and make sure he ate seconds. There were nights when he would hardly eat at all. There were nights when all the food was gone and all the money, and he sat cursing, running dirty hands through the locks of his hair.

The girl climbed on a chair and surveyed the kitchen cupboards. There was still some cheese, a jar of pickled cucumbers, and a half-loaf of old bread that she could toast for him. They had no butter left, but the clay bowl was half full with pork lard that her father had brought back from work Monday last, and there were a quarter of a cabbage and some carrots for soup. Satisfied, she took out the lard and the bread and clambered down; made a sandwich for herself, ate it, then drank deeply from the tap.

Her hunger sated, she looked under the sink to see how many bottles there were left. Her father got angry when they ran out, and it was her responsibility to look after supplies. She counted one bottle of schnapps, and five of beer; three fingers' worth of Hungarian wine. It would do, but she'd have to run and buy some more tomorrow after school from the fat, smiling vendor across from the church. The money and ration coupons were in the drawer in the hallway commode. She fetched them over to the kitchen table and counted out how much it would cost, set two pennies aside for a coil of liquorice and three boiled sweets. Her chores completed, she ran into the bedroom where she slept all by herself. Her wooden catapult was there, and the little teddy she called Kaiser San for reasons even she could no longer explain. She curled up with him underneath her blankets, made a cave for herself and her little friend. There she lay and pondered, got into an anger with herself.

'I shouldn't have said anything,' she said out loud and pressed the teddy to her chest.

'It was only because he said that I was clever,' she explained to Kaiser San.

'It wasn't a lie though, and nothing you have to tell the priest. It was more like bragging because I don't really know. But Frau Vesalius said it was Shine-a-man for sure.'

She fell silent then, happy she had been able to explain herself, if only to a teddy who she knew herself was not quite real. Nonetheless, she took him along when some minutes later she got up again and opened the door to her father's bedroom. The room was dusty, smelled of cigarettes and dirty laundry. She wasn't allowed to clean in there, and felt illicit now, clambering through a pile of dirty clothes and crumpled papers. The bed was as large as she remembered it, the cotton sheet sweat-stained only on one side. The other side was very smooth: was dusty too, it must be said, but devoid of any imprint, as though the mattress here was good as new. At the top of the sheet lay an unused pillow stuffed into a cotton case the girl could not remember having ever been changed.

But she wasn't there to stroke her mother's linen, though she touched it briefly, with a timid sort of haste, as though reaching out to pet an unknown dog. Then she fell to her knees before her father's dresser. Here, under the button gaze of Kaiser San, she opened the drawers, one by one, and ran a careful hand through their contents, a book, some socks, an album of photos. She found it at last tucked into his undershirts, took it out and opened the blade: remembered him holding it, clutching his midriff, its point drawing a dimple in his pale and hairy skin.

'He wouldn't,' she whispered to the teddy. 'Surely, he wouldn't.

'He never ever would.'

When Kaiser San didn't answer her, she took him into her hands and pushed a finger in the hole where the stitching had come loose at the base of his neck, dropping his head forward, into a perpetual loll. 'He looks hunchbacked,' her father had told her, not drunk enough yet not to know what he was saying. She folded the blade back into the grip, then pushed the knife in through the hole until it had quite disappeared. Satisfied, having squeezed the teddy for evidence of the lump, she tucked him under one arm, closed all the drawers, and tiptoed out the room.

It was a quarter past seven. Her father wouldn't be back for another half-hour. A radio voice drifted in from the window, angry and insistent, and she passed the time in front of the mirror, timing her lips to speak along with the bark. There were gestures to go with that voice, and a rectangle of black moustache: a boy had shown her (furtively, behind a tree) in the schoolyard after class, hands curled into fists and shouting nonsense at the sky. She tried it now, her back bent like her teddy's, a dollop of shoe polish smelly underneath her nose, and fell into giggles when she thought she had got it right. She would show her father later, and there would be laughter, along with the booze.

TWO

Carl Friedrich Wilhelm Großmann met his victims in the area around Andreasplatz, in the Berlin district of Friedrichshain. Many of them were women travelling alone; not all were professional prostitutes. The neighbours saw these women go into his flat; none of them seemed to stay very long, though it was hard to say when exactly each had left. In the witness reports, compiled after Großmann's arrest, some suggested they had seen him with as many as fifty different companions. He offered them lodgings, and food. It was a part of town well acquainted with the idea of trading shelter for the pleasures of the bed. No one will have been surprised by the attendant noises. They heard nothing as straightforward as a plea for help.

Carl Großmann was a butcher by training. He ran a sausage stand at the train station, always had meat. There were only three murders with which he could be charged; a body found still bloody in his bed. One can picture the detective, peeling back the sodden sheet, cringing at the way it stuck to her cold skin. Großmann's judges had no time to reach a verdict. He hanged himself in his cell on the 5th of July 1922. All this happened in Berlin: far from Vienna, where no comparable figure has ever been tried.

CHAPTER 1

It was a quarter to ten. She called earlier on this, the second night, and called more fully dressed, in a starched house dress and woollen shawl, her fake pearls sitting dull upon the fabric.

'Frau Vesalius,' he greeted her, noting her eyes, her mocking smile, the abject tone that framed her response.

'Dr Beer. If you please.' Her hand pointed downwards, into the ill-lit shaft of the hallway stairs. 'So sorry to impose.'

She turned around without waiting for an answer, and shuffled forward to the head of the stairs.

There was no need for him to fetch his doctor's bag. It had lain packed by the door the past two hours, and he had bent to retrieve it no sooner than he heard the ring: had worked the deadbolt with its handle hanging heavy from his wrist. All evening he had hurried himself, had taken a hasty dinner, followed by a hasty bath, impatient for the call that he knew would come. He'd gone to town especially to make sure he would not be disturbed, then felt the hours yawn before him like a valley that had to be traversed. He had tried reading, had fetched down a volume of a medical journal that had long called him to its study and sat down, legs crossed before him, on his favourite armchair by the corner lamp. It was little use. All he managed to do was spill tea on its learned pages, and later, having changed his beverage, a half-snifter of brandy. It was hard to tell why the girl's prospective summons excited him so. Any onlooker might have thought he had fallen in love like some grammar-school oaf, his notebook full of maudlin verse. The very thought was absurd. All it was, he reassured himself, was that he savoured a mystery. Beer's life had been dull since his wife had left and he had quit the hospital. He had lost contact with a good many friends; some had filed requests to join the Party.

They walked as they had the previous evening, the housekeeper leading the way with a ponderous rheumatic step until he brushed past and took the lead. Once in the flat, he turned to the right quite automatically, and was flustered when he saw the girl emerge from her room. She was still in her day clothes, though the blouse hung dishevelled from the waistband of her skirt and gaped at throat and chest. Perhaps she had fallen asleep wearing it; had emerged now for a glass of water, or to empty her bladder. When she caught sight of Beer, she stopped in her tracks and raised her hands to her hair, as though to search it for forgotten curlers. She had not known he would be fetched.

'This way, if you please,' mumbled Vesalius, and gave his sleeve a firm little tug. 'The Professor begs a word.'

Surprised, compelled, Beer turned his back on the girl. Vesalius led him to the left, deeper into the flat, to a set of double doors that separated the rooms overlooking the main street from the rest of the apartment. Her hand shot up to knock, a flow of rapid little raps that hammered home her delicacy of temperament. Then, not waiting for an answer, she pulled open the door, grabbed the doctor's arm and pushed him through the foot-wide gap, shutting the door on his heel. Her grip, he noticed, was extraordinarily strong; it stung him through the layers of his coat and shirt. He stood for a moment, rubbing his arm, and surveyed his surroundings.

He was alone. The room was large and well appointed, dimly lit by a six-point chandelier, each limb crested by a yellow, timid bulb. There was a grand piano on his left, and a dining table to its side; a cluster of armchairs underneath a row of windows, closed against the autumn night. Books filled the walls behind him, stood on cherry-wood shelves that rose high towards the twelve-foot ceiling, some four or five hundred volumes by his instinctive guess. He recognised some of the medical literature, long rows of clothbound periodicals alongside the classics of anatomy and aetiology, Benedikt and Koch, Näcke's *Atlas of the Brain*. There was little in the room that pointed to its owner's present occupation. A print of Dürer's *Rhinoceros* hung gilt-framed from the picture rail not far from the settees; underneath it, a serving table with an assortment of crystal flasks, their contents' amber accentuated by a candle.

'Ah, Dr Beer. I did not hear your knock. Very kind of you to come at this late hour.'

His host emerged from a door on his left and stood framed by the brighter lights behind him. He made a gesture to follow him into what turned out to be his study; took position not far from his desk, stood upright, shoulders squared and hands raised before him, as though steadying a lectern. He was an old man, gone seventy, bald on top, the face framed by an old-fashioned beard; still had his teeth, yellowed and somehow wet, as though covered by a film of mucus; ears bushy with the steel-wool bristles of old age. Speckstein was dressed formally in woollen trousers, jacket and waistcoat, the tie double-knotted in the English manner, his wire-framed glasses enlarging a pair of kindly eyes; the shoes worn and sensible, signs of fraying at his trouser cuffs and elbows. When he spoke, he had an old-fashioned Viennese musicality that brought back to Beer the Professor's lectures at the university: the patient fluency with which he had explained his points, the voice making quiet music out of '*mons veneris*', '*vulva*', '*pe-ri-ne-um*' and hardly a giggle from the rows of young men to whom these designations

66

remained mythical, signposts to secrets their hands had brushed in the dim light of some strumpet's abode. This was before the anatomy room stripped the female body of its mystery: queues of half-grown men, taking cuttings from a womb, their awkwardness now drowned in Latin. Speckstein had no longer been around to watch them then. He had sat in court, defending his honour against some 'beastly accusation' as the papers quoted him as saying, defended it in vain as it turned out, and was lost to the profession. It had taken the *Anschluss* to suggest a change of fortunes.

'Please, Doctor. Make yourself comfortable.'

The old man turned around for a moment to close the room's sole window, shutting them off from the noise of the street. It afforded Beer time to look around. The room was much like Speckstein's living room, furnished in the tasteful pomp of an empire now defunct. There were more bookshelves here, a long-case clock, and a gynae-cological chair of the type that had been popular in the 1890s: green uphostered leather and ebony leg-rests to assist the parting of the knees; the headrest shiny from long years of use. The desk was strewn with notebooks and clothbound files, the bronze head of Mozart weighing down a sheaf of notes. There was a Chinese vase, chipped at the rim, and a tasteful charcoal nude; Speckstein's portrait, arm in arm with his mama. Behind them, from the hook on the half-closed door, hung his uniform, like the shadow of another man. Beer found a chair standing near the wall and pulled it into the centre of the room before sitting down. His host, he noticed, remained on his feet.

'A drink, perhaps. Brandy, or a glass of wine?' Speckstein gestured towards his living room, then dropped his arm when Beer shook his head.

'My apologies. You must be wondering what all this is about.' He sighed good-naturedly, smiled, clasped his hands behind his back. 'I understand you have been seeing to my niece's ailment.'

'Your housekeeper called for me late last night.'

'Yes, quite right. And your diagnosis?'

Beer shifted in his seat, looked up at the smiling man.

'I have not come to any definite conclusions.'

Speckstein nodded, raised his hands before his chest, as though soothing an upset child.

'You can speak quite openly, I assure you, Dr Beer. Do you think she's play-acting? I tried to examine her myself, you know, but she would not stop screaming until I left the room.'

'It's hard to tell,' Beer answered after a momentary silence, unsure whether he was committing a breach of confidence. 'Your niece strikes me as the sort of person for whom the real and the fantastical converge. I doubt she is malicious, if that's what you are asking.'

Speckstein nodded, wet his lips. 'I believe it puts her under some strain. Living in my house, that is. Her father thinks me an opportunist, and a pervert.' He smiled at the last phrase, ruefully, but not without a depth of feeling, the smile crumbling into a mask of old pain.

'You know, of course, what I am talking about.'

Beer shrugged, embarrassed for the old man. Nonetheless he found himself pressing the point. 'Why did he send her to you then? Her father, I mean?'

'The university. He asked me to find her a place. He has a dream that his daughter should become a doctor, too.'

'An only child, I take it.'

'The sister died when they were children. Do you think her cut out for study?'

'I have only met her once, Herr Professor.'

Speckstein nodded at that, as though he appreciated Beer's caution, turned around all of a sudden, picked up a folder from his desk.

'I hope you can help her, Dr Beer. I really do. But there is another reason I wanted to see you.' His face grew tender, eyes melting behind their wire frames. 'Somebody killed my dog. I have reason to believe they may be after me.'

He held out the folder, then took hold of Beer's hand as he reached for it and cradled it in his own, the gesture old-fashioned, avuncular, strong. 'I should like your opinion on the matter.'

He let go of Beer's hand before his touch became an imposition; turned to compose himself; fetched Beer a box of cigarettes as he leafed through the papers; then took upon himself the 'honour' of lighting the match, in every gesture the tact of a bygone generation. Beer was embarrassed by it, choked on the smoke he inhaled, sat coughing into photographs.

The pictures were of the dead. The dog's carcass came first, photographed from a variety of angles. It was followed by a crime-scene sketch drawn with coloured pencils that itemised the bloodstains in the yard and classified their splatter patterns according to the principles set down by Hans Gross. Next was a man in uniform, stabbed through the eye, slack chin sagging against the bulk of his chest. He had died in the open, five blocks from this room; there was a corner store there, selling spirits and beer; a schoolyard and a church, a fountain with a broken spout. Further photos followed, the blood dark as ink in their flashlit black-and-white. Tucked in with the prints were folio pages with typed autopsy reports; detailed records of witnesses questioned and dismissed. Beer leafed onwards, to the end. He counted four dead in all.

'These are police files,' he said, returning the papers to the folder. 'I have no right—'

Speckstein interrupted him; drew close again to stand by his shoulder, one hand on the back of Beer's chair. 'It is entirely at my discretion. I asked for the files especially. From the Chief of Police. I have some influence, you understand.'

'I don't see what use I can be. I am merely a family practitioner.'

'You are too modest, Dr Beer.'

70

Speckstein walked to the bookself, ran his fingers over a volume that stood at eye-level, its spine embossed with a golden script. Beer recognised it at once.

'Your dissertation was a remarkable piece of work. A great advancement in the field of forensic psychology. Not to mention your articles on pathological cruelty towards animals; the lecture on comparative pathography you gave during the Bergen Congress. I believe Aschaffenburg singled you out for praise in his review in the *Monatsschrift*.'

He looked over to Beer, folded his palms before his lips, as though in prayer.

'Somebody killed my dog, Dr Beer. Slaughtered it. Right here, in the yard across the road.'

'Walter,' said Beer, somehow moved despite himself.

'Yes. Walter. All I ask of you is to cast a look over the files. And have a talk with the police. A certain Boltzmann. Like the physicist. With your permission, I will ask him to drop in on you and discuss the case.'

Beer acquiesced with a nod and a shrug of the shoulders.

'If you think I can help—' he mumbled, trailing off, then stood to take his leave from the man. For a moment he was unsure how to go about the process.

'I must get going,' he said vaguely, and was startled when Speckstein rushed over to once again take hold of his hand. He held on to it, too, between both his palms, his knuckles dotted with black moles.

'I am much obliged,' he muttered, seeking out Beer's eye, then turned abruptly and walked back to his desk, gave himself over to a frenzied search.

Beer found himself rushing to the door, but was unsurprised when Speckstein chose to speak again.

'One more thing, Dr Beer,' he said, his voice lowered to impress upon Beer the change of subject. His hands, the doctor noted, had found what they were looking for: another sort of file, its clothbound covers marked in inch-high ink with the address of their building. This was not a police file, strictly speaking, though its contents might easily be passed on to the police. It belonged to the realm of activities that, in recent years, had renewed Speckstein's social prominence, with the help of a notepad, and a host of informers.

'I hope you will forgive me if I remind you to be careful. In everything. These are' – the old man searched for a word – 'uncharitable times.'

Beer stood for a moment, trying to divine what precisely Speckstein was telling him. His face seemed open, free of malice, soft eyes gleaming behind their glasses. It was only the teeth that looked ugly; yellowed, clothed in spit. From where Beer was standing, already halfway in the doorway, it was impossible to see the uniform, hanging freshly pressed from its iron hook. It took only a moment to find the right words.

'Certainly, Professor. *Heil Hitler.*'

'*Heil Hitler,*' said Speckstein, smiling sadly as Beer took his leave as a good German should. Neither man raised his arm to complete the salute.

CHAPTER 2

When Beer stepped through the double doors that separated the Professor's apartment from the rest of the flat, both Vesalius and Zuzka were there, standing to either side of the entry. The door had been opened a few inches and he wondered briefly how much they might have heard, standing there, eyes locked and leaning against opposite sides of the wall. The girl's face was flushed and she was shivering, spasms running through her neck and limbs. He stepped close to her, and as he reached up to check the temperature on her cheeks, the doctor's bag he had been clutching all along bumped awkwardly into her shoulder.

'You are cold as ice,' he said, surprised, and heard a wheeze run through her lungs.

Behind him, Vesalius snorted, then gave voice to his thought.

'You must examine her at once, Herr Doktor.'

'Yes, I think I'd better,' he mumbled and took hold of the girl's elbow. Together, they walked to her room, where he sat her down upon the bed.

'A hot-water bottle if you will,' he said over his shoulder, and met the housekeeper's stare.

'At once, Dr Beer. So fortunate to have you here.'

She turned with a bow, and Beer instructed his patient to change into her nightdress, then stepped out into the corridor. He wished for a moment that Vesalius had been there to witness his display of tact, report it later to her master, but she was gone, making noises in the kitchen, the splutter of water as it was poured down the gullet of a kettle. The girl called him back long before it had boiled, lay on her bedding with her body exposed, the nightdress too thin to think of her as other than naked.

'You must keep warm,' he said sternly and watched her roll herself into the bedding, dragging one arm and one leg, it seemed, her lungs labouring over every breath.

'Have you lost any sensation?' he asked her, and picked up her calf, then dropped it abruptly when he heard Vesalius's step behind him, already far too close.

'The hot-water bottle,' she said, and handed it over like an infant for the burping. 'She will be all right, won't she? One can hardly sleep for worry.'

Beer sent her out without another word, then closed the door on her, wondering how long she would stand there, hanging on their every word. There was little he could do about it, and so he turned around to his patient; drew up the chair he'd sat on the previous night, reached under the quilt to place the hot-water bottle, then took hold of the girl's wrist and measured her pulse. It seemed to have calmed a little, and her skin was getting warmer. Only her lungs seemed to trouble her still, a rhythmic wheeze that rose in the room like the whistle of a far-off train. They sat, not uttering a word, conscious only of her breathing, until Beer gradually became aware of its echo, similarly regular and gathering in urgency. It came in from the open window, slowly rising in pitch, the rhythmic moan of a woman making love. They listened to it silently, avoiding each other's eyes, the girl's breathing now but a whisper underneath that steady, searching gasp. The pace quickened, then broke. One could almost taste the final grunt of satisfaction. When it was over, Beer got up stiffly and closed the window. Before he sat down again, the girl shifted her legs under her down quilt, its surface moving with the scissor of her thighs. There was in her gesture something so clumsily deliberate, he was tempted to walk out on her. He looked at the floor and left it for her to find a way past their awkwardness. She took her time. At long last she sat up, wrapped the bedclothes around her frame.

'I feel better,' she said. 'Thank you.'

She got up slowly, trailing the edge of her quilt as she walked, and drew to the window he had so recently closed.

'I should go then. Let you get some rest.' Beer rose from his chair, then bent to retrieve his bag along with the file Speckstein had given him.

'I'll be back tomorrow to take blood. You might have an infection.'

'Stay,' she said, reaching out a hand and dropping half the quilt in the process. Her fingers almost touched him now, but the motion stopped, a half-inch from his shoulder.

'Stay the night. There is something you should see.'

He hesitated, trying to gauge her intentions, and wondering what Speckstein would say.

She guessed at his thought.

'It's important,' she pressed. 'You can say I had a fit.'

He shrugged and nodded, put down his bag. The closed window reflected her face to him, showed him her smile. Her eyes were trained outwards, past the reflection, into the yard.

'What are you looking at?'

'The girl. She is sad tonight.'

'Why?'

'Her father.'

She pointed and he drew closer, shared the space before the narrow pane. Across from them he saw Anneliese framed between two flowerpots: she raised her hand in greeting when she recognised the doctor. In the window next to hers, Beer found her father. He was sitting at the kitchen table's clutter, his face buried in the crook of one arm.

'Asleep?' Beer asked, but Zuzka shook her head.

'Crying. He gets like that some nights. It upsets the girl.'

'She should be in bed by now.'

'I agree.'

She freed her arms once more from under the quilt, folded her hands underneath her cheek, telling Anneliese to go to sleep. To his surprise the little girl obeyed: nodded, as much with her torso as with her head, blew them a kiss across the yard, then turned around, a teddy dangling from her hand.

'Let's stay here a moment, while she falls asleep. She can see us from her bed.'

They stayed where they were, crammed too close before the little window, looking out into the dark. Only a small number of windows showed any evidence of life, thin strips of light leaking from drawn curtains, their seams aglow like cracks within the night. In the silence that had settled around them, Zuzka began to count them off, counted under her breath at first, but soon took to speaking at her normal volume, and collapsing a finger with every name she called.

'Family Berger,' she intoned, pointing to the row of windows directly above the little girl's. 'That's their boy, Lutz, with his light on. He just turned fourteen. I saw him try on his shirt earlier today. *Hitlerjugend.* He's been singing their songs. And there' – she pointed to the side wing, a third-floor window on their left – 'that's Klara Kovacs. She's divorced, they say, and makes a living giving English lessons. She has a little tabby, sits in the sunshine all day long. Frau Vesalius told me English isn't all she's teaching.' She paused to lick her lips. 'And right above her, that's Egon Kopp. Lost a leg in the war. I have never seen him leave his flat. They say he was a painter, back when he was young. The only time he's visible is around ten at night. I see him at the corner of his window, peeking out from behind the curtain. All you can see is the top of his head. I think he's watching Frau Obermann undress.' She pointed to the apartment above them, and smiled. 'Herr Novak told me, when he was drunk, that she never draws the curtains. Two windows to the right, it's Gerhard Neurath, but he's out now. Works as a night watchman. He used to be a waiter at the Café Central, I heard, but they kicked him out on account of his bad cough.'

She stopped to catch her breath, then wet her lips again, long tongue tracing the outline of her mouth. Beer took advantage of the pause.

'Do you ever hear a trumpet player?' he asked.

'A trumpet player? Why yes. Somewhere in the attic, I think. I listen to him practise sometimes. I have never seen him though.' She dropped her voice into a whisper. 'He's an Oriental, Vesalius says. From the other side of the world.'

'Shine-a-man,' said Dr Beer. 'Shine-a-man plays the trumpet.'

'You know him?'

'No,' he said, shaking his head, then turned around demonstratively, and sat down on his chair. 'You shouldn't do this, you know. It's what your uncle does: stand at his window at night, keeping a tally of the neighbourhood. It doesn't become you.'

Her forehead creased with displeasure. 'What's wrong with looking out the window? It's what everybody does. You think things were so different two years ago?'

He shrugged at that, brushed off his trousers with the back of one hand. 'Too many suspects in any case.' He caught her looking at him confused, and consented to explain. 'If this was a detective yarn, I mean. A reader cannot remember more than two or three.' He smiled, rolled his shoulders, bent for the bag. 'You should go back to bed. And I should be leaving.'

'You promised you would stay.'

'So I did.'

She returned to her bed, knelt down upon the mattress, then pounded her pillow into some agreeable shape, the straps of her nightgown falling from her shoulders with the violence of her movement. In all her gestures, she seemed half child, half village tart. Another sort of man, Beer thought, might long have contrived to hasten the transformation. He stared inside himself and saw his blood was cold. It hit him as a sadness, almost, and for a moment he wished he could explain. But there were no words for his feelings. So he stood to help her bring some order to her bedding instead. Together, they soon had her buried beneath a low rise of down.

'Good?' he asked her and she nodded, freed her arms, laid them down on top of the bedding.

'Just a little warm. What did my uncle want from you?'

He hesitated. 'You already know. You were listening in. Along with the housekeeper, like two children at a dinner party creeping up on the adults.'

She made to deny it, then burst into a laugh. 'Just imagine the scene, both of us standing by the door, pretending not to notice the other. She kept glowering at me, and I kept glowering back. We heard every word. *"Do you think she is play-acting?"* She was pleased with your answer, if you want to know.'

'Were you?'

She scratched her nose, like it didn't much matter to her; answered with a question.

'What did you make of the Professor?'

'I thought he kept the *Zellenwart* well under wraps.'

'The *Zellenwart*.'

She repeated the word that, eighteen months ago, neither of them had used or even known about. It came to them from the north, and denoted a kind of public spy, in charge of a whole row of buildings, each of them home to a lesser specimen of his breed, armed with a notepad, a

Party pin, a sackful of spite. It was, in Beer's estimation, a crude sort of job, performed by crude men. There were few professors in Speckstein's present line of work.

'My father says he raped a little girl. Years ago. That's why he had to resign. He was lucky not to go to jail.'

Beer nodded, hid behind a cough. 'Something like that. But he was very civil to me.'

'You liked him.'

There was no way to mistake her tone of accusation. Beer endured her glare and considered this; thought of the uniform hanging from her uncle's door.

'I suppose I did. Until he bid me goodbye, that is. And told me the police were coming to my home.'

He picked up the file he had been given. 'You have seen this before, haven't you? Last night when we talked, you mentioned four dead. And that you drew a map. There is a map like that in this file. Four dead, all within a few blocks of here, just like you said. I was surprised you would know in such close detail. From hearsay, that is.'

She blushed, pursed her lips.

'So I didn't draw it,' she said sulkily. 'It's true, though, isn't it? Somebody's killing Nazis.'

'Perhaps. I don't know. You should sleep now.'

'There is something you need to see.'

'Where?'

'It's too early yet. At four or thereabouts.'

'Sleep. I will wake you.'

'You will stay?'

'I promise.'

'Thank you, Dr Beer.'

And with that she went to sleep: drew the bedding up over her chin, closed her eyes, and soon drifted off, all tension leaving her body, and her breathing clear now, like the breeze across a field of rye. He watched her, watched her lips curl over a dream, a lovely, thievish, wicked smile; watched the ardour that passed like a ripple through her face, and the mischief, and the want; watched her lips move and her eyes roll, thick lids bruised from long and wakeful nights; and her left foot wiggle free of quilt and bed, pointing sideways up into the room, then hurry back into the shelter of the down.

Dr Beer watched all this, sitting on the hard, wooden chair not a foot away, his fingers leafing through the pictures of the dead. It wasn't long before he fell asleep himself.

CHAPTER 3

When she woke, she was surprised at first to find him there, slumped low in his seat, his chin on his chest, and a line of wet where he was leaking from the mouth. His hands had dropped to either side of the chair, hung lifeless, like the limbs of a marionette. It was easy at this moment to think of him as hers, to play with at her leisure, and she reached out at once to touch his beard, like a schoolgirl on a dare. He was handsome even in his sleep, perhaps more so: a closed man, buttoned up in his soul, the eyes like peeled almonds, half hidden under the broad brow. It was tempting to spend an hour just touching him; lie there, slide a hand on to his thigh. Then she remembered why she had asked him to stay the night and shot up in her bed; shook his shoulder in passing and ran to the window.

'We are too late,' she hissed. 'He's already got rid of his face.'

To her left, on the other side of the yard, lay the lit-up stage of her obsession. A threadbare curtain billowed in the breeze.

She heard Beer get up behind her, stumble to her side. Together they looked over at the young man across. He had just finished taking off his clothes. One saw the reflection first, staring waistup from his corner mirror, then the man himself. He stretched, both arms thrown up towards the ceiling, then began to pace the length of his room; lit a cigarette that dangled careless from one limber arm. She breathed and swallowed, excited that he took his time like that, parading for them without haste. The man was well built, and naked. The electric bulb caught the ridges of his shoulder blades, and, upon his turn, the sculptured line where the belly veered to avoid the hip and narrowed to the pubic bone below. His manhood was heavy, half-aroused, a purple knotting on his otherwise pale body; was familiar to her from long nights of watching, and shameful, too, for him and for her. Once he seemed to grab for it; scratched his thigh instead; turned with gusto to send flying that blood-engorged member. The girl and the doctor cowered in the window like soldiers in a trench: it was what she imagined war to be like, two snipers waiting for their cleanest shot. As they stood and watched, she reached over and took hold of Beer's hand.

'I'm married,' he whispered nervously, but she did not relent.

'I know,' she said, and placed a cheek against his shoulder. His jacket smelled of cigarettes, and day-old cologne. It upset her when he pulled himself free with sudden violence, and reached across her face to draw the curtain, cutting them off from the yard. There was to his face then that unsavoury quality – at once superior and benign – that she often found in her uncle: the paternal mask of enlightened discipline, calibrated in its wrath. Beer was getting ready to tell her off.

'Is that what you do every night?' he asked. 'Watch a man prance around?'

She nodded, smiled, was pleased to feel the tightness of spasm rush into her lungs.

'Every night,' she said, then let fly the ragged whistle of her breath. Beer steadied her, walked her quickly back to bed.

'Just a few hours ago you intimated that poor Frau Obermann was a trollop – and anybody watching no better than her.'

'Did I really? How inconsistent of me.'

'I'm through playing games.'

He moved the chair noisily, retrieved his bag and the file that had slipped from his knees and had scattered its contents across her floor.

'With your permission.'

He rose, bowed, walked briskly to the door. She gave him time to almost reach his destination.

'There was blood,' she whispered at his back. 'On his knife. The day the dog died.'

'Blood?' he asked.

'Yes. And he has a woman there. He keeps her hidden. I think she's not allowed to leave.'

Beer turned now, first to her, then to the window, pushed his head through the curtains to gaze across.

'It might be nothing,' he said. 'It might be his wife.'

'Nobody has ever seen her. There was blood on his knife. And people are dying all around the house.'

'Four,' he said. 'Only four dead. And only one of them a woman.'

'Will you go talk to him?' she asked.

'I will think about it.'

'You must, you know.'

'I could call the police. Or tell Speckstein.'

She caught his eye and saw that he wouldn't.

'If I was a man,' she said, 'I would go knock on his door. As a doctor, you see. Make out I was concerned.'

He seemed to consider this, searched his pocket for a gold watch, pulled it out and looked at the time.

'I need to go now, get some sleep,' he said. 'It's Friday. I will be doing house calls all afternoon. The young man across' – he gestured back to the window – 'he can wait for the weekend. Most likely it's nonsense in any case. A young man with a sickly wife. And a girl' – he smiled at her, condescendingly, tenderly, she wasn't sure – 'with too much time on her hands.'

'Call for me,' he added, 'if the paralysis recurs. And stay away from the window.'

He left hurriedly, before she could say another word. She heard him at the apartment door, fumbling with the deadbolt and the lock. Twice he put his weight against the door, trying to wedge it loose, the reverberations running through the walls. It dawned on her that Vesalius must have locked it from the inside: slipped shut the bolt and locked it for good measure, hung the key back on its hook. Zuzka swung out of bed, smiling, pleased at the thought that he could not escape her so easily, and made her way down the corridor in total darkness. The doctor had not dared to put on the lights, unwilling to wake the housekeeper. She was about to round the corner to the main hallway, when she heard Frau Vesalius's shuffle in the kitchen behind her: stopped and pressed herself into the gap between two hallway cupboards; smothered her breathing to a quiet rasp. The widow passed without the slightest hesitation and rounded the corner. Zuzka imagined Beer must have jumped when he heard a sudden voice call out at him in the dark.

'Just a moment, Herr Doktor. Let me find the switch.'

Light flared in the milky bulb above the door, chased shadows down the corridor. To Zuzka, who remained hidden around the corner, they turned into a play put on for children: she could make out Vesalius's hair, unruly like the wreath of snakes that crowned Medusa, and the square-cut shoulders of the doctor's coat; her crooked posture, arms wrapped around the bathrobe gape, clutching to her bosom the hard-bought reputation of her chastity; his listing, leftward stoop as his bag imposed its weight upon his balance. They stood too close for comfort, the doctor rattling weakly at the door.

'It won't open,' he said imploringly, as though he had exhausted his allotted range of tether and now longed for nothing more than sleep.

'It's locked, Herr Doktor. Here, let me find you the key.'

The widow took her time sorting through the row of hooks and hangers from which hung a variety of implements. Beer literally stamped his feet in impatience.

'Here. This one, I believe. My eyesight, you understand. It isn't what it used to be.' She shuffled to the door ignoring the doctor's outstretched hand. 'Ah, yes.'

The door opened slowly under her guiding hand, but she had yet to step out of the way, her body blocking the exit, the doctor pressing from behind.

'I heard something, you know. That night, I mean. A sort of bleating, high-pitched, shrill. More like a sheep than a dog.'

The doctor finally passed the threshold, thus stepping out from under the doorway light. His shadow simply disappeared: shifted, then collapsed on to itself, leaving Zuzka alone with Vesalius's shade. It was a surprise, therefore, to hear him speak again. He must still have been standing there, out on the landing, pinned down by the old woman's words.

'You heard the dog? When?'

'The night it was killed. An hour after midnight. I had trouble falling asleep.'

'And it came from the yard across the road?'

The shadow shook its head. 'No. It rose within the building.'

'From our courtyard, you mean.'

'From within the building, Dr Beer. It was like the stones whispered it.'

'But that's absurd.'

There was a silence then, and once again Zuzka wondered whether Beer had left; whether Vesalius was standing there, door-knob in hand, quietly watching as he walked up the stairs. But again he spoke.

'Did you tell the Professor? And the police?'

'The police?' Vesalius answered. 'Who wants them in the house?'

The widow turned her head to stare deep into the flat. 'I thought it better to mind my own business. Know what I mean?'

'Yes,' said the doctor, and Zuzka saw his shadow re-enter the doorway in order to shake Vesalius's hand. It looked to the girl like they were congratulating one another on their prudence.

'Goodnight, Frau Vesalius. Rest assured this will remain between you and me.'

'Thank you, Herr Doctor. So good of you to come.'

And with that she shut the door on the departing doctor. Zuzka used the cover of its bang to slip back into her room.

CHAPTER 4

S he did not come to a decision until halfway through the day; stayed in bed, in fact, complaining of ailments whose symptoms she enumerated to a sour-faced Vesalius. The idea itself was an old one, had been conceived in the depths of her, quietly, through those long nights of watching. It was the doctor who had brought it to the surface: the weary caution with which he took the measure of all action. *'If I were a man,'* she had told him, prodding him onwards like a donkey. Her idea paid no heed to her sex's frailty; it would ride with hussars, feasting on raw meat.

Once she had embraced it fully, she acted quickly, her cheeks flushed now by her own daring. She ran to the double doors that separated her uncle's set of rooms from the rest of the apartment: opened them quietly and sneaked down the corridor to the bathroom on her left. Once inside she turned the key, ran a quick eye over the shaving paraphernalia that lay spread out on the sink. As a girl she had liked to play with her father's razor: had cut shavings off the top of her fingernails, and collected them in a jam jar by her bed. At night, they would plant them, her sister Dáša and she, in the soft dirt of the herb patch, in the vague hope of growing an enamel child. Even now her nails had little divots at the centre, ragged, like the mark of small teeth. When she painted them, something of which her uncle disapproved, the polish would pool there, then harden and flake.

The image of her red-dipped fingertips returned her to the man with the painted face, and hence to her plan. She turned away from the sink; found a perch on the edge of the bathtub, then reached over and opened the medicine chest that hung screwed into the wall right next to the door.

She came to it often, would sit on the tub and study the array of pills and powders; had spent many an hour plucking the stoppers out of the brown pharmacist's bottles and sniffing at their contents. There was morphine there that, on a handful of occasions, she had dared drip on to her tongue; powdered Veronal piled up in a jar; castor oil and iodine (she had once smeared her breast with it, painted a circle around the nipple); a brown paper bag marked 'Acetylsalicylic acid' in Speckstein's careful hand. More than half the medicines carried no identification other than a series of letters and figures, and sometimes the date. The poisons were marked by a bright red skull, the alcohols by the jagged suggestion of a flame.

At times, on one of those long afternoons when there was nothing for her to do, she had picked a bottle at random, uncorked it and then upturned its neck on to the skin of her thumb. She had burned herself on acid once, and made herself giddy with the fumes of some potent type of ether. It wasn't much of a game but it carried with it a whisper of risk: some years ago, back in her father's house, she had read a story in which Russian officers held a revolver to their heads without knowing whether or not the chamber was loaded. It was a game she should have liked to play, but only if she knew in advance that she would live. It was the sound of the hammer bearing down upon the chamber that spoke to her, not the violence of the bullet. Her father used to say that there clung to her 'the faintest whiff of brimstone'; would kiss her then, after he said it, to take away the sting, the palms of his hands sitting warmly on her ears and shutting out the noises of the world.

It took her a good few minutes to pick a drug. She reached for the ether first, then decided its fumes were too familiar; dabbed a spit-wetted pinky into an unknown powder and brought it to her lips, then spat the foul stuff into the sink. In the end she settled on a harmless solution of colloidal silver, putting a little into an empty bottle whose glass-and-rubber stopper doubled as a pipette. She found a length of masking tape, stuck it on the bottle, and boldly marked it with the letters 'Ag-H$_2$O (Lq)' in a manner that approximated her uncle's mode of classification. Her preparations complete, she closed up the medicine chest, unlocked the bathroom door, and quickly returned to the safety of her own room, where she stuffed the bottle into a leather handbag and chose a topcoat to wear out. There was no need to alert Vesalius to her leaving. She took the spare key off the hook in the corridor, slipped out on to the landing, and quietly turned the lock.

Identifying the correct door proved harder than she had imagined. She knew that his apartment was on the second floor of the building's side wing, its windows facing into the courtyard. But when she climbed the narrow staircase of the side wing – itself very different from the elegant revolutions of the main flight of stairs – and came out on a cramped little landing, she found that all three of the doors before her might plausibly lead to a set of rooms with courtyard windows diagonally across from her own. Not one of the doors bore a name. There were no mail slots and no bells, just crude knockers set into the flaking paint. In the top quarter of each door, an inch above the crown of her head, a small window of green milk-glass replaced the lacquered wood, and bled faint traces of light on to the landing.

She stood around for some minutes, unsure of herself, then was startled when a corpulent man in a dirty tuxedo pushed up the stairs behind her, and brushed her buttocks as he squeezed his way past. She turned around after him without speaking, and he stopped halfway up the next flight of stairs, his features in darkness.

'May-I help you?' he shot out, the accent odd to her ears.

'I am looking for the man with the painted face.'

This seemed to puzzle the stranger, who came down a step, the lower half of his face entering into the light. His skin was rough and as though yellow, the cheeks fleshy and pockmarked, full lips framed by the wisps of a beard. It angered her briefly that he had not bothered to remove his hat. She noticed now that he was carrying a case under one arm, black and cylindrical in shape. Its handle seemed to have fallen off.

'Pain-ted fa-ce,' he said, in his oddly accented German. 'You-are look-ing for the clown.'

'I don't know what he is.'

'There,' said the man, pointing his free hand at the door to her left, then raising it upwards to lay a warning finger across the swell of his lips.

'Bet-ter don't disturb. He works all-night. And sleeps in daytime. Just like my-self.'

He chuckled at that, and, as he threw back his head to grant space to his mirth, she saw for a moment the contours of his face, unusually wide, the eyes slanting upwards under the heavy bones of his brow.

'Thank you, Herr—'

'Yuu,' he said, 'simply Yuu,' and finally doffed his hat to reveal a head of black hair, cut very short above the ears and somehow jagged, as though he had done it himself. He bowed, turned,

96

and was off, the leather heels of his dress-shoes loud against the staircase's naked stone.

She waited until she heard him enter an apartment high above her in what she surmised was the garret, then reached out to rap the knocker of the door on her left. There was no answer. She waited, reached out again, wishing now that she had brought a warmer coat, for it was chilly on the narrow landing. A third rap was answered by a squeaky noise as though of a man sitting up in his bed. A fourth rap got him moving; she heard him stand up, cast around for clothes. When the door swung open, his hands were still busy buttoning his trousers. He wore no shirt and had pulled his braces over a ribbed, cotton vest, the shadow of old sweat forming a wedge between the muscles of his chest. His feet were bare, turned on their sides to limit their exposure to the floor-boards' chill, the toenails chipped and dirty.

'What do you want?' said the man, and leaned an arm against the door frame, exposing to her the dark tangle of his armpit. 'You lost or something?'

She shook her head and stared at him. The first thing that struck her was that he was much shorter than she had thought, more muscular. There was a deep solidity to his arm and shoulder, to that compact body underneath the dirty, sleeveless shirt. His face, too, was alive with the movement of his muscles, the eyes open and passionate: the face of a boy itching for a schoolyard brawl.

All this surprised her. He had seemed so calm behind the shelter of his make-up.

His eyelashes, she thought, were much longer than her own.

'Can't you speak?' he asked her, more gently now, though the gentleness dissipated as soon as she had forced her tongue into an answer.

'I am here about your wife.'

'My wife?'

'Yes. I heard that she was sick.'

'My wife is sick? That's what you have heard? Where?'

'I'm not sure,' she said. 'I suppose Dr Beer told me. In passing, you know. He probably doesn't even remember.'

'Dr Beer told you my wife is sick?'

'In a word, yes. I bring medicine.' She reached into her handbag to produce the bottle she had so carefully marked. 'It is sure to give relief.'

It was hard to make out all the emotions that ran through his face as she spoke. There was anger there, and scorn; fear, too, as he leaned out the door and shot a glance up and down the stairs. She wished he would open the door further and allow her to see more of the room. His sink, for instance, was invisible to her, as was the bed; the pile of magazines about whose contents she had so often wondered. All she could make out was an edge of the windowsill, and an ashtray that stood overflowing not far from the heels of his still out-turned feet. His armpit filled the air between them with the smell of his sweat. She found herself intrigued by the smell: it seemed to her, at that moment, more intimate an imposition than if he had stooped to grab hold of her hand and kissed it. Not that he seemed in the mood for gallantry: his anger was palpable, a physical presence, like a dog straining at the leash. And yet there was, in all his gestures, an odd awareness of her. She saw it in his eyes, which made a survey of her chest even as they glowered, and in the cock of his narrow hips. It was something her mother had once tried to tell her about, before embarrassment had slipped a gag into her thoughts: she had whispered a phrase about their milkman's 'quiet hunger', and dropped her bony hands to rest a moment on the swell of her thighs. All of a sudden it struck the girl that this was the closest she had been to a man, unsupervised, if one disregarded her father, that is – and Dr Beer. The thought brought home to her her own audacity. She would have to find someone to whom she could brag about it later.

He took his time in any case, stared at the bottle with intense suspicion, then grabbed it from her without touching her hand. He unscrewed the stopper, drew the pipette out of the liquid, and squeezed a drop into his hand.

'What's this?' he mumbled, then shot another glance into the dark of the staircase behind her.

'Medicine. I'm afraid I forgot the name. I can make enquiries. But I'm sure it will do your wife no end of good.'

'I have no wife,' he said, harshly, and shoved the bottle back into her hand. 'Who the hell are you?'

This drew her up short. There had been, in all her preparations, no plan for an answer. All she had imagined was this: her talking to the man across the yard. He should have thanked her by now, invited her in to meet his wife; or broken down and confessed to her the nature of his crimes. She had not reckoned on the menace of his physicality, the spastic bunching of his fists. It called to mind the blood she had seen washing down his sink, and she took a step back.

'I am very sorry,' she said. 'I was told you live with your wife.'

'Who are you?'

'I live in the house. With my uncle. Main wing, first floor.'

She watched him turn his head to the window, work out her provenance. His face was very dark now, muscles bunching on cheeks and chin.

'Did Speckstein send you? Is he watching me? Are you his maid or something?'

'No, nothing like that,' she said, then became uncertain. Perhaps it was better to signal that she wasn't on her own. 'Though he knows I am here.'

She paused, swallowed, stepped closer yet to the top of the stairs. 'My room faces the yard,' she said. 'There was a woman—'

He grew angry again, eyes flashing in his bulging face. It cost him a great effort to speak. 'You have been watching,' he said. 'Whatever you think you have seen . . . I'm an artist, you see. An artist. I perform . . . There are important people, you understand. They come to see me. My show, it uses props – mannequins – you understand?'

The door had opened more widely during his tirade and left unobstructed the view of the room, and the room beyond. She found herself staring past his shoulder, trying to catch a glimpse of the unknown. He followed her gaze, then lifted a fist before his face. For a moment she thought he would leap out, smash her head in, but he quickly jumped back and closed the door until it stood open no wider than a crack. Only one eye remained visible to her.

'There is nothing here,' he hissed. 'Nothing of interest. You hear?'

'Yes,' she agreed, drawing closer again to the door. They stood breathing as though after a fight, his eye hanging head-high in the gloom.

'Where do you perform?' she whispered across the silence that had risen between them. 'Perhaps I could come one evening, and—'

He slammed the door in her face: put a shoulder to it and slammed it, the wood cracking under his weight. She stumbled back as though she had been slapped, lost her balance on the stairs and fell down four or five steps, bruising her ankle and her buttocks in the process. *If Dr Beer comes tonight*, it ran through her head, *he'll find my bottom black and blue*. The giggle escaped her before she could stop it: a single high peal that ran up the stairs. She wondered whether the angry man heard it, standing barefoot behind his door, and whether it made him angrier still. As quickly as she could, she stood up, and hobbled down the stairs, into the warmth of the courtyard. As she crossed it, her eyes still scrunched against the brightness of the light, she thought about what she had seen over the man's shoulder in that short moment when he had opened the door wide enough to grant her access to the flat. A foot was little to go by. It might have been dead, or made out of wood, the stain on its heel nothing but dirt.

Right there, out in the yard, her legs still shaky with her triumph and her fall, it occurred to her what she must do in order to find out.

CHAPTER 5

All afternoon she waited for the man to leave: a clot in her stomach, pins and needles running up her spine; one ankle swelling, the other leg numb; bruises stirring deep within her rump. At first she stood by her window, peered anxiously across the yard. To see him clearly she had to draw close; press her face to the glass, or open it up, push her head into the open. He had drawn the curtains, tattered, threadbare rags that billowed in the breeze and revealed as much as they hid. He tugged at one such curtain to slide it across a foot-wide gap and succeeded only in pulling it down, his face blackening with anger. To his side, in the back room, the other set of windows remained in utter darkness: perhaps, she thought, he had painted the panes, or nailed some blankets to the window frames. They might hide a darkroom, or a slaughterhouse.

Then, the ripped fabric of his curtain still in his hands, he caught her watching him. The brow shifted, muscles moving through his meaty face. He dropped the rag and leaned out into the yard – head, shoulders, breast all threading through the woodwork – and shouted something she didn't hear, his hand rolled into a fist; shook it too, high over his head, with the violence of a man wielding a club, cotton vest sweat-soaked from his efforts. She recoiled from the window, bit her lip; drew close again after counting to a hundred, and found his eyes still peering across, the hand raised, ready to punch. His stare poured into her: her lungs caught it and met it with a wheeze; pushed it downwards, to her stomach, where acids rose to drown it. She burped a sour burp, then licked the spittle from her lips; checked the window again and found him there, staring darkly, waiting to pounce.

So she shifted to the kitchen. The angle was bad, and Vesalius was there, busy with tomorrow's lunch, but she found she could watch the side wing's door from there, sitting in the shadows of the wall. In time she relaxed a little, put water on for tea, then sat, both hands around her steaming cup, eyes on the yard, and was lulled to peace by the noises of the house. The sounds here were different from those that collected in her room: running water, the growl of a flush, then the angry phrases of an argument, raining down from high above, a man and his wife having it out about his mother. She listened and imagined the scene, her body calming with each moment; reached in her mind to that other marital sound that had flown in through her window in the depth of night, its origins opaque to her, unspeakable. She had spent much energy unravelling its mystery, had once watched two horses couple in the country, and stolen books down from her uncle's shelf. The mystery had not lifted with these instructions in anatomy. One had to marry to learn what made a woman bark her pleasure rudely out into the yard. The doctor had borne the sound as one bears a whipping, shoulders rolled into his chest, palms on his trousers, as though to steady his thighs. He didn't wear a wedding ring. Perhaps he found it interfered with his duties. She wondered if Speckstein had worn one, back when his wife was alive and he had made a living looking up his patients' skirts. Behind her, Vesalius dropped a saucepan lid and dissolved the argument upstairs in its clean, insistent ringing. She bent low to pick it up by its wooden handle, then swore and held her back in sudden agony; dropped hard into a chair, the lid still ringing in her lap, and smothered its song between her palms. At the centre of the gesture there sat a hard little sound when her ring-finger collided with the metal. Zuzka noticed it, looked up into the old woman's face, found nothing there but pain and spite. It puzzled her, and she decided to ask, making sure she sounded polite.

'Frau Vesalius,' she asked. 'Were you ever married?'

The other woman swore, rubbed the soreness in her spine, nodded.

'Twenty-seven years.'

'Twenty-seven years,' the girl echoed, finding it easy to summon her wonder. 'How was he?'

Frau Vesalius stopped her movements to consider this, fingers still dug into her spine.

'A good husband,' she said at last. 'Never missed a day of work, then lost all his savings all the same. He had hands like a schoolgirl.'

She stretched out one of her own, hard as a shovel. The ring was silver, tarnished; cut deep into a fold of skin. Her knuckles dwarfed it, trapped it, each finger knotted like a root. Zuzka looked from hand to face and found the same hardness in each. Her own hands lay soft upon her knees.

'Was he, you know – faithful?'

She threw it out quickly, fearing reprimand, and was surprised to see that Vesalius refused to take insult.

'On the whole,' she said. 'Had an eye on my sister. As a young man, that is. It goes after a while.'

'It?'

'Don't play daft.'

They locked eyes for just a moment, until Vesalius got up, set the saucepan lid down upon the counter and took a knife to a cluster of beets. Her fingers were soon running with their juice. It provoked the girl, being ignored like this; there were other things she longed to learn.

'How did you know?' she asked in the end, of this woman she didn't like, had never liked, not from the day she'd come to the house, two months ago and more. 'Before you married him. How did you know you were in love?'

'Love,' Vesalius said, and sneered across one shoulder. 'That's what we're after. The good doctor, is it?'

The girl had no choice then but to march off, back to her room, and leave the woman to her cackle. Tears of fury almost made her miss her man.

By the time she had dried her eyes and was back at the window, he was already halfway across the yard, his hat hiding his features, a duffel bag heavy in one hand. She recognised him by his movements, the angry roll of his shoulders, feet stomping as though he sought to punish the ground. Even so, she wanted to make sure, and sneaked into her uncle's bathroom whose high narrow window afforded a view of the main road. She climbed upon the bathtub's rim, pressed her nose against the narrow vent, and watched him walk up to the tram stop: light a cigarette, his features crude in the late-afternoon sun. When it was clear he wouldn't return, she clambered down again and ignored the throbbing in her ankle; fetched a coat and tied a scarf over her hair. Vesalius saw her leave. She stood in the kitchen door, the beet knife still in her hand, and watched her slip out. As Zuzka descended the stairs, the snap of the deadbolt followed her down.

The janitor was not in his flat. She rang the bell, then walked into the yard, staying close to the wall, in the hope of avoiding Vesalius's gaze.

The metal door led down into the odour of wetrot. She listened, hoping he would be alone; heard nothing apart from the shuffling of feet. The door to his workshop stood ajar: she saw his back, bent at his workbench, a bottle of beer standing open by his feet. An odd sort of table stood pushed against the wall, its sides elevated, two wood-planers cluttering its surface.

She knocked and pushed through the doorway. It wasn't until she had entered completely that she noticed the child. Lieschen was standing in a chalkmark circle she had drawn upon the floor, was red-faced and somehow dishevelled. When the girl saw Zuzka, she squealed in delight and spun her body into a pirouette, careful not to step outside the circle's confines. She got through a turn and a half before she lost her balance and had to throw out a leg to take her weight; panted and laughed, and pushed her braids back over her shoulder's hunch.

'Fräulein Zuzana,' she shouted. 'I'm learning to dance.'

The janitor had turned around, and he acknow-ledged her presence with a mumbled '*Grüss Gott*'. He rose now, kicking over his bottle, then bent hurriedly to pick it up from the floor: stood licking beer off his dirty fingers while he eyed her with suspicion. She noticed the smell that clung to him and cut through the mildew: gamey, cloying, as though of aged meat. He moved slowly, shook wood shavings off lap and chest.

'Fräulein Speckstein,' he said at last. 'Does the Herr Professor need anything?'

She hesitated, looked again at the girl. 'What is she doing here?'

The man shrugged. 'She came after school. Agitated. Some children found a dead body in the bushes.'

'A dead body? Who?'

She had asked the janitor, but it was Lieschen who answered.

'It was a woman,' she sang out, after another pirouette. 'Sepp said she was naked.'

She raised two hands before her chest and cupped them in imitation of the boy's gesture. 'The policeman wrapped her in his coat.'

'How perfectly awful,' said Zuzka, and crouched down by the side of the girl. 'Don't you think you should go upstairs now? Get some rest? You must have had quite a shock.'

Lieschen looked at her: clear, open eyes, painful in their trust.

'It *was* awful,' she whispered, 'though I didn't really see. There was a man there and he cried and cried and cried.'

She slid down to her knees and erased the chalk circle with the heel of one hand.

'I'll wait for you and then go up.' Her movements were simple, direct. There was no way of avoiding her scrutiny. Zuzka turned to face the janitor.

'My uncle requires the spare keys. To the house, I mean.'

The man took it in, shrugged, walked over to a metal box that hung screwed into the wall. 'Which ones?'

'All of them.'

'All of them? But why?'

She shook her head. She had always found it easy to lie. It was just a matter of believing what one said.

'I really cannot say. He just barked at me to get the keys. He has' – she paused for effect, found real fear spreading through her body – 'a temper.'

The man nodded as though this made sense to him, then took three iron rings from their hooks, each of them threaded with a dozen keys.

'Front wing,' he said, lifting up the first ring, then repeating the gesture with the other two. 'Side and back. The keys aren't labelled.' He pointed to coloured pieces of string that he had attached to each key. 'My own system, helps me tell them apart. Do you need the keys to the basement as well?'

'My uncle didn't say,' she answered cautiously. 'He asked for discretion,' she added, then saw the man was baffled by the word. 'To keep quiet. Party business, I suppose.'

'Yes. Of course.'

She had expected the janitor to be more difficult, but he was meek as a lamb; passed the keys over without further ado. His hands were large, the cuticles stained by rust or blood. *Too many suspects*, it came to her head all of a sudden. She smiled and curtsied, wished him a good evening.

'I will bring the keys back when my uncle is done with them,' she told him when she was already at the door, the child following her with a ballerina's mincing step.

'Of course. A good night to you. And good health. Dr Beer tells me you have been sick.'

'Yes,' she breathed, and reached back to take the girl's hand. Together they ascended the stairs and re-emerged into the yard. It was past six o'clock, the whole courtyard in shade. Lieschen was looking up at her with an odd expectancy. Zuzka bent down to her, took her hands in her own, felt the stick of chalk that she had buried in one palm.

'Is Herr Speckstein going to spy on someone, Fräulein Zuzana?'

'Call me Zuzka. It's nicer that way.'

The girl smiled at that but wouldn't let go of her question. It stood there, in her red little face. Her mouth curled around it. Zuzka made another effort to throw her off scent.

'You should go home now. Your father will be back soon.'

Lieschen shook her head. 'Not until eight, he won't. So who is he spying on? My father says he spies on everyone.' She lowered her voice. 'Even on us.'

'And do you have any secrets?'

Once again the child shook her head, then

stopped herself. 'One,' she said after some thought. 'I have one. But it's only for me.'

'You won't tell. Not a single soul?'

'Only when I want to But not before.'

She smiled at the thought of her own vigilance, raised her chin proudly into the air, her body following the gesture, the neck welded to her chest. Zuzka watched her, returned her smile.

'Well, the keys are a secret, too, you see. No one must know.'

'Not even me?'

'Not even you.' She hesitated, licked her lips, allowed her anxiety to win out against her better judgement. 'Not unless you promise to help.'

The girl's face lit up. She nodded with great earnestness, then raised a hand to her heart to seal her holy oath.

'I promise, promise, promise,' she whispered, and danced another pirouette in the half-dusk of the yard.

Quickly, without speaking, Zuzka took Lieschen by the arm and led her over to the side wing. They entered cautiously: paused in the open doorway for just a moment and took their bearings. The entryway was long and narrow, the staircase to their left, the door of the hallway toilet ahead, the ghost of a light creeping through its cracks. They stood and listened, then stepped inside.

'Here, Lieschen,' said Zuzka, having marched the child up to the turn in the staircase, halfway to the first-floor landing. 'You stay here and wait.

If you hear a noise – if I shout for help, or if someone comes in after me – you run like the wind and get help.'

She waited until the girl had sat down, smoothed the dress down over her knees. 'Can you do that for me?'

'Yes,' said the girl, again with that earnest rocking of her body, her face so serious it made her look old. Zuzka smiled, turned around, then back, gave the girl a quick little kiss.

'Most likely I'm just being a silly goose,' she whispered.

The keys were jangling in her hands.

She knocked first: walked up to the landing, found the door, made sure to knock. Just in case, that is: in case he had returned while she was in the basement; and in case it *was* his wife back there, sick with the flu, indifferent to rescue. Then she tried the first key: chose it at random, a yellow string double-tied through the hoop, tooth jagged like a crone's. It fit but wouldn't turn. She tried another, and a third, the noise of her failures loud in her ears. The seventh key fit: she knew it even before the lock snapped open and the door swung inwards under her pressure. 'Hello,' she called ahead, half shout, half whisper, her tongue dry against her gums. The flat beyond lay in semi-darkness, looked large, mysterious, the back room blocked from view.

She stepped in and turned to close the door; felt her breath fail at the sound of the latch clicking shut. She reopened the door, looked out, saw the girl; shut it again (the snapping of jaws), and locked herself in, all the time looking over her shoulder, fearful of what was in the second room. Perhaps, she thought, it was better to have a clear path of escape. She unlocked the door again, opened it. The girl remained sitting on the steps, the stairwell silent, empty. This time, she turned the key without closing the door first: leaned the door shut against the deadbolt, then dragged a chair there, to lean against the handle and give her warning in case someone should follow her in. All the while her heart was in her mouth. She had never understood the phrase: had read it in her father's Homer, been puzzled by it, dismissed it, a poet's tall tales, all until now, when her lips and palate had acquired a pulse.

The door secured, she turned and walked across the room: stayed away from the windows, threading a path through dirty clothes. His smell was everywhere, the smell of sweat and something oddly fishy, old smoke clinging to the walls. She stopped once to bend and pick up a magazine; found a naked woman staring back at her, fat stomach rolling underneath two giant breasts. The woman lay sprawled across an armchair; looked cramped, uncomfortable, one buttock puckered like a wind-bruised sea. She laid the magazine down again, circumvented the bed, the crumpled sheet, blankets crusty with old dirt. The second door was only a step away. She reached and held its handle like the hand of a friend; gently, that is, for comfort and strength. Her fist rose: she knocked, drowning out the wheezing of her lungs.

There was no answer.

It wasn't long before she opened the door, and waited for the light to follow her inside.

CHAPTER 6

Nine-year-old Anneliese Grotter was sitting on the stairs leading up to the first-floor landing of the building's side wing and wishing she had brought Kaiser San along. Zuzka had long disappeared through the door at the top of the landing: had struggled with the keys for a while, her breath a broken whistle groping for a tune. Then silence had fallen, a silence full of muffled sound, steps in the ceiling, the murmur of the walls, the tinkle of pipes, all far too loud in the girl's straining ears. Twice she'd stood up, stretched out her legs; crept up to the door to find it wasn't locked but leaned shut against the dead-bolt. Lieschen had put a hand to it, applied some pressure, felt a weight shift on the other side. Afraid, excited, she'd gone back to her perch upon the stairs; pulled her dress over knees that were bumpy with cold, gave herself over to the passing of minutes. She tried to count them, found herself racing through the seconds; used the rhythm of her heart (Father had shown her, three taps for every two seconds, one had to count out loud or soon lose track), but found it, too, was racing through its beats. It might have been three, it might have been twenty: two lines of spittle running down her chin. At some point, she had pulled a braid into her mouth and started sucking on its strands.

Then a racket roused her, scared her, a rush of water underneath her bum. She leapt up, nearly choking on her hair; recognised the flush of the hallway loo, the tread of a man stepping out. Before she could move, he had walked into sight: stood head bent, hands still busy with his belt, a rolled-up newspaper jutting from his pocket. He wore a black hat and evening clothes, his features creeping with the hallway's shadows. In the dim light the only thing Lieschen was sure of was the slant of his eye. Another moment and he would turn; see her, search his pocket for a knife. She was two yards above him, three yards to his left; a measly foot from the shelter of the staircase's turn.

Her feet obeyed her. Later, in the safety of her room, she would feel grateful for their courage, would praise and spin them through another pirouette. Just now she simply stepped away, was on the staircase one moment, and up on the landing the next. She heard him follow her, a heavy man's shuffle, had a second to make up her mind, crooked neck trained down into the stairwell. She could run or she could hide.

The door gave under little pressure: a chair slid aside, making no noise, her fingers guiding shut the door behind her. She fell to her knees and pressed an eye against the keyhole. The big man was walking towards her, then turned sharply to his left; stopped at the bottom of the stairs (she could nearly read the headline on the newspaper peeking from the pocket of his coat), broke wind, and carried on, his leather soles making a racket on the stone. The knife he carried remained safely in his pocket.

Lieschen exhaled, relieved. She jumped to her feet and turned around, expected Zuzka there, glaring at her, ready to scold. But the room was empty, save for its clutter, and smelled like her father's, of alcohol, cigarettes and sweat. At the far end, another door stood open upon a shadow of movement. She drew closer, curious, slipped on some magazines that lay littered across the floor, their pages open at some pictures. A bent-over lady stood looking at her, adjusted her stocking; a beer bottle lolling just left of her rump. The girl stepped over it – and her – and on to the thereshold. The braid was long back in her mouth.

The second room was dark. A pair of curtains blocked the sole window, hung heavily, as though weighted by lead. The bed stood against the far wall, narrow, a body spread along its length: Zuzka standing in front of it, her shoulders rolled into a hunch. She was reaching down to the body with both hands, had lifted one of its arms into her chest. It was dark, and Lieschen didn't see much, just Zuzka's movement, her left hand holding on

118

to the woman's elbow, the right hand pinching along her naked bicep. She'd grab a twist of skin between forefinger and thumb and turn it, turn it hard, it seemed to the child, up and down that long naked arm. The only other things visible to the girl were a foot, sticking out from under the sheet at one end, and a face sticking out at the other. But what a face! Lieschen had a picture book of angels who looked like this: bones fit for birds, stretching smooth the elfin skin, the long, thin face of a fairy, running to a point on a dimpled chin. Her eyes were big and hungry and green: it was as though a patch of moss had sprung up amongst the lashes, the only thing of colour in the half-dark of the room. They did not move.

It was hard to tell whether or not she was dead.

Then she blinked, both lids coming down over her eyes, blinked once, unhurried, the skin so thin you'd think that it might rip. Zuzka saw it, too: let go of the arm, a cry of anguish falling from her lips. She tore off the sheet that covered the woman, found her naked on a rubber mat; put both hands on her hip and rolled her slowly on one side. The skin, so white on chest and arms, turned raw and livid on the back: holes the size of Lieschen's palm, staring out the midst of her, pink at the edges, their centres liver-dark and wet. She was slick with moisture from the waist down. It was only now that Lieschen saw it that the girl recognised the smell of rot and urine standing in the room. The woman's hair had been cut, roughly, into a two-inch tangle that ran from scalp to ear to nape. The spine looked like a row of knuckles gathered for a punch.

Zuzka dropped her. She should have eased her down gently, rolled her over on her side, but did not seem to have the strength for it: dropped her, slipped and lost her balance, crying, turning, finding Lieschen standing there and gathering her in her arms.

'The swine,' she murmured, hugging Lieschen hard, 'the swine.'

Their cheeks were side by side, the child's chin flat against her crouching friend's shoulder. It left free the view of the stranger in her bed, eyelids blinking from their perch upon the pillow, one flutter, then two, then three.

'Beer,' Zuzka said into her shoulder. 'We must fetch Dr Beer.'

She lifted Lieschen up and carried her, legs dangling, away from the room and out on to the landing, then dropped her back to her feet intent on locking the door behind them. The child watched her as she stood searching for the right key: she dropped the key ring twice, had trouble finding the hole, was muttering to herself, the evening light from the windows starting to fail, her breath a penny rattling in a tin. When she dropped the keys yet again, Lieschen stooped to pick them up for her, tried one in the door. It fitted and the lock turned under the pressure of her hand.

'What's wrong with that woman?' she asked as she handed the keys back to her friend. Zuzka took them, held on to her hand.

'A man lives in that flat,' she said. 'He' – she paused, uncertain – 'he's bad. A bad man, you understand? But you must go home now.'

She turned, dragged Lieschen behind her down the stairs, ran out into the courtyard.

'You must go home,' she repeated, but wouldn't let go of her hand, dragged her behind her instead, into the main stairwell and up the sweep of the stairs. It was all Lieschen could do just to keep up. She didn't think she had ever run quite as fast as this.

CHAPTER 7

Anton Beer opened the door to the bell's shrill ringing and found Zuzka and the child there, standing winded hand in hand. Zuzka reached out a palm and – mistaking the gesture, his mind still busy with the files he had been studying – he took and shook it, gave the ghost of a bow. Then he felt her tug, jerky and insistent, and became aware of the spasms in her breathing. Beer searched her face, found her habitual nonchalance wiped from her features. She had been crying, he saw, the cheeks were still wet, tears and sweat beading on her upper lip.

'What is it?' he asked, but was answered only by her tug.

'But you must come inside,' he murmured, shaking off her grip and stepping to one side. It was the child who marched in, crooked neck bent forward as though she were leaning into the wind.

'There is a woman who is lying in bed,' Anneliese told the doctor, her own emotion audible only in her lack of modulation. 'On the other side of the yard. Her back's full of holes, and she has lovely green eyes.'

'But where?'

'Come,' she said. 'I will show you.'

Without waiting for Beer's reaction, she chose a door at random and headed left, into his study. His desk was there, standing at the centre, the chair facing into the room. The desktop was covered with police files, a glass of brandy rising from their midst, his cigarette still smoking in its ashtray.

The child spent no time taking in her surroundings. She ran to the window, parted the curtains, stuck her head through the open frame. 'Over there,' she shouted, rising to the tips of her toes and pointing deep into the courtyard, her chest pressing hard into the windowsill. 'But you can't see, 'cause the tree is in the way.'

'You mean the side wing?'

'Yes. Shine-a-man lives there. I saw him tonight.'

He nodded, confused, made to return to Zuzka whom they had left in the hallway, still gathering her words. He nearly collided with her in the doorway to his study.

'We must go at once,' she said. 'Help that poor girl.' Again she reached for his hand. This time he let her.

'Is it the man with the trumpet? Has he done something to her?'

'I pinched her,' said Zuzka, 'to see if she was alive. She didn't even flinch.'

'But who? You really must slow down. I can't understand a word you're saying.'

The fingers in his palm were cold and hurt him with their pressure. It was very different from how she'd held on to him the previous night. Beer pulled himself free, took the glass of brandy from his desk and placed it into Zuzka's hands.

'Here, drink this. And sit down on the couch. Now tell me what is going on.'

Slowly, by increments, he got the story out of her. She told him how she had gone across the yard that afternoon to talk to the man they had observed; how she'd offered him medicine for his sick wife ('Medicine?' he asked, incredulous. 'Colloidal silver,' she told him, as though expecting he would praise her for the wisdom of her choice); how she had been turned away, rather rudely, but seen enough to notice a body lying at the back of his flat. So she had decided to return, had broken in, in fact, and found a woman there; had thought her dead until she'd opened her eyes. ('Did she say anything?' 'Nothing at all. Her back looks like she's been whipped.') He refilled her glass and listened to her description of the injuries; the green of the woman's eyes; the image in some smut magazine she had found lying around on the floor. Even now, in her agitation, she was wresting poetry from those moments of fear, spoke more than she had to, paused for effect. She was less effusive when he pressed her for answers on some matters of fact.

'How did you get the keys?' he asked her just now: earned a shrug, a sip of the brandy, the whispered insistence that they 'must go right away'.

'But where did you get them?' he asked anew, unwilling to let the matter drop.

'The janitor,' Zuzka told him. 'I asked for them in my uncle's name.'

'Christ,' he said. 'Does your uncle know?'

'What do you think, Dr Beer?'

'And Anneliese? How did she end up in the flat?'

'I don't know. I left her to stand guard, and then there she was, all of a sudden, staring at me across the room. Just look what she is doing now.'

Anneliese had been quiet through their exchange, and, turning around, Beer found her, feet planted on the leather of his chair, in a low stoop over his desk. She was holding a photograph, had raised it right up to her nose. For just a moment he wanted to shout at her, tell her to get her dirty shoes off his leather, and impress on her that she was meddling with highly sensitive information. Then he saw the sadness on her face, mingling with the strain of whatever had happened across the yard. He stepped up to her gently, giving her time to feel his presence by her side, then took hold of her by the waist, and gently stood her back on the ground, the photograph still in her hands. Her eyes rose, found his.

'They take photographs of the dead,' she complained softly and looked to him for confirmation.

'Yes,' he said. 'They do.'

'That's nasty,' she said, and he couldn't tell whether she was referring to the practice or to the images themselves, four human corpses and a dog. She was holding a print of Walter, her thumbs careful to avoid the shape of the prone beast, as though touching it would hurt his soul.

'Will you put it back?' he asked her gently.

'Yes,' she said, sliding the photo on to his desk. 'It doesn't belong to me.'

He reached down to touch the crown of her head, smoothed her hair. 'We must go now,' he told her. 'I need to have a look at the woman you found.'

'She is beautiful,' said Lieschen. 'And ugly. Her back is.'

She reached behind herself clumsily, her twisted spine limiting her range of motion, pointing to her shoulder and the bony ridge of hip.

Behind them, Zuzka rose, placed the glass upon the desk, then walked briskly to the door. Beer followed her along with the child once he had retrieved his doctor's bag. They walked down the stairs, not speaking, passed Frau Novak, who eyed them with pre-emptive hostility. The yard was almost dark. Beer headed for the back wing first, guiding Anneliese by the shoulder.

'You go up now,' he told the child. 'You have had enough excitement for one evening.'

To his surprise she did not argue, turned instead to embrace Zuzka's legs in a clumsy hug, then did the same to his own.

He stopped her before she could run off.

'One more thing,' he said. 'You mustn't tell

126

anyone what you saw. Fräulein Speckstein would get into trouble, you see, and we don't want that.'

The child nodded, gestured for him to lean closer, then whispered in his ear.

'Zuzka,' she said. 'She said I can call her Zuzka.'

'That's nice,' he whispered back.

'I'm sure it's all right if you do, too.'

She curtsied, then smiled, then ran off into the house and tore up the stairs with a broken, jagged gallop. They watched her go, then walked over to the side wing, hoping the neighbours had better things to do than stare out into the yard.

She led him up with good composure; found the right key almost at once; locked the door behind them. It was only when they reached the doorway to the second room that she hesitated.

'In there?' he asked, then walked briskly ahead. Zuzka followed him. He took his bearings, the shadows so deep he could barely make out the woman upon the bed; looked over at the curtains, gauging how much light they would block. There were three or four layers, some of them heavy brocade. It was unlikely that anything would seep through.

'Close the door,' he said. 'I want to switch on the lamp.'

She followed orders like a good nurse, then winced when cold electric light filled the room. There wasn't much there beyond the cot and a dresser, just crumpled-up towels littering the floor. He stepped over to the cot and drew up the lone chair; felt Zuzka's breath on his neck and barked at her to give him some room. Only then did he put a hand upon his patient.

She did not flinch.

He began his examination. From habit, he started talking, asking questions first, then announcing what he was about to do. The woman did not react, though her lids stood wide open, eyeballs travelling to scan his face. She was in her early twenties, malnourished, her skin so dry in parts it had formed into clusters of scales. She was also astonishingly beautiful, pale and delicate, so thin as to be nearly androgynous, small pink nipples rising out of the suggestion of breasts. Only her hips flared, wide and womanly, forked downwards into a pair of long and skinny legs. Slowly, lifting her thighs and the small of her back, he rolled her on to her belly, studied the wounds that were scattered across the white plain of back. He counted three deep sores, one of them open to the bone, the black smudge of dead tissue filling much of the crater. A number of smaller ulcers could be found on elbows, neck and heels; the skin livid there but dry. The woman was wet, had emptied her bladder, a puddle running down the rubber sheet. The smell that rose from her was frightful.

Beer stood up, leaving her on her belly for the moment, walked to the door and switched off the light. The sink was located in the front room. He found a towel, wet one half of it, then returned to his patient, Zuzka watching him with dark, brooding eyes. He wondered briefly what she made of all this, his professional gestures enacted upon another. There was a question written in her face, but she gave no voice to it. She simply closed the door behind him, turned on the light.

Beer knelt and began to clean the patient, starting with the feet and working upwards. He wiped her skin with the wet end of the towel first, then rubbed her dry with the other. When he had got as far as the lower thighs, he felt Zuzka kneel beside him. She reached for the towel, tried to take it off his hands.

'Let me,' she said.

'I can manage,' he murmured.

'It's not a job for a man.'

He wanted to protest, tell her he was a doctor, and married, but kneeling there above the cleft of the woman's buttocks, he did not find the words.

'Be careful with the sores,' he said instead. 'They are prone to infection.'

He left the room briefly to wash his hands in the sink.

When he returned, he slid the chair over to sit near the woman's head, then bent forward until he was in her line of sight.

'I don't know whether you can hear me,' he said, repeating words he had already spoken a half-dozen times, 'but I'm a doctor. My name is Beer. With your permission, I will have a look at your teeth now.'

The drop of one lid was her only reaction. He took it to indicate assent, lifted her head slightly, stuck two fingers through her dry and perfect lips, and ran them through the curve of both gums. Next he forced open the jaw as wide as he could and moved his body out of the light: stared down her throat like a peasant buying a horse.

'He brushes your teeth, then,' he said to himself, too softly for either woman to hear. He laid her head back, arranged the pillow for comfort, waited for Zuzka to finish cleaning her up. She took her time: went out to rinse the towel once, switching off the lamp while the door stood open, thus leaving him in darkness, then found a clean shirt in the closet and used it to pat her dry a final time. Beer lit a cigarette and started pacing the room.

'What now?' asked Zuzka when she was finally done; coughed a little when a breath of smoke caught her in the face.

'You must return the keys before they are missed. And make up an excuse why you are late for dinner.'

'What do I say?'

'To the janitor? What were you planning on saying?'

She frowned, then shrugged, wrapped her arms around her chest. 'That it was all a big mistake. A misunderstanding. Something like that.'

'Say that then. And remind him that he had no business giving you the keys. I don't think he likes

130

your uncle much. He might be inclined to forget about the whole thing.'

She nodded, still thoughtful, arms locked in their double embrace.

'What about her? Has he—' She lowered her voice. 'Raped her?'

He shook his head, started to answer, then thought better of it. 'She needs help,' he said. 'I will stay here and talk to the young man who lives here. See what this is all about.'

She waited for more, but he fell silent, let her figure it out. At last it dawned on her that she wouldn't be privy to his diagnosis. Some colour returned to her cheeks.

'He's a clown,' she said, sulkily.

'A what?'

'He paints his face white, and puts on black clothing.'

'A mime,' said Beer.

'Yes, that's the word. An angry sort of man. He killed the dog. He might try to kill you.'

'Return the keys,' he said, soothingly. 'If you like we can talk tomorrow. It's a Saturday. I can drop in after lunch.'

She switched the light off in a huff and ran out into the front room. There was no need to tell her not to lock him in. She simply threw the door shut behind her, then could be heard making a ruckus down the stairs.

Beer chuckled to himself and sat down near the woman with the green eyes.

'Forgive her manners,' he said to her, reaching down to brush some lint from her hair. 'She's temperamental, and young.'

He was answered only by a flutter of eyelids. It would have been churlish to see in it anything other than a smile.

THREE

Friedrich – 'Fritz' – Haarmann worked with a partner. They had met, he later testified, at the Hannover railway station. It is unclear whether Haarmann approached Hans Grans, or whether it was the young man who actively offered his services; certainly he had worked as a prostitute before. A friendship sprang up from these inauspicious circumstances. Within a matter of weeks, the two men began to share lodgings. Once Grans had become aware of Haarmann's activities, he agreed to supply him with a string of men straight from the trains: young, handsome strays who were new to the city. Afterwards, he received their clothes in payment. There is no evidence that he partook in the murders, despite Haarmann's sworn statement to the contrary. Both men were executed in the spring of 1925.

During the investigation and trial, much was made of Haarmann's physicality, his long fingers and soft hands, the full moon of his face. Court records describe him alternately as strong, masculine, and coarse; then as pliant, soft-bodied, feminine. He liked to smoke cigars and enjoyed baking; during conversation he would keep licking his lips. His homosexuality was well known to the police.

After Haarmann had killed his victims by means of throttling them while simultaneously biting through their Adam's apples, he cut open the abdominal cavity to remove the intestines into a bucket. The organs would follow. Denuding the bones was, by his own testimony, sickening work. He kept the flesh in a wax-cloth bag, and spent many hours soaking up and scrubbing away the blood. Those remains which had no commercial value he threw down the toilet or dumped in the river.

In the years prior to his arrest, Haarmann had worked as a police spy. A psychiatric examination, performed early in his life, concluded that he was 'eighty per cent incapable of gainful employment' on grounds of 'congenital feeble-mindedness'. Haarmann distinguished himself during his military service. His father was an engine-driver. He married in 1900: a 'large, pretty girl' named Erna Loewert. When the first of the skulls was discovered, by a group of children playing by the river, the authorities suspected that they originated from the Göttingen anatomical institute. Close to six hundred boys and young men were reported missing in the Hannover area during the early 1920s. Haarmann was sentenced for twenty-four counts of murder. He blinked a lot. His moustache was a light shade of brown. He wiggled his bottom. He died at the age of forty-six.

CHAPTER 1

Anton Beer settled in for the wait. He turned off the light, opened the curtains, gave his eyes time to adjust to the spare glow of the moon. His feet hurt from an afternoon of house visits, and he wondered how he would while away the hours. There were two chairs in total, one in each room. He tested both of them for comfort, found them unsatisfactory. They were cheap, barren things, badly put together. One wobbled, the other had a nail protruding through the seat, threatening to snag his trousers. He returned his attentions to his patient, cleaned, as best he could, the wounds upon her back, whispered to her about the therapies he was planning to attempt. There was time, he thought, to return to his quarters and fetch rubbing alcohol, prepare an antiseptic; pick up a cushion, some reading matter for himself. But he was afraid to leave the woman; afraid, too, that the door would bang shut behind him, or that one of the neighbours would discover it open, and run to the janitor. He found himself stuck here, stooped over this silent woman and searching for ways to excise her dead flesh.

'We might try maggots,' he whispered to her, bending low so she could see his face. 'It sounds worse than it is.'

Beer could have sat on the ground, but it seemed undignified in front of a patient.

Once upon a time he had taken well to waiting. Beer thought himself a patient man. It had infuriated his wife, and impressed his professors, the calm placidity of a man of science who understood there were things beyond his control. Now his bladder tugged at him. He did not want to step out and use the hallway toilet and fought to suppress the urge; felt queer at the thought of pissing down a stranger's sink. He excused himself from the bedside, took to pacing the rooms, found a chamber pot in the near darkness that, once disturbed, grew vivid with the stink of old urine and to which he now found himself compelled to add his own. The noise was loud in his ears, embarrassing; he had made up his mind that the woman next door could hear just fine, that her paralysis stopped at the neck and left unaffected the senses of the head. And yet she couldn't speak, or felt disinclined to do so; had a cared-for mouth and healthy tongue, pink and narrow like a cat's. Her toenails had been recently cut. In his brief examination, he had found no evidence of sexual assault.

Having passed his water, Beer straightened, slid the pot back under the bed with a careful push of one foot. There was a bar of soap on the sink, a shaving brush and razor. The basin itself was covered by a film of white grease; the mirror and fixtures rust-eaten and mouldy. The rag that served as a hand towel bore the parallel lines of a dark stain. Beer stood washing his hands, then took the rag off its hook and walked over to the window, held it high into the moon. The stains looked as though someone had wiped a knife with it: a single movement over a four-inch blade. Even with the better light he could not be certain it was blood.

The sight stirred memories in him, of the photos that lay scattered across his desk, and of other such photos that he had studied in his life; of lectures, heard at the University of Graz, that searched for meaning in the patterns of a smudge. It also worried him: called to mind the dangers of his chosen course of action. In her summary of the day's events, Zuzka had told him of the stranger's anger, had used the word a half-dozen times, the tremble of awe lending spice to her story-teller's voice. And he had seen him, stripped down to his socks, strutting his brash virility across the length of his messy room. If the man chose to attack, Beer would be no match for him. He returned the towel to its hook, and slowly, feeling uneasy about the violation of privacy it implied, began to search the man's room for a weapon. Beer considered the razor, but found it at once too feeble and too deadly; it would be no help in keeping the man at bay, and might kill him in a single, unlucky stroke. A club would be better, some sort of long stick, but Beer could find nothing with sufficient heft. There was some cooking equipment next to a corner stove, but all of such shabby quality that it seemed to have no weight at all, the frying pan drooping from its handle and the saucepan hammered from a penny-sheet of tin. He moved to the bed, considered the table lamp with its broken, cheesecloth shade; opened the wardrobe to find nothing apart from two cotton vests, stiff with dirt, and a change of underwear so threadbare he could see the glow of his own palm as he ran it through its knit. On a shelf near the washbasin he discovered a parcel wrapped in newspaper that responded to his touch with an odd spongy softness. Disconcerted, his mind still haunted by images of the dissected dead, he carried it to the window; opened it gingerly, a handkerchief wrapped around the tips of his fingers. But all he found was a hunk of smoked fish, the eye staring dark and oily into the moonlit sky. The newspaper itself, four weeks old, was a copy of the *Kronen-Zeitung*. Its headlines announced the Russian occupation of eastern Poland; the encirclement of Warsaw by the *Wehrmacht's* might. The picture of Hitler had been altered by a lead-pencilled squiggle, his moustache grown to resemble Stalin's Cossack brush. For a moment Beer experienced a rush of sympathy for the fish's owner, and he felt ashamed of his dogged snooping. Then he shook the thought, and

140

returned the fish; bent low to a box he'd seen stashed near the bed, and pulled a screwdriver from its clutter. It was big and heavy and crude; there was no edge to it, but a flat, rusty head that if need be could be raised to threaten a man's eyes, or be jammed into the softness of his groin. He weighed it wearily, the oath of his profession falling from his lips.

'*Primum non nocere.*' First, do no harm.

At long last he shrugged, shoved it in his pocket, and bent down again to sort through the other items in the box.

Beer found nothing of value. There was a torn handbill announcing a cabaret act in Munich, with a picture of a long-legged woman hitching her skirt high over her knickers; five or six leather balls, sand-filled, with some seepage at the seams; a pack of cigarettes, and a pound of sugar wrapped in a brown bag; two crumpled tubes of grease-paint; and a pair of thick woollen trousers, tied into a bundle with a belt. He also found some photos, a series of three, all taken on the same day in a photographer's studio: the backgrounds changed, from a monochrome curtain to a painted vista of the Alps, but the clothes stayed the same. It was a family of four, the boy and the girl of similar height, neither of them much older than Lieschen. Both parents and son were cheaply if neatly dressed, the Sunday outfit of a working family, starched white linens erupting from the coarse fabric of their trousers, jackets, skirt. Only the little girl was different. In the darkness of the room it was impossible to make a study of her features, but Beer saw enough to notice the little fur cape that had been thrown around her shoulders, from which issued a dress that looked like a crude imitation of an evening gown. Her eyes were outsize, bruised with eyeshadow, small lips vivid as though painted on to the blank little face. The feet were strapped into a pair of narrow boots that grew out of a two-inch heel. In all three of the pictures she held hands with the little boy, her legs spread shoulder-wide, as though struggling for balance. Puzzled, Beer returned the picture to its box; exchanged it for the pack of cigarettes, which he prised open after a moment's hesitation. He had long since smoked the last of his own. Of all his impositions this seemed the least offensive to him, and he lit up the cheap tobacco, having carefully turned his back to the window before he struck the match. It was then, smoking, coughing lightly into one fist, that he returned to his patient's bedside and sat down again on the edge of her bed. She had not moved, but her eyes were wide open. In the patch of moonlight that fell on her face, her features looked fragile, as though made from glass.

He sat and he talked. An hour passed, and the moonlight disappeared behind a drift of clouds, left only the residual glow of the city. Beer was unused to silent patients and found his repertoire consisted largely of questions, which he reeled off into the dark. At times her wink seemed to answer him, and, at a moment's inspiration, he begged her to move her eyelids once for a yes, and twice for a no, then bent close to catch her answers, felt her breath upon his cheek and lips. In this manner he confirmed that she could indeed not speak, nor move her limbs; that she wasn't in pain. When he asked her whether she feared the man in whose flat he had found her, she closed her eyes with what seemed like deliberate torpor and kept them shut. After a while her breathing suggested that she must be asleep. Beer shrugged, lit another cigarette, found he wasn't done talking.

'You must think me queer,' he said into the darkness, one arm stretched to touch her in that bony curve where neck meets skull. 'Sitting up all night in a stranger's place, without so much as asking permission. I'm afraid it must strike you as impertinent.'

And a little while later: 'My wife left me. I suppose I deserved it.'

The woman slept through his comments, her breathing even, the boyish hair thick and knotted underneath his petting, soothing hand. In the morrow, when she was awake again, one would have to comb it out. When he moved, to regain the circulation that had been lost to his left leg, the screwdriver he'd shoved into a trouser pocket bit sharply into the flesh of his thigh. He cursed, stood up, and waited for the mime to hurry up, come home.

CHAPTER 2

The man returned to his flat at what might have been a little after four. It was too dark now for Beer to read the pale dial of his watch. He had managed to stay awake through much of the night, dozing off only once or twice, and then coming awake with a start as he felt his body falling forward towards his patient. Every ten minutes or so he had got up, paced the rooms, looked across the yard to where he assumed Zuzka might be watching. He saw nothing of her, and avoided standing close to the window for more than a few seconds at a time. A light breeze had struck up, drew a coy little dance from the tatters that served as curtains in the first of the two rooms. Beer had smoked ten or twelve of the man's cigarettes, his throat raw with their tobacco. In his boredom he'd found himself clearing up a little of the front room's clutter, had picked up socks, magazines and newspapers, and stacked them in a corner near the bed, then wet his hands, his face, the back of his neck.

When he finally heard steps approach the door, followed by the jingle of a set of keys, he was back

144

at the woman's bedside, crouching low next to her sleeping features. Quickly, abiding by a decision he had made some hours before, he moved a step or two into the other room so that the man might see him at once. Beer had no desire to surprise or frighten him, and felt certain he would not sound any alarm. His hand was shoved down his trouser pocket, fingers wrapped around the screwdriver. It took an age for the man to understand the door wasn't locked. It was possible, Beer thought, that he'd had too much to drink.

When he finally entered, he did not deign to notice him at first: shrugged his coat off near the door, threw down a cloth bag no larger than a school satchel, reached behind one ear to retrieve a cigarette that was wedged there against a dark tousle of hair. His neck, torso, arms and legs were all dressed in the same jet-black cloth; even his hands were covered, rose invisible in the dark. It was only the cigarette that moved, left its perch and was thrust into the centre of a ghostly face. A match was struck, lit up his eyes, dark, bulging orbs that stared across the distance of the room. The man had yet to close the door. It occurred to Beer that he was making up his mind whether or not he should run. He took his sweet time.

It puzzled the doctor.

In the hours of the wait, going over in his head what Zuzka had told him, and walking amongst the squalor of his room, Beer had resolved that this was a primitive man, easily angered. He'd expected shouting: a drunk and clumsy charge. But the man who was walking towards him now was composed, the white face a wall, unreadable, dark eyes staring from it with a wet sort of passion for which the doctor could not find a name. He was heading for Beer, his eyes fixed beyond the intruder, on the doorway to the back room. As soon as Beer realised the man's intent, he got out of the way, took three, four quick steps to one side, his hand sweaty against the screwdriver's grip. The mime disappeared: Beer heard him step up to the woman's bed, then quickly turn to draw the curtains, the spare light growing dimmer yet. When he returned to the front room, he was holding a pocket knife, the blade opened over a handle made of bone. It might have been four inches long. The bone shone white in his gloved hand: it seemed to reflect the pallor of his face. Beer spoke, wishing to forestall the man's decision to attack.

'Is she your wife?' he asked.

There might have been better places to begin.

The mime just looked at him with that blank of a face. His forearm rose, the one with the knife, wiped hard across the length of his lips: greasepaint staining the cuff of his black sweater. A mouth emerged, thick, heavy lips gaping open like a wound. All of a sudden his anger was obvious. When he spoke, the words rushed out amongst a shower of spittle.

'Who the hell are you?'

The knife was stretched forward, pointing at Beer.

'I'm a doctor. I live in the house. Anton Beer.'

The man nodded at the name, as though he'd heard it before. The upper half of his face remained as unreadable as before.

'How did you get in here?'

'All I want is to help your wife. We can call the police if you like.'

With an effort of will, Beer let go of the screwdriver and showed the man both his palms. His fingers looked thin to him, the knuckles chapped and swollen. He must have lost weight in the past few months. The man observed the gesture, but did not lower his knife. Only the mouth showed emotion, a tremendous, quivering anger. Regardless, the doctor pressed on.

'She will die if nobody sees to her. I know you don't want that. You—' He searched for something definite, something that would convince the man. 'You brush her teeth. Even the molars. It must take a lot of patience to do that. A lot of love.'

Slowly, gradually, the man relaxed his arm; bit his lip and tucked away the knife, slipped it into some invisible pocket of his trousers. The anger remained on his mouth, and, as though to master it, he turned away, walked over to the sink, stripping off his gloves and sweater as he walked. Beer watched him as he bent low over the sink and began to wash his face. The mime's eyes never left the intruder, were fixed on the mirror. Halfway through, he flicked on the bulb, and they both of them winced at the sudden flood of light. A mix of grease and water was travelling down the man's muscular chest and back, left streaks upon his skin. When he was done, there remained only a thread of white, framing his hairline and the cut of his chin. The face that emerged looked raw with emotion. Whatever composure he had was washing down the plughole. Even the voice seemed changed, seemed coarser, Bavarian vowels laying siege to his Viennese.

'She's not my wife,' he said. 'She's my sister. Eva.'

Beer remembered the photo, nodded. 'You two are close?'

'Twins,' said the man, though his face looked nothing like the woman's, looked meaty and boorish and burdened with anger.

'Why do you say that she'll die?'

'She has bedsores. From lying still for too long. Some of them are very advanced. Very dangerous. They are prone to infection.' Beer paused, trying to gauge whether the man was following what he was telling him. 'How long has she been like this? Paralysed, I mean?'

The mime shrugged, ran his fingernails along his chin, scraping off flecks of paint that were hiding there.

'She'll die from lying still?' he murmured, something passing through his face that took Beer a few moments to place: the thought, light and evil, of a life without his twin.

The doctor nodded. 'She might. She needs medical attention. How long has she been paralysed?'

'Ten years.'

'Ten years? And she doesn't speak?'

'Not since she was thirteen. Mother used to care for her. Now she's with me.'

'And nobody knows she's here?'

The mime shook his head. 'I carried her in at night. A friend helped me. We pretended she was drunk. She wasn't sick then.'

'She is now,' said Anton Beer and reached for a cigarette. While he stood there, lighting it, he noticed the man notice that the cigarette was one of his. His face darkened with the thought of the doctor rifling through his things. For a moment it threatened everything: his fists bunched, the weight of his body shifting into shoulders and arms. It cost the mime great effort to unclench himself, and accept the half-empty packet that Beer held out to him.

'You must decide what you want to do. We could bring her to a hospital, but—'

'They'll kill her.' It came out as a snarl; in his eyes once again that sly look of longing. It passed through like a wedge of geese giving chase to summer: you'd blink and they were gone. The rest of his face was busy with his anger and his grief. 'I've heard stories.'

He gestured widely with his hands, cigarettes scattering from the open pack. Beer didn't contradict him. He'd heard stories, too. They had been there even before the war had started. By now they were taking on a more definite shape.

'Yes,' he said simply. 'They might.'

He took a breath, made his play. It wasn't until the words were out that he realised how anxious he was for their acceptance.

'You have to leave Eva in my care,' he said. 'She needs to be turned, four, five times a day, and massaged head to toe. The wounds have to be seen to, the dead tissue removed. I live in my practice. You can't help her. Nobody needs to know.'

The man took it in, brow creased in thought. His hand rose, thumb and forefinger taking hold of his nose. He blew snot into his open palm, then wiped it on the seat of his trousers: a fluid gesture, untroubled by breeding. Next Beer knew, that same thumb and finger had come together once again and hung in the air rubbing one another, in a gesture as old as the gods.

'How much—?' the man began to ask, but Beer interrupted him.

'You needn't pay,' he said. 'It is my duty as a physician.'

The phrase came out pat: it irritated the man. Beer could see he was struggling with the implications of his offer. He wondered how long it was that he had been his sister's only caretaker. It remained hard to believe that they were twins.

'We better carry her up right away, while it's still dark. The fewer people know, the better. We don't want anyone to call the hospital. Or the police. If we do meet someone, we'll say she fainted and we are taking her to my practice.'

'All right.'

With two words, the man had settled it. He turned away from Beer, thus hiding his face, and walked his dark passions over to his sister's room.

They were busy lifting the woman out of her bed, Beer holding the feet, and her brother steadying head, neck and shoulders, before he spoke again. He had put his sweater back on, and turned off the light; was a smudge of skin suspended in the dark.

'If you touch her—' he said, and pursed his lips in a manner calculated to give meaning to the phrase.

'You needn't worry. I'm a doctor.'

'If you touch her,' he resumed as though Beer had not spoken, 'I will come break your neck.'

Beer told the man he understood. He wondered when would be a good time to ask him whether or not he had killed Speckstein's dog.

CHAPTER 3

The janitor saw them carry the body across the yard. He did not recognise them at first. The night was very nearly black, dawn still some hours away, the city around them leaking a faint yellow glow. All he could see was the shadow of two men, a bedsheet between them, in which lay rolled the body of a slender corpse. They almost dropped it as they tried to open the door that led to the main stairwell; there was a stumble and an oath. The janitor recognised the voice, and put a name to the first of the shadows. Otto Frei. He had shown up not a month back, secured a sublet from the previous tenant who'd gone home to live with his mother; had paid extra for a second bed, for 'women friends' as he'd nervously explained. A man in his twenties, shifty like a vagrant. Thus far, the janitor had not seen him bring home any tarts. He worked at night and slept during the day, had brought his own curtains and hung them out back. The night watchman, Neurath, had told him that he worked as a clown. He couldn't be earning much more than he ate.

The second man he recognised by his movements.

There was something slow about the doctor. It was there even now, when he was bent on haste, a pair of ankles in his hands and a man for company who was little other than a bum: the leaden patience of a man who thinks before he steps. The janitor remembered Beer's wife: a striking, long-limbed woman, very much a lady. Once, some weeks before she left, Frau Beer had stopped by his cellar workshop to complain about the plumbing, and led him to their private toilet with a proud self-assurance that did not flinch when he lifted the lid upon her pungent mess. She'd looked tired then, a little heavy in the midriff. One story went that she was pregnant with another man's child: Frau Vesalius had told him that while she beat a carpet in the yard. Perhaps it was true, but the janitor did not think so. The bricks, they told another tale. It was now thirty-seven years that he'd been working in their service. At times they spoke to him directly, whispered to his fingertips as he ran them past their frames of mortar. Or else it was the house's dead who came forward, a story on their lips: the little babe who'd died of suffocation, four days old, the inquest queasy about the bruises near its neck; or the fat old woman it had taken four to carry out, a judge's daughter he was told, gone to seed on cream puffs and morphine, hand-delivered every morning. Lately, it had been the dog that came sniffing: nipped his feet sometimes when he had nodded off, or crawled under the blanket in search of warmth; talked to him quietly, in whimpers and in growls. You had to kick it, make it shut its bloody gob, a trail of pee when it ran yelping to its grave. Of course, all it was: his head was growing soft. He drank too much, often started in the morning, talked to himself, heard voices. 'Janitor', he called himself, 'Janitor', the tag of his profession. Seventy years old and a frame on him like he was thirty; chasing the murmur at the bottom of an earthenware jug filled with rowan-berry schnapps. He had been working through much of the night; had stepped into the yard just now to breathe the air and smoke a cigarette, an apron tied around his neck and waist. Out came the doctor and that bum of a clown, carrying a corpse, whispers, stories, rising from its linen sheet.

His instinct was to follow them, see where they were going: up to the fourth floor and the doctor's rooms, or out the main door, into the street. The janitor took a step, plodding, soundless, the way he knew how, then remembered his apron, the blood smeared across his stomach, chest, and hands. It was drying now, drying into skin and cloth; smelled of metal, sea and salt. The taste was so thick, he wondered whether some had strayed into his face. The cigarette smelled of it, as though it had been dunked in blood; he had yet to light its tip. So he stood and he listened, and heard precisely nothing: not the slamming of a door, nor the twin tread of men, carrying a dead-weight up

154

the stairs. The janitor looked up and found the doctor's rooms, waited to see whether he would turn on a light. He didn't. The minutes passed, dawn inching nearer, a breeze in the chestnut leaves, picking up force. Behind him, in the darkness, the janitor became aware of the swing of the cellar door, heard the wheeze of Neurath's breath rising laboured from his wasted lungs: a wet sort of breathing, a man drowning on clean air. Fräulein Speckstein had breathed like that, just a little, bringing back his keys.

'We better get back to work,' Neurath said. 'I need to be done by sun-up, return to my post.' He spoke softly and fast, caught his breath after each phrase.

The janitor acquiesced, followed him in, the smell of blood growing thicker here, along with that of boiling fat. He would let the air out later that morning, once the kitchens got going, two dozen households frying cauliflower, potatoes, pork liver and *Speck*. He'd ask Neurath to return at the end of his shift, help him clean up the mess. Together, they walked down into the cellar workshop, and as they passed the game table that had taken him three days to build, the janitor indulged himself by running two knuckles across its smooth and polished surface. After school, little Lieschen would come, and they would have themselves a game.

CHAPTER 4

And just like that, he was gone out of her life. For three whole days, all Zuzka saw of Dr Beer was a few minutes' worth of interview when she sent Vesalius to fetch him to her sick bed: perfunctory visits in which he took her pulse and advised her curtly to 'pull herself together'. She went up to his apartment, mid-morning on the day after she had brought him to the green-eyed lady, and again after dinner, but he saw her off at the door, explaining that he was 'quite simply snowed under with work'. She asked, of course, whether he had sent for the police to arrest the man who had so mistreated the woman, but was told, with a heat that surprised her in the doctor, that she had misunderstood the whole situation.

'The man is her brother. Otto Frei by name. I am seeing to the patient.'

And added, in a tone at once conspiratorial and patronising, 'Better not mention it to anyone. Especially your uncle. Frei has reasons to keep quiet about Eva. Reasons one should respect.'

It stung her, this 'Eva', thrown in with a familiarity

that contrasted sharply with the hurried formality with which he treated her now.

'I will come with you when you go to see her next,' she pleaded, swallowing the sharper words that had risen to her tongue, but was met once again by his shaking head.

'It's simply no longer your concern, Fräulein Speckstein.'

And then, with an avuncular benevolence that only served to irritate her further: 'Look here, the winter semester has only just started. There may still be time to secure a place; no doubt your uncle can pull a few strings. If you are so keen for patients of your own, there is no better place to start.'

She began to protest, but he simply closed the door on her, closed it gently, without haste or anger, as one does with a pedlar whose tawdry wares one has declined. Never in her life had she been so summarily dismissed.

Nor could she gather any more information by keeping up her surveillance of the apartment across the yard. She had watched it on the night Beer had waited for the mime's return (this despite a deep exhaustion that beset her like a fever), but had not been able to see much beyond the glow of a cigarette, moving up and down the length of the two rooms. For a brief interval – it must have been gone four o'clock by then – the light had been turned on and she had watched them talking, Beer and the stranger: the latter angry, stripped down to his waist. Then they had turned the light off again, and she, overcome by the many hours at the window, had thrown herself on to her bed and fallen asleep, pins and needles running through her calves and lower thighs. The next night, she stood guard from midnight onwards, only to discover that the mime had acquired somewhere a new set of curtains for the first of his two rooms. He drew them just as soon as he came home; poked his head through once, puffed on a cigarette, his face paint still in place, then disappeared again behind their heavy cloth, a cold, sudden rain bearing down into the yard.

She turned to Lieschen next, the only other bearer of her secret; wondered whether she had heard something, seen something; was keen to rekindle in herself the feeling that she stood at the centre of this mystery. Zuzka found her on the street outside the building, skipping up and down the pavement, alternately hitting or avoiding all the many puddles left behind by the rain, the hem of her dress sodden like a dishcloth. A dirty little teddy bear, much worn by use, was dangling from her wrist: it seemed she had tied it there with a piece of string. As soon as she caught sight of Zuzka, the girl smiled and ran towards her, then stopped and blushed as she drew close; raised a hand over one eye, the teddy rising with it, hanging upside down before her face. It was from behind the shelter of this impromptu patch that Lieschen addressed herself to her friend.

'Fräulein Zuzka!' she called, putting special emphasis upon her name. 'Is it true that it's a Czech name? Imagine, we have been friends all this time and you never told me.'

Zuzka smiled, charmed as ever by the girl's good nature, trying to make out what Lieschen was hiding with her hand.

'Yes,' she said, 'it's Czech. My sister was Dáša – Dagmar – and my mother, Milena.'

The girl nodded excitedly. 'Janitor told me. He says when you are Czech it's *"Pani"* and not *"Fräulein"*. Is that right?'

'Yes,' she said. 'What else did the janitor tell you?'

She shrugged, shook her head, laughed. 'Something I didn't understand. About politics and so forth: *"protect-or-rate of bloody shwaykes"*. But you should've said something. I said it wrong all along. So it's *"Pani Zuzka"*. *"Pani, pani, pani"*. It's much nicer than *"Fräulein"*.'

In her joy at her discovery, the girl let drop the raised hand and spun herself into a clumsy little pirouette. One of her feet hit a puddle and splashed not only herself but Zuzka, too, with a spray of muddy water.

'Look out,' Zuzka called, jumping back. Then she caught sight of what the girl had been hiding.

'But how did this happen?'

No sooner had Lieschen recovered her balance than she realised her secret was out. Her first instinct, clumsily deceitful, was to throw her hand back up to her face and deny that anything was wrong; her lips were set for the lie, eyes hardening with a fierce sort of pride. But almost immediately something else won out, and Lieschen lowered arm and teddy once again and stood gazing at her adult friend. A blush spread, started at neck and cheeks and shot upwards, to the roots of her hair. Zuzka noticed it, felt moved, her own childhood stirring in her, inarticulate and grave. She lowered herself into a crouch to look more closely at the discoloration that covered Lieschen's cheekbone and sat in a loop around the eye: green, yellow, blue, the elusive colours of an oil slick spread against her fragile, childish skin.

'How did this happen?' she repeated, more gently now, and took hold of the girl's shoulders. 'Did you get into a fight at school?'

The girl shook her head, then shrugged. She seemed very much ashamed of something, was fidgeting under Zuzka's hands.

'Your father then?'

Again the girl shrugged, wet her mouth: pink tongue lingering on the bow of her upper lip.

'He's very sad,' she said at last. 'More than usual.'

'He's drunk, you mean. Did he beat you when he was drunk?'

The girl hung her head and dug around in the pocket of her dress, retrieving a handkerchief still carefully folded, as though it had been purchased like that and not yet been spread out.

She pointed to its pattern with a strange insistence, and held it up for Zuzka to admire.

'It's pretty, isn't it? So many colours.'

'Your father gave you that?'

The girl nodded, her eyes pleading for something that Zuzka couldn't quite grasp. She was about to tell Lieschen that it was monstrous, buying her off with a gaudy piece of cloth bought from some penny vendor, and promise that she would have words with her father – or with her uncle! – when it dawned on her that the girl was beseeching her to let it drop. Lieschen was not ashamed for running around with a black eye; she was ashamed that people would realise her father had hit her: in this, it seemed, she sensed some terrible humiliation. It was almost as though it was she who had done the hitting. Touched, exasperated, Zuzka straightened and offered the girl her hand.

'We need to put some meat on the eye. A steak or a pork chop. That's what my mother did when somebody got hurt in the face: put meat on the bruise. I don't know why, but it seems to work.'

'A steak?' Lieschen asked dubiously.

'Yes,' said Zuzka. 'Come, we'll go upstairs to Frau Vesalius's kitchen and fetch one. I dare say you'll look funny with a steak over one eye.'

The girl smiled at that, took Zuzka's hand, and allowed herself to be walked up to Speckstein's flat.

It might have been better to buy a steak at the butcher's shop, but Zuzka did not want to spend the little money she had. Also, rationing had started some weeks ago, and she had no access to the household's coupons. Perhaps it would be possible to take the meat without Vesalius noticing: Zuzka had no interest in explaining it to her, and had avoided the widow since their conversation about marriage some three days before. She asked the girl to wait outside on the landing and let herself into the flat, the hallway carpet swallowing the sound of her tread. She was in luck: Vesalius was not in the kitchen just then. Zuzka ran to the larder, searched the meat shelf, found a stack of cutlets wrapped in red butcher's paper. She took the topmost, felt the cold, spongy moistness of meat. It called to mind, for a moment, the strange woman's back: the blackened holes that gaped at hip, bum and shoulder blade. Disgusted, momentarily dizzy, she felt a stab as though of something cold deep in one lung; felt a rash of goosebumps charge up one leg; stood wheezing by the kitchen window, recovering her wits. It was there that Vesalius found her. The widow stepped into the kitchen and saw her holding the packet of meat. Something ran through the housekeeper's face, it might have been worry. It was soon expunged by her habitual sourness of expression.

'That's tomorrow's lunch, that,' she said gruffly, and moved to take it from Zuzka's hand. Zuzka would not let her, tore it away from the woman's grip, then clasped it to the shiver of her bosom like a letter from some beau.

'I will bring it back,' she shouted and broke into a run, slammed the door on the way out, then stood upon the landing searching her blouse for stains.

'Is that the steak?' asked Lieschen, her hands raised over her ears, startled by the bang of the door.

'Pork chop,' said Zuzka and quickly dragged her down the stairs.

Out in the street, Zuzka's breathing calmed, and sensation returned to the toes of her left foot, which, for some minutes, had lain stuffed in her shoe as though dead. They walked half a mile until they had reached the grounds of the hospital, where there was a row of park benches shielded by trees.

And so they sat, Zuzka and the girl, on a bench watching invalids take the air, Lieschen with the unwrapped pork chop placed over one eye, its juices running in thin rivulets down her face and chin, a bloody moustache forming in the down over her upper lip. It did not take long until they both broke out in laughter at their adventure. It rose in Zuzka first: she thought of Vesalius, the scene in the kitchen, their wrestling like fishwives over a pound of flesh (in her imagination they stood, legs spread for balance, arms bloodied to their elbows, tugging at either end of half a pig), and then of her desperate gesture as she cradled the meat against her breast. When the laughter burst out of her, Lieschen was, at first, surprised.

She looked up from under the chop, blood drops like tears streaking down her cheek, then fell to laughing herself, hesitant at first, unsure why Zuzka was so merry, then – the floodgates opened – with ever greater energy, until she drummed her feet into the ground and dropped the pork chop into her lap. It was only the stares of passers-by that convinced them to calm down, little by little, and then the slow onset of a cold rain which bid them leave the bench and make for home.

Once they had arrived inside the building, Zuzka took back the chop and wrapped it up again in the red butcher's paper in order to return it to Vesalius's larder. Before she took leave of the girl, who stood wet and shivering in the front hallway, peering into her father's letter box, she remembered why she had sought her out in the first place and quickly asked her a question: had Lieschen heard any more about the green-eyed lady with the torn-open back, or seen anything to do with the man the doctor claimed was her brother? To her surprise, Lieschen had. In quick, simple phrases, she told 'Pani Zuzka' that, early in the morning when Zuzka was still sleeping, exhausted by the long hours she had stayed awake, she had watched the 'sad, angry man' walk up the main staircase just as she was on her way to the bakery to fetch some rolls for breakfast. Curious, aware that this was the man who lived in the flat where Zuzka and she had found the 'beautiful angel who doesn't move', Lieschen had followed and watched him go into Dr Beer's practice; and this not just that 'first' morning, but 'yesterday, too' and 'once again this morning': she had waited for him out here by the letter boxes, even though it made her late for school.

'He kept on yawning and didn't even raise his hand like one does when one has manners,' Lieschen said, proud of all the knowledge she had managed to accrue. 'Is he really very bad?'

Zuzka shook her head. 'I really don't know,' she said, bowed down to the girl and kissed her on the crown of her head. They took their leave then, young woman and girl, each of them off to rest a little and change into dry clothes.

CHAPTER 5

She went to talk to Beer the next morning, determined to show him that she would not be shut out of his secrets. Her first step was to beg her uncle for an alarm clock and then set it for the break of dawn: she wanted to see for herself how Otto Frei called on the doctor. Speckstein obliged, but seemed out of temper. He'd spent much of the afternoon on the phone, and had gone out around six, not wearing his coat, to return half an hour later with a look of restrained frustration. At dinner, sitting across from one another at the dining-room table, sharing a plate of cold cuts and cheese, he had spoken little apart from enquiring after her health, his tone quietly contemptuous as it always was when addressing his niece. She declared she was 'somewhat better' and told him she might be able to enrol at the university this semester after all, or in any case audit a number of lectures. He made a note to contact an old colleague, producing a leather-bound diary for the purpose, and urged her to rejoin the Party youth group Faith and Beauty, now she was in better health. Zuzka was in bed an hour later and listened to the tinny bleating of the Oriental's trumpet, rehearsing mourning in the confines of his garret. When she pressed her hands to her ears, reaching vainly for sleep, she was surprised to find the melody persisted undiminished.

The alarm clock woke her, rang first in the distant reaches of her dream, then spat her out into a rainy dawn, her curtain open, water streaking down the windowpane. Zuzka sat up, silenced the bell with her hand until she found the little lever that shut off the action of its clapper. She was dressed and waiting by the window long before she saw Otto Frei's figure step into the yard. He passed their front door not two minutes later: she stood at its peephole, caught him trotting past, hair tousled, sleepy, a cigarette jutting from his fleshy lip. Otto stayed at the doctor's for a quarter of an hour, then returned. Zuzka was back at her window, watched him cross the yard and open the door to the side wing. She had long put on her shoes and jacket, and now left her room at once; had dressed, on purpose, in the oldest of her clothes, a blue cotton blouse and mouse-brown skirt, twice mended where moths had eaten through the fabric. At the last moment, walking out of the flat, she opened the hallway cupboard and took out the short coat with the fur collar which her mother had given her, to wear to the opera', and which she very much liked but had not had any occasion to wear. Why she took the coat she could not herself say, other than a vague sense that she wanted, after all, to look good before the stranger, and this despite having decided it was best to approach him 'humbly', in the oldest of her dresses. Zuzka was outside, crossing the yard, before it struck her how ridiculous she must look, in the shabby, twice-mended skirt and fur collar, running to avoid the rain, but it seemed too late now to turn back, and in any case, what did it matter? She was meeting a man who might be a murderer, never mind what the doctor said. It took a minute to climb the stairs to Otto Frei's door, and ten to find the courage to knock. He opened almost at once.

Otto Frei was dressed in dirty trousers and the black sweater that he wore for work. His face was sleep-creased, blotchy; he was drinking coffee from a blue tin cup. Zuzka noticed at once that the door to the back room stood wide open; that the room was light, its curtains open to admit the day; that there was no foot that would stick out the end of the bed. Otto followed her gaze, shrugged. He turned around and walked a few paces into his room to fetch a packet of cigarettes; leaned against the wall lighting one, clearly feeling much at ease.

'What do you want?' he asked.

She did not answer, found just then she had no voice, her gaze still fixed on the back room, and the questions it implied.

'She's gone,' said the man, some of his anger re-entering his voice. 'The doctor says you know and will keep your trap shut. But come in, see for yourself.'

So she crossed his threshold, stepped into the room, closed the door. His smell was everywhere, cigarettes and sweat, the piles of magazines. It seemed pointless to inspect the back room and she gave it only a cursory glance, saw the rubber sheet rolled up in one corner, a pair of men's underwear thrown carelessly on the ground. Quickly she returned to a position close to the front door, all the while staying away from the windows. She did not want to be seen by the neighbours, standing alone in a strange man's room. All the same she found that she was grateful that the windows stood wide open; if she had to scream (and she was preparing her body for just that, breathing more deeply than was necessary, a stiffness spreading through the muscles of her neck), people would hear her, come to her rescue. She wished he would speak to her, explain who he was, and what was wrong with his sister; tell her why her illness was subject to such secrecy. But the man simply stared at her and smoked his cigarette. In his coarse features amusement could be read. He had yet to offer her a seat.

Agitated, focusing on his discourtesy, she cast around for a chair, and noticed instead the knife lying open on the sink, the handle made of bone. The sight of the knife unlocked something in her, and, turning around to face the man, half her mind busy with locating a chair, she found herself talking: not about the woman he'd kept hidden in a darkened room, nor about the man himself, but the murders that she'd heard about, and the killing of the dog. The deaths had not occupied her much of late, there was so much else that had clamoured for attention, but now, as she stood in the stranger's room, Lieschen's words came back to her, about the naked woman in the schoolyard, and the death of her sister, too, was tied up in it somehow, and what came out was precisely this, some babble about the 'dead woman' whom the policeman had to 'wrap into his coat', 'lying naked, quite naked for schoolboys to stare at', and about her uncle's dog, 'left butchered in the yard across – killed with a knife'. By the time she had finished, the man was laughing at her quite openly, scattering cigarette ash from his grinning mouth.

'You laugh,' she said, her temper rising, 'but I saw you wash the blood down this very sink.'

It wiped the smirk off his face.

In the first moment, she thought he might run at her and hit her. He pushed off from the wall, and dropped the cigarette; took two steps towards her, hands rolled into fists. But then he halted, thinking, the muscles of his jaw and brow bunching with the effort.

'You think—' he started to say, then stopped himself. 'But maybe I just cut myself.'

He paused again, looking for words, when a new thought seemed to occur to him. 'You didn't tell anyone,' he muttered, more to himself than to her, then stared at her as though he saw her for the first time, some strange calculation running through his features. 'Not even Speckstein.'

She shook her head, perplexed by his changes of mood, wishing to appease, even to please him.

'I only told the doctor,' she said, almost a whisper, 'and he knows how to keep a secret. Your sister is with him now?'

'Yes.'

'And she is called Eva? It's such a lovely name.'

She thought he would smile at that and hasten to agree, but he merely frowned and continued to watch her, chin pushed forward as though itching for a fight. Zuzka had never had a conversation with a man such as this. It was as though they were talking across some great chasm: all her social mannerisms, acquired at her father's table, in the society of lawyers, teachers, country doctors – they all seemed useless with this man. He was immune to social graces, and seemed impregnable as a result. At home, through the years of adolescence, Zuzka had learned the art of charming men by taunting them with an audacity they were too chivalrous to repay in kind. It seemed to work with Dr Beer. It didn't work with Otto Frei.

And then, just as she was thinking this, holding on to the smile she had affected at the mention of his sister's name, his stare changed and became somehow very insolent. It was as though, brazenly – wishing her to know just what he was doing – he was picturing her naked body underneath her jacket, blouse and skirt, and was arranging it into various poses and positions, evaluating them in his mind's eye. His excitement was obvious, and she quickly stepped away from the sink, made as though to run for the door, but in the end she took no more than one little step. It only brought her closer to this man and his hunger. She, too, found herself remembering his naked body, half-aroused, pacing up and down this very room.

'So what do you want?' he asked again, a crude suggestion vivid in his gaze. 'Why are you here?'

'Dr Beer won't let me see Eva,' she said, squirming under his gaze, and aware at once how childish it sounded. 'It isn't good,' she quickly added, 'leaving a woman with a single man.'

'What do you care?' he barked, though she saw at once that her last remark had stung him: blood shot to his face, sat there like a rash. He turned away from her, released her from his insolent eyes.

'I'm also sick. Not like your sister, though perhaps – Dr Beer is at a loss.'

She said it as a lie, from self-importance, and because she had long taken a fancy to thinking herself sick, but once the words were out she found she believed them, and believed, too, that there might be a connection, a mysterious connection, between herself and the paralysed Eva Frei.

'I thought, perhaps, that a pair of sympathetic hands – a woman's hands, you see . . . and, besides, I am studying to become a doctor myself.'

'And you won't tell Speckstein?' He had sat down on the bed and leaned against the back-board, put his dirty feet upon the sheet. Where ten seconds ago he'd been bulging first with lust, then anger, he seemed at ease now, his eyelids lazy and as though drooping into sleep.

'Not about the blood and not about Eva,' she said. 'But why the secrecy? After all she's merely sick.'

He looked up at that, nodded, seemed ready to launch into an explanation; barked out a half-dozen phrases, about the 'public-health doctor' and the 'health court', and something about the son of a landlady, 'that rotten swine', then stopped as though sick of the whole topic and spat on the floor with no regard for what he might hit. 'Ask the doctor,' he said after a pause. 'He explains it all very well.'

'And she really can't move at all?'

This, too, created a reaction. He swung his feet off the bed, walked briskly to the window, patted down his pockets for another cigarette. For a moment he looked like a boy, lost in the role of playing a man. It was impossible just then to recall the stare with which he had appraised her flesh.

'Sometimes,' he said, grinning nervously from behind a breath of smoke. 'Sometimes, I think there's nothing wrong with her at all.' He coughed, as though embarrassed, swore, scratched between his legs. 'But it's out of my hands.' His eyes found hers, were soft now, boyish. 'I had no choice, you see. The doctor says she is dying, just from lying still. It eats holes in her skin.'

She nodded, smiled a little at the simplicity of his phrase, then bit her lip for being so unfeeling. And still she pushed on with her questions.

'How did it start, her illness?' she asked.

'There was a – She was only a child, we both were. She was performing, you see, and then. There was –'

Something happened to his train of thought, it seemed to have got stuck somewhere, then turned muddled. He tried to straighten it again by beginning to pace the room, his body thrown forward, one arm swinging like a pendulum. The anger was back in his voice and face.

'Your uncle touched a young girl. Did you know that? He was thrown out of university because of it. Ask anyone.'

'But your sister –'

'To hell with my sister,' he shouted all of a sudden. 'Ten years we took care of her, Mother and I. To hell with her. It's all yesterday's snow.'

His anger cowed her, drove her over to the door. She grabbed the handle, started turning it, was halfway out the door before she turned to reassure him.

'You love her very much, don't you?' she said to him, her voice very gentle, as though shushing a babe. He stood, legs planted wide amongst the magazines and dirty socks that littered his floor, a man looking for balance: his features trapped between anger, lust and pity. It was a mixture so peculiar it brought a thought to her head, at once flattering and enticing. *There is a man underneath,* she thought, *who is wounded and noble.* She would make it her task, she decided, to guide him to the surface.

CHAPTER 6

Beer found he liked the little things, the way her eyes moved, following the passage of the shadows as the sun inched forward through the hours of the day; and the flutter of her lids, now fast and imperious, now slow and almost coy, inflecting her answers with impatience or irony or quiet passion, just as she chose. She was not always responsive. There were times – minutes, hours – during which she seemed asleep with her eyes wide open, and would react neither to his continuous banter, nor even to the touch of his hand. This bothered him, filled him with fear, and he was, in those moments, unable to refrain from reaching down, laying two fingers on her narrow throat and reassuring himself as to the beating of her pulse. Beer found that he could talk to Eva, could spell out truths, or at any rate grasp at them with a boldness that he did not otherwise allow himself. She listened with equanimity, and sometimes a wink. Of course it was also possible that it was a purely physiological phenomenon, and that her mind was as empty as a drum.

On the first afternoon after her arrival, he had

set up an impromptu operating theatre in his examination room, sterilised his scalpel and two pairs of tongs, and excised most of the rotten flesh from the two bedsores where the destruction of tissue was at its most advanced. Beer had spent considerable time arranging her bed, going so far as to make a sketch of the three positions between which he had decided to rotate her body, then took pains over finding her a nightgown that would give her a semblance of modesty as well as a little pleasure. He had rejected two of the more risqué gowns his wife had, towards the end of their relationship, ordered from Paris, and settled on a simple but nicely adorned piece made from a double layer of cream silk that lay loosely around Eva's slender frame.

In the days after Eva's arrival, there were a number of vexations. First, his laundry, urgently needed, did not arrive, and, when he called by the shop, the door was locked, with no note to explain the absence. Then Otto Frei came every morning, arriving several hours before his first patient. Otto would cast a quick glance at his sister, then insist on sitting in the kitchen and agree to a cup of Beer's morning coffee. He spoke little, sat sullenly before the steaming cup, and yet was in no hurry to be on his way. In the end some queer little question would flow out of him – How much did one earn as a doctor? Would Eva learn to speak again? What did Beer think about what the papers called the science of 'he-re-ditty'? – or else an anecdote, choppily told, though not without a suggestive power, about work and his past and the life of a performer. It was the telling of these stories that provided occasions, fleeting seconds, when, freed for a moment from the torrent of emotion and the selfish cunning with which he sought to become its master, Otto's coarse features became almost beautiful and a vague resemblance emerged between the two twins. These woke in Beer the wish to see Otto Frei perform, though, of course: he couldn't leave Eva. When he stepped out, as he did one night to go to town and look after some of his own affairs, he did so hurriedly, making sure to return within the hour.

Then one evening Speckstein came to visit, wishing to learn whether the police detective had called, and pressing Beer for his opinion of the 'case'. He was visibly put out when he learned that Beer had not yet been contacted by the police, and unhappy, too, at Beer's cautious answers concerning the contents of the files. All through their talk, Beer's main preoccupation was that Speckstein not find any reason to ask to step into his bedroom, which he had given over to Eva's use (he himself slept in his living room). Three or four times, in his own answers to Speckstein's probing questions, he noticed an obscure allusion either to paralysis, to the permanently crippled, or to the bedroom itself. At another time, the mind's unconscious urge to betray itself through careless words might have amused him, but now he found himself breaking out in a sweat and searching Speckstein's face for signs that he had somehow latched on to the hidden meaning behind his answers. When Speckstein left, bowing to Beer with all the formality of his outdated manners, he promised again that a detective would call in the next few days 'for certain'. Beer assured him that he would offer every assistance, then closed the door and returned to Eva's bedside, rearranging the pillows, and rubbing alcohol into her skin.

On the fourth morning after Eva Frei's arrival, only a handful of patients presented themselves in Beer's waiting room. By eleven o'clock he had whittled them down to two men: the first the neighbourhood greengrocer, who hobbled into the examination room, then rolled up his trouser cuff to reveal a torn-open calf, crudely bandaged in a tea towel (he insisted that there was no need to trouble the hospital); the second a man of about forty years of age who complained about stomach cramps. He was a tall man, big-boned and awkward in his physicality: the hips bigger even than his shoulders, with long, flabby legs, and little islands of coarse hair that clustered on his knuckles. He had a thick shock of hair that could not be anything other than a wig. Jet black, it sprang in a double wave from a crisp parting high upon his scalp, then stopped abruptly above the shaven side of his ears and neck. The face was commonplace, doughy; the eyes almost black, the lips very thin and very red. It was as though a hole had been clawed from his face, then circled by a line to mark the mouth. The suit he wore was almost new, yet worn somehow in a slovenly manner; brown lambswool, too thick for the season. When he unbuttoned his shirt, to let the doctor at his gut, Beer was struck by how big his nipples were, clinging oddly to his flabby chest.

'So what is it, Doctor?' he asked after repeated prods, each of them answered by a low and almost comical groan. 'Is it very bad?'

Beer asked a few routine questions, then gave his verdict. 'You have nothing to worry about. It's just wind. It can be very painful.'

'Farts,' laughed the man, though his eyes took on no lustre. 'And here I was expecting a death sentence.'

He swung around, sat with his legs dangling from the examination table and listened to Beer's dietary advice, his hands busy with his shirt buttons. When he was done, he stood up, put on his jacket, then neither pulled out his insurance papers nor made any movement towards the door but simply stood there, looking about the examination room, and especially at the shelf of books that Beer had moved there, feeling that the presence of some volumes was expected by his patients. He passed a hairy hand over the names embossed on the spines, and even took the liberty of fetching down a volume of basic pharmacology.

Beer was about to object, but the man cut him off with a question.

'You used to work as a neurologist, didn't you? Or a psychiatrist, I never quite understood the difference. You have read Dr Freud, I suppose? The Jewish doctor.'

The black eyes took a hold of Beer.

'His books are forbidden.'

'Yes, but you've read them. They are in your field, wouldn't you say? An interesting fellow. You are familiar with his theory of repression? He is speaking about people who keep everything welled up inside. It's like a cork they've stuffed into their souls. In a strong man, one might call it stoicism.'

'Repression,' said Beer, feeling that the man was laughing at him somehow, and experiencing an urge to show him up. 'It's a mechanism, not a personality type. We all have it. It keeps ourselves hidden from ourselves, for our own good. Otherwise it might be hard to carry on.'

'Ah, so you *have* read him.'

The man picked up a pencil and a piece of paper from Beer's writing desk, and, with remarkable self-assurance – as though he were standing in his own office, helping himself to his own stationery – scribbled a note, put a date next to it.

'Force of habit,' he smiled, folding the paper into his jacket. 'I'm sure you don't mind.'

Beer watched the gesture with a sinking heart.

'You are the detective,' he complained. 'You should have said.'

181

'Let's sit down somewhere,' said the man. 'Professor Speckstein assures me you are a font of wisdom when it comes to murder. Perhaps you could ask your maid to put on some coffee. But I forgot. I am told you don't have a maid. Nor a receptionist. Somewhat peculiar, wouldn't you say? I suppose you will have to put it on yourself.'

Beer led the man into his study, then had no choice but to leave him while he put on the kettle. When he returned, the man was standing at his bookshelves, taking down some titles on the same piece of paper on which he had recorded Beer's cognizance of Freud. They were all of them books that 'violated the precepts of National Socialist science', or however the phrase ran. Beer watched him do it, until the hiss of the kettle called him back into the kitchen. He brought the coffee in upon a tray. The two men sat down, stared at each other across the file-littered desk. For a moment Beer thought of Lieschen holding the picture of dead Walter, and almost smiled. He wondered what would happen to Eva if the man should choose to arrest him. His name was Teuben, Franz Teuben; not half an hour ago Beer had taken down his details on an index card. An address in the fifth district: too far away for an ordinary patient. The man took up his coffee cup, tasted the brew without adding milk or sugar, gave a nod of approval.

'You're here about the dog,' Beer said quietly. 'I expected a Boltzmann.'

'Boltzmann is sick,' answered the man, then smiled. 'So, Dr Beer. Here I am: investigating a dog killing and imposing on your hospitality. And all because of a *Zellenwart* who used to be a professor, of all things. Before he was caught with his hand up a girl's cookie jar, that is. And here *you* are, some kind of expert.'

He retrieved a number of loose pages from his jacket pocket, unfolded them.

'Anton Beer, thirty-four. Denomination: Catholic. Six semesters of law, before switching to medicine. *Summa cum laude*. Three years in Germany, it says here, before we became Germany, that is. Hannover and Düsseldorf, a stint in Berlin. In-depth studies of the Haarmann and Denken cases – you had to go north to find a murder you liked, it seems; our own were too boring for you. A paper on Kürten and dog slaughter. Groundbreaking, in the Professor's words. Wife in Switzerland, taking the waters. Either she or you were screwing someone else, I suppose. Voluntary resignation at the hospital. A lot of praise there, though your political outlook is described as "backward"; a humanist, I am told, even somewhat to the left. The words of a jealous colleague, perhaps – short man, cheeks like a pig, the sort of man that's always sweating. What else? The Chief of Police calls me personally last night, tells me to involve you, no holds barred, and can I kiss his ring while I'm at it? You know' – he stopped himself, took a sip of the coffee, his thin lips looking very red against the china – 'if I wrote all this up in a report, you'd make a lovely suspect.'

Beer sat quietly throughout the man's speech, observed his impertinence, the lack of movement while he spoke. The man did not shift in his chair, nor move his arms; did not gesture or rush his words but simply sat, with his flat little eyes, the papers spread out on the desk before him. When he raised the coffee cup, the liquid inside barely quivered; he returned it to the saucer without a sound.

'Well, Dr Beer, I see you've studied the files. What's the verdict?'

Beer sighed, shook his head. 'I'm hardly competent to comment on police matters.'

'Yes,' said the detective, and a smile broke on his drawn-on mouth. 'The Professor warned me that you were a coward. Circumspect. That was his word. "*He must be pushed to get involved.*" A fair assessment, would you say?'

'What else did he say?'

'He passed on his notes; writing as a *Zellenwart*, that is. He even has a little file. "Anton and Gudrun Beer." Nothing much in it, I'm sad to say.'

He picked through the papers in front of him, located a torn-off sheet on which he had scribbled three or four comments.

'"*Humanist in internal emigration. No suspicious activities. Receives visitors all times of day and night. Not unusual for a doctor. Works in self-imposed obscurity.*" A little vague, don't you think? What sort of visitors, of what sex, how many, when? I mean if we are going to spy on you, we should do it properly. The problem with a man like Speckstein is that he's a creature of the Empire. He's in the Party, of course – since '37, or so he claims – but not of the times. Even the name, *Speckstein*. Sounds Jewish, don't you think? It can't be, of course, not for five generations, but then again, you never know. And that niece of his! A neurotic, I understand. Father a country lawyer, married a Czech girl, beneath himself. A romantic. That may explain it. The neurosis, I mean. Slavic blood and too much poetry. Or don't you hold with race science, Dr Beer?'

Beer sat through all this, wondering how much more it would take to push him from irritation to rage. He was not a man much prone to anger, but here he was, something dreadful rising in his chest. He drank some coffee, held it in his mouth as long as he could, then launched into a summary of the files.

'Four murders, Herr Teuben. The first victim male, twenty-two, member of the SS and recently arrived from Linz. Found leaning against an oak tree in Josefstadt, stabbed through the eye with an oblong, pointy object such as a fencing sword or bayonet. Right-handed assailant, a single clean thrust, and a very shoddy autopsy report. The blade penetrated deep into the frontal lobe and left a mark on the interior wall of the left parietal bone. No other signs of trauma. No wife, no enemies, though a witness mentions gambling debts.

'Second victim, electrical engineer, forty-one, active in the Labour Front. Suspected homosexual. Blunt-force trauma to head, torso and lower body. One arm broken, heavy bruising down one shin. Also an irregular stab wound just above the pubic bone, some glass splinters found during autopsy. The body was found in some bushes near the hospital gardens, probably dragged there from a nearby location. Had his wallet in his pocket, twenty marks and change, and a folded picture postcard of a parakeet.

'Third victim, a young woman, subject to sexual assault, found naked in a factory yard near the Jörgerbad swimming baths. Death by asphyxiation with some sort of strap. Several abdominal wounds, caused by a small knife, post-mortem. The girl was sixteen, wore a BDM uniform; father apolitical, a drug-store clerk, mother a housewife with an older brother who's been a Party member since 1931.

'Fourth victim, a university student of law, twenty-four years of age. Found stabbed in an alley near the Gürtel, not half a kilometre from here. Six wounds, in the chest and neck, a four-inch blade, swung from below and from the side. Punctured carotid artery. Additional facial wounds caused by a blunt object, probably a boot. Member of the Teutonia fraternity prior to *Gleichschaltung*; Party application pending. A

Hernals boy, upwardly mobile; the father an engine mechanic, deceased; the mother rents to lodgers.

'And the dog, of course. Cut up pretty bad, no known political affiliation. If you want my professional opinion, Detective Teuben, I think these are all totally unconnected. A spree of violence at the start of the war.'

He did not mention the curious pattern in which the girl's clothes had been distributed, nor the white stain visible on the law student's sleeve; did not dwell on the details of the dog's wounds; crossed his arms instead to gesture he was done with it all, then pulled out his watch and checked the time.

Teuben studied him, smiled, drank coffee, sat still.

'An excellent summary,' he said at last, the eyes as flat as when he had called Beer a coward. 'It has the merit of being accurate. I am not sure it will please the Professor, however. Nor the Chief of Police.'

Beer stood up, spilling coffee as he did so, walked to the window. 'I heard there has been a more recent murder. Another woman found dead. Perhaps there is a connection there, I don't know. Speckstein hasn't given me the file. I will have to ask you to leave now, I'm afraid. I have another patient coming in a few minutes.'

'Ah, yes, Frau Langenkopf. Afraid of open water. Can't tell whether you're screwing her or just robbing her blind, but she'll have to wait. No point interrupting a conversation among men.'

CHAPTER 7

Teuben refused to leave. There was to him a self-assurance that Beer had never before encountered: he took the liberty of always speaking the truth. For ten minutes or so he was content to sit in silence, then asked the doctor to see whether he had some beer in his larder, and some rolls left over from breakfast. Beer tried to ignore the request, remained standing at the window, staring out into the yard. Through the branches of the chestnut tree he saw Anneliese, playing alone in the rain, her hair and face wet, and showing no sign of going in out of the cold. Frau Langenkopf arrived, and was displeased when Beer announced they would have to reschedule.

'I had a setback,' she complained, and begged the doctor to admit her.

'I cannot,' he found himself saying. 'I have the police in the house.'

The phrase chased her away without further ado.

When he returned to the study, Teuben was standing at the window in the same position Beer had recently abandoned and had lit himself a cigarette. A piece of notepaper was in his hands. He did not mention Anneliese in the yard, but simply repeated his request for 'a bite to eat, if you please, and something to wash it down'.

'What more do you want from me?' Beer flared up, but Teuben ignored him, went out into the corridor, made use of the doctor's telephone.

'A man will be over with the missing file,' he told Beer once he had hung up. 'The second dead girl. Did I mention we have a suspect in custody? He has a pretty good alibi for some of the dates in question. Might be difficult to make all the murders stick.' He shrugged, reclaimed his seat in Beer's study. 'I really am starving, you know.'

Beer relented and went into the kitchen to butter some rolls. His hands were shaking and twice he dropped the knife.

When he returned to the room this time around, carrying a tray with beer, cold cuts and Kaiser rolls, Teuben was gone. He hastened back out into the corridor, still holding the tray, and saw at once that the door to the bedroom was open. Running now, one of the bottles overturning and spilling across the rolls and ham, he entered the room. Teuben was standing at its centre. The curtains were drawn, Eva lying in the semi-dark, eyes closed, her shoulders turned to them, the wounds hidden at her back. Her bare arms looked very thin jutting out from the white fabric of her nightgown, her head sunk deep into the pillow and disclosed only by its brush of hair. The dark fabric of the blanket, its lip sitting just above her waist, set off the pallor of silk and skin. Teuben was about to step closer, but Beer got in his way, and used the tray to push him backwards, towards the door. To his relief, the detective allowed himself to be steered out, and even closed the door.

'Who is she?' he asked, a semblance of life waking in his flat, dark eyes.

'Who do you think?' said Beer. 'A lady friend.'

'I thought for a moment she was dead.'

'Sleeping draught. She was – not feeling well this morning. I told her to stay in bed.'

Teuben looked at him, the ghost of a smile on his red lips. 'It didn't say that in the file,' he muttered to himself, as though amused at the hidden depths of man. 'But the hair—'

'What about it?'

'Cut off.'

'She wears wigs. It's what she does.' Beer pursed his lips, astonished by the fluency of his lies. It was as though he had prepared them long ago, and now found them ready at his beck and call. 'I rather like it.'

'She's a prostitute?'

Beer shook his head.

'A widow. I spilled the beer. Why don't we go into the kitchen and get another? And then I will assist your investigation in any way possible.'

Teuben seemed to consider this: stood a foot from the door, eyes fixed on its grain, thinking it

190

through, one arm outstretched as though getting ready to re-enter the room.

'I will need a name,' he said at last.

Beer had one ready. 'Evelyn Huber. Please, I'd prefer if nobody was to know. My reputation—'

Teuben waved him off, walked ahead of him to the kitchen, located a jar of sour gherkins and another one of pickled fish and placed them both on the table.

'Let's forget it for now, Dr Beer,' he said, sticking his hairy hand down the brine to retrieve a cut of herring. 'A secret among friends. Good for morale.'

He gestured for a bottle of beer, then drank from it without waiting for a glass.

'Kreuzwirt should be here presently. My assistant. Bringing us the file.'

Beer nodded, sat down across from him, and watched him lick the brine juice from his fingers.

When Teuben finally left, an hour and a half later, Dr Beer sat down next to a newly repositioned Eva Frei, picked up a book he had glanced through the previous night, and slowly, his heart heavy and feeling as though dyspeptic, began reading out to her the Hippocratic oath, of whose precise wording he had wished to remind himself.

'"Every house to which I come I will enter only for the good of my patients, steering clear of all ill-doing and all seduction, and especially of the pleasures of love, with women or with men, be they free or be they slaves."'

He looked up wearily and thought of Teuben. 'But what a liar you have made out of me.'

Eva heard it, moved her eyes, and winked.

That evening Zuzka called on Anton Beer, insisting that 'Otto had given her permission' and stayed for an hour, talking to Eva; and the next day, around lunchtime, the laundry boy dropped by, his long horse-face sullen when Beer asked him where the hell he had been.

It felt nice to put on a fresh shirt.

PART II

MARVELS

ONE

The patient came to him on the recommendation of a mutual acquaintance. He was working as a neurologist in Munich then: it was the early 1890s. The woman was shy at first; shook his hand and took to calling him 'dear Baron'. She suffered, she explained, from a compulsion to masturbate, and was able to achieve orgasm without any physical stimulation whatsoever, simply by contemplating the ocean or other manifestations of the grandeur of nature. When Albert Freiherr von Schrenck-Notzing touched her skin during his routine examination, her sexual climax was near instantaneous. Like Sigmund Freud, the Baron had studied hypnotism in Paris and Nancy; his monograph on the efficacy of suggestion therapy for this and related cases of sexual pathology was received with great interest by clinical psychiatrists across the German-speaking world. By the late 1890s the Baron was best known for his role as expert witness in a string of high-profile court cases. He demonstrated that a frightening proportion of court witnesses suffered from a 'suggestion-induced falsification of memory' and had never experienced the events to which they testified in court. Financial independence, the result of his marriage to the daughter of the lacquer-paint manufacturer Gustav Siegle, allowed Schrenck-Notzing to increasingly turn his attentions to the scientific exploration of paranormal phenomena. In the course of 1904 he published a series of articles on the phenomenon of Magdeleine Guipet, the French 'dream-dancer', who gave pantomimic interpretations of musical scores while in a state of deep hypnosis. During the half-decade prior to the start of the First World War, the Baron spent several years studying the 'materialisation phenomena' of the medium 'Eva C' who, in trance, was able to produce a gauze-like, translucent substance from various bodily orifices, most typically her mouth and nostrils. At times this substance, dubbed 'teleplasm' by Schrenck-Notzing, would take on the shape of faces, phantoms, ghostly limbs. Eva C endured repeated cavity searches and was asked to perform naked in order to eliminate the possibility that she was merely excreting a substance previously hidden on her form. Unlike her contemporary Mina Crandon, she was never accused of having had her genitalia surgically altered to conceal an additional limb that would account for the various phenomena she was able to produce. Schrenck-Notzing's resulting monograph is considered one of the classic studies in this field. Amongst his most vociferous critics was the neurologist Mathilde Kemnitz, née Spieß, the later wife of Erich Ludendorff. Dr Ludendorff was a noted feminist and theorist of the Völkisch Movement known for his attacks on Jesuits, Jews and Freemasons. The Baron died in 1929, twelve years before the National Socialist Party prohibited parapsychological research throughout the Reich.

CHAPTER 1

The boy brought it to school in a box. It was a shoe carton stolen from his mother, three air holes drilled into its lid so that the animal could breathe. The children noticed it at once, and in the short break after the first lesson they crowded around Josef, urging him to show what he had brought.

'My uncle gave him to me,' the boy announced as he began to raise the lid with great ceremony. 'He found him in the woods.'

The lid wasn't quite off yet when a dark little snout poked through the gap, narrow and triangular, a twitchy black nose at its tip.

'What is it? Let me see, Sepp, let me see!' cried the boys, jostling for space (the girls had long been pushed aside, stood on tiptoe, looking over the boys' shoulders). The lid was off, finally, and everyone stared, looking at the woodland creature that lay revealed upon a bed of straw and waiting for some definite reaction, something from one of those boys who were considered boldest and shaped opinion, here in this *salon* of children of classroom 4B.

'Oh, but it's only a hedgehog,' a freckled boy called Gernot pronounced at last. He was much admired for his nonchalance and his deadly aim when spitting pips. 'How boring!'

'Yes, boring.'

'That's exactly what it is.'

'A hedgehog. Our garden is full of them.'

The crowd quickly dispersed, not without some curious backward glances at Josef and the hedgehog. Two or three girls stayed behind a little longer, to test the sharpness of its salt-and-pepper spines, then scattered like pigeons when one of them, knock-kneed Petra, whose father drove a Benz, got herself pricked, jumped back dramatically, and started sucking on one finger (though not the one that had touched the hedgehog), unsure as of yet whether to wrinkle her nose in disgust or let fly with some tears. (Some of the other girls liked to call her a cry-baby, though there were others who'd reward her tears with tender hugs and even kisses, in imitation of their mothers.) Josef stayed behind with his box, whispered sweetly to his hedgehog. He was a 'good sort', his report card read, 'not particularly gifted'; the youngest in a family of eight. Before long the teacher returned, and everybody sat down at their desks.

It wasn't until the lunch break that Lieschen approached him, slyly as it were, while he was sitting by himself, offering a carrot to the animal with considerable vigour. After two, three pokes the frightened creature had had enough and rolled itself into a ball. Lieschen crouched down next to him, watched him stab the carrot into the wall of spines, the smear of her bruise lending a peculiar whiteness to one eye.

'You're doing it too hard,' she said. 'See how he's scared.'

'He likes spiders best,' the boy explained, taking no heed of her advice, and continuing to jam the carrot into the hedgehog's spines. 'I go into the cellar to hunt them. You have to take off three or four legs, so they can't run away from him.'

Lieschen was silent for a moment, asking herself if she considered this mean. 'You just rip them out?'

'Yes. Spiders don't bleed.'

'Why not?'

'I don't know. They just don't.'

She pondered this, then nodded her approval of his feeding strategy. Josef gave up on the carrot, and some minutes later, the hedgehog began to unfurl itself, its little black eyes looking up at them in beady submission.

'Have you given him a name?' Anneliese asked.

Josef nodded. 'Of course,' he said. 'Eckhardt.'

'That's a stupid name. You should call him something nicer.'

'Like what?'

'I don't know. Something that sounds nice. Prince Yussuf, for instance.'

'Prince Yussuf. But nobody's called Yussuf.'

'Somebody is. It's a real name. I know it for sure.'

'And can he really be a prince?'

'Why not? Can I pick him up?'

'Yes. But he belongs to me.'

Gently, cupping both hands as though she were scooping water from a pond, the girl collected the hedgehog and raised him up before her face. The animal was very light and sat in her hands calmly twitching its nose.

'Prince Yussuf,' she whispered gently, then pointed her chin at the teddy that was dangling from her wrist. 'Meet Kaiser San. He isn't real, but it doesn't matter. I like him all the same.'

Slowly, as carefully as she had picked him up, she placed Yussuf back on to the straw that lined his box and stood up to tower over the sitting boy.

'What do you want for him?' she asked, putting her hands on to her hips like she'd seen the women do at the Naschmarkt when they were complaining about the price of food.

Hearing her businesslike tone, Sepp, too, stood up, his large feet straddling the box.

'He isn't for sale.'

'Go on. Your uncle will get you another.'

'You don't have anything I want.'

'And if I had a knife?'

'A knife? What kind?'

The boy's eyes showed his curiosity. A decent-sized knife was much prized amongst the boys, the bigger the better. Lieschen turned around and,

204

shielding her action with her body, dug through the stitching on Kaiser San's neck. She sunk two fingers into the stuffing and soon managed to pull out the pocket knife, its horn handle covered in lint. Quickly, wishing to show off the knife as advantageously as possible, she wiped it clean on the cotton of her dress, then unfolded the blade and turned around to the boy.

'You see,' she said, handing it over. 'It's very sharp.'

Josef held it well out in front of him, as though afraid that he would cut himself at any moment, admiring its size and weight.

'It's really big. Where did you get it?'

'It belongs to my dad.'

'Won't he be angry?' the boy asked, not wanting to get into trouble.

Lieschen shook her head, bit her lip, a dark cloud of blood rising to her cheeks.

'He's got a new one now.' She paused, as though waiting for the blush to subside. 'So what do you say?'

Sepp thought it over, his eyes fastened on the knife, then handed it back with some reluctance.

'I'll tell you tomorrow. I have to ask my older brothers first. My uncle gave him to all of us. Eckhardt. He said we had to share.'

'Tomorrow?' Lieschen asked, distraught. 'Why not this afternoon? You can talk to your brothers and then meet me somewhere. Or I'll come home with you after school.'

The boy shook his head. 'I have to go *there*,' he said, meaning the *Deutsches Jungvolk*, which he seemed to dislike.

'But isn't it fun?'

'Sometimes,' he said, pulling a face. 'You'll see for yourself soon.' Josef knew her birthday was coming up.

'And if I don't like it?'

'It's cont-pulserry. That means you have to go. Especially now that we've been fighting with the Polack.'

He shrugged, heard the school bell, picked up the box. 'It's not all bad. They teach us new songs.'

Together they walked back to the school building, then stopped again before entering its double doors. In front of them the corridor yawned: a gaggle of children running to their class-rooms, the sticky smell of floor polish rising from the linoleum.

'Tomorrow, then?' Lieschen asked, stuffing the knife back into her teddy and holding out her little hand.

'Yes.'

They spat on their palms and shook on it, and promised one another that they would reconvene at the start of the next school day, to complete the transaction upon which they had commenced.

CHAPTER 2

Zuzka found Lieschen in the hospital gardens. It was four in the afternoon, the sun sitting low amongst a smear of clouds; moisture in the air and the lawns very muddy, the result of autumn showers that had been coming down at intervals throughout the day. Zuzka had been out window-shopping, delighting in the bustle of the city and the lack of supervision she enjoyed since coming to live with her uncle. She did not feel ill today, had stopped off at the university and wandered its busy hallways, young men talking, laughing, calling out to one another under the gaze of Meynert, Boltzmann and Krafft-Ebing, cut in marble along the courtyard cloisters. Coming back on the tram, she had jumped out two stops early, made a detour through the hospital grounds. It was pure chance that she happened upon Lieschen. The girl was standing at one of the benches along the gravel path that led deeper into the gardens and was talking to a man of about forty. He had taken off his hat to signal that he considered himself in the presence of a lady, and his thick blond hair was weirdly bisected by a long scar that ran from the base of his skull all the way to his left eye, which sat dead and glassy in his face. Lieschen was talking with great animation, throwing her hands about as she did so, the teddy jangling at her every motion. Her dress was muddy, her shoulders and hair wet from the last rain shower, her satchel weighing down her crooked back. This last detail surprised Zuzka. Most days, the girl ran home first, got rid of the bag: she had told her once that it hurt to carry it around. Zuzka drew closer, unnoticed by the girl, who was crumpling up one little fist in illustration.

'That's how small he is when he rolls himself up. But when he stretches he gets to be four times that big. And anyway, tomorrow he's mine. I have to feed him spiders. Only I've got to pull the legs out first.' She made a face, then noticed Zuzka. A smile took shape underneath the yellow-purple bruise.

'*Pani,*' she called out. 'Look who I've met!'

'Good day,' Zuzka nodded to the strange-looking man, who returned her greeting with an odd sort of mutter, his dead eye fastened on her chest. It appeared that he could move only half his mouth. The live eye looked weepy and too old for his face.

'I'm afraid we have to go.'

She pulled Lieschen away without awaiting a reaction, and quickly walked her out of earshot.

'Imagine,' the girl told her breathlessly. 'He's got

a steel plate in his skull. Right here.' (She gestured.) 'A grenade hit him in the last war, cracked a hole in his head, and they fixed him up with a steel plate. Isn't that wonderful?'

'But did nobody tell you you oughtn't to talk to strangers?'

'Why not?'

'It's dangerous, that's why.'

'But he was just sitting there. I told him about Prince Yussuf. He says he had one, too, when he was young. Karsten. That's almost as stupid as Eckhardt, don't you think, *Pani*?'

'Here, let me take your satchel. Good God, that's heavy. And you've been carrying it around all day. Why on earth didn't you drop it off at home?'

This silenced the girl's chatter, and for the rest of the way she walked quietly, as though in deep thought.

When they arrived in their own yard, Lieschen asked Zuzka if she would like 'to play a little'. Zuzka agreed, but sent her up to change her dress first.

'You're all wet,' she admonished the girl. 'Just look how your collar is all soaked.'

Lieschen nodded, looked at the window of their flat, then shook her head, her lips rolled inwards across the rows of little teeth.

'It's almost dry,' she murmured. 'We could go play in the Pollaks' yard. I know a way in.'

'You will catch cold. Go change. It'll only take a moment.'

'But I don't want to! If you don't want to play, I will go by myself.'

Zuzka watched this display of temper with consternation and glanced up at the girl's flat, trying to judge whether the lights had been turned on. There was little one could see from the yard.

'Is your father home?' she asked the girl, who had begun to pull at the satchel in Zuzka's hand, repeating that she would play by herself.

Lieschen let go of the heavy bag, hung her head with something like shame.

'He's sick,' she said.

'He's not been going to work?'

'No.'

'Is he – drinking?'

The girl shrugged, looked up into her face, eyes moist with her plea. 'Let's go and play, *Pani*.'

'I tell you what,' said Zuzka, anxious that Lieschen not catch cold. 'Why don't we go visit Fräulein Eva? She is the woman with the bad back.'

'The angel?'

'Yes. She's living with Dr Beer now. We can towel you dry there. Of course, it's all a big secret.'

'A secret!' smiled the girl, and reached to take Zuzka's hand.

Together they climbed the stairs to the doctor's surgery.

CHAPTER 3

Beer's waiting room was close to full when they entered through the propped-open door. They quickly walked past the stares of curious patients and sat down in the living room, across from the surgery, waiting for Beer to emerge. He came out, noticed them at once, frowned. A young doctor who had worked out of a practice just a few buildings down the road had been conscripted, and suddenly, from one day to the next, Beer's patient stream had close to doubled. He was overworked, and concerned what sort of impression the arrival of a young woman and child were making. Nor was he sure that Anneliese should have access to Eva: she was, after all, barely ten years old. About Zuzka, there was nothing that could be done. Otto himself had confirmed that he wanted her to look in on his sister, a strange glimmer passing through his eyes that struck the doctor as unpleasant. In any case, since they were already in the flat, he found he had little choice but to wave them through to his bedroom, looking over one shoulder to make sure none of the patients was watching them. He supposed he should have hired both a secretary and a nurse. In the past, he had been put off as much by the operating costs as by his innate need for privacy; now, with Eva in the house, it was out of the question. Resigned, he walked to the waiting room and called the next patient into his surgery, a toothless little man who began to complain about his gallstones before Beer had even had a chance to close the door.

In the course of the next two hours, Beer took every opportunity to step for a moment into his bedroom and see how his visitors were getting on with Eva. Each time, he found them in nearly unaltered poses, Lieschen sitting on the bed, her feet tucked under her, an odd sort of glow lighting up her little features. She was chattering away to Eva, and once in a while reached out to put both palms upon the woman's face, very gently, as though she were laying on hands. Beer wondered briefly whether it bothered Eva, but did not have the heart to tell the girl to stop. If I was lying paralysed, he thought, I should like a little girl to touch me just like that. Anneliese winked at Eva, and Eva winked back: caught the glance, soaked it up, then bounced it back when you least expected, from the left eye and *just so*, for the girl to catch with sudden laughter. It was like a game of tennis played with love. No doubt each of them was keeping score.

As for Zuzka, she had no part in their game. She sat further away, upon the chair, her arms crossed in front her, and somehow as though angry with herself. Whenever he came in, he would see her straighten in her chair: lean forward, towards Eva, stretch out an arm maybe, to smooth the blanket covering one leg, or place her chin into her hands, and remind the girl to be gentle.

It took Beer two or three visits to figure out what was going on. *She is bored*, he thought. *She would like to be the good nurse, but the truth is this bores her, this Eva, unmoving like a stone.* To his surprise he found he liked her better at that moment than he'd ever done before. It seemed to him a very human struggle that Zuzka was waging with herself and he flashed her a smile as he left the room, then was taken aback at how eagerly she answered him, her whole face flushing with excitement. Beer quickly closed the door behind himself.

At the end of his next little visit – no smiles this time, he made sure to look preoccupied – she rose from her chair with great vehemence and announced that she must go and would it be all right to leave behind the girl. Beer had only two patients left and enquired whether she'd mind waiting another twenty minutes. But her patience had evidently run out, and she even seemed upset, her eyes wet not with tears but with some kind of inner tension that puzzled the doctor. Vexed, but also feeling a little guilty (he could not account for it himself just then), he ran to the desk in his office to fetch his spare key, then drew her into his kitchen when, already dressed in hat and coat, she came marching down the corridor with great speed.

'Here, take this,' he said. 'It's only for emergencies, of course. I expect you to ring the bell. The fact is, the police were here, and you never know. So, just in case. If it looks like I've been – detained. She needs to be turned every four hours: there is a sketch on the night table outlining the positions. Don't worry, though, it won't come to it. All the same, it's better someone has a key . . .'

Zuzka did not reply to his instructions: stared at the key, then pocketed it, her face in shadow under the brim of her hat. They stood for another moment; then she ran off, down the corridor and through the propped-open door. Beer looked after her and called for the next patient. The clatter of her heels down the stairs reminded him of his wife: it was what she'd sounded like, leaving, whenever they'd had a fight. Of course, truth be told, they'd never had very many fights at all.

When Beer had seen off his last patient (a tax inspector's plump wife, who thought she might have caught scarlet fever from her young daughter and appealed to the doctor to drop by and check on the girl), he locked the front door behind her, poured himself a glass of wine, and joined Anneliese and Eva in his bedroom. The girl had stretched out on the bed next to Eva and was telling her something about a friend of hers called Yussuf, who would come home with her 'tomorrow without fail'. The shortness of her neck was very noticeable just then, coming up on her from behind, the twisted line of her shoulders and back. When she saw the doctor, she quickly sat up and showed him her feet.

'I took my shoes off,' she called, as though expecting him to tell her off. 'It's nice here in bed. Do you sleep on this side or the other one?'

The doctor smiled at that and lit a cigarette. 'I sleep in the living room. But isn't it time you got yourself home? Your father will be worried.'

She did not answer, but after some hesitation swung her legs over the edge of the bed and began putting on her shoes. Once she had managed to fasten both buckles, she stood close to the doctor and gestured for him to bend his ear to her mouth.

'Is Fräulein Eva very ill?' she whispered.

Beer nodded.

'Will she die soon and go to heaven?'

He almost responded with the truth, then caught himself short. 'I am not allowed to discuss my patients with others. It's a very important rule.'

Her brow darkened and she sucked her lips over her teeth. 'You mean that she will die.'

'No,' he said. 'I mean what I said.'

'The doctors thought that I would die,' she confided. 'When I was small.'

'How do you know?'

'Father talks about it often.'

'What does your mother say?' he asked, before he realised his mistake.

The girl took it in her stride.

'She ran away. Same as your wife.' She seemed unaware of the barb in her remark.

Beer stood up, embarrassed, felt a stiffness come into his manners.

'You should go now,' he repeated. 'It's very important you don't tell anyone about Eva. Not even your father. Nobody at all.'

The girl ignored his command, remained where she was, at the foot of the big bed, looking up at Beer. He noticed that her satchel stood leaning against the wall, her teddy propped on top of it, its head lolling like a drunk. Resolutely, he stepped over to the bag, picked it up, and headed for the door.

'But why shouldn't I tell?'

For an agonising moment he thought Lieschen had realised he was in her power and decided to blackmail him in some childish manner. But when he turned, her face betrayed only confusion and an earnest desire to understand. He sighed and set the satchel down again.

'It's complicated,' he said.

'Tell me, please.'

So he explained it to her, using much the same words he'd used when explaining it to Zuzka a few days earlier, only this time he found it difficult to follow his own thread, the girl's eyes boring into him, uncomprehending.

'It's like this,' he said. 'Every doctor who treats a patient like her is obliged to report it. To protect

216

public health, you see. Frei says she's already in the system – she's been recommended to a public-health facility, and scheduled for sterilisation. Only it wouldn't come to that – there are cases, quite a few cases, of systematic neglect. And now that the war has started, there is a rumour going around . . . a lung infection, that's what they are going to say. And there's also Otto to think about. He'd be put under scrutiny. He's been to prison, you see, and his father was a syphilitic – it's a type of sickness, a terrible sickness – and by the rules of heredity—'

He broke off suddenly, faced the girl's stare, eager, patient, the smudge of a bruise rounding one eye.

'They'll take her away and she will die,' he said curtly.

It took an effort to suppress that part of him that wanted to add: *Maybe. I don't know anything, and who can tell these days?* He didn't and nobody could. And yet he believed it. 'They'll take her away and she will die.'

The girl nodded, satisfied, stepped forward to collect her satchel, then stopped herself, looked up again.

'She wants to live,' she said, and gestured to the bed.

Beer was struck by this, the solemnity of the phrase, thought it a question. 'Yes,' he said, said it too quickly. 'I suppose so.'

Lieschen nodded once again, picked up the bag,

stepped into the corridor. 'Can you see our flat from your window?' she asked as they were walking to the front door.

'Yes,' said Beer. 'From the living room.'

'Can I look?'

'Of course.'

She ran there quickly, pressed her nose against the glass. It was dark outside, and her father's kitchen was lit up, the curtains wide open: a man in his undershirt working his way through a bottle, his elbow planted on the table, the palm supporting one weary cheek. Contrary to what Beer expected, Lieschen seemed pleased by what she saw, or at any rate reassured.

'I'll go home now,' she said. 'Can I come sometimes, play with Eva?'

'Yes, you may.'

He helped her pull the bag on to her crooked back, ran some fingers through her tangled hair, wished her a good night. At the front door, she turned around one more time, a new thought on her face (and how many questions there seemed to be living in that misshapen body of hers!).

'Do you know who killed Walter yet?' she asked. 'Was it Shine-a-man?'

'The Chinaman,' Beer said, 'is Japanese, and called Yuu. Herr Masuko Yuu. But no, I don't know who killed Walter.' He paused, dug in his jacket for a cigarette. 'Do you remember, the first time I met you, there was a man who came into the basement to talk to the janitor. He is called

Neurath and coughs a lot. They seemed to have some business of some sort. Do they spend a lot of time together, the janitor and he?'

The girl shook her head. 'I don't know. He comes to the basement sometimes.'

'Never mind.'

Beer lit the cigarette, unlocked the door, his thoughts running in several directions all at once. Lieschen was looking at him, waiting to see if he would say anything else.

'It's just that – Have you ever noticed, Anneliese, that, sometimes, in the bath, when one is singing, I mean, or maybe whistling to oneself, you hit just the right note and some pipe overhead will start to sing along, and it will travel through the whole house, and the whole house will hear your singing? It's got to do with the pitch, the vibrations of the pitch. It's why an army cannot march across bridges.' He smiled, blew smoke. 'But I'm not making sense, am I?'

The girl shrugged, unsure of what to say, then countered with another question of her own.

'Which one do you like better?' she asked. '*Pani* Zuzka or Fräulein Eva? They are both very pretty.'

He laughed, hid behind his cigarette, opened the door.

'Time to be off,' he said, and hurried her through. 'Goodnight.'

'Goodnight, Anton Beer.'

Beer stayed at the peephole another moment, watched Anneliese run down the stairs. Then he returned to the bedroom, arranged Eva into a new position, and wondered for the hundredth time whether it wouldn't be better to move her somewhere else, somewhere nobody knew, not Zuzka, not Lieschen, and not the detective.

'But where?' he muttered to himself. 'And besides, he won't be back. I'm done with Teuben. And he's done with me.'

After dinner, still agitated, he left Eva alone for an hour and went to town. It wasn't a wise thing to do, but just for a little while he needed to get away. All the same, his movements were governed by the usual precautions.

CHAPTER 4

After leaving Anton Beer's flat, Zuzka went straight to find Otto. It was the third such visit since their morning meeting the previous week. She would go over in the late afternoon, when Otto was awake and already dressed to go out – with laced-up boots, wearing his coat indoors, the collar turned up as though against the wind – but would tarry for another hour, drinking beer, smoking, leafing through newspapers and magazines. On the first of these visits, he had stood in the door with great hostility, but had admitted her nonetheless, assuming, perhaps, that she brought news from Beer and Eva; had barked at her to say what she wanted, and been taken aback by her admission that she'd come 'simply to talk'; had shrunk from this announcement (as she later put it to herself) like an animal accustomed to abuse, then at once found refuge in a brazen leer and begun to study her body with great purpose.

'Talk then,' he'd said, flopping down upon his unmade bed, and had answered her questions briskly, distractedly, watching her movements, especially her shoulders, neck and breasts.

All she had learned from him during that first visit was that he was working at a place called the Kasperl Club, 'just across the bridge from Schwedenplatz', not a cabaret but some sort of 'gentlemen's club' (the difference eluded her); that his sister, too, had worked as a performer, 'done magic tricks, told the future', had been 'famous, almost famous', at a time he designated only as 'before'; had hinted, too, that Frei was not their real name and that, one day, he was going to 'return it to the graveyard that it came from' (he seemed somehow especially proud of this remark and laughed at it like a man who wanted to hint at some great cleverness, then frowned and scowled at her as though he had already given away too much). She'd left him shortly after, avoiding his touch as he held the door for her on the way out, his hand stretched forward as though to pet her head or touch her neck, the palm cupped and his fingers square and blunt and dirty, she pictured them all through her dinner and late into the night.

On her second visit Otto opened the door without surprise, asked her in and even offered her a chair, then found himself at a loss as to what to do with himself. After a moment's hesitation, he bent down to retrieve a magazine that lay upon the floor, sat upon his bed and began reading (she herself was talking, telling him about Lieschen's father and how he beat the girl for no reason other than that he was a drunk). She was about to steer the conversation towards Eva, had hardly uttered her name, when she saw him jump back to his feet and fly into a rage at something he'd read. In response to her question as to what had upset him so, she was shown the photo in his magazine, already three months old, of a happy family taking their breakfast, the father wearing a black uniform, his son of twenty sinking healthy teeth into his buttered slice of bread.

'There're oranges on the table,' Otto said, jabbing into the depths of the murky photograph, obviously struck by this evidence of wealth, then punched a finger through the young man's face in renewed fury.

'You don't think he'll have to go, fight the Frenchies! A nice office job for him.'

Next she knew he had thrown down the magazine, was opening a beer.

'Here, have some, wet your whistle,' he said, and poured a mouthful into a dirty cup, then watched her sip it with that peculiar and burning greed, his hands dug deep into his pockets, sifting, counting his loose change. She stayed for another cup, then grew nervous when he began to tell some story about a singer at his club who had gone to a midwife, to take care of her problem, 'you understand', only now she'd become infected, and 'you could smell her all the way from the changing rooms to the stage'. Quickly, gulping down her drink, she excused herself, and washed out her mouth before joining her uncle at the dinner table.

'You seem distracted,' the old man said politely, but left her alone when she pleaded a headache and rushed off to bed. Through the open window came the whinny of a muted trumpet; she threw it shut but was unable to rid herself of the melody.

Had Zuzka been asked about the purpose of her visits, she would have been unable to give a clear answer. The question tormented her. She lay in bed at night, no longer probing the extent and nature of her illness (her symptoms were quite gone), but straining instead to comprehend her relations with that man Otto Frei. At first she thought what drove her was mere curiosity, the desire to learn something about the sick woman that went beyond Beer's pedantic warning to keep her presence a secret, and gave flesh to the ghostly face she had watched smoking through so many nights. But her visits did not provide any answers: he seemed a man incapable of conversation, had no focus, slid away from topics as freely as a child; was furtive, too, without any reason she could name, his brow heavy-knit against the things he must not say, then suddenly let slip some sugges- tive detail behind which cowered his life's tragedy (that it was indeed a tragedy, Zuzka had long resolved). Then, too, there was that sense of danger he exuded, of violence, and – she had trouble with this last part, picked at it as at a scab – of sex. It was with horror and delight that she thought of those sudden flarings of desire (for her body, that is, for that body hidden away under her clothes)

224

that would take hold of him and darken his gaze, her lungs ever ready to rise up in scream. She did not love Otto Frei. Of this she was quite certain: he was too coarsely made. And yet he seemed alive to her, like no man she had ever met. Certainly more so than Anton Beer. It was best, she resolved, just as sleep caught up with her, tugged her under like the tide, if she took care not to return.

The present visit started like the last. He let her in and offered her a chair. This time she did not speak; her mind was heavy with the image of Eva, lying motionless under the child's playing hands. Dreamily, she recalled how she'd seen her for the first time, emerging (for a moment only) between the drawn curtains of the back room window, into the drizzle of a late-summer rain, held aloft, she now knew, by those fat and dirty fingers; an act of charity, of love, performed against the dictates of prudence, *just so*, because Eva might enjoy a change from the ceaseless sameness that was her life. Zuzka pictured it (raindrops falling on an open eye) and, taking her head into her hands, remembered also her own boredom in that room across, a boredom she had the courage neither to dismiss as unremarkable, nor to accept as characteristic of her soul. Tears sprang into her eyes, for herself, for Eva. She found a handkerchief tucked deep into her sleeve and blew her nose. Otto sat on the bed and stared at her in silent wonder. It took her some minutes to translate her emotion into speech.

'I saw Eva just now,' she said, snot still clogging up her nose. 'If I was like that, sick, I mean –' She paused, searched for a phrase, something tender that would mask the revulsion that she felt, found nothing, just the truth, callous like a knife. 'God, I'd want to die.'

'Can it really be –' she added an instant later, recalling with sudden clarity his earlier confession that there were times when he himself doubted that Eva was sick. 'Can it really be that she's making it up somehow?'

She thought for a moment that he would flare up, shout at her, but he leaned forward instead, waved her closer so that, moving her chair to the side of the bed, she could smell the beer on his breath.

'Two years back,' he said, quietly, sharing a secret, 'in the winter, I put her in the bath. She was better then, could move her neck a little and sometimes one arm. Mother was in hospital, and I was alone with her, the whole house was empty, everyone out at work. I put her in the bath. Made it nice and hot. I had planned it all out. All week, at night, I planned it; couldn't sleep, pictured it, the bath down the hallway with white little tiles. So I put her in, the head bent over the rim so she won't drown, open the window a crack, *to let the steam out.* That's what I tell her. Casual, like. And then I pretend I hear a noise, down in the cellar, take the bath brush that's hanging from the wall (like a club, you see, in case it's burglars), say I'll be right back. And then – nothing. I go down the stairs, sit down in a corner. Don't make a noise. A whole hour, and the cold coming in through that crack in the window (I had to force it open, because of the snow). And I hold my hand over my mouth, wondering how long can she stand it. And then—' He made a gesture, vague in its meaning, almost catching Zuzka with the back of his hand.

'You pulled her out.'

He shrugged, nodded, reached for the dirty pillow at the end of his bed, then stood toe to toe with Zuzka, who rose from her chair and took a step back.

'Sometimes, I stand over her with a pillow. Just like this. And I tell her, close your eyes, just close your eyes and I will do it, and she lies there, looking at me, and when I turn away—' He threw down the pillow. 'That's when she closes them. And then at night I hear her move about.'

'Move about?'

'Yes. Like a ghost.' And he fell to laughing, an odd, hoarse heave of a laugh, angry and sad, that sent a spray of spittle on to her good blouse. 'I run to her, and I swear I sometimes take the knife.'

She winced, stood her ground, smelled his beer-breath and his sweat.

'So why not just give her up, let the hospital take care of her?'

'Shut up,' he shouted, stepped close and shouted it, his chin pushed forward, raining spit upon her own.

'Shut up,' he shouted, but his hands did not rise and he did not seem very angry, only the voice was loud, his mouth just inches from her own.

She blushed, turned away finally, saw herself reflected in his dirty mirror, spots of greasepaint livid like a rash. To her side, growing out of the slope of her shoulder, was his face, meaty and muscular, coarse skin ruddy with emotion.

'The last place we were living, there was this man sniffing around her. The landlady's son. He knew I didn't want the police to come.'

She swallowed, waited for him to continue, their eyes meeting in the mirror. 'What did you do to him?'

He flashed her a smile, it might have been called cruel. 'What do you care?'

It should have stopped her, goaded her on instead. 'And what about Speckstein? Why did you kill his dog?'

He shook his head in denial, but she wouldn't accept it; stepped to the sink and picked up the knife with which he'd done it, the handle made of bone.

He watched her try the blade with her thumb. The blade was quite blunt.

'What was its name?' he asked, a schoolboy's question, the cruelty gone, though kept within reach. 'The dog?'

'Walter.'

'Walter?' He laughed. 'What a stupid name.' Then added, 'What was it like?'

She shrugged, put down the knife, wiped her fingers on her skirt. Then, theatrically, recalling words that Vesalius had used: 'An old dog, it pissed everywhere.'

'Pissed, eh? I thought you was a lady.'

He bent for a beer, poured some of it into a cup, handed it over.

'To Walter.'

She drank, coughed, drank.

'You killed him, you bastard.'

But in her heart she did not mind. What love had she for that dog?

Otto shrugged and smiled.

'I have to go,' she said, wiping her mouth. 'It's dinnertime.'

'Yes,' he said, 'I'm going to work.'

She stepped out quickly, trying to gain a head-start into the yard. The janitor was there, on the way to his cellar workshop, carrying a sack lumpy with its heavy load. He looked up when he saw her, mumbled a greeting, then watched the mime emerge from the door she had just fled. It was impossible, she thought, that he did not notice the fury of her blush. Upstairs, her uncle waited, cheese and cold cuts spread upon their table. Zuzka ran in, hung up her coat. Vesalius watched her, poured out some wine, and left them to bless their food and eat.

CHAPTER 5

It was night, gone ten-thirty. Zuzka was lying on her bed in darkness, wrapped only in her dressing gown. She had come out of the bath more than an hour ago, hot and flushed, and had lain down on the bed with the window half open, staring out into the sky. It was raining, a patter of drops falling on the sill. The door opened, a strip of light fell into the room, caught her bare heels. Frau Vesalius stepped in, squinting into the dark. Zuzka did not stir, pretended to sleep. The old woman closed the door behind herself, bent down to pick up the clothes that lay scattered across the room, Zuzka's underwear and the yellow silk shift; her woollen skirt and the tan stockings. The housekeeper made two piles, one of dirties, the other one of clothes that needed to be aired and put away. Zuzka watched her every movement in the weak light from the yard; she wondered what had made the housekeeper come in here for a task that she usually left for the mornings. Vesalius's whole bearing was marked by spite and disapproval. The hands looked overlarge in the faint light, were threaded by a web of ropey

230

veins; the eyes very dark and devoid of animation. Her head shifted, and immediately Zuzka closed her eyes, gave an even rhythm to her breathing. She had no wish to talk. In this self-imposed darkness, she heard Vesalius move about the room, then draw closer; felt her bend down over her body, the stale stink of kitchen smells clinging to her housecoat.

When she spoke, the voice was quiet, close to her ear.

'You have to stop,' Vesalius told her. 'You don't honestly imagine that nobody's seen you. Half the house knows, and soon the Professor will, too.'

She paused, waited for a reaction. Zuzka kept her eyes firmly shut.

'Such rough trade, too. You'll get pregnant and end up in the street. Your uncle is planning a reception in two weeks' time. He told me today. For Party dignitaries, very fancy. If you are looking for a man – just ask him to buy you a nice dress.'

Again the woman paused and gave Zuzka the chance to be done with her charade. Zuzka heard her sigh, then straighten (her back actually cracked); the solemn shuffle of her feet as she headed back towards the door. She opened her eyes, saw Vesalius hesitate, halfway between bed and door, her back old and bent. Just then she looked harmless, concerned for Zuzka's virtue. It softened Zuzka. She had questions burning on her mind.

'How long?' Zuzka asked. 'How long have you been with my uncle?'

The housekeeper stopped, turned around, large hands dangling by her side.

'Twelve years next month. I started after Manfred died. My husband.'

'So you were there, when –' She stopped, cast around for a phrase. 'Everybody says he raped a girl.'

'You want to know what happened?'

'Yes. It's important, somehow. Because of the dog. Walter.'

Vesalius snorted at the mention of the name, stared at her across five feet of darkness.

'I can show you if you like,' she said.

'Please.'

'I'll be back.'

The old woman left the door wide open.

When she returned, Vesalius was holding a thick, square book, some sort of album, bound in green felt. She undid the lace ribbons that held it shut and leafed through the pages until she came upon a folded piece of paper. Its edges were crisp and clean: it had not been unfolded very often. The old woman handed it to Zuzka, who sat up in her bed and turned on the bedside lamp.

'She was what they call a *medium*,' Vesalius said even before Zuzka had a chance to commence reading. 'A scientific experiment. All sorts of famous people came to watch.'

It was a page cut from a newspaper and was dated September 1927; its columns intersected by the neat lines of its folds. Zuzka tried to

232

concentrate, the words swimming before her eyes, but all she could make sense of were the headlines that introduced each of the paragraphs, promising sensation.

'Thomas Mann was there,' she read, confused.

'Your uncle was asked to examine her. See, it says here.'

'Why him?'

'In case she had something hidden on her body.' Vesalius paused, pursed her lips. 'It says somewhere that "*it called for a physician familiar with the female form*".'

Zuzka scanned the page for the quote, unsuccessfully, then looked back at the housekeeper, those hard, mocking eyes. It had never occurred to her that Vesalius, too, despised her uncle.

'You've kept this all these years?' she asked, giving voice to her surprise.

'Have it,' said Vesalius, turning away from her with sudden vehemence and pressing the album to her chest. 'I have no use for it. And stop seeing that Gypsy.'

She left before Zuzka could either thank or ask her.

What did she care whether or not Speckstein's niece managed to disgrace herself?

Zuzka waited until Vesalius had closed the door and she could hear her shuffle down the corridor before returning her attention to the article. The paper felt cheap in her hands, flimsy and grey; as she examined the page, some of the print began to smudge and stick to her fingertips. The page she was looking at constituted the opening fragment of a longer trial report; it cut off abruptly at the bottom. The cover page overleaf was dominated by a collage of images that began just under the title lettering and extended all the way to the bottom margin. She realised with a start that it was for this, the artist's impressions of the courtroom rendered in small, feathery lines, and flanked by hand-lettered captions, that the page had been preserved. There was a total of three scenes, very lifelike, each depicting a different moment of the trial, juxtaposed for maximum effect. At the bottom of the page sat the members of the jury on the tiered, railed-in benches peculiar to their office, listening to the expostulations of an expert witness. This expert witness, a short, fat man with impressive moustaches, was rendered in profile, his right hand extended towards a propped-up poster-board upon which the outlines of female anatomy had been delicately sketched (all details that would have offended public taste had been carefully omitted, or else were blocked by the expert's gesture). Above the jury, the space was cut in half. On the right cowered her uncle, looking ten years younger, his hair full and dark. He sat hunched in the dock, his hands neatly placed in front of him. His eyes were lowered and his brow creased as though in repentance or in shame. To his left, on the witness stand, a girl in her early teens, skinny and pale. She was wearing a plain black dress with a white collar. A cross was visible high on her breast. Her features were distorted by fear and disgust, the lips pushed forward and sealed; the left hand thrown over her eyes, fingers spread to reveal one tear-rimmed eye. Her right arm was extended, broke the boundary of the thin line of ink that separated her from the defendant, and reached across to point an accusing finger at her tormentor's hunched figure.

'Struck dumb by the assault, Evelyn Wenger testifies with her hands,' the caption read. 'The Professor awaits the verdict.'

'The jurors are instructed about the results of the medical examination by Professor Dr Kiefer.'

Zuzka stared and stared at the little girl's face. She knew at once that it was Eva.

Zuzka turned back to the article, willed herself to read the text. She grasped it in snatches of bold type and quotation, but was unable to keep her mind focused through the whole of the piece: there seemed to be altogether too many words for one simple truth.

Vesalius had not been gone ten minutes when Zuzka began dressing, folding up the page back into its neat, tidy square and stuffing it into a handbag to take along. She closed the door to her room behind her, tiptoed into the hallway and searched for her coat in darkness. As she approached the front door and felt for the keys on the hook, she grew convinced that the house-keeper was behind her somewhere, staring at her from the door to the kitchen, or standing behind the hallway wardrobe, disapproving and silent. Zuzka did not turn around. Outside, the air was cold, rain coming down in a spluttering drizzle. She hurried to the tram stop and then onwards, towards Schwedenplatz and the Kasperl Club.

CHAPTER 6

She would have liked to take the tram. It was far to Schwedenplatz – more than a mile down Alser- and Universitätsstraße, then a quarter of the way clockwise along the Ring – and she would have liked to take the tram, only she wasn't sure whether the tram would still be running at this time, and when she got to the station there was no timetable and nobody waiting whom she could ask. So she set off, thinking she could always find one at Schottentor, and some minutes later the tram flew past her, its windows brightly lit, three, four passengers sitting on the benches, staring out into the street. It was cold and it was raining, the night sky covered in cloud. Only now and then the wind blew a gap into the clouds and revealed the sickle of the waning moon, cut to pieces by the web of wires that hung suspended above the tracks. Halfway down Universitätsstraße, she was startled by the clip-clop of horses as a carriage drove past, heading home towards some outlying stable. She arrived at Schottentor, saw a crowd of drunk men clustering around the sausage stand, eyeing her up and down as she drew close, placing her, a solitary woman out late at night. There was no tram in sight, and, rather than wait under the eyes of those men, she walked on, turned left on to the Schottenring, towards the Stock Exchange, her coat growing heavy with the rain, her footsteps ringing on the cobbles. A policeman passed her, paused, and removed the cigarette from his thin lips long enough to give a shrill, insinuating whistle; two other men, old and shabby, stopped an argument as she walked past and stood shoulder to shoulder, watching her legs pick their way around the puddles, before resuming their hostilities. She left the Ring, chose a short cut, then got lost in the little alleys around Judengasse until she found a flight of steps that led down towards the canal.

The rain let up while she was crossing the bridge, once again flinching under the gazes of men who moved about in packs of two or three. A car drove past, caught her in its headlights; slowed down (so it seemed to her), men's faces darkened by the windscreen, their talk inaudible out on the bridge; then a howl as gears were changed, and the spray of a puddle gunning for her shoes. She hurried on and entered Leopoldstadt, the second of the city's twenty-one districts. Once, she had read, it had been the Jewish ghetto, separated from the city by the waters of the canal. Now it was the place where men went to drink and to buy love.

Zuzka found the Kasperl almost at once. The club was in a side street, two blocks from the bridge. A painted sign announced the venue, hung brash and new upon a yellow flaking wall. There was little traffic here, no line for the door, just a tired old man in a barman's waistcoat sitting on an upturned bucket and having a smoke. The door itself stood ajar.

She walked up to it, heard noise travel through the gap; reached out with fingers tingling from the damp and pushed it open. There was a narrow hallway, its walls thickly plastered with handbills, and a staircase leading down into the cellar. Against the wall leaned a man in something like a porter's uniform: gold-trimmed royal blue. Epaulettes made from thick, yellow thread dangled from both shoulders. He was a tall man and quite impressively fat. When he caught sight of her, he immediately appraised her face and figure. She expected him to say something, but he just stood there, his thumbs wedged behind his belt, sucking on a short-stemmed pipe. The clamour of bar noises travelled up the stairs, followed by a scatter of applause.

'Is this the Kasperl Club?' she asked, blushing. 'May I come in?'

The man sucked on his pipe. 'Are you a guest or trade?'

'I – I am here to see – the show.'

'Alone?'

'Yes.'

'There's a cover charge. Eighty pfennig. You have that?'

She nodded, dug in her handbag, could not locate her purse. Her eyes filled with tears.

'It must be somewhere,' she said, stepping closer, into the hallway's light. The porter stooped over the handbag with her, blew pipe smoke in her face.

'No money, no entry, Missy,' he guffawed and his epaulettes shook with his laughter.

'Ah, go on,' said the barman, who had finished his cigarette and picked up the bucket. 'Such a nice lady, and the place half empty tonight. I'm sure someone will buy her a drink.'

His accent was Styrian, soft and melodious; nicotine stains on his fingertips and teeth. 'What do you care if this one gets in for free?'

The porter shrugged, and the barman took her elbow and pulled her along with him, down the cellar stairs.

'What would you like, sweetheart?' he asked as they stepped into a long if somewhat narrow room filled with several rows of round tables and chairs. The floorboards were bare and very dirty, littered with cigarette ash and mud. There was a long bar on their left, and a raised stage to the front, the latter screened by a set of red curtains. The light was dim, made dimmer yet by the cloud of smoke that clung to the low ceiling. Just about half the tables were taken, mostly by solitary men, though there were some brightly made-up women to be seen. In one corner, near the stage, a group of six or seven young men sat together, wearing SA uniforms, the table in front of them overflowing with glasses. The atmosphere was muted, almost tense. Just then a hush came over the crowd, and the lights were further dimmed.

'The show is starting,' the barman whispered to her and led her over to the wooden counter. 'Beer or wine?'

'Wine,' she answered, grateful, and sat down on a stool. Otto Frei had taken the stage.

He came on without announcement: parted the curtains and stepped out, dressed in black from head to toe. He was carrying a chair. It was only when he had crossed the stage, put down the chair and sat himself down that the house lights were switched off. All that remained was a single spotlight that sought out his face, and the glow of cigarettes amongst the guests. Everything that she knew about his face – the brow, the cheekbones, the fat, sensual mouth – was just the same, but it had been bleached of all emotion. A canvas remained, startling in its blankness; the large eyes cold and emptied of their passion. He stared out into the audience for an endless minute, his face disembodied in the dark.

'Who's first?' he asked.

The voice had not changed. It was coarse and full of anger, the weak link in his act. For a moment he seemed human: a man with a painted face. Then the lips closed and silence reclaimed him.

'Rudolf,' a voice shouted, amongst the group of

241

SA youths. 'Over here! He's reporting to barracks tomorrow, and soon it's off to war!'

A second spot came into being, scanned the faces of this lively gang, half a dozen fingers pointing at someone sitting in their midst. The light settled on the man they indicated, a blond lad of twenty, his face drained of colour by the light. Now there were two death masks, one on the stage, the other rising from amongst the gaggle of his peers, staring one another in the eye.

'All right then,' said the young man, lips forced into a smile. 'How will I fare?'

The mime did not react at once, but peeled back both his gloves and set them beside him on the chair. He stood, the light following his every movement, the hands falling lifeless from their cuffs. The next moment, they took on a rhythmic movement, up and down, forward and back, and in a moment it was clear the mime was marching, though his feet did not stir and he made no progress across the stage, just the hands moving to the inaudible rhythms of some drummer boy. The face meanwhile was proud, imperious, a soldier about his duty, only there was fear in it, too, a trembling right around the lips, and the occasional sideways glance to check on how his comrades were getting on, just to see whether they, too, were marching fearless to their likely death, or whether he had been fooled into taking to the road alone. A shell hit. It made no sound, but it hit all the same: the mime's eyes caught it as it came hurtling into his line of sight. He dropped to his knees, raised his hands to cradle his ears, a soundless scream falling from his lips. More shells fell, the heat of battle, and the mime in their midst, hands curled to fists, stoppering up his painted ears. Then, the battle over, he stood, a frail, handsome smile spreading on the parchment of his face, shy at first – could it be that he was alive? – then young and carefree, though he kept his eyes up, not caring to look at what lay littered on the field. The mime sat down again, his chin raised in triumph. One hand turned around upon itself and became the hand of another man, pinning a white cotton ribbon on the black nothingness of chest. No medal had ever been better earned: the face said it, had long forgotten its fear. Then the hands disappeared within their gloves, and a great solemn blankness descended upon the whitewashed features of the mime. He was Rudolf no more.

The room exploded into laughter and applause.

'And his girl?' somebody shouted. 'Will she be faithful?'

The mime heard it, shushed them with a finger laid across his lips. His eyes opened wider, became pretty, the mouth soft and round. The gloves came off again, and the mime-turned-girl began to write a letter, tender words that left their imprint in her tender smile. She had not finished with her composition, was labouring, her tongue between her teeth, to find phrases that did justice to her virgin love, when a knock interrupted her: she looked up, startled, waved one hand to usher in her guest. That it was a man, a stranger, one knew at once by the caution that crept across her face. She shook her head twice, gave curt and hurried answers to some unheard question, each answer mouthed by pale and displeased lips. The man would not leave, drew nearer, put a hand upon her arm. She tried to shake him, struggled, beat a fist against his chest. Then, little by little, a change stole over her, some sort of slackening of the will. At first she hung lifeless and endured his groping, her lips tightly sealed against his kiss. But slowly, moment by moment, caress by caress, something else woke in her, old and powerful and born of the body. It would not be denied. She gasped in surprise as she watched herself yield: a stretching of the throat and jaw, eyes swimming with the knowledge of her need.

The act finished with the mime enacting her passion, the heavy braying of a beast in heat, made all the worse for its total lack of sound. When he was done, shouts and whistles followed him off the stage. He stepped through the gap in the red curtain, dragging his chair behind himself like a rag-and-bone man dragging home his cart. He never even bothered to bow.

'He's good,' said the barman, and refilled her glass. Zuzka had not realised she had drunk it. 'Three days back, he told some fat man he would die on the crapper.' He wagged his chin. 'Heart attack. Just as he was reaching for the paper, to wipe his old arse: out pop his eyes and his ticker goes bust. It nearly came to blows.'

She smiled back at him and drained her second glass in three quick sips.

'Where is he now?' she asked.

'Backstage. The door over there. You know him?'

'Yes,' she said and her heart beat as though she were pleading guilty to some unknown crime.

She got up, made her way towards the stage and past it, to the metal door the barman had indicated. Some of the men looked up from their tables, followed her with their eyes. She was still wearing her wet coat and hat, the leather handbag dangling from the crook of her arm. The sign read 'No Entry' but the door wasn't locked. It opened upon a black, heavy curtain, designed to keep out the light. She closed the door, stood in darkness looking for the gap in the curtain, then stepped through into a brightly lit corridor with linoleum flooring that reminded her for a moment of a hospital corridor. A mop stood in an empty bucket in one corner, a number of doors led off to her left and right. She stepped up to the one closest to her (it stood ajar) and pushed it open a little wider. A woman, stripped to the waist, was stepping into a cocktail dress. Her chest and ribcage were covered with old bruises, her painted face looked haggard and worn. Zuzka had not seen another woman naked since puberty and was taken aback by the sight. She was particularly struck by the smallness of her breasts and nipples, and the sickly cast of the woman's skin; the knobbly protrusion of her belly button that clung to her belly like a tumour. She had a cluster of moles over her left hip.

'What is it?' the woman asked, fastening the dress at her waist and pulling its top over her naked frame. Her voice was tired, not unkind. 'You lost, honey?'

'I'm looking for Otto. Otto Frei. The mime.'

'You his girlfriend or something? Third door on the left. Unless he nipped out for some air.'

Zuzka left her, followed her instructions: a door with a crack in its lacquer running from handle to hinge. It, too, stood ajar; behind it, Otto, sitting on a stool. The room was large and barren, held no mirror and no sink, a tube of make-up lying crumpled on the floor. He rose when she stepped in, a cigarette jutting from the painted lips.

She expected him to say something, welcome her, offer her a seat, but he remained as he was, silent, the face white and washed of all expression. With a tremor she recalled why she was there, and dug the newspaper page from out her handbag.

'Evelyn,' she said, not without triumph. 'Her name is Evelyn. Not Eva. I know why you killed the dog.'

Her hand was actually trembling.

He accepted the article with great carelessness, laid it next to him on the table that served as his

246

dresser. There was a bottle of spirits there, standing open; an ashtray overflowing with butts. She wished very much that she could see his face behind the paint. She needed to know if she'd hit her mark.

'Admit it,' she tried again. 'There's no use denying.'

He rose and took her by the wrist.

Any moment now, she thought, he was going to tell her the truth.

'My uncle,' she said, filling the silence between them. 'Speckstein. He's giving a party. Vesalius told me to buy a new dress.'

He shrugged and pulled at her, used her weight to slam her back into the wall.

Her breath was knocked out of her. In that instant, she was sure he would beat her, cut her open with his knife. He was so close, she could see down his mouth, the gums very red behind the white of his lips. Then she felt his knee, forcing apart her thighs, the weight of his body crashing down upon her chest. He did not kiss her, not on the mouth, though she felt his teeth travel up and down her neck. 'Oh God,' she murmured, and it fell from her lips lifeless and abstract, like a line from a play read out by the prompter. One hand (he was still wearing his gloves) reached around to cup her buttock, and she realised in wonder that he strove to be tender in his lust. He had yet to lift her skirts. Over his shoulder she became aware of a presence, the woman in her cocktail dress. She was standing in the door, unembarrassed, watching their embrace. All she saw was a colleague kissing his girl, her long neck smudged with the white of his make-up. Otto became aware of her, pulled his leg from between Zuzka's thighs; he stepped back from the wall, one hand still pinning her wrist above her head.

'Do you have any cigarettes?' the woman asked, and Otto nodded, passed her his pack, then let go of Zuzka and offered her a light, the match catching fire between cotton fingers black as tar. Zuzka used the moment, grabbed her handbag, slipped over to the door. She wanted to run away but felt abashed somehow, needed to tell the woman that things were not as she assumed. 'We're not –' she began and stopped herself. 'I'm not – He just grabbed me, and I—'

The woman smiled, blew smoke and watched it drift across the room. 'Just close the door next time, honey,' she said. 'There's no need to get embarrassed.'

Zuzka turned and walked away then, through the club and up the stairs, headed homewards through the night. Once, near the Fleischmarkt, she saw a man step out of a house in a hat and coat and for a moment she thought it was the doctor, squeezing the hand of someone unseen, but she hurried on, fearful, ashamed to hope that it was he.

TWO

Rudi Schneider was eleven when he first manifested supernatural powers. The year was 1919: March. His sixteen-year-old brother, Willy, who had already begun to draw the attention of Schrenck-Notzing and like-minded researchers, was performing a seance in his father's house in Braunau am Inn, the birthplace of Adolf Hitler. When in trance, Willy gave himself over to a 'trance personality' called Olga, whom some identified as Lola Montez, the Irish-born dancer and erstwhile mistress of King Ludwig I of Bavaria. On this particular night Olga demanded Rudi's presence. The parents, concerned for their child's sleep, refused to wake him. When Rudi stepped out of his room a few minutes later – with tousled hair, no doubt, wearing a nightshirt handed down from his sibling – he was in a state of deep trance. From this day forward, Olga attached herself to the younger and more gifted Rudi. In a Munich facility purpose-equipped by the Baron von Schrenck-Notzing, he was subjected to one of the most intense and scientifically rigorous testing cycles ever developed for a spiritistic medium. Separate test series took place at the Institut für Radiumforschung der Akademie der Wissenschaften in Vienna and at the National Laboratories for Psychical Research in London through the 1920s and '30s. Large numbers of interested laymen, including doctors, scientists, artists and professional stage magicians, were invited to attend the seances. The young medium was particularly adept at the telekinetic manipulation of objects and the manifestation of 'teleplastic' limbs that bore only a rudimentary resemblance to human arms and legs. In his spare time Rudi completed his apprenticeship as an engine mechanic. By the mid-1950s he was living in Meyer, Austria, working as a driving instructor and running his own driving school. He died in 1957, a young man of forty-nine.

CHAPTER 1

More than a week had passed, the autumn growing grey and cold. Throughout this week, Lieschen's father stayed at home and drank. He had stopped shaving some time ago, slept at the kitchen table half the nights, stank. Every afternoon the bent little girl went up to Dr Beer's practice and played with Eva, then ran into Beer's living room to watch her father down his drink. She counted the bottles lined up by his arm, rapt in her attention, then would pick a sudden moment – seemingly no different from all the rest – when she'd tear herself away and go darting for the door.

It took Lieschen less than a minute to run down the stairs, across the yard, and up the staircase to their flat: and still it seemed too long for her. She was afraid of what might happen in that brief minute and tried to shave off seconds, taking two, three steps with every leap; arrived breathless, stars before her eyes. For more than a week now she had opened the door to their flat with a special sort of trepidation, expecting some kind of unnamed catastrophe to welcome her as soon as she had crossed the threshold; always she stopped, still on the landing, and pushed open the door with both her hands, the hedgehog sitting in its box at the tips of her feet. She rarely left him at home now, Prince Yussuf, took him to school and on to Dr Beer's practice, kept dead spiders in a jar that she carried in her satchel. The doctor had told Lieschen to keep the animal boxed when she went in to visit Eva, and made her wash her hands in the big sink in his kitchen with a special sort of soap (he'd had to find her a stepping stool so she could reach). It wasn't that the doctor did not like Yussuf. But he suspected him of carrying germs, which she pictured to look much like woodlice, but smaller, with yellow pincers growing from their heads. Beer told her the hedgehog might be hiding them amongst the spines upon his back. She looked, of course, but Yussuf proved too clever for her and hid the vermin far too well.

When she came to the doctor's practice after school that day, Lieschen found the door locked and a handwritten note, placed much too high for her (she had to step back all the way to the other side of the landing and read it squinting from afar), announcing that Beer 'begged his patients' pardon' but had been summoned 'on an urgent house call' and hence had to close the practice for the afternoon. Her heart sank. She shrugged off the heavy satchel that was pulling at her back, sat down upon the topmost stair and took Yussuf from his box (Kaiser San, who shared the

254

hedgehog's kennel, was sitting straw-littered in one corner, his button eyes a little sulky because he was playing second fiddle to a prince). The hedgehog stood still upon the staircase landing, twitched its pointed, mobile snout, then ran back towards its box. The girl scooped him up and put him back amongst the straw. It was best just to go home.

This time, she was in no hurry to cross the yard. Nobody was about just then, the washing lines hanging empty, no carpet being beaten under the branches of the chestnut tree. The day was wet and raw, the clouds sitting dark and heavy in their rectangle of sky, fixing to rain. She tried the door to the janitor's basement but found it, too, was locked; no sound of his labours reaching up into the yard. Lieschen might have walked over to the hospital grounds to talk to the man with the steel-plated skull, but knew she'd get soaked on the way, arrive shivering and cold. That, and the satchel bothered her, dragged at her back. She'd just run up and drop it off.

There were twenty-five steps to their front door: two fewer than to Zuzka's, who lived in the front of the building where the steps were wider and flatter, for rich people's feet. As she climbed, the girl reviewed her morning. Petra had come to school that day with a pair of new lace-up boots. During break time, a red-faced Sepp had told her that his older brother had 'buggered up' the knife; he'd shown her the broken-off blade and they'd buried it a foot deep in the schoolyard sand. Sepp's brother was called Adolf: like the butcher, like her mother's father in the photograph with the torn edge, like the man who shouted on the radio and wore the stump of a moustache. It was a stupid name, but pretty, too, because like hers it started with an A. The girl arrived. She put down Yussuf, unlocked the door, pushed it open with both hands.

As always, Lieschen called ahead into the flat and – as so often – she received no answer. All was quiet, only the music of a gramophone carried from across the yard, French horns calling horsemen to the hunt. The girl picked up the box with the hedgehog, stepped over the threshold; closed the door with a shove of her hip. There was a bad smell and she told herself she must open the windows, let in the air, though Father said how much he hated a draught. She kicked off her shoes, drummed her toes against the floor. There was a smudge of blood on one wall, level with her face, and another, bigger than the first, a few steps on. The blood led to the left, towards the kitchen and her father's bedroom, but Lieschen turned right first, towards her own room and the window-less closet with its thick yellow rug and the old iron washstand, the towels and bucket and floor-soap and lye. No tremor ran through her burdened hands.

Once in her room, the girl laid the box on her bed and, not knowing herself what she was doing, took out the hedgehog and the hunchbacked teddy, placed them both upon the floor, then opened the satchel, unscrewed the jar and shook out some spiders. Then Lieschen straightened, lingered, ran into the closet to fetch a washcloth and a scallop of soap. Some vague notion that she should scrub the stains from off the walls must have occurred to her, for she moved back out into the hallway, walking gingerly, on tiptoe, her shoulders very bent just then, head and arms jutting stiffly from the crooked trunk. The floor was cold beneath her naked feet.

The girl walked to the kitchen, then the bedroom, where she had to force the door because a dead-weight leaned against its hinges. She saw what she saw and did not find the breath to shape a scream; got her dress dirty, and the heel of one foot, and the hand that later pushed some hair out of her face. She did not stay long. Outside, out on the landing, it took no thought to reach up and shove the key into the lock. She had no plan, no care for what came next; her face was pale except for the smudge left by that careless hand. The door locked, she tried the knob once more as was her habit, then took the stairs in an awkward running stumble; heading down, that is, towards the yard. At the bottom of the stairs she got all tangled up and fell; pulled herself back to her feet, stumbling, running down the hall. There was a window in the door that led outside, and already she could see the heavy drops of rain pelting down on to the yard: she longed for them keenly, hurried forward, one foot wet with sticky blood. Then a face darkened the window – she was but two steps away – and the door was pulled open from outside, a man pushing in his chest-heavy girth. It was too late to stop, something working on her legs more exacting than momentum. She collided with his stomach and his groin, bounced back, and once again fell hard on to the ground. His pockmarked face was rain-washed as it bent towards the fallen girl.

Shine-a-man plays the trumpet.

Japan is four islands, far off to the east.

He bent down to her, water dripping from his hat, and it was now, at last, she thought that she might learn to scream. She lost her senses instead; big hands taking hold of her, at the armpit and the neck.

Nobody saw Yuu carry her off.

CHAPTER 2

More than a week had passed. The fuse burned out half a dozen times, threw his practice into darkness; patients treated by the light of day, weak, glum, overcast, the city always between rains. Beer worked from eight-thirty to six; a round of house calls on Friday afternoons and Tuesday nights. There were visitors. Otto dropped by every morning, looked in on Eva. Then came his patients, then Anneliese, then Zuzka. They all had their rituals. Otto liked his coffee with lots of milk, no sugar; brought some rolls on occasion, or two or three eggs in a gesture of friendship or of payment, it was hard for Beer to tell. Anneliese brought her hedgehog and pressed her nose against the living-room window every day before she left; spun round, shouldered her satchel, then ran out the door like the wind. Zuzka came only when the last of the patients had left and he stood heating his dinner at the stove. She came to talk, it seemed, though often she said very little. She'd sit silent at his kitchen table and watch him eat, then burst out with some snatch of thought, half formed,

259

random, following lines of association he sat down to unravel only after she was gone.

The first time she had come like this – after hours, not asking after Eva or the girl, but brushing past him at the door and heading for the kitchen where an omelette lay frying on the stove – he had thought at first she must be drunk. A smell of beer clung to her breath. She took a seat, watched him run a spoon along the rim of the frying pan, then flip the omelette on to a plate before sliding it back into the pan. Her cheeks were blotchy, marked with red. She seemed to be in a state of great excitement.

'So what is it?' he asked, and poured her a glass of water from the sink. 'Shouldn't you be at dinner with your uncle?'

She nodded, drank the water in long, greedy gulps, then sat brushing at some drops that had fallen on her blouse. Beer gave her time to find an answer.

'I went back to him,' she said at last. 'Even after –' Her eyes rose, glared at him, strangely defiant.

'I stayed by the door, you know, holding on to the handle. Afraid, I suppose, ready to run, not looking him in the eye, but at his legs, his thighs, thinking he might pounce. I had a speech prepared, too, and let him have it. About honour and such, and how did he dare. It came out just as I rehearsed. And you know what he says to me? "*I thought you liked me.*" Just that, sulky, pulling a face. And off I am running down the stairs.'

She frowned; shook her head in wonder.

'I saw his show, you see. It's like someone else is hiding in that tube of paint.'

The doctor turned off the gas, poured himself some wine.

'The show,' he repeated, catching on. 'So you went out all by yourself. But that's –'

'Dangerous, I know.' Her eyes flashed with anger, then filled with tears.

'I asked Frau Vesalius once how one knew one was in love.' She laughed, mirthless, ran a sleeve across her face.

'What did she say?'

'I don't remember. I think she told me that you were already married.'

He sat down across from her, took a sip of his wine.

'You don't love me, Fräulein Speckstein.'

'No,' she agreed, all too easily. Another man would have been stung.

'But you think you love –' He paused, picked through his words. 'He's a dangerous man, you know.'

'I know what he is,' she returned, angry, impatient with his conventionality.

His wife had told him once that every good woman loved a rake. There, too, it had been a matter of complaint.

'I have to go,' said Zuzka.

She stood and he hastened down the hallway ahead of her, held open the door.

'You mustn't come here all alone,' he said to her, pressing her hand. 'The neighbours will talk.'

Her laughter rang up to him as she ran down the stairs. On reflection he realised he might have said it just to conjure that laugh.

CHAPTER 3

Zuzka came every night after that; came, Beer surmised, straight from some rendezvous with Otto, stayed fifteen minutes, then headed off to dinner with her uncle. On occasion he persuaded her to sit with Eva for a moment, believing somehow that exposure to Eva would soften her and make her better, the effect Eva had upon himself. Zuzka agreed but performed it as a duty, her thoughts turned inwards upon herself. Beer found her much changed, this young woman who had called him to her bedside to treat an illness he'd soon diagnosed a sham. Back then she'd been playfully mischievous, proud to be *in charge*; manipulative like a child. Now she seemed to him as though transfixed: pinned to the spot by some force stronger than herself. Another girl might have run away from that which held her, but she'd been born with more courage than good sense. It was useless to warn her; when he tried, she ceased to listen, drank her water, wished him a good night. He wondered obliquely whether he should be giving her advice on contraception, but reassured himself that this was premature. Her reputation suffered from her visits, so he felt, but the rumour served as cover for the truth.

For all his concern, the bulk of Beer's energies went elsewhere. He was absorbed in a struggle for Eva's life. There had been setbacks in these past few days, necrosis spreading within a sore along the bony parts of her right shoulder blade. When he spoke to Eva (quick, murmured statements of what might be called confession) it was about himself, not Zuzka. Eva answered him by winking. It was all he'd ever asked.

On Monday, Beer missed Zuzka's visit. He had been called out to an emergency around lunchtime; closed down the practice and stayed away until late, all the time fretting that he'd left Eva alone for too long. Tuesday, Lieschen did not show. This, too, caused him some worry. He stared across the yard into her father's flat, but the curtains were drawn. Perhaps they had gone away. Zuzka came during dinner, cold cuts and a hunk of bread: he let her in, his napkin drooping from his hand.

'Have you seen Anneliese?' he asked, but she did not seem to hear, ran to the kitchen, drank from his wine.

'My uncle is out tonight,' she announced. 'I told Vesalius I was eating with you.' Her eyes looked wild to him, some great disturbance running through her mind. She had yet to remove her coat; it hung open and weary from her girlish shoulders.

'And Otto?'

'Gone to work. He kissed me today.' She winced, unfastened the hook at the top of her blouse, showed him a collarbone marked by a bruise. 'I closed my eyes and pursed my lips, saying he may.' She poured more wine, downed it. 'Turns out he bites. Then he stood waiting, that look in his eyes.' She blushed. 'Like he thought I knew what came next.'

'What did you do?'

'I—' She straightened in her chair, patted down some strands of her hair. 'I ran away, of course. Though first I invited him to my uncle's party. The big soirée. You must help me tell him.'

'Your uncle's giving a party?' Beer muttered, confused. 'But you can't invite Otto. It's impossible. You must tell him you were joking.'

Zuzka nodded at that, but he could see she wasn't listening to him. She kept drinking more of his wine, her face flushed, frightened and drunk.

'I haven't seen Lieschen for two days,' he tried again, hoping to call her to her senses, but again she simply nodded, then cut him off, not having heard a word.

'Three or four years ago,' she said, 'Father brought us to Vienna for a week. We went to all the museums, and to the theatre every night. *Hamlet* was playing. Some famous actor, too old and too fat, bulging out of his tights. I remember his legs most of all, staring at his legs, and at the front.' She gave a manic sort of laugh and made a gesture down past her abdomen where her legs stretched scissored at the groin. 'The play was awfully long. One part, though, struck me very much, when the actors performed the play within the play. I found it and read it later, in my father's library, Karl Kraus' translation, Dad had marked the section with a postcard from the Alps. *The Mousetrap*, it's called: the moment Hamlet lets his uncle know how much he knows. He went pale, poor Claudius, white as a sheet upon his throne. I couldn't fathom how he did it. The actor, I mean: how he willed the blood to leave his face. I literally thought he would fall over and die.'

Zuzka looked over to him, as if to see whether he was following her line of thought. She seemed reassured when she saw that he did not.

'You mustn't say anything to anyone, isn't that right?' she asked with great abruptness. 'Because you're a doctor, I mean.'

Her eyes, he noted, pointed past him, deep into the flat. All at once he understood. She was thinking of Eva. There was no man easier to blackmail than Anton Beer.

Again she poured from the bottle of wine.

'But what is it that you want from me?' he asked, dismayed.

She took hold of his hand, dragged him out of his seat and out of the kitchen, towards the living room, where he slept at night upon the leather couch. She let go of him, threw herself face down upon its cushions, slid a pillow under her hips;

her coat and skirt riding up mid-thigh, the stockings drooping on her doughy legs.

'Have me,' she said.

It was as though she were asking him for a cigarette, or another glass of wine.

He stared at her stiffly and ran to the window to close the curtains.

'Zuzka,' he said, kneeling down beside her elevated bum.

The doorbell rang. They both turned their heads. It was like a scene from some cheap farce.

He thought at first he might be able to ignore it. Beer expected no visitors that night, and it seemed important to see to this: an unhappy girl, hip-cocked, crying, a heave and shiver running through the muscles of her back. But the ringing was insistent, soon joined by the loud banging of a fist. Beer excused himself, rose to his feet and stepped into the hallway, making sure to close the living-room door behind himself. Five steps took him past the coat rack. He looked through the spyhole, then opened the door. It was Teuben, detective inspector of the criminal police.

CHAPTER 4

Detective Inspector Teuben made himself at home. '*Grüss Gott*,' he said, '*Heil Hitler*,' not raising his right arm; walked into the kitchen first, bent to find a beer at the bottom of the larder, pushed out the cork with a flick of his thumb. Beer marvelled again at the thinness, the redness of his lips; the jet-black wig that cut off in a line above the ears and neck; the awkward physicality in the new but shabby suit. His shoes were wet from walking amongst puddles; muddy footprints soiled the floor.

'Halfway through dinner, I see. May I—?' And the big hand reached forward to cram a slice of boiled ham into his mouth.

'You wouldn't have any horseradish, Dr Beer?'

Silent, yielding, Beer stepped over to one of his cupboards, and retrieved a jar of pickled *Kren*, unscrewed it, plunged a little spoon inside. Teuben watched him with open amusement.

'You're quite the housewife, Dr Beer. I'm impressed.'

'What do you want, Detective Teuben? It's late, I'm tired.'

The man smiled, clicked the grease off his finger and thumb.

'Why don't you have a look at this, Dr Beer?'

From the pocket of his coat, which he had thrown across an empty chair, he pulled out a folded-up envelope. Inside was a typed police report, detailing an assault against a young woman named Gisela Kirsch.

'She's a maid in a doctor's household. Surgeon by the name of Rupp; proud member of the SS. You know him?'

Beer shrugged. 'I might have met him at a ball.'

'Ah, the physicians' ball. How splendid! Middle-aged wives looking like meringues; selling off their daughters to the highest bidder. But I suppose it's part of the game. Making contacts and all.' He scoffed another slice of ham, cut himself a piece of bread. 'The attack took place in the Volksgarten. Miss Kirsch says she "just wanted to take the air". Middle of the afternoon, would you believe? Not a lot of people around, because of the rain. The assailant dragged her into the bushes. Notice the leather strap he tried to put around her throat. We took pictures of the bruise. It's a wonder she got away. A hardy girl, big juicy arse.'

'So now you think you have a serial murderer after all.'

Teuben raised his brows, his hairline twitching with the motion. 'That's why I come to you, Dr Beer. The criminological genius, German methods and all. Take your time, though, read it in peace. We can talk about it all tomorrow.'

He stood, wiped his hands on the tablecloth, finished the last of his beer. 'There's another reason why I came.'

'Yes?'

Teuben took his coat over one arm, stepped into the hallway, then turned to walk into the flat rather than out. He was heading for the bedroom.

Beer ran after him.

'What are you doing?' he asked, laid a hand on Teuben's shoulder, stopped him with a sudden tug. The thin lips spread into the knife-cut of a smile.

'Following a hunch.'

They stood like this for a moment, front to back, Beer's face close to the spot where neck and throat grew into ear, the detective's head half turned so as to present a perfect profile, his dark, soft eye and sagging chin, the purple strip of a shaving bruise clinging to the bottom of his jaw. Teuben's smell rose between them, a masculine mixture, not unpleasant, of aftershave and sweat. The hand Beer had raised to the detective's shoulder now sat there with the limpness of a lover's parting touch; its passion spent, it lingered only as a reminiscence, marking time. Teuben stared at this, the doctor's hand, and waited him out.

It did not take long. Beer withdrew his arm, stuffed the useless hand into one pocket: it found a hanky there, and some old button sewn from

270

folded bits of leather, worn smooth and greasy from long years of use. The detective smiled once more and carried on towards the door; swung it open with a sudden push. Beer followed him into the room, gherkin juices rising to his throat. In front of them lay Eva, stomach down upon his bedding; her neck was bent so that she faced them, the pillow wet with a patch of drool, green eyes large and reflecting back the sudden light of the hallway bulb. A sheet covered her from foot to naked shoulders; the nightgown's straps pretty with their lace against her pallid skin.

Teuben took a breath and eased himself into the chair that stood by her bedside, level with her chest and face. He reached and touched her, shook her, then creased his brow in wonder.

'What's wrong with her? Why doesn't she move?'

'She can't. A temporary condition. I'm treating her.'

Teuben bent forward until his face hovered only inches above her covered back. He sniffed, then straightened. 'She smells,' he complained and pulled back the sheet to reveal the first of the bandages, easily visible through the gown's thin gauze.

'Please,' said Beer. 'She must not be disturbed.'

'And she really cannot move? Not even her arms and head?'

'No.'

'How wonderful.' He touched her face, ran a hairy thumb along her lower lip.

'Detective. You mustn't. This woman is very sick—'

Teuben turned to him then, his thumb still pressed to Eva's mouth, prising open her lips in a gesture that was openly obscene.

'Dr Beer,' he said with some formality. 'The last time I was here you told me this woman was your lover, and asleep. You lied very well. I had my suspicions, of course, but told myself to let it go; what use was it to me to see you troubled, and besides what good is a man who doesn't whore? In short, I had other things on my mind. But then, some days ago, I find myself thinking about this woman in your flat. I only had the briefest glimpse – a shorn, dark head, a skinny arm, sleeping soundly in your bedroom – but something stuck with me, some sense of line' – he gestured through the air as though he were a painter – 'and I find myself thinking perhaps I'd like to meet the girl myself. So I make enquiries. It doesn't cost anything, I'm the police, so what the hell. The name was fake, of course, I half expected it, though common enough in Vienna that we tracked down two and asked them awkward questions just to make sure. Then, this afternoon, just after I have taken down Fräulein Kirsch's statement and hence was thinking of paying you a visit, I remembered that Speckstein mentioned a divorcee in this building whom he suspects of "unlicensed prostitution" in his stuck-up little phrase. Teaches English, a deaf old crone as chaperone who wouldn't know it if she banged an army out back. I go for a visit, profess an interest in some foreign tongue. Turns out she's a handsome little lass with a gorgeous head of hair; skinny, shapely, knows how to smile. So for a moment I think it's her, I've solved your riddle, and am even a little disappointed. The divorcee is pretty, don't get me wrong, but in the light of day she lacks the mystery that I remembered: she wasn't worth, in short, wasting my thoughts on for nigh on a week. Just to make sure I tug at her hair. We're face to crotch by then, she thinks me a customer, looking lovely with her lips around my swollen cock. And what do you know: it's not a wig. I nearly yank her head off, I do, and with it my pecker, she bites down in pain. So I apologise and let her finish; have a think. I've a good mind to come over straight away, put a boot right up your bum, but then it's office hours and your patients might be in the way. So I tell the driver to take me back to the station. I pick up the report – two birds, one stone – go out for a beer, make bets with myself what it'll be. Most likely, of course, the bedroom is empty; crumpled bedsheets needing a wash and the wardrobe filled with Frau Beer's old frocks. At worst, I figure, I'll get a new name out of you, and an address that fits the bill. But then, there's a chance there is more to it after all: the shorn-haired girl caught sleeping in your bed. I drink a second beer and wonder is she a Gypsy – a thief, a bum, a

Communist? – run away from one of our camps? And then – I order a schnapps to congratulate myself! – I remember you worked at the hospital, keeping tabs on the mad. So all of a sudden I have this romantic notion that you have a nutcase here, pretty like the night. And just like that everything makes sense: your sudden resignation, wife gone to Switzerland, the quick, confident lie. You are screwing a loon, the type the propaganda tells us we'd do best to put a bullet through their heads. I took a cab here, will you believe it, rather than waiting for a station car to be available. Excited like a little boy.'

He laughed, straightened and withdrew his arm, wiped his wet thumb on his tie. 'But this, Dr Beer, this I didn't expect! A girl who can't move, big old plasters on the back. Pretty like an altar boy chewing his first wafer. And anything you say about it, Dr Beer, it's bound to be horse-shit, so please don't even start.'

He stood, rounded the bed, slipped a hand under the sheet and took hold of one of Eva's feet. 'You haven't just shot her full of morphine, have you? No, you'd keep her tied in that case, making sure she didn't wake and make a nuisance of herself; and I can't see any straps.'

Through all of Teuben's speech, Beer stood head bowed, helpless, the taste of gherkins in his mouth. He dearly wished to spit and wash his mouth; to strike Teuben, push a spike through both his eyes. His right hand remained clenched around the contours of the leather button. It seemed scarred to him, sown together from leftover scraps. A surgeon's fingers might have admired the stitching.

'Tell me,' Teuben said, still holding on to Eva's foot, and raising her leg beneath the bedsheet. 'Is it still customary to examine female patients through their clothing? I nearly fell out of my chair laughing when our old coroner told me. He was talking about the difference between the live patient, and the dead.'

His eyes found Beer's. There was no malice in them, the doctor thought, just hunger. It took him a moment to gain control of his voice.

'It's no longer customary. Not among the younger generation.' He paused. 'Don't hurt her.'

'Hurt her? But why should I? She's – perfect. God's idea of woman, when he whittled on that rib.' He smiled, pleased with himself, red lips parting over neat white teeth. 'Leave us, Dr Beer, why don't you? Fix some coffee, perhaps, and a glass of brandy.'

Beer remained where he was, halfway between bed and door, feet spread wide for balance. He became aware of his own breathing, the detective's gaze upon him, awaiting his reaction. Beer had a strange sensation as of a noise rising in his ears, like the shouts of many voices, the words just out of earshot and conjoining into the seashell whisper of the tides.

'You can't,' he said. 'I won't.'

Teuben shook his head, raised a hand to scratch within his wig.

'Dr Beer. 'There is only one way this can end. If you were doing something legal, you'd have thrown me out by now, made some noise about your *rights*.'

'She has an acute infection. She could die at any moment.'

'Nonsense.'

'Have a look then.'

The doctor stepped up to the bed, and folded over the lip of the sheet, revealing the back of the nightgown. The voices grew louder in his ears; he wondered what would happen if they suddenly broke into intelligibility. With swift, tender movements he undid the topmost clasp and pointed to the bandage.

'Go on, peel it back. It's loose, so the wound can breathe.'

Teuben reached forward with surprising delicacy. He raised the corner of the adhesive tape with one fingernail, then peeled it back slowly, trying not to hurt the skin. The bandage came off, revealing the crater of the wound, looking fresh and pink like the gums of a newborn. Inside the half-inch hole there was a wriggle of movement. Teuben bent closer, trying to see, then leapt back to the window, his face suddenly pale.

'Maggots!' he said, appalled.

Beer readjusted the bandage, buttoned up the gown. They stared at each other across the bed.

Teuben looked thoughtful, white under his wig. All his blood seemed to cling to his lips.

'But what is that noise?' he said, and turned around to the window.

'You hear it, too?' Beer asked, surprised. Just then a whistle joined the hubbub of voices. It sounded from outside.

The two men stepped to the window. All was quiet in the street, two lamps casting cones of light on to the pavement. A flow of pedestrians, not all of them in coats, was heading for the building's front door, which had been propped open with a brick.

'It's coming from the courtyard. That's a police whistle, that.'

Teuben turned abruptly and headed for the corridor. Beer followed close behind, cast a parting glance at Eva, her eyes open and unmoved. Her foot was sticking out the bottom of the sheet where Teuben had held on to it, the toes curled inwards, into the sole.

In the corridor the two men ran into Zuzka, emerging from the door to the living room. Teuben stared at her, standing there in her grey woollen dress, one stocking flapping down around her ankle, then burst into a sudden laughter.

'You're full of surprises, Herr Doktor.'

Zuzka brushed past him, took a hold of Beer's arm. He noticed with irritation that there was a stiffness to her walk that recalled one of her earlier symptoms: she dragged the left leg. It struck him as a bad moment to indulge in childishness.

'There's been a murder,' she murmured, fear in her eyes. 'Across the yard. Lieschen—'

A gust blew from the living room behind her (she had opened the window to have a clearer view of the yard) and carried with it the sharp trill of a police whistle, unmistakable now in its pitch. Even Teuben started at its sound. Without another word all three of them rushed forward, out the front door, and could soon be heard running down the stairs. Outside they were met by a dense crowd of neighbours and strangers, held in check by the police.

CHAPTER 5

Zuzka stood in the yard and shivered. She had left her coat in Beer's living room upstairs, where she'd taken it off and flung it to the floor some time after the doctor had run to answer the door, hoping he would see it upon his return and read it as a clue to her displeasure. It had been a long half-hour that she'd spent, alone, having offered up her virtue and been spurned. She'd lain on the couch and cried a little, embarrassed, stung at having been abandoned at a moment such as that, abject and unhappy, though some small part of her was listening, exercised as to who had dared to ring the bell. It was a single man who entered the flat, and from the few words that carried from the kitchen she formed the dim understanding that it was a policeman working on the killing of the dog. When he and Beer walked past into the bedroom, she opened the door a little and thus overheard much of the policeman's long and filthy speech, then grew aware of the hubbub of voices floating up from the yard. Distracted, her mind clinging to the image of a woman kneeling before a man's unbuttoned fly, she ran to the window and drew back a corner of curtain. Right away – before, even, she'd become aware of the crowd that pressed together in the rectangle of yard – her eyes sought out the flat inhabited by Lieschen, marked as it was by the sudden flash of a photo camera inside. Even after the flash the flat stood brightly lit. There was no mistaking the uniform of the man who leaned against the window, staring down on to the crowd. A second flash, behind him, lit up the kitchen and threw his shadow across the yard. The crowd stood with their heads thrown back, staring up as though they were admiring a firework display. Two further policemen, their hands busy with their truncheons, secured the door to the back wing. Zuzka opened the window; snatches of conversation drifted up to her. The word 'murder' hung in the air: 'once again with a knife'; someone talked loudly about 'the Zellenwart's dead cur'. She listened further, the cold contracting her fair skin. 'Lieschen,' somebody said, and again, 'Lieschen,' fingers pointing at the flat. She recognised among the crowd the man from the hospital gardens with the scar and the dead eye. He was eating a sandwich, talking as he chewed. Vesalius was there, and old Frau Novak; the Bergers; the Obermanns; the English teacher with her head of auburn locks. Half the crowd was smoking. In the half-dark of the yard the glow of the cigarette ends hung like fireflies on a summer's eve. A group of men were shouting questions at the policemen guarding the back entry. A schoolgirl laughed and was loudly told to shut her trap.

When the first of the whistles sounded, Zuzka flinched and left the window. A glance at the mirror would have told her that she looked dishevelled: the eyes red from crying, puffy skin around the cheeks, blouse and stockings in some disarray. She stopped at the door, heard another whistle rise behind her, then stepped on through, nearly colliding with the policeman in the hallway, big-hipped, ugly, with large hairy hands. What she said to Beer, she could not later recall. The stairs received them, the staccato click of her heels, the men running ahead of her, gaining ground with every step. Her left leg gave her trouble, would not quite move; a tightness in her chest that had not bothered her in days.

Outside, the two policemen parted for the detective and for Beer, then closed ranks before she had time to cross the yard. She craned her neck, saw a third flash spill from the lit windows, which threw the crowd into relief. It occurred to her that she'd have a better view from her own window, but realised at once that her key was in her coat. Vesalius would let her in. Vesalius was standing talking to Herr Neurath, a fur-lined cap upon her head. Zuzka shivered and stayed where she was. Someone next to her offered her a cigarette. It was a worker in overalls, a patch of grease clinging to his cheek. He did not seem offended when she declined. Someone at the back started singing a tune; another voice soon inserted a dirty verse. Half the crowd seemed to be drunk; a fairground spirit mingling with the fear.

A half-hour passed, new bodies entering the press, and now and then a whistle sounded from its thick, calling to order the drunken and the bold. Zuzka looked through the crowd for someone who might hold some information. Her eyes fell again on the divorcee who was said to make a living teaching English: the made-up face under the tumble of her hair, a little blue hat pinned into it and serving no purpose other than to add a dash of contrast to the ample locks. She wore a long black coat and lace-up boots, looked respectable and fragile, leather gloves on her hands. Her name was Klara Kovacs. Zuzka pushed through to her, avoided looking at her lips.

'*Grüss Gott*,' she said, blushing. 'Can you tell me what is going on?'

The woman inspected her, turned up the collar of her coat, frowned.

'There's been a murder. Up there in that flat. Where the little cripple lives.'

'Lieschen. Is it she who—?'

'I heard it was the father. The door was wide open. Blood everywhere. A man told me he wasn't the first such victim. Somebody killed Speckstein's dog, cut him open with a hatchet.' She gave a little shiver, reached for a handkerchief to dab her nose.

'Yes,' said Zuzka. 'So I've heard.'

Something was happening near the door to the back wing, at the other end of the yard. A movement went through the crowd, irresistible, like the swell of the sea, at first rushing in on the space, then swiftly parting to grant passage to a group of men. It was the detective, followed by Beer, a man in uniform walking by their side. As soon as Frau Kovacs became aware of the little group, a hardness crept into her eyes and she turned abruptly to vanish into the crowd. Zuzka was left standing alone in the press of men. When she noticed that Beer was headed in her general direction, she raised her hand until he caught sight of her. The detective by his side was talking at him, his small mouth inches from the doctor's ear. He stopped speaking as soon as she was in earshot. She noticed that he had threaded a hand through the gap under Beer's armpit and was holding on to his arm. They both came to a halt in front of her.

'What happened up there?' she asked.

'Lieschen's father is dead.'

'But how? Who—?'

Beer was about to answer, but stopped himself short when the hand around his arm tightened. One could see him wince under the detective's grip.

'It's under investigation,' he began again. 'The autopsy is tonight.'

'And Lieschen?'

'Nowhere to be found.' Beer paused, looked up

283

to the detective as though seeking his permission. 'The body is some days old. When did you last see her?'

'I can't remember. Two, three days ago.'

'We must try to find her.'

Zuzka was about to ask for further details when she felt Beer's attention shift to somewhere behind her. She looked around and saw her uncle march through the door that led from the front of the building into the yard. He was dressed in coat and tails and had evidently been drinking. His face was very flushed.

'Somebody at the police station found me at the Mayor's reception. He said there'd been a murder in my house.'

He peered over to the policemen who stood barring the way to the back wing, then focused in on Teuben. 'Are you in charge?'

'Yes, Professor. Detective Inspector Teuben. The Chief of Police will have my report first thing in the morning.'

'Come now, my man, no need to be coy. What happened here?'

'We have to wait for the post-mortem. Impossible to give you a sense of the case before.' He seemed to be speaking more to Beer than to Speckstein, his knuckles white against the doctor's coat.

'But there must be some details you can give me.'

The detective shrugged, gave Beer's arm a final

squeeze, then led Speckstein a few yards to one side and began talking to him in rushed whispers. Beer and Zuzka gazed after them. The doctor looked tired and pale.

'I should go back and look in on Eva,' he murmured. 'She needs to be turned.'

'We have to find Lieschen.'

'And where do you propose we go look for her?' He sighed, took her hand in his own, then dropped it quickly, aware of the crowd that surrounded them. 'But you are shivering.'

'I forgot my coat upstairs. In your living room.'

'I'll go fetch it for you.' He paused, caught sight of Speckstein, who was waving at him with the magnificence of a king, a little drunkenly, that is, curling his fingers in their white glove. 'Just a moment. Your uncle wants to speak to me.'

Beer seemed relieved to leave her presence. She wondered whether he would be avoiding her from now on. Stung and stubborn, she followed him and stood behind his back while Speckstein instructed him to 'take full charge of the medical side of things'. There was a large, brown stain on the expanse of her uncle's shirt-front, in the shape of a teardrop. It surprised her. He was normally the most fastidious of diners.

A voice distracted her. Later, she would marvel that she was able to pick it out from the din of the yard. She turned around and saw Otto, in his black clothes and shabby coat, standing a few yards behind her, asking questions of an old man in the crowd. There was no greasepaint on his face and something of his sister stared out from his large, expressive eyes. A flood of thoughts and feelings rushed her, all connected to this man: about their daily awkward meetings, almost wordless now, filled with a tension neither one of them seemed willing to relieve; about the article from the magazine (she had long asked to have it back) with its strange and silly words – 'spatial clairvoyance', 'ideoplastic materialisation' – that somehow pointed to his sister, that living corpse that the detective wished to own; about the memory of his performance, the whitened lips, the silent moans, the knee he slipped between her thighs. There was no telling how long he'd been standing in the yard, nor whether he had noticed her, drifting through the crowd. He finished his conversation and set out for the side wing, passing within a yard of where she stood.

'You aren't working?' she asked him quietly when he drew level, taking care not to step any closer. It was to her as though the entire yard was staring at them: had hushed, stood straining, ears cocked for his reply. Otto stopped and shot her a glance.

'They closed the club. Something about the paperwork. The owner's been arrested.'

His features reflected deep confusion.

She wished that she could touch him then, just as Beer had touched her a few minutes ago, reach over, hold his hand. They sat like that sometimes, up in his room – tenderly, she thought, his palm in hers – though in his face there often ruled a bug-eyed anger. He shrugged, resumed his journey, then was brusquely stopped by a hand that grabbed his collar and pulled him off balance so that he stumbled to one knee. The hand was large and it was hairy. It was Teuben's.

If the crowd had seemed hushed to her before, it fell silent now, intent upon this scene of sudden action. The silence spread in quick concentric circles at whose centre fell the pebble that was Teuben's hand. Only towards the back did the fairground atmosphere continue, were coarse jokes shouted, ditties sung, did people talk to trade the gossip. A ring formed around the four men, Teuben, Otto, Beer and Speckstein. Zuzka found herself in the foot or so of empty space that separated spectators and spectacle, the only one amongst the watchers who knew herself to be exposed. From high above a trumpet sounded, high-pitched, human, like a baby's wail, then was quickly scattered by the wind. All eyes were on Teuben.

'Who are you, my friend?' he growled, aware of the audience, enjoying it. 'I've seen you before. You live here?'

Otto nodded, pointed over to the door to the side wing. He seemed to have immediately understood that the man belonged to the police: did not struggle against the hand upon his coat, kept his eyes away from him, fastened on the ground.

It came to Zuzka that he had been arrested before.

'But how is it that I know you?'

'I'm a performer,' Otto muttered. 'At the Kasperl Club. Perhaps—'

Teuben pulled Otto closer yet, stared down into his face, then dropped his eyes further to his chest and legs, the jet-black clothing of his trade.

'Well, I'll be damned. You're the mime.'

Otto nodded.

'I saw your show two weeks back. Magnificent. I laughed so hard, I nearly bust a gut.'

'Thank you, sir.'

The detective's hand remained on his lapel. 'But what an extraordinary face.'

He turned to Beer and Speckstein, swinging Otto around with him and adjusting his hand which came to sit behind his captive's neck.

'It seems you have an artist living in your midst, Professor. Have you seen his show? No? You should, it's magnificent.'

He paused, licked his lips, shot a gaze across the crowd.

'I'll tell you one thing, Professor. You should have him at that party of yours that the Chief of Police keeps talking about. Some entertainment for the guests. After dinner. Raise the spirits a little.'

Speckstein looked at him embarrassed, gathered all his dignity.

'I'm afraid there won't be a party. It might not be safe, given recent events.'

'Nonsense,' said Teuben, speaking louder than was necessary. 'We must keep up the Germanic spirit. Stoic in the face of danger, chin out and *marsch*. Tell you what, Herr Professor, I will see to the security myself. Just leave it to me; I'll blend in with the guests and nobody'll be the wiser. Dr Beer is coming, too, I presume – your esteemed colleague? Yes? Wonderful. And a bit of cabaret to go with the dessert. How about it, Herr –?' (and here he snapped his fingers at the mime).

'Frei.'

'Herr Frei. Are you free on Saturday night? For a private performance, I mean?'

'Yes.'

'Then it's all settled. What do you say, Professor? A little entertainment for your guests, and Beer and I to make sure nothing untoward is going on. Or are you worried that it'll be too vulgar? High and low, it's all a nonsense of the past. There is no such thing as class – only Germans! Go on, Comrade *Zellenwart*, it'll be a blast.'

Speckstein excused himself soon after, struggling for dignity. He grabbed Zuzka's wrist and dragged her after him, and was quickly followed by Frau Vesalius whom he ordered to draw a bath and bring his pipe. Teuben and Beer returned to the scene of the killing. The crowd in the yard dispersed after another hour, when it started to drizzle.

Later, the back wing was reopened, the door to the victim's flat sealed with a wax stamp. It was the night of the 31st of October 1939. When Zuzka sat down on her bed, still wearing all her clothes and shivering from her hour in the cold, her body failed her and she found herself unable to move either of her legs.

CHAPTER 6

Beer told Eva. He sat on her bed, had rolled her on to her left side, held on to an arm and was massaging its muscles, all the while talking, catching her eye. She blinked now and then, moistened her gaze. He took it for a sign she understood. It was late, almost morning; the doctor looking haggard and worn.

'So he marched me over to that house of death,' he told her. 'No, that's not true. It wasn't Teuben who was marching me. I wanted to go, the moment we stepped out into the yard and saw the crowd there, craning their necks. I was just the same as them – I wanted to see first hand. And then I wondered, what if something had happened to Anneliese? Her father was a drunk, you know; she watched him from the window every day. Sometimes, a man like that, he doesn't need a reason, love will do it the same as hate. For violence, I mean: to do the girl harm. I was afraid of what we might find.'

He broke off, licked his lips, fingers kneading Eva's skin.

'On the way up the stairs, I kept calling her

name. We were both of us running, Teuben in the lead. He turned once and told me to shut the hell up. Up on the landing, he grabbed hold of my arm. I wasn't sure then, was he steadying me, or holding me back? We entered like that, walking arm in arm.

'The door was wide open, the front hallway trampled with fresh mud. You'd think they'd know better, respect the crime scene, but they had barged right in, first the neighbour who had found the corpse – a war vet by the name of Kopp: he was sitting in the hallway on a chair, a leg and a half stretched out in front of him, answering the same questions over and over for different men – then the policeman whom he'd fetched from down the street, wet and surly on his beat. Three leather soles and the rubber peg of a crutch: they had come in together, trailing in mud, and had found a second neighbour who had chanced upon the open door, his hands deep in the dead man's pocket – looking for his passport, he said, which he read is what you do. The policeman left the two in charge while he went to find a telephone. What else was he to do? Nobody was to enter the flat while he was away.

'The door hadn't been forced. That's the first thing I noticed: that the door hadn't been forced. I used to study these sorts of things, you know, when I was still half a boy, and anatomy bored me. Kept a copy of Gross's *Handbook of Criminal Science* by my bedside, read it whenever I could.

That's before I discovered psychiatry. It seemed more elegant than blood-splatter patterns and bullet trajectories, more suited to the type of man I sought to be. I took a fancy to the criminal mind. It led me to Hannover and Düsseldorf, and from there into Teuben's arms. I should have studied ophthalmology, but then that's not a young man's choice.

'The lock, in any case, had been picked or opened with a key, sometime between four o'clock and six, in the stretch of time when Kopp had left the building to wet his whistle in a bar. He passed a closed door on the way down; found it open on his return. There was some blood near the entrance, looking old, I thought – days old, not hours – though at this point I wasn't yet sure: two or three smudges just about halfway up the wall. We followed them into the flat, Teuben walking me along, telling everyone I was an expert, which I suppose is somewhat true. The kitchen was a clutter, the table overturned, broken bottles on the floor, and a jack-knife in the sink, five inches long, with a two-tone handle made of horn like you can buy in any old *Tabak*. It was lying on a pile of unwashed dishes. Someone must have picked it up, then thrown it back quite recently. On the topmost plate there was a broken crust of dried-in blood.

'The man himself was in the bedroom. From the way he was lying it was clear he had been moved. The body was stiff, bent at the waist, its hands pressing a crumpled-up jacket to the belly, black now, sodden, made of wool. I guessed it had been twenty, thirty, forty hours at the most: a body old enough to play host to flies, yet young enough to remain locked in *rigor mortis*, lying in the charnel smell of rotting blood. The strange thing was that something about him – the stubble, the lips, the greasy, thick hair – still clung to the memory of life; he was pale and he was dead, and he wanted a cigarette. That, and he looked like his daughter, the same sort of bones. Teuben laughed when I tried to close his lids.

'Most of the blood was at the midriff, and there was a cut visible through his unbuttoned shirt. For some reason I kept staring at his shoes. They were house shoes – slippers – made from ancient suede, the leather torn and bruised, soft soles bloated with his blood. We laid him on a stretcher, under a sheet, though he would not easily unbend. It was work and we got sweaty, our shirt-fronts stained inside and out. I noticed something then: that Teuben is the sort of man who does not mind handling the dead. Neither do I, but I'm a doctor. Perhaps I am allowed.

'Another thing I noticed: there was no hedgehog. His box was in the girl's bedroom, along with the teddy she carries around, its head askew upon the loose-stitched neck, and I even found some paw marks, it had come to the kitchen and trodden in the blood, but the animal, it wasn't there, I looked under the beds and under the cupboards and asked the police guard had he seen it scuttle about. He told me there were no hedgehogs in the city. I almost called it by its name, Yussuf, like a dog, to see if it would come.

'And then there were those footprints, amongst the trailed-in dirt: three sets in all, criss-crossing the kitchen in a pattern it took some time to figure out. I made a quick sketch of them, like the *Handbook* says: spread a piece of paper on the kitchen table and copied down and numbered every stain, three policemen craning over me, laughing, I suppose, though one offered me some coloured pencils he carried in his coat, to give some colour to my art. (I took them and thanked him, and marked red all the blood.) The first set of prints belonged to the man's own slippers, a broad, flat-footed oval, frayed at either side. He got his toes wet first, then slipped in his blood, moved forward and back in no order I could discern. A dancer might have left a trail like that, or a man fighting a ghost. At one point he fell and left his handprints on the ground. From then on he chose to crawl.

'The second kind of print was of a naked heel, small enough to belong to the child. It trailed away from the bedroom, out the front door. I lost track of it halfway down the stairs: it disappeared in the dirt. I suppose this means she's alive, and I smiled a moment, crouching low upon the stairs, my dirty fingers picking at the floor. But where, I ask you, can she be without her shoes?

'The third set, it was fresher than the other two. There was a single print right near the body, of an old and worn-out boot. The blood had dried by then and barely stained this stranger's sole. Whoever it was, he noticed it and rubbed his boot clean against the bedroom's door frame, then left no other trace. The print did not belong to either of the neighbours who had discovered the corpse, nor to any of the police – I lined everyone up and looked at their soles just to make sure. Teuben watched me through all this, bemused. His only words to me were this: "Not a word until the autopsy."

'And that's where I was for half the night, in the basement of the city morgue, washing down a sticky corpse, then cutting him open, who was already cut. We got there late, had waited for the crowd to thin out in the yard before we moved the awkward body, still sitting more than lying on the canvas of the stretcher, the sheet with which we covered him kept sliding to his hips. By ten the rain had washed away the curious, and the men carried him down into a waiting car. We followed. I did not want to go, Eva: I'm no pathologist, have always been clumsy with the knife, but he insisted, Teuben did, stood in the room and threw out the assistants, while I smoked and did my bloody work. For every cigarette I smoked, he dug a fresh mint out his pocket; watched me, didn't speak or move, hummed strains of the *Horst Wessel Lied*. It was three-thirty by the time I finished: cold out, raining, no light in the sky. Teuben took it upon himself to drive me home, him talking, about the Chief of Police and Speckstein and God knows what else. Every time he changed gear, the engine howled, he drives very badly, stalled the car twice.

'The last thing he said to me, as he pulled up outside and I got out: 'Don't think about moving her,' he said, meaning you, of course, his fingers clamped around my arm. 'If you do, I'll throw you in jail and beat you stupid with a rubber hose.' He gave me a mint then, and sent me on upstairs. The car drove off and I raced up, to clean you, turn you, tell you my woes.'

He rubbed his face, exhausted, searched his pockets for a cigarette, found an empty packet that he crumpled in one fist.

'Who would have guessed?' he murmured, laid her palm against his cheek. 'You've made a talker out of me.'

She closed her eyes then and did not open them again until he left. Beer turned off the light and went to bed.

PART III

CRETINS

ONE

Herbert Gerdes' 1936 film Erbkrank – 'The Hereditary Defective' – was screened in all of Germany's five thousand cinemas. By law, each screening of the silent documentary had to be accompanied by a speaker accredited by the National Socialist Racial and Political Office. Through the documentary, the German public was granted access to the wards of a mental asylum. Among the film's exhibits there were patients who were 'hereditarily deaf and dumb'; 'two brothers, both sexual offenders, with deformed hands, the younger of whom had committed a sexual murder'; 'an idiotic Negro bastard from the Rheinland'; 'an epileptic brother and sister'; a 'thirty-seven-year-old fraudster'; a 'frequently convicted alcoholic'; a 'forty-four-year-old epileptic guilty of multiple sexual murders'; 'four feeble-minded brothers and sisters'; a 'foreign violent criminal'; and an 'illegitimate idiot' who had been 'in institutions for the last twenty-two years'. Erbkrank had a running time of twenty minutes. It was the third in a series of six films promoting the July 1933 Law for the Prevention of Hereditarily Diseased Offspring that gave the State the power to initiate forced sterilisations. Not one of these films openly advocated the killing of the mentally or physically handicapped. The feeling persisted amongst Party leaders that a segment of the German and Austrian population would resist the open adoption of such measures. Other films made in Germany in the same year as Erbkrank include Luis Trenker's Western The Emperor of California, Victor von Plessen's documentary The Headhunters of Borneo, Carl Lamac's Sherlock Holmes mystery The Hound of the Baskervilles, and George Pal's 3-D animated short Four Aces So Close You Can Touch Them.

CHAPTER 1

'Here, have a cigarette.'
It wasn't yet 8.30, the morning keen and bright. Rain had given way to sunshine: it glared in puddles and was caught in the streaky glass of windows; dried the mud that caked the gutters; warmed the skin but not the bones.

'Go on then,' she said and watched the man tap one from the crumpled pack. His fingers were thick and calloused, the cuticles and fingernails blackened with dried blood. He was wearing a white smock, freshly pressed, and clean apart from the stain at the bottom of his chest pocket, no bigger than a coin. Had he been a teacher, one would have thought his pen had dripped: red, the colour of correction. It was fifty years, now, she'd been done with school. They had known each other even then. Somewhere along the line he had dropped the familiar 'Martha'.

'Here you go, Frau Vesalius,' he said, then resumed their earlier conversation. 'The whole place was a terrible mess, is what I hear. My nephew works in the police, called me first thing this morning. Blood everywhere, he says, signs of

305

a fight. Killer cut him open like a fish, from the bladder to the ribs.' He paused for a puff. 'But I suppose you know all that.'

She shrugged non-committally. 'The times we live in,' she offered.

'Why, yes, the times.'

'They cut the Professor's dog up just the same.'

'Not quite. Multiple stab wounds is what my nephew says. More pincushion than dog.' He pointed at his abdomen with the air of a man who knows what he is talking about. His name was Gehrke. He was the butcher.

'I hear they called a headshrinker in,' he continued. 'A Dr Bern.'

'Dr Beer. He lives in the building, you know. His wife left him.'

The butcher weighed this information, his big hand rising to pluck the cigarette from his lips.

'A good man, this Beer?'

Vesalius shrugged. 'He looks after the Professor's niece.'

'Oh yes? What's wrong with her?'

'She needs a husband.'

He laughed, and she joined him, stubbed out her cigarette, half-smoked, against the wall of his shop, then pocketed the stump. They were standing in the expanse of courtyard outside the shop's back door. She had come early and asked for a minute of his time.

'What is it you want then, Frau Vesalius? Meat for the party, I suppose.'

'So you've heard about the party?'

He grunted, flicked his cigarette into the dirt. 'They say the detective invited himself last night. Brazen, they say. A man like a pig. But then, I wouldn't mind going myself. They say the Mayor might be coming.'

'Here's what we need.' She passed him a list she had written on the back of an old envelope.

He studied it and frowned.

'I'm not sure I can get all this. What with the rationing—'

'He has special dispensation.'

'Even so.'

She nodded, put a hand out in farewell.

'Get what you can, butcher. I'll see to the rest.'

'Will do,' he said, his big hand swallowing hers. When they'd been eight, she had given him a thrashing once, for lifting up her skirt in play, and kissed him, too, in the doorway of a church: her lips on his rosy cheek.

She went to the baker's next, ordered a cake and bought two *Topfengolatschen*, for which Speckstein had a special passion.

On the way back into her building, Frau Vesalius stopped for a natter with the janitor, exchanging the same gossip and settling some items of business, all with a minimum of fuss. Upstairs, she found the flat empty. She stored the shopping, then crept through each of the rooms, making sure she was quite alone. A furtive trip to the row of Speckstein's crystal decanters provided her with

307

a half-glass of apricot brandy. She returned to the kitchen, sat down by the window, and took one of the *Golatschen* from the brown-paper bag, a buttery pastry filled with curd cheese. It was still warm. Eating it quickly, sipping at the glass of brandy, she looked out across the yard. Frau Berger was sitting at her window, peeling potatoes in the sun. She looked tired. Her youngest was in hospital with a bad case of measles. Yesterday's crowd had left cigarette butts scattered all across the yard. A street hawker strolled in, placed his box near the trunk of the chestnut, and got busy collecting the soggy fag ends into his upturned hat. The Novaks' wireless was playing, as always too loud; Frau Novak singing along in her flat voice. Somewhere in a nearby yard a carpet was being beaten, its rhythms breaking up the song's, and a child bawled shrilly for its mother.

As she was finishing the last of the liquor, Vesalius peered across to the Grotter flat, now the scene of a great crime. The police had left the curtains open, and when she strained her eyes she thought she could make out a dark stain on the wall near the window. She washed the glass, replaced it, then carefully wiped up the *Golatsche*'s crumbs. If the Professor asked her why she had brought home only a single pastry, she could always claim the baker had sold out. After all, it was wartime. There were hardships to be borne by all.

CHAPTER 2

It was his lunch hour. Anton Beer sat at his desk, typing up his report, first detailing the trauma to the body (a single knife-thrust to the upper-right quadrant of the abdominal cavity that had punctured the liver at the height of the gall bladder, resulting in fatal levels of blood loss), then reconstructing the events in Grotter's flat. 'Angle and type of wound are consistent with self-injury,' he typed. 'Width and profile of wound match the knife found at the crime site. Victim's blood-alcohol level indicates advanced state of inebriation at time of self-wounding. Blood patterns and position of body point to panic and severe disorientation. The victim evidently hoped to stop the bleeding by pressing his jacket to the wound, then attempted to barricade himself in his bedroom (perhaps hiding from his daughter, Anneliese Grotter, age ten). Verdict: accidental suicide.'

Beer finished typing, picked through his prose. It made no effort to comprehend the level of despair (of drunkenness, of folly) that would induce a man to draw the curtains and cut into his body with a bone-handled knife, and failed to sketch the mad urge that had sent him from the kitchen out into the corridor, searching for God knows what, then compelled him back into the bedroom, where he'd huddled behind the closed door, watching the blood fill up his coat, his numb, flailing legs dragging over first a chair and then one corner of the heavy bed in the vain effort to seal the door. He had left no note of explanation, nothing but the photo of his wife that they had pulled out of his jacket pocket, stained to the point where all one could see of her was a naked leg jutting from the bottom of a bathing costume. At least Beer assumed it was his wife. The leg had been flabby, sand-freckled, white. She had, Teuben had told him, long left the country: had gone to the Americas and left behind no known address. There were no other living relatives. A life-insurance policy for some paltry amount had been found among the dead man's papers and contained the usual clause that excluded suicide as a valid basis for claim. At work, Grotter had gone on the sick; a liver condition not unconnected with the drinking. A younger Beer would have felt compelled to construct from all this some narrative of motive; at thirty-four and tired, he was content to simply type up the bare facts.

Beer signed the report hastily, glanced at his watch, and ran to unlock the front door. It was nearly two o'clock: his afternoon hours were about to begin. Two women were already queuing on the landing and followed his request to take a seat in his waiting room. One held out an envelope to the doctor, saying she had found it leaning against the front door: she'd picked it up, she said, so that it wouldn't get stained. Beer read the enclosed note while he prepared his surgery.

'The little girl is in the hospital,' it read.

The words were clumsily written, the note unsigned. He stuck it in his pocket, threw on his doctor's coat, called in the first of the patients. The sun lit up the dust and grime upon his window. It was time he had someone come and clean the flat.

Beer had just begun to put some questions to the patient (the old woman had launched into a long story about her overworked son and had yet to mention any ailment of her own) when the phone rang. Beer excused himself, stepped out into the corridor. He was unsurprised to hear Teuben's voice.

'I've finished the report,' he said brusquely. 'I can drop it off at the station later if you like.'

'Never mind that, Doctor. I'm sending a man over to pick you up. He'll be there in ten, fifteen minutes. Kindly wait for him on the street. There's something I'd like you to see.'

'It's impossible. I have practice hours, Detective.'

Teuben chuckled. 'But Doctor. It's a matter of public safety. Surely you can't refuse.'

'I will lose all my patients over this nonsense.'

'Hardly. Once the war gets going good and

311

proper, half the doctors in the city will be called to the front. Plenty more patients coming your way. One way or the other.'

He rang off, not waiting to hear any further objections. Defeated, Beer ran back to his patient. The old woman was sitting on the examination table where he left her, her knotty legs dangling like a child's. Her hat was in her lap.

'There is nothing wrong with you,' he barked at her. 'What is it you want from me?'

'My son is hungry.'

'Why doesn't he come himself?' he yelled, but had already grabbed the form that attested to the need for improved rations, signed and stamped it, his face reddening with anger. He saw her off, then stepped into his waiting room, which was slowly filling up with patients. Four faces were looking at him.

'I'm afraid I have to close,' he said. 'An emergency.'

The people grumbled, but stood up at once. Only one of them lingered, a young man with puffy eyes and dark, lank hair whose cheeks were flushed with a high fever.

'Tomorrow?' he asked, embarrassed by his dire need.

'First thing,' Beer promised. 'I'll open a half-hour early, make up for lost time.'

'Bless you,' said the man, eyes smiling from their swollen sockets.

Beer closed the door behind him, ran into the bedroom to turn Eva, then quickly took to the stairs.

Outside, the police car had yet to arrive, and he stood smoking for a minute, hands in his pockets and gazing up into the sun. *The little girl is in the hospital,* the note had read. He hoped this meant she was all right.

CHAPTER 3

Teuben met him in his office. It was a large, whitewashed room with a near-empty desk standing at its centre; two bookshelves filled with files and many yards of empty space. Dustballs danced upon the parquet flooring when Teuben's secretary opened the door for Beer, then settled once he'd stepped into the room. The windows were thrown wide open, cold air pouring in along with the sun. Teuben stood motionless, leaning the backs of his thighs against his desk. He wore a cardigan today, buttoned up to the knot of his tie, looked pale and somehow very happy, unbruised by their near sleepless night. Beer handed him his autopsy report. Neither of them had uttered a greeting.

'Ah, the report.' Teuben cast a glance at it, then placed it face down on his desk. 'It is hard to believe a man would kill himself with a knife, don't you think? Stick it in his guts, I mean, rather than just cutting his wrists or throat.'

Beer shrugged. 'It happened all the same,' he said stiffly. 'And besides, he was drunk. Perhaps the idea had stolen into his head with all the rumours going around, everybody talking about knives.'

'An *idée fixe*. Next you will tell me there's a precedent. In the literature.' He smiled, fished a mint from his pocket and slipped it into his mouth.

'More than one.'

'But you are missing the point, Dr Beer. All I said was that it was hard to believe.' He turned, located a cube of marble that served him as a paperweight, placed it on top of the report, then walked over to Beer, dustballs scrambling to avoid his tread.

'Here now, come with me.'

Teuben led him out into the corridor and down a set of stairs. At the bottom, uniformed policemen opened a door for them, allowing them entry to a row of cells, recognisable at once by the heavy metal doors that lined the walls. Each door was equipped with a rectangular slit at eye-level that could be opened or closed from the outside only. No noise was audible at present. A row of benches lined the gaps between the doors.

'Holding cells?' Beer asked, a note of anxiety in his voice. How easy it would be for Teuben to keep him there; to take away his keys and go to Eva. He would protest, and earn a truncheon to the teeth for his troubles. Teuben seemed to notice his fear, and smiled.

'Holding, interrogation, whatever is needed. There are more on the other side of the building. Where the Gestapo do their work.' He slid open the peephole on one of the doors, then dragged Beer over by one arm, gently, as though walking a debutante on to the dance floor.

'Do you know him?'

It took Beer a moment to recognise the man. He was sitting on a cot, in a room not much larger than a broom cupboard, lit by a single naked bulb that hung high from the centre of the ceiling: arms wrapped around his knees, his heels drawn up and planted near the buttocks, he was rocking and humming a low tune. His lips looked large and pursed on his long and horse-like face. A welt near the temple and the inflammation of one ear were the only signs that he'd been beaten.

'But it's the laundry boy,' Beer realised at last.

'Yes. Wolfgang Fromm is his name. I noticed you were on his client list. We held him before for a day or two, but got nothing definite out of him, so I decided to let him go.' He gave a snort, as though to mock his own stupidity. 'I had him picked up again this morning.'

'What has he done?'

'For all I know – nothing. Or everything. He's half an idiot. We pick the idiots up first, you know, see what we find.'

Beer stared uncomprehendingly as Teuben slid the metal cover back over the peephole.

'You see, Dr Beer, the mistake I made all along was this –' He smiled, it was meant to look sheepish, red lips parting for his mint-fresh breath. 'I was chasing the actual culprit, would you believe? Old habits. Childish, wasn't it? And then I decided that the deaths were unconnected, and Speckstein a damn fool. Got snappish about it, too, pissed off the Chief, made all sorts of blunders.'

He took a seat upon one of the benches and gestured for Beer to join him. Mechanically, the doctor peeled a cigarette from the packet. Teuben watched him, spat out the mint, helped himself to cigarette and match.

'Then it dawned on me last night, right there, in the dead man's kitchen. I had been trying to dig up the truth, while what was called for was initiative. *Auf den Führer zuarbeiten.* Working towards the Führer. It's the watchword of the age. Speckstein wants a serial killer, someone who also killed his dog. He's more than half convinced the Chief. And Hitler is waging a war on cretins, anti-socials: the stupid, the useless, and the mad.'

He paused, made a flourish towards the cells, the cigarette cupped in his hand. '*Voilà!*'

Beer heard it and put his head in his hands.

'You'd charge an innocent man?' he asked, his protest meek, his forehead cool against his palms.

'Who is to say he isn't guilty? A little time with us, and I'm sure he will confess.'

Teuben rose, lifting Beer up by his elbow, walked him out the corridor and back up the stairs. His office was as they had left it, desolate; a stack of paper on his desk, face down, burdened by a stone.

'Of course it does not have to be the laundry

boy. There is someone else who comes to mind.' He paused, raised his hands in front of his chest, palms out, as though leaning them against an invisible pane of glass.

'The mime.'

'Yes, the mime. Otto Frei. Might not be his real name, incidentally. Something fishy about his registration papers. I had them brought to me this morning. Also, there is the matter of his sister –'

Beer looked at him, gauged his smile. 'A sister?'

'You didn't think I noticed?' The smile widened. 'I saw it at once: something about the eyes. Subtle but distinct. He'll look more like her once he drops forty pounds. The thing is, if I arrest him, he might blab about her, and what happens then?'

Beer was silent, watched as Teuben retrieved the report from under the marble paperweight, read it, then folded it carefully in half.

'Barbiturates,' he said to the doctor. 'That's how I'm told they do it. At the hospital. They add barbiturates to their diet, little by little. Within a few weeks the patients catch pneumonia and die quite naturally.' He folded the report a second time, down to the size of an envelope, and threw it into the bottom drawer of his desk. 'Of course, now that the war is on they may expedite things. War is an impatient business.'

Beer swallowed, noticed that his hand had started to shake. He pushed it down one pocket. Inside, his fingers brushed against a handwritten note.

'Your report needs reworking,' Teuben said. 'I'm relying on you. All the forensics have to add up. Something incontrovertible. So we know what we want the culprit to confess.'

Once again he took Beer by the arm, and slowly walked him out of the office. The policemen on duty stopped to watch them as they passed but left them well alone, eyes darting to avoid the detective's. Perhaps it should have reassured the doctor that he was not the only one who feared this man.

Outside, the massive bulk of the police station at their backs, Teuben flagged a driver, then turned his attention back to Beer.

'I'll visit tonight,' he said. 'We can speak further. And look in on your patient.'

'Don't. The maggots –'

'Yes, I called the hospital about that. Talked to an internist there, a certain Dr Wolf. He tells me it's a form of therapy that the Americans are fond of. He recommended a 1931 article by a certain Dr Baer, from the University of Johns Hopkins, then got flustered when I asked was Baer a Jew. Baer and Beer – a funny co-incidence, don't you think? In any case, Wolf assures me it's a sign of the patient being on the mend.'

'All the same, Teuben, you can't come tonight.' Beer tried to leave, was unable to break the detective's hold on his arm. 'Eva has a bad infection.'

'Eva.' The red lips took the flavour of the name. 'Nice. I'll tell you what, Dr Beer. The party's in three days. It gives you time to figure out what we need to finish the arrest. The laundry boy, or Otto, just as you please. Three days, too, to get her healthy. I'll want to see her then, tête-à-tête.'

He released Beer, watched him get into the car.

'And no funny stuff, as they say in the radio plays. *Heil Hitler*, my friend, see you soon. Better dust off your dinner jacket.'

He waved after them as the driver steered the car into the road.

They hadn't yet gone more than three blocks when Beer asked to be let out. He waited until the car was out of sight, then climbed on the tram and got off at the hospital. There was a note in his pocket on which he wished to follow up.

Later that afternoon – after he had looked in on Eva, and fixed himself a bite to eat – he could be found standing in the yard, eyes closed, neck thrown back and face raised to the sky, listening for the buzz of a trumpet high above.

CHAPTER 4

And what after all is a trumpet? In purely physical terms it is a long piece of brass tubing of cylindrical or conical bore, twice bent to render it an oblong oval, opening into a bell at one end, and into a much smaller 'cup' – the mouthpiece – at the other. The earliest trumpets are ascribed to an ancient civilisation living by the River Oxus in the third millennium before Christ, though, lacking valves, they might best be considered precursors to the bugle. There were valveless trumpets made from precious metals found in Tutankhamun's tomb in Egypt: one imagines Howard Carter dusting them off with his archaeologist's brush and staring first uncomprehendingly, then with sudden recognition at the tuliped mouth emerging from the slender pipe. The ancient Chinese knew it, as did the Moche of Peru. Its shrill and cutting sound commended it to generals, who used the trumpet to direct their fortunes on the battlefield. So useful was its signal sound, and so vulnerable the army to the cry of enemy bleaters, that trumpet playing grew into a guarded art, protected by the ordinance of a guild:

no layman was to learn the secrets of embouchure. The instrument did not shed its military connotations until late in the nineteenth century, when composers began to invite it to their concert halls with increasing frequency. By now the valve had been invented, a simple piston mechanism that would extend the length of tubing when depressed. Three valves taught the horn chromatics; a fourth was sometimes added, to battle the vagaries of intonation. In 1864 Jean-Baptiste Arban published the first edition of *La grande méthode compléte de cornet à piston et de saxhorn par Arban*. By the end of the 1920s, Louis Armstrong, satchel-mouthed, Storyvilled, and in complete ignorance of the Frenchman's method book, was plucking high Cs from the skies like so many stars. It is said that one trumpeter can recognise another just by looking at his lips. The embouchure leaves its mark upon the muscles of the mouth, and the steady pressure of the metal rim distorts the lip itself. The modern trumpet is equipped with a lever that allows the player to pour accumulated moisture from the instrument, and thus the trumpet can be found expectorating in philharmonic orchestras across the world. Its spit collects around the feet of those condemned to sit amongst the brass, dress shoes tapping on horn-moistened floors. When playing the trumpet, it is said, one needs to blow as though aiming to cool one's bowl of soup; cheeks puffy like a baby's. The trumpet can be muzzled by a mute: it changes its tone, but will not censor its speech. It is a curious fact of acoustics that a toilet plunger, skilfully waved before the open bell, can transform the trumpet's sound into that of the human voice. It is a versatile instrument. The trumpet can ring of the whorehouse, or of God on high; can hail the King, or stand weeping at his infant's grave. Ellington used it for the catcall of the urban jungle; in the second Brandenburg Concerto it is said to take the part of Pheme – Fame – who guides the august to Parnassus. Everywhere it travels the trumpet finds friends, supporters, lovers; those who pour their pains and triumphs through its twisted tubes. Herr Yuu is one of its disciples. Just now he has placed it in its leather case, the insides of which are dressed in satin and shape a padded hole precisely measured to its size.

CHAPTER 5

Herr Yuu was a contemplative man. He liked books and he liked mirrors, both of which were on display in his tiny garret room, though the former outnumbered the latter by a ratio of five to one. Besides the bookshelves and the many reflections of himself (the mirrors, most of which were no larger than the cover of a pocket Bible, were nailed to the walls at various heights and quite surrounded him), there was in Yuu's room a bed, a chair, a music stand, and a little wooden table. On top of this table rested the trumpet in its open case. A lampshade fell from the slanting ceiling and was made from green velvet; its heavy material smothered the bulb so that the room was only very imperfectly lit. A small window opened to the courtyard, and a strip of flypaper hung from the ceiling near its frame, coated with lint rather than insects and trembling in the breeze. In one corner there stood a metal wood-stove, unlit, a dozen logs of firewood stacked on top. Yuu himself was sitting on the bed and musing on the history of trumpets. He played for dance bands and had recently had trouble finding work. His looks were doing him a disservice, though they had once been seen as a welcome curiosity. He was Japanese, which is to say he belonged to one of the world's Master Races, but such subtleties of Nazi anthropology seemed lost on the managers of Vienna's dance halls. They held to an older wisdom: that in times of war, the foreigner was suspect. He had not eaten since dawn, and was wearing his hat against the draught.

Yuu heard the movement on the stairs and landing long before the knock. What surprised him was the length of time that separated the two sounds, and he registered the hesitation this implied. He himself took a breath before admitting his guest and practised a ninefold smile in as many mirrors.

'En-ter,' he called.

The door swung open. It wasn't locked.

It was Dr Beer who stepped in, and immediately the room felt cramped. The bookshelves, the lampshade, the slant of the ceiling: they all seemed designed to push the visitor towards the bed, upon which throned the burly figure of the Japanese. After a moment's thought, Beer ducked to the left and took a seat upon the lone chair. The table was right next to him, three wobbly legs, and on its top the trumpet in its battered case. Looking at it now, he was struck by the instrument's complexity. There seemed to be an awful lot of little parts.

Beer looked at Yuu. It was the first time he had

seen the man up close. He was intrigued by his skin, its colour and texture, acne scars dimpling his cheeks and giving them the appearance of mottled wood. The sparse beard contrasted starkly with the fullness of his hair, unevenly cut and shaven above the ears so as to show a strip of stubbled scalp. The eyes were foreign and rather becoming, the elegance of a single-folded lid. Yuu's brow was bony, prominent, and his whole figure exuded an air of firmness and strength. Beer judged him the sort of fat man whose weight sits in the bones. He might starve, but would never grow thin.

Yuu for his part studied Beer with close attention and was struck above all by the symmetry of the doctor's features. He wondered idly whether he was the sort of man with whom women fell in love. Other than that he seemed to him a study in pent-up emotion, leaking lightly from the eyes. Yuu was a scholar of the trumpet, and of men. Beer was the kind of man he liked. He carried secrets. Both men removed their hats in greeting. The doctor spoke first.

'You sent me a note, Herr Yuu,' he said. He didn't phrase it as a question.

'Yes.'

'I went to the hospital as you suggested. They told me a man left an unconscious girl in the waiting room two days ago and then ran off. One of the nurses said she remembered he was foreign. When pressed, she indicated there was a slant to his eyes.'

Yuu nodded, his hat in his hands. 'Is the girl well? There was blood on her clothing, and on her face.'

Beer ran a hand through his hair, an elegant gesture, and somehow effeminate.

'She ran away. Woke up, screamed, and wouldn't give her name. They had administered a sedative and were inclined to think her stupid. She was transferred – for observation – and then she ran off. An institution at the edge of town. She was not wearing any shoes.'

'I see.'

'Tell me what happened, Herr Yuu. She's all alone and her father is dead.'

Yuu related his story. He had been practising the trumpet, he said, sitting by the window and playing scales. One couldn't see an awful lot from up here, but the one thing that one could not help but see was the bedroom window of Herr Grotter. The angle was steep, and through the half-drawn curtains all one could make out was the floor near the window and one corner of the bed. The day was overcast, Yuu's spirits depressed, and he'd registered almost in passing that Herr Grotter was in the bedroom and was lying next to the bed in such a manner that only his feet were visible. Yuu thought nothing much of it. The man was a known drinker and may have rolled out of bed, senseless, sleeping off the liquor. He'd paused in his practice and eaten some boiled potatoes.

When Yuu reclaimed the chair by the window

and was about to attend to some further exercises, he saw the little girl, Anneliese, cross the yard. His eyes followed her quite mechanically, and found once again her father's feet. Only now it struck Yuu that the feet – the shoes – were wet and perhaps bloody. He hesitated until he saw the feet move, jerkily, as though someone was trying to move the body or wake up the man. There was something so unnatural about the movement that he concluded at once that it must be the girl, either pressing against the bedroom door, or against the body itself. He might have remained where he was in sudden horror had not the rain come pouring down just then. It released him and he ran downstairs and through the door into the back wing. The girl came flying towards him in the hallway and quite simply passed out. He bent down to her, found her bloody, and feared she had injured herself. In his initial panic he rang a doorbell on the ground level but received no response. He was about to ring another when he came to realise what the situation might look like. To leave her lying in the dirty hallway seemed unconscionable, and so, not knowing what else to do, he carried the girl into the yard instead, into the steady rain. Had he seen anyone out in the yard, he would have explained everything at once, but there was nobody about, and given the proximity of the hospital he thought it best to bring her there. By the time he arrived, the blood had washed off her face. She was still unconscious but looked otherwise fine. Yuu left her slumped on a bench in the hospital corridor and returned home to his trumpet. He had been wondering what had happened to her ever since.

Beer listened to the man's high, accented voice with some misgivings. For all its idiosyncrasies of intonation, it had the fluency of an actor's. Beer had never heard a foreigner speak the language as well as this, and that alone spoke against him somehow. And yet his story might be no more than the truth.

'Why not come to me?' he asked, when Yuu had finished and sat smoothing the crease of his trousers above the thighs. 'When you found her passed out.'

'I thought-you were a doc-tor on-ly for the head.'

Yuu put a finger to his temple, the people's gesture for a madman. Again the fluency of his response grated on Beer; it reminded him of himself, lying to Teuben. There was nothing else he wished to ask, and yet he found himself reluctant to leave, looked around himself, found his gaze reflected in the mirrors. Yuu watched Beer watch himself and stretched his lips into an insinuating smile.

'I-know who kill-ed the dog,' he said without preamble, leaning forward on his bed.

'So do I,' answered Beer. 'You saw it?'

'Yes.'

He listened to the man's account in silence. It helped confirm what he had surmised.

'Why did you not tell the police what you saw, Herr Yuu?'

The fat man wagged his head from side to side, as though shaking water from his ears.

'For the same rea-son I did not tell any-one about the girl. No-need to get caught-up in thes-e things. Not as a for-ei-gner. The police learn every-thing any-way. Soon-er or la-ter.'

'Not everything,' said Beer. 'Some secrets live right under their noses.'

He paused, weary, cast his eyes down on the table. 'Play something for me,' he added, pointing to the trumpet. 'Something quiet.'

Yuu nodded, and gestured for Beer to pass him the case. He watched Beer eagerly while he attached the mouthpiece, then warmed it in one fist. 'It-is an an-cient instru-ment. Did you-know the Egyp-tians played?'

'Please,' said Beer. 'No lecture on the trumpet. Just play.'

And Yuu did, strains of Händel rising from his horn. Beer listened for a quarter of an hour, unmoved, unmoving, fingers folded in his lap, then suddenly leapt up and ran out of the room without uttering a word. Yuu looked after him, still playing, double-tonguing arpeggios to the rhythm of his receding steps.

CHAPTER 6

As Beer sat listening to Yuu's playing, a strange agitation took hold of him. The numb restraint that had helped Beer through the day dropped away from him and was replaced by a manic sort of energy, inarticulate and hostile to all thought. He ran out, possessed by the need to be by Eva's side, then faltered before he reached the door to his bedroom that was now her sick chamber. Beer dived into his study instead, found his desk littered with photos, dead bodies staring up at him, heads and limbs outlined by blood. He poured a brandy, sat smoking with the snifter in his hand. A fleck of cigarette ash fell into the glass, hung suspended in the liquid. He sent a finger to its rescue, watched the laws of optics break it at the knuckle, the liquor burning on his skin. A noise startled him: he pushed back the chair, ran into the corridor, stood dog-like, his head cocked to one side, limbs unmoving, in the stillness of the hunt. It was not the first time he'd thought he could hear Eva shift within her room. She had woken him, two nights ago, and he had lain there on the couch, fully expecting her to float into the room, his wife's lace gown too large for her and tripping up her little feet. Angry now, elated by this sudden clarity of anger, he stormed into her room. The open door threw a shaft of light across the bed. It found the outline of her buttocks and her upper thighs, stiff under the whiteness of the sheet. Deflated, unwilling to abandon his suspicion, he scanned the features of the bedding. Her pillow seemed more crumpled to him than he had left it, the folds around her feet more pronounced and as though recently disturbed. He pounced, dug out her foot, held on to it in search of warmth brought on by recent movement. How often, he wondered, had Otto stood like this, one foot between his angry hands, begging her to be a fraud, or stuck a needle through the surface of her skin just to see if she might flinch? He moved around to the side of the bed, found her face, her green eyes open to his stare.

'Are you awake?' he asked, too loud for the room.

She waited a heartbeat before she winked: from tiredness, or from flirtation, or because her sickness had long hollowed her into a cretinous shell.

'I saw Teuben today. The detective.'

She closed her eyes.

'He wants a date.'

The phrase appalled him. He wished to see her cry, a sob to rend her listless chest, but all she did was lie there, breathing, eyeballs roaming under her thin lids. She gave no reaction when he dropped his face into the scraggy, inch-long stumps of unwashed hair and rooted around for a place to press his lips. He thought he loved her, but even this seemed false to him, devoid of focus and desire, and he quickly stood to turn her and to change her diaper, his movements gentle, absent, disconnected from his rage.

Two hours later, restless, Dr Anton Beer left his flat and headed out to town. 'Life is short,' he said to Eva, as he turned his back on her and stooped to retrieve his hat that had fallen from his fingers.

'I'm sorry. I'll be back soon.'

On the way down, midway between the third and second floor, he stopped at the large window that looked out on to the yard there, and was surprised to find Otto's painted face staring back at him through the chill and rainy night. The greasepaint surprised him. It had been his impression that the mime was out of work. Nor was he sure why he would stand there, playing idly with his knife. The tip of his cigarette flared red as Otto inhaled. Beer turned and continued on his way.

CHAPTER 7

O tto took a last drag, then threw the butt
out into the yard.

He drew the curtains, turned to the
mirror, raised the knife. He'd held it like this when
he had killed the man, his left fist dug into his
jacket: underhand, the grip reversed so that the
edge would point up into the wound; his right
thumb pressing hard into its base, splitting the skin,
his own blood trickling down on to the handle.

It was just as well the knife was blunt.

He swung the knife on a trajectory that started
level with his hip, then curved inwards and up:
mimed the impact while his left hand reached to
grapple with his unseen foe, fingers curled around
the collar of his coat. Up ahead, in the gleaming
square of the soap-flecked mirror, his movement
made a pretty picture, balletic and savage all at
once. Otto repeated the motion three or four times
until he was sure of its effect: the weight of the
slumping body pulling down the drooping blade.
It was thus that he had killed his man.

He supposed that one might kill a dog in a
manner much the same.

He practised it: raised his left elbow instead of reaching forward with his hand, to protect his throat from its approaching jaws; slipped down to one knee, adjusted the angle of the blade and cut low into the plain where haunch flows into belly. The furry triangle of its retracted cock near snagged the knife as he cut across. Walter. He'd been a boxer, a neighbour had told him, stood hip-high to his master. He tore upwards until the ribcage caught the ripping blade, then dragged the carcass to one side by its hind legs; bent to wipe his hands upon the matted fur. When he rose again to face the mirror he could almost hear the crowd's applause. His face was a plaster cast of apathy. Otto folded up the knife, placed it on the sink, then sat down on his bed and lit another cigarette. His stomach was grumbling; he had neither food nor beer.

A magazine distracted him. It had always been like this for him: one thought flicking to replace the next, oil-slick with its urgency and bloated with emotion – Otto Frei, eternal citizen of the now. He snatched the magazine from the heap upon the floor. Dried-in beer had crinkled its pages, made them brittle, a corner coming loose in his impatient hand. For a moment he sat entranced – brow knit, spine rolled forward into itself – by the half-page advertisement for a body cream that guaranteed the rapid swelling of the breasts (there was a drawing there, of a long-haired woman standing in profile, her black sweater rising like a leavened clump of dough); then he threw it aside, leapt from the bed, and planted a handstand between washstand and door. Upside down, face flushed beneath its mask of white, he wondered whether Zuzka would come. Since the closing of the club, she had called on him thrice: obliged him to draw the curtains, then threatened she would scream should he approach. She'd watched him, touched him, told him he stank; had raised her skirt once, to rearrange a garter, drinking in his stare. She said she knew now how a woman might please a man using only her mouth; wrinkled her nose then, in deep disgust. On two occasions they had kissed. His hands had searched her body and had felt her break away; his spit wet on her chin.

'I mustn't get pregnant,' she'd said.

And: 'Tell me how you killed Walter.'

Always her conversation returned to this, the death of the dog, and then to Eva, whose broken body she thought he had sought to avenge. When she had shown him the article outlining Speckstein's trial, he had read it first with fear, then with a sly sort of excitement. He knew the story: it had struck him a blow when he was a mere child. Their father had talked of it, a mute, crying Eva listening in. She had still been able to move back then, hobbled along dragging her left leg, one arm dead and falling stiffly from its shoulder. It had been six months since the attack, and they'd had hopes she would recover, though none that she'd agree again to earn the family's bread. For a week or two they'd followed the trial and their father had kept cuttings in the cabinet drawer. After Speckstein's acquittal in court and his subsequent resignation from his post at the university, the newspapers' interest faded, as did Otto's. He was learning to breathe fire then, and to vanish a canary by collapsing its cage and quickly replacing the dead bird with its mate. It was the year he had started to smoke.

When Otto had moved into the building, he'd recognised Speckstein's name at once; had been beset by a renewed rage at what had happened to his sister; then had dismissed it as the coincidence it was, and had henceforth thought of the Professor only as the eyes and ears of a hostile State from which one did best to hide. Then Beer had shown up with his odd questions, and Zuzka had brought him a page from a newspaper as though it held the answer to some urgent riddle. In the club, when she'd come to visit, he'd paid it no heed and assumed only that she came to him as a woman comes to a man. It was only after he had returned to his rooms that he'd read it, his make-up running down the clogged and stinking drain.

Otto was not a thinking man. 'Your stomach does your thinking,' his mother had once told him, hugging him from behind and placing her hands across the broad front of his chest. And also: 'Your stomach is quite clever.' She had not praised him often, and so he remembered it, trusted in his stomach and the pressure of his glands, and looked upon all his actions as both necessary and good, with a satisfaction unknown to a more considered man. What became clear to him upon his reading of the newspaper report with its vivid pictures was that Zuzka mistook Eva for the girl Evelyn, who had not dared to speak the name of her tormentor, but mutely pointed at the Professor when asked if he was present in the room. He understood, too, that this was why she thought he'd killed the dog. It was impossible to calculate what would be the harm or benefit of disabusing her of the notion. Denial might cost him her favour, and he feared her retribution, for there were things he sought to hide more damaging than the slaying of a mutt. She professed a hatred for her uncle, to whose party he now found himself invited, and whom he held to wield great power. All he wanted was to live: to eat, and drink, and maybe poke this girl who was so young and pretty, smelled of perfumed soap, with not a callus on her little hand; and not be thrown into some prison, or go tempt bullets in some foreign war. His stomach told Otto to remain silent and admit to nothing. At most he would trade a charade of slaughter for the favours of her fanny, though it was as she had said: *She mustn't get pregnant.*

Nor must she complain.

It'd be best if he held his new act in reserve: dog killer, to be performed – if ever – only to a naked audience of one.

A sound reached him, still upended, sent him spinning from his handstand into a tumbler's roll. Someone stood outside the door. He'd heard some steps upon the stairs, too dimly to be certain whether they were walking up or down, and now they had stopped some inches from his door. Otto did not hesitate. He took hold of the handle and swung open the door, reached to grab her by the wrist and pull her into the room; touch her, kiss her, before she could object. His hand shot forward and hit the brim of a black felt hat that hovered in front of him at the height of his navel. Beneath it, on the square yard or so of landing, kneeled a man, fat, tuxedoed, busy with his left shoelace. The man looked up into the greasepainted face, eyes like tadpoles buried behind cheeks of fat, then re-aligned the angle of his hat.

'Good-evening,' he said. 'I was-just la-cing my shoe.'

Otto found himself laughing in response.

'You're the trumpet player. You gave me quite a scare.'

'Herr Yuu,' the fat man nodded. 'You would-not have in your kit-chen some-thing to eat?'

'To eat?'

'Yes. Or a glass-of beer per-haps.'

'I haven't a thing.'

'A-pity. I had-no dinner.'

They studied each other a moment longer until Otto turned to snatch his cigarettes from the bed.

'You want one?' he asked and proffered the packet.

'Much o-bliged.'

They stood smoking in the stairwell, eyeing each other's clothes and recognising each other as performers. When they were done, Herr Yuu offered him his hand. Otto shook it.

'You are-a clown?'

'A mime. I don't speak.'

'No voice.' Herr Yuu nodded. 'Have-you used mu-sic in your-act?'

'Never.'

'Per-haps it is some-thing you-should try.'

'You have your trumpet with you?'

'All-ways.'

And Yuu came in and sat on his bed; laughed at the girl in the body-cream ad whose breasts looked inflated like balloons, and played a slur, a whisper, then a thump for every step that Otto took and every transformation of his face. He played shyly at first, then with growing confidence, until they moved in perfect harmony and it was to Otto as though it was his body that was playing the trumpet, and that every crease of brow sang with a certain pitch and temper; and little trills to greet each flutter of his glove.

CHAPTER 8

And it was this music that greeted her, not the same night but the next, past three o'clock and less than forty hours to the party. It was cold out, no longer raining, the street lamp shedding orange light. The child had a key to the building's front door, but her fingers were frozen and it took her a while to work the lock and slip into the hallway. There was no hurry to her movements. She had already spent two idle hours in the yard in which they'd found the dog; had lain down briefly (though the ground was muddy) in that sideways sprawl that bared the stomach, thinking with this gesture rather than her head. To think – to speak! – was dangerous, could set on you like the shadow of the Wolf (from the age of four or five she had pictured it as never more than a dark shadow, and in that darkness lived a yellow eye). Her dirty brow was flushed with fever. Cold sores caught the snot upon her upper lip.

The chill had driven her across the street, and drove her on now, into the courtyard.

She looked around. The yard seemed small to

her, as though shrunk. Someone had overturned the rock under which she used to hunt for earthworms. She stuck a toe in that place, felt clammy earth and the twisted knot of a big root. A neighbour had chained a bike against the chestnut tree, and a pile of leaves sat clumped together on its seat. On the metal frame which was used to beat the dust off carpets there sat a magpie, chattering. There were no people around.

For that, at least, she was grateful.

She feared this place, feared conversation, words that would make official all she already knew: and yet her eyes strayed upwards, first to Zuzka's window, then to Anton Beer's, both of which were dark. As for her father's kitchen window, she avoided it, for was it not possible that he was still awake, drinking, the curtains open and his merriment visible for all to see? A memory came to her, brisk and tidy like a postcard, of the moment when he'd beaten her for having stolen his knife, then bought her a handkerchief patterned in orange, in black, and in blue. She wore it now, over her hair and ears, though at this instant she pulled it down and thrust it in the pocket of her dress, as though to hide the present was to hide the thought of him (of him, of knives, of darkness shrouding their four windows at which she laboured not to look, and failed, and failed, and failed again).

It was then – one hand in her pocket, eyes darting from the windows to the yard – that she caught the music, that peal of a trumpet coming from an unaccustomed room. The trumpet continued, bent the note into a sort of snort; farted, apologised, whistled away the sudden stench. The girl did not smile. Her naked feet were wrapped in rags.

A light caught her notice, no more than a glimmer, coming from the cellar door. It had been closed but had not locked. The thought of the cellar seemed to cheer the girl, and for an instant her arm described a motion in which the wrist flicked away from her at the height of her chest. It was as though she were striking a match away from her body, or throwing a marble underarm across the yard. Her tongue followed it with a single click. She walked to the door, pushed it open, descended the stairs. There was nobody in the janitor's workshop, but noise and light spilled from the door at its back. En route, passing the game table, she noticed a wicker cage sitting on top. She ran up to it, and stared with great emotion at the animal that crouched inside, a leaf of lettuce between delicate paws. Five more steps brought her to the half-closed door. She stopped to look through the gap, saw two men, one of them the janitor, both bending low over a bath tub. Their arms were cut off by the bath tub's rim; they wore aprons, were cursing, shirts upturned to the elbow and beyond. When they straightened, their hands and wrists were slick with dark blood; they wiped it into rags before it had a chance to stain their clothes, though one of them, coughing, held on to a clump of solid, dripping flesh, mottled and spongy, like a large ball of moss. The girl saw it, turned around and left.

Outside, a voice screamed down into the yard. 'Quiet, for God's sake,' it screamed. 'There're honest people trying to sleep here.'

As for the trumpet: it sang on.

CHAPTER 9

Frau Vesalius woke her. She did not knock or announce herself, but simply stepped up to her bed and pulled off the bedding, exposing her, the nightgown riding up beyond her hip. She woke from dreams – something about a blind man peeling potatoes, an insurmountable pile, and in her nose the moist and cloying smell of dirt – then saw the housekeeper, those mocking eyes aglow with something wholly new. Assuming she was still asleep, the old woman began to prod her shoulder with one knee, all the while whispering her name. Zuzka flailed, leapt out of bed, then noticed the girl, half hanging from Vesalius's hand, dirty, writhing in the light of the housekeeper's lone candle.

'Lieschen!' she exclaimed; kneeled to crush her in a hug, but saw the girl shiver and withdraw, her small, twisted body struggling in Vesalius's grip.

'I found her outside the door. She was scratching it. Sitting on the floor and scratching it. Like a dog.'

It was hard to tell whether Vesalius was disgusted

or moved by Lieschen's behaviour; she pulled at her like an angler hauling in his catch, the girl's arm taut and straining at the joints.

'She won't say a word, the stupid thing.'

'Leave her be.'

Quickly, interposing her body between the girl and the old woman, Zuzka gathered Lieschen's head into her stomach.

'Let her go, I said.'

Vesalius did, and the girl slumped in Zuzka's arms, then slid on to the floor. Her mouth was encircled by sores, mud stuck to her clothes and hair, the childish eyes filled only with suspicion. She whispered something. Zuzka fell to the ground beside her, pressed her ear to her lips.

'A bath tub full of blood,' she mumbled. She was having nightmares.

'What time is it?' Zuzka asked the housekeeper, who had not moved and was staring down at them, massaging the hand that had held up the girl.

'After four.'

'He makes them into sausage. Down in the cellar,' the girl whispered, then hummed a snatch from a popular song.

'I will go bring her to the doctor,' Zuzka decided.

'I can take her up if you like.'

'No.' Zuzka pulled a skirt and cardigan over her nightgown. Her eyes never left the prostrate girl. 'She doesn't trust you.'

Vesalius flushed at this last comment, but did not reply. When she had finished dressing, Zuzka pulled Lieschen up by the armpits, marched her out ahead of her. In the hallway she slipped into a coat and wrapped a shawl around the girl, both to warm her and to hide her state of disarray. Zuzka had not seen Beer since the night Lieschen's father had been found. It was no longer clear to her who had avoided whom.

They mounted the stairs. The girl was hot with fever and sluggish in her movements. She walked ahead of Zuzka, was prodded on by Zuzka's hand at her back, and kept repeating odd snatches of phrase under her breath. Her gait was oddly clumsy; she had tied some rags around her feet, and they kept slipping off and trailing, until Zuzka bent down and tied them in a messy bow. Up close Lieschen smelled of wet clothes and unwiped bum.

When they passed the stairwell window, the trill of a trumpet reached them from afar. It was Otto and the Chinaman making merry behind half-drawn curtains. 'Rehearsing,' he'd told her when she called that morning and found them laughing, sitting tired on his bed. She had allowed him to touch her breasts once the Chinaman was gone. He'd unwrapped them, pinched a nipple, then slipped his knuckles in her crotch. 'Dogs have bones in their peckers,' he'd told her while she buttoned up her blouse. 'It's difficult to draw a knife across.' She had left when he'd asked her would she lend him some cash.

They reached the door, and Zuzka pressed down

on the bell. Nothing happened. She tried again, and was again met by silence: no ringing could be heard on the other side. A dim memory stirred in her of Beer complaining about the house's faulty wiring. Annoyed, she knocked instead. The thick door seemed to swallow up her rap rather than amplify it. She knocked harder, hurt her knuckles, but got no response. Next to her, the girl sat down awkwardly, her twisted neck pulling her chin into her chest. She might have been crying, or fallen asleep. Zuzka knocked again, then remembered the key Beer had given her an age ago, in case of emergency. She wondered could it be that he had been arrested. All at once she was angry with him, for not being there when she needed him.

She searched her pockets, she was wearing the same coat. The key was rattling with the small change, was marked by a black leather string. She slipped it into the lock and entered, reached out for the light switch and flicked it, to no avail. There was no electricity.

'Hello,' she called ahead, feeling awkward now, and again, 'Hello,' a little louder. Behind her, Lieschen entered, which is to say she stumbled in and broke into a sudden run: towards the bedroom and Eva, foot cloths flailing in her wake. Zuzka followed, pushing the door shut behind her, then crashed into the girl when Lieschen came to a sudden stop. The living-room door stood open: the girl was staring inside, one hand rising to commence the picking of her nose. Light flared, a phosphorous flash that filled the room, then collapsed into itself. Beer had struck a match.

For a moment, then, the scene was brightly lit, before the shadows scuttled back and reclaimed the room as theirs. What Zuzka saw was quite simple. Two men were lying squeezed on to the couch that Beer had converted into a bed, their naked white chests jutting from the bedsheet that they shared. The stranger was just waking. Beer was pulling himself up, a wedge of dark hair filling the hollow beneath his breastbone. When the match had burnt down to his fingers he blew it out. In the dark, all she could see was the outline of the two men's skin. Beer sought to rise, then, staring down at himself, fell back on to the couch. It was clear to her that he was naked.

'Fräulein Speckstein,' he said, stumbling, looking for another match. 'My friend, he was thrown out of his lodgings.'

Then, weaker still: 'It isn't what you think.'

'The girl is sick,' she said, turned on her heel and ran away.

TWO

Werner Heyde met Theodor Eicke in the early days of March 1933. It is easy to imagine their meeting, the young doctor coming into the room, a clipboard in his neat and well-groomed hands, the patient sitting in his hospital pyjamas, a warden by the door in case he should prove violent. Heyde was thirty-one then, was a ward doctor at the Würzberg psychiatric clinic, a talented man with excellent grades and a bright career ahead of him. Eicke was some years older, a man of forty, a Great War veteran who had spent years running I.G. Farben's internal security in Ludwigshafen. He was also an active member of the NSDAP and had joined the SS in 1931. The man responsible for his present incarceration on grounds of 'dangerous lunacy' was Josef Bürckel, the Nazi Gauleiter for a section of the southern Saarland and the future Reichsstatthalter for Vienna and regions. The two men were close political rivals, and Eicke had made open threats of 'purging' the Party of its internal enemies. After several weeks of observation, Heyde concluded that Eicke 'displayed no signs of insanity or brain disease, nor of any abnormal personality traits consistent with psychopathology'. Eicke was released in June of 1933 and made commander of the Dachau concentration camp in a matter of days. By May of 1934 he had instigated a wholesale revision of concentration-camp administration and initiated the formation of an SS unit of concentration-camp guards, later known as the SS-Totenkopf units. In the same summer, he and his adjutant personally shot the SA leader Ernst Röhm as part of the Night of Long Knives. Dr Heyde, meanwhile, had joined the Party in May 1933 on Eicke's personal recommendation. In 1935 he entered the SS as a medical officer and was soon put in charge of the eugenic examination of concentration-camp inmates. By May 1940 he had been put in charge of organising the secret programme of terminating 'undesirable' life known as 'Action T-4' after the Tiergartenstrasse 4 address of its Berlin operational centre. Most T-4 killings were performed by introducing carbon monoxide into fake shower rooms. The gas was delivered by I.G. Farben, Eicke's erstwhile employer. I.G. Farben also held the patent for Zyklon B, a cyanide-based insecticide, an odourless version of which would later be used in the systematic murder of inmates of Nazi extermination camps.

CHAPTER 1

At two o'clock in the afternoon on the day of the party, Professor Josef Hieronymus Speckstein was sitting at his desk and taking his blood pressure. He had slipped the inflatable cuff over his upper arm, and was holding on to the little rubber ball that served as its pump. The foot-high mercury column stood on the desk in front of him; he had put on his reading glasses to better observe the numbers. The stethoscope was clasped around his neck and caught the sunlight streaming through the open window. The Professor's posture was very erect, as though he had just sat down to perform an *étude* at the piano; his necktie neatly knotted at the collar. Having inflated the cuff sufficiently to cut off the circulation of his blood, Speckstein reached for the stethoscope's earpieces and eased them into place. Gently, he began to let the air out of the cuff and waited for the sudden whoosh of circulation, the first of the five Korotkoff sounds. Ahead of him, through the open door, he saw Vesalius enter his living room, then turn into his study. She stopped when she saw that he was busy, having approached no further than the door. Suspended from her hand, on a wire hanger of the sort used by professional laundries and visible through a layer of thin paper in which it had been wrapped, hung his dinner jacket. At the bottom, the final few inches of the trouser legs peeked out from the protective paper, their outer seam decorated by a braid of lustrous black silk. The Professor gestured to his housekeeper to wait for a moment while he attended to the important task of ascertaining his health. Within two minutes he had read both his systolic and diastolic pressure off the mercury column, one hundred and ninety one over ninety-five. He wrote down the numbers in a little clothbound notebook, then replaced it in his desk drawer, along with the stethoscope that he had gently prised from his ears.

'Please,' he said, looking up with his most charming smile. It took close familiarity with his physiognomy to understand he was annoyed.

'Very sorry to disturb you, Herr Professor. Your dinner jacket has come back from the cleaner's. Shall I hang it in your bedroom?'

'Naturally. Much obliged.' He hesitated, licked his lips. 'Did you have my uniform cleaned as well?'

Frau Vesalius did not answer right away. He could very well see that she hadn't. The uniform was hanging from its peg at the back of his door from which it had not moved in more than a week. The old woman shook her head, then laid her hand across her mouth to indicate she was aggrieved.

'Are you not wearing your dinner jacket then?'

'But of course. Only, perhaps I won't. After all, the event does have its – official – dimension.' He hesitated, picked up the mercury column, weighed it in his hands. His fingernails were perfectly groomed. 'Give the uniform a sponging and a brush, if you will, Frau Vesalius.'

'Certainly.'

'And I think we had better forget about the sit-down dinner. We will make it a buffet affair, push the dining-room table to one side, let people help themselves to food. There will be some additional guests, you see.'

This item of news drew a reaction from Frau Vesalius that was no longer mocking but openly distressed. She had been told there would be twelve, perhaps fifteen, gentlemen coming for dinner; had already mentally arranged the crockery on the blue damask tablecloth and worked out a way to seat everyone with dignity; had rinsed the crystal wine glasses she had taken from their locked cupboard and polished them to a shine, and prepared most of the dishes, including liver-dumpling soup, a platter of cold ham and thinly sliced Hungarian salami, and eight pounds of boiled beef in cream sauce. Now all her plans had been undone.

'But who –?' she began to ask.

Speckstein cut her off at once. 'Some of the

gentlemen are bringing friends,' he said a little stiffly, then gestured for her to take charge of the uniform.

'A buffet will be less formal. More dynamic.'

He paused, his displeasure showing more and more in the colour of his cheeks.

'Also, it might be better not to bother with the table silver. But no, do use it. Only make sure it's the – well, the gentlemen who handle it.'

Frau Vesalius had recovered her habitual air of nonchalance, and retrieved the uniform from its hook, stood holding it with both its legs trailing on the ground.

'The gentlemen?' she asked with great innocence.

'Yes.'

'But who else is coming?'

He made an impatient gesture to intimate that surely she understood. Vesalius returned his gaze with one of studied incomprehension.

'Worthy men,' he said at last, 'only some of them are lacking in – That is to say, they make up in vigour what they lack in – well, in social grace, I suppose. I am sure you follow what I am saying, Frau Vesalius.'

'Yes, Herr Professor. Silver for the gentlemen. The weekday cutlery for the riff-raff. How many can we hope to expect?'

It was clear to him that Vesalius was laughing at him, though her face remained serious and as though downcast at the news. He had not the strength to admonish her for her choice of words.

'Thirty, maybe forty,' he said curtly and waved at her to leave. She snorted, turned on her heel and rushed into the kitchen. Within minutes the flat was filled with the banging of big pots. Speckstein listened to it with a vague sense of satisfaction. It well expressed his own emotion.

The truth was that ever since that oaf Teuben had invited himself to his party, Speckstein had received cards and phone calls from various sources thanking him for his gracious invitation and asking him whether they could bring along 'a friend or two, all impeccable Party comrades'. The Professor suspected this was Teuben's doing. The man seemed bent on mobilising a social element which, apart from its indubitable devotion to the Führer, had little place at his table and had spread news of the party to such an extent that every brazen little *Blockwart* and SS ensign thought himself entitled to invite himself. Conversely, six or seven of the guests on whose company he had counted had called to cancel at short notice, claiming that a sudden cold or a professional engagement prevented them from attending. When the Vice Chancellor of the university rang to indicate he would only be able to 'stop by for a moment or two', Speckstein finally lost his patience and called on the Chief of Police in person to complain about Teuben and the rabble he was dragging into his house. The Chief commiserated with him, but indicated that 'important Party dignitaries' were pleased to see that he was throwing open his doors to the Party faithful irrespective of their social background, and that Teuben, for all his failings, had promised to deliver this very week the killer who had been terrorising the city and was on the verge of becoming an important and respected personage to whom promotion would doubtless have to be granted. It was hardly the time to enter into conflict with the man. When Speckstein began pressing the Chicf nonetheless, he was curtly reminded that he should endeavour to bury his Hapsburg prejudice against the little man, and was told that he would no doubt benefit from rubbing shoulders with the *Volk*. The Chief himself, alas, would have to leave right after dinner, but the police service would be well represented even in his absence. In short, Speckstein had long lost control of his own celebrations, and his dream of conducting a dinner party reminiscent of those that had punctuated his life as an academic dignitary, where brilliant conversation had been exchanged over choice cuts of veal and a selection of fine wines, had been quietly perverted. Now he would be playing host to a Party rally better suited to a beer hall, with a *clochard* clown for entertainment.

It was with a sigh, then, that Speckstein locked away the blood-pressure meter in a cupboard adjoining his bookshelves, and with a sense of trepidation that he began walking around the flat, inspecting it as a general might inspect the field on which he had been forced to give battle, and moving out of sight various valuable trinkets on display. He looked in on the kitchen, where Frau Vesalius was busy cutting up strips of tripe for an impromptu soup. On the kitchen counter there sat a long thin loaf of *Strudel*, still steaming from the oven's heat. For a moment he stood in the doorway, watching the housekeeper wield the heavy knife and taking in the aromas of cinnamon and baking apple; then his restlessness rushed him on down the corridor, past his niece's closed door (he was undecided as of yet whether he should urge her not to attend the festivities or simply require her to withdraw by nine o'clock), into the small drawing room that was used for little more than storage, and then back again towards his office. The thought of his niece stayed with him, and in a sudden burst of energy he got out his pad of writing paper, gold-embossed with his name and title, and retrieved his favourite fountain pen from the gilt holder on his desk.

'Dear Brother,' he began.

> I am writing once again to report on your daughter's health. Do not be alarmed when I say that the recent signs of recovery have been superseded by new bouts of nervousness. I remain of the opinion that hers is a routine case of neurasthenia brought on by overstimulation, and that she would benefit from being removed from the city with its noise and pollution, and the questionable

company its cramped situation thrusts upon its denizens. Health and virtue are as one, as you well know, and it is to both that I perceive a threat which is further aggravated by her idleness. The semester has started some weeks ago now, and despite two or three haphazard outings to the university, Zuzana has given little sign of taking up her studies in earnest. When I asked her, she told me straight out that her fellow students did not interest her much. I retorted that it was the subject of medicine and not the look and manners of her peers that should wake her interest, whereupon she gave me a morbidly enthusiastic description of the anatomy room (whether she took her details from that which she had witnessed or culled them from a book I was unable to ascertain). In short, I find it doubtful that she will make a proper fist of the study of medicine at this point, and am anxious lest she contract a moral and physical disease from which it will take her years to recover. My advice, dear brother, is to recall her, surround her with the support of a proper family (something that I, by myself, am hardly able to do), and, if she should formulate the wish to enter the medical or any other faculty at the start of the next semester, to send her to Salzburg or to Graz, where she will find herself in a more tranquil environment that will benefit her nerves. As for myself, I am well and am preparing for my party tonight, which promises to be a great social success.

He hesitated, wondering whether to add a word or two about his anxiety concerning his ever-expanding guest list, but found himself unable to find a formulation that was neither politically insensitive nor demeaning to his own sense of worth. 'Give my love to Milena,' he ended. 'Your devoted brother, Josef.'

Speckstein read through the letter one more time, admiring the even flow of his penmanship, then carefully folded the sheets of paper into tidy thirds and eased them into an envelope. Two minutes later he slipped into his coat and left the flat to buy a fresh book of stamps and personally put the letter in the mail.

CHAPTER 2

In her room, propped up against her bed's wooden headboard, and using a world atlas that she held pressed against her pulled-up knees as her desk, Zuzka, too, was engaged in the writing of a letter. It was addressed to her sister, Dagmar. Over the years she had written many such letters to her dead sibling; there was a box in her room at home where she kept them under lock and key, and once or twice a year she would take them out and read through this record of her childhood years.

Zuzka wrote. 'My dearest, dearest Dáša,' she wrote.

About six or seven months before you left me alone upon this earth, you told me one morning that you'd overheard the neighbour's maid say that mothers expect their daughters to bleed during their wedding night. It was summer then, and the neighbour's daughter had just married. The maid had been doing the laundry, and all the family's bedsheets were hung out in the garden to dry in the sun. We walked, hand in hand, and sat down under the still-moist sheets. There was a breeze and I remember the flap of cotton, quite loud at times, like the snapping of a whip. Bleed how? I asked you, and you said you didn't know. Maybe the husbands hit their brides, you suggested. We ran in to look at Julia, but her face was not bruised. Are you happy? we asked her. She smiled yes, a little stiffly, and walked quietly away.

I don't know myself why I am writing to you about this now. I figured out long ago what the maid was giggling about, and have giggled about it myself since. It turns out, however, that it's not a laughing matter. Uncle has written an article, would you believe, on 'Pathologies Pertaining to the Perforation of the Hymen'. His own copy is covered with notes that he scribbled in the margin. Some doctor he quotes gives an estimate of the quantity of blood. I forgot the amount but it's not very much. There is no mention in the article of any pain. It's that word Father is so fond of using when he's being high and mighty. 'Implicit'. Isn't it unfair that women should be cursed with childbirth *and* with this? And yet they say there is great pleasure in it all (and of course there is – I hear my neighbours braying through the night!).

You will have guessed by now that I'm in love. He is a simple man, though honourable; gentle but strong. I thought for a while I loved another but as it turns out he has other attachments (I nearly walked in on him with a lady friend the other night in a situation that might have been compromising). In any case he is too old for me, and a strange ugliness clings to him, behind the handsome looks. My lover is a better creature, roughly hewn, yet gentle, gentle. He seals with kisses any wound he might inflict. Tonight he is coming to Uncle's party. I thought about *Hamlet* when I invited him but now I don't know. It's lonely in this city, and my legs and lungs, they give me trouble. Perhaps it would be best just to go home.

'The truth, dear Dáša,' she concluded, 'cannot be written. Even to hint at it is to go too far. I remain, for ever, your loving sister, and long to kiss the rough stone of your grave.'

She signed off, struggled to read the letter through her tears, then jumped up and ran over to the little table where she kept matches and a candle. The paper caught fire at once, burned brightly and fast, and singed the tips of her fingers. She threw it down with a cry, watched the flame dance upon the floorboards, reaching (it seemed to her) for the corner of the bedsheet near which it had fallen. Afraid now, she raced for the water glass that was standing on the floor at the other end of the bed. She grabbed it and poured it, heard the sizzle of smothered flame: black ash rising up to her, gliding gently through the air and brushing her bare arms. It was four o'clock in the afternoon. Zuzka was still wearing her nightdress. It now became speckled with trails of black soot. Involuntarily, her bare feet standing in the puddle upon the floor, she raised her eyes up to the window and looked over into Otto's flat.

His curtains were open, and he and the Chinaman were standing by the window. She'd given him what little money she had and they had invested it in food and beer: the knotty stick of a cured sausage lay between them on the windowsill, along with his knife and a loaf of dark bread. Bottles of beer were in both men's hands.

She turned around quickly, lay down on her bed, and tried to master the sobs that took hold of her body, the whistle of her breathing soon filling the room.

CHAPTER 3

Detective Inspector Teuben had long finished dressing. He had donned his parade uniform along with his newly polished boots; had threaded the needle of his Party pin through the cloth over his heart; had shaved and applied cologne not only to his jowls, throat and wrists, but even dabbed a little on his stomach and inner thighs. It was a quarter to six, too early yet to set off, and so he was sitting in his armchair rereading a scrap of old newspaper clipping that two days of research had produced. The name had come first: it had been a matter of tracing a string of addresses and comparing signatures on various registration papers. Fortunately, Otto Frei was attached to his first name, a fact that did much to narrow the search. And then, too, he was a performer, easily identifiable by his work. It had not been Teuben but an assistant who had hit upon the idea of telephoning all the managers of well-known nightclubs to ask if they had ever hired Otto or any other member of his family. Specifically, Teuben was interested in his sister. When he caught trace of her, he was astonished that her exploits were remembered after more than a decade. Her career had been remarkable, in a side-show sort of way. It had stopped overnight. Teuben had found no shred of information that would have told him why.

All this research into Otto Frei and his sister had been accomplished in the breaks Teuben took from the interrogation of his prisoner. This, however, progressed at a much more satisfactory pace. The laundry boy was eager to please. There was a moment, it was true, when their research into Otto produced a tantalising link between him and one of the victims. It suggested that they might do better focusing on him rather than the laundry boy. But the lad proved to be so simple and cooperative a soul that Teuben was loath to abandon this most natural of suspects. The boy was willing to sign anything; even when he recanted, as he did periodically, in moments of a near-animal stubbornness, his explanations were so incoherent and contradictory that they only served to implicate him further. It was best therefore to keep private the details of Otto's file, above all from Beer. The doctor would have much preferred to put away a guilty man, even if he made for a less convenient defendant.

A child came into the room, nine years old, his hair jet black like his father's. He had a milky and somewhat sickly complexion and was prone to coughs. Quickly, with light, rapid steps, he walked up to the seated man, pressed his face into the

369

sleeve of his uniform, then began to clamber on to his lap. Teuben was indulgent with his only living child and helped him gain his perch. The boy was light for his age. When still an infant he had fought a protracted battle against croup. His name was Robert, after a maternal uncle. They called him Bertl.

'What are you reading, Daddy?' Robert asked, scanning the newspaper article and the pages of notes Teuben had assembled on his desk.

'I am reading about a girl only a few years older than you.'

'Is she a thief?' It was an article of faith for the boy that his father was interested above all in thieves.

Teuben shook his head. 'No, Bertl. A sorceress.'

'A sorceress? But that's marvellous! Can she do magic?'

'A lot of people believed she could tell the future. She was quite a sensation, back in her day.'

'With a crystal ball?'

'With cards. She was something like a Gypsy.'

The boy took in all this information and a look of wonder spread through his pale face. He reached to pick up the old clipping, stared at the murky photo, in which a young teen in a party dress and heavy make-up was raising both her arms above her head, as though soliciting applause. She looked big to the boy, much older than he.

'What's her name?' he asked, trying to read it for himself but failing to make sense of it.

'Hrobová,' Teuben answered, himself stumbling a little over the double consonant up front.

'A stupid name.'

Teuben shrugged, half inclined to agree.

'The father was a Slovak. It means "grave" or "tomb". *Eva Grave*. Not a bad *nom de guerre*, I suppose.'

Robert nodded, not willing to admit that he did not understand the phrase, still studying the photo. He was about to ask something else when his mother showed at the door. She was younger than Teuben and still handsome if not exactly beautiful. Unlike the boy she was plump and ruddy, in sparkling good health. She saw her son sitting on his father's lap and flashed a smile. The trust he showed in Teuben's paternal protection always astonished her. As for herself, a quiet fear governed her relations with her husband that she alone mistook for respect. There was great harmony to their conjugal relations.

'You look nice,' she said to him now with genuine admiration. 'Make sure you don't crease his uniform, Bertl. I've just had it pressed.'

She took some steps into the room, then stopped well before reaching his desk. 'Do you need anything before you go?'

'No. In fact, I might as well get going.' Teuben swung his son from out of his lap and on to the floor, then gathered the papers on his desk and locked them away in the top drawer. 'I want to stop by the office on the way.'

He ruffled his son's hair, patted his wife good-naturedly on the rump as he passed her, and even took a certain pleasure in her smile as she bid him goodbye. In each of his words and gestures, and in the simple, direct movements with which he put on his hat and coat, then walked out into the mildness of the evening air, there was already a hint of something joyously impatient, the light, teasing touch of sexual anticipation. It was as Beer had said to Eva: Teuben was out on a date.

CHAPTER 4

Those of the guests who had received a written invitation had been asked to arrive at Speckstein's party at seven o'clock sharp, for pre-dinner drinks. Anton Beer did not number among this select group. At a quarter past seven, he was still sitting in his study and had yet to get dressed. His dinner jacket had been pulled out of the wardrobe and hung in the open window to air; and yet he was quite sure that he would not go down to join the party at all, would send a card communicating his regrets the following morning (not to send anything seemed to him ill-bred). At present, he was occupied by writing out the alphabet in large letters on to pieces of cardboard that he had cut to about four times the size of an ordinary playing card. He was using a blunt-tipped coloured pencil and was at pains to invest his labour with a certain formal beauty. Cards that bore the letters A to M lay piled to the right of him; he was working on the N, enjoying its sharp, dramatic angles, and adding ornamental scrolls to both the beginning and the end of the lightly sloping letter.

The girl Anneliese was sitting not far from him. She kept to the floor though he had twice offered her a chair, and had accepted only the comforts of a blanket that he had fetched from the living room and spread out for her in one corner of the room. There she sat, her legs splayed before her, drawing clumsy outlines of people and animals on a pad of paper and colouring them in. At present she was working on what might have been a zebra or a horse. Its lines ran in strict vertical order. If it was a horse she was drawing, it was dressed in prison garb. The girl's fingers were dirty from the oil pastels she was using.

Beer had tried to talk to her several times over the past few days, and through tender insistence had learned some details about the days she had spent since the death of her father, Tobias Grotter. By putting them together with what the doctors had told him at the hospital and at the clinic, to which he had placed several calls, a picture had emerged, too vivid perhaps to be entirely realistic. He saw her waking in the hospital ward, sullen and in shock, and running at once for the door. A nurse had restrained her, asked her questions, while the girl pressed her hands over her ears and stamped her frightened little feet. No parent came to claim her, nor were the police looking for her. A hospital doctor who spent half his time working at a clinic on the western edge of the city had her transferred there: they had a children's ward. She escaped almost immediately, climbing out a bathroom window when her registration was still incomplete, then made her way back into the city, barefoot, disorientated, avoiding the questioning glances of strangers. Beer could not fathom whether she had got herself lost or had deferred her home-coming on purpose. The girl, so talkative but a week ago and boundless in her confidence in strangers, had become suspicious and withdrawn. Beer wondered to what degree she understood what had happened to her father, and whether it wouldn't be best for her if she were gently forced to acknowledge the truth. He had already made several attempts in this direction. He had also tried to reassure her with regard to the janitor, whom she had seen 'draw a bath with blood, not water', as she had told him when he'd stood her in his own bathtub and rubbed her down with a sponge and tepid water.

'I went down and talked to him at length,' he'd said. 'He's a good man, really. You have nothing to fear from him.'

The girl had merely nodded and asked to please be towelled off.

As for the scene she had witnessed two nights previously, when she and Zuzka had appeared in his living-room doorway: about this, the doctor and the little girl had not exchanged a word. He felt that anything he could say to her would but burden her with yet another secret, at once bewildering and without consequence. She seemed oblivious in any case, and since neither Otto nor

Zuzka had shown their faces in the past few days, and Anneliese liked to spend all her time either in his study or in Eva's bedroom, there was no possibility, at present, that she might say the wrong thing to anyone and put him in immediate danger.

Sighing, taking a break before embarking on the O, Beer stood up from his desk and crouched down next to the girl, one knee joint creaking in complaint. He pointed to the wall, where the hedgehog the janitor had sent up for Lieschen was sniffing at the window curtains, but the girl was impassive, refused to give so much as a smile. He had seen her play with the animal a few times, but mostly she had ignored it and had even thrown a pen at it on one occasion, then watched it roll itself into a ball.

'Prince Yussuf,' he said gently. 'Isn't that his name?'

She shrugged her crooked little shoulders, then nodded, never looking up at Beer.

'Don't you think he looks a little lonely?'

Again the girl shrugged, sucked in her lip, threw a glance over to the animal.

'Maybe,' she said.

'And you? Are you feeling lonely, Anneliese?'

This time she gave no response at all. Frustrated, he settled one knee on the floor, laid some fingers on her shoulder, half expecting her to pull away.

'You don't talk as much as you used to.'

The girl wrinkled her nose, stopped colouring. 'Eva doesn't talk.'

'Eva is sick. Look here, Anne—' He paused,

corrected himself, struggled for a phrase. 'Lieschen. You found your father, didn't you? Before you woke up in the hospital.'

Her body went still, the eyes staring into him without emotion.

'I know it must have been terrible. You mustn't be afraid, though. It wasn't – murder. Your father was very sad, and he was drinking far too much. And then he – That is to say, there was a kind of accident. He hurt himself.'

She shrugged yet again, raised the pencil she was holding and drew it, point first, across the front of her dress, leaving a bright purple mark. He had seen her make that movement once before: in the janitor's cellar, when Beer had asked what had happened to poor Walter. Back then she had fanned her fingers before her abdomen to suggest the spilling of the animal's guts. This time she eschewed such drama.

'It's a good way to go,' she murmured. 'For a dog.'

Beer heard the phrase and knew at once it wasn't hers. Its callousness stung him, and he leaned forward to be closer to the girl.

'Is that what your father said?' he asked. 'When they found Walter?'

But Lieschen simply went back to her colouring, drawing a person this time, fat of body and of limb; drew slits for eyes and a wide-mouthed, yellow funnel that jutted from its red-lipped mouth. Beer's knee gave another creak as he stood up. He felt he couldn't help the girl. It shamed him to admit that she was the least of his problems that night.

He walked into the kitchen. On the table there stood an array of beer bottles, five in number, placed in no particular arrangement and looking for all the world as though they had been plonked down at random. One of the bottles was open, the porcelain cork dangling from the metal hoop that attached it to the neck, and a third of the contents was missing. Beer fetched a glass, placed it next to the bottle, poured out an inch or so. It stood there, the foam first rising then settling in the narrow glass. He turned his back on it, took two steps out of the kitchen, only to run back and throw the beer down the sink. He did not want, in some unguarded moment, for the girl to come sampling what stood poured out on the table. When the time came, he thought, he would have to lock her in the study so that Teuben did not see her. She was vulnerable now, an orphan. As there were no living relatives, she would end up in an orphanage: the hunchbacked daughter of an alcoholic suicide. It would have been much better to remove her from the flat, but Beer was not sure where he could bring her. The janitor might have been happy to look after her, but she seemed so crushed and traumatised he did not dare suggest it, and after a fashion it was true: the man drew baths of blood and not of water. When the time came, he would have to lock her in. The thought repeated itself. When the time came. He replaced

378

the glass on the kitchen table, a smear of dried-on foam climbing up its side. The clock struck eight. It was time to turn Eva.

He entered the bedroom without haste and went about his nurse's business. Eva endured it without so much as a wink. While he was changing her nightgown into one of plain cotton, his eyes neither lingered on nor avoided her naked form. He had expected himself to be seized by agitation, but felt preternaturally calm instead, and found himself thinking that – one way or another – things would come to a rest that night. *It's the gambler's moment of repose,* he thought: *when all the bets have been placed and the ball is spinning around its wheel.* And he was strangely happy about this, the inexorability of fate, and strangely indifferent towards Eva, whom he'd worked so hard to save. It was as though all his feeling for her had long been exhausted and he was reduced once again to nothing more than his function, a doctor looking after his patient. He smiled at her without warmth, tucked the sheets up to her chin. A noise travelled in through the window he had opened, of young men talking loudly on a floor below. Beer turned, opened the door, lingered a moment to light a cigarette. And then, in that very instant, his hands still in his pockets, searching for the matches, a new tenderness rose up in him, fresh, livid, unexpected. He gave a cry, whipped around, fell to his knees beside the bed, green eyes watching him with the sadness of the damned.

'Oh Eva,' he whispered.

She winked at him to say she understood.

He stayed another hour. They did neither of them cry. Beer spoke a little, his lips bowed low over her ear. He was holding Eva's hand.

'It's like this,' he told her. 'All your life you keep yourself hidden. Even from yourself. Your brother, now – Otto – he's the type of man who lives at the surface of things. He has to paint his face to disappear, and seal his lips. Everything he says, it's indiscreet, even when he's telling lies. I think that it's a gift of sorts. These days, of course, it might just help to get him killed.

'But I – I never speak, not really. I use my words to hide behind. I don't speak and I don't act, even when I'm out and pursuing my vices. I feed them, it is true, but it's only so that I keep them in check. All of my life I have been calculating the odds: an economics of prudence, buying off desire so I can live in peace. I am doing it even now, speaking to the living dead. But it's better than not speaking at all.

'I'm sorry, Eva,' he told her. 'I'm so sorry.'

The clock struck 9.30. Exhausted, unable to bear the wait any longer, Anton Beer ran out of Eva's room, threw on his dinner jacket, locked up Lieschen in the study, and went downstairs to join the party.

CHAPTER 5

Beer was met by the first signs of the party no sooner had he stepped out his door. Noises rose within the stairwell, of drunken men shouting, laughing, breaking into song. Halfway down, a youth of eighteen, nineteen years was sitting on a step, his body bent double, clutching his thick flaxen hair. A companion, some years older and swarthy in complexion, was squatting next to him and whispering ceaselessly into his ear. Both men were wearing brown shirts and armbands, had tucked their trousers into thick woollen socks. Beer stepped past them without greeting and continued towards the noise. On the next landing three policemen in dress uniform were passing a carafe made of cut glass back and forth, trading snatches of popular songs in which they had substituted the lyrics for pornographic equivalents. Just then, one of them dropped the carafe's heavy stopper and watched it bounce down the stairs, then drop into the central chasm and shatter on the floor below. All three of them burst into laughter. Beer passed this group, too, without so much as a word.

When he turned the next bend of the large and littered staircase, he saw from afar that the door to Speckstein's flat stood wide open. Laughter rang out from it, followed by a trumpet's comic whistle. In the doorway, straddling the threshold and leaning casually against the doorpost, stood a tall, thin SS officer with a pointy chin and finger-wide moustache. A cigarette was smoking in his long-boned, handsome hand. When the doctor tried to walk past him, he reached out with a sudden movement and took hold of Beer's arm.

'Are you sure you are invited?' he asked, eyeing the dinner jacket with some suspicion, then leaned in close to blow cigarette smoke into Beer's face. Before Beer had time to formulate an answer, the man let go of him again.

'But what the hell. Go ahead. Most of the food's gone, but some of the lads brought beer and spirits. You might just catch the tail end of the show.'

Inside, the flat seemed strangely empty until Beer reached the doorway that led to Speckstein's living room and study, where a tight press of people stood shoulder to shoulder and were pushing and shoving for a better view. The air was hot and stale here, a mixture of smoke and sweat. Muttering excuses, and taking advantage of a group of three or four elderly gentlemen who disrupted the crowd with their attempt to leave, Beer managed to squeeze past the outermost row of spectators and slip inside. All eyes were directed to the far end of the room, where Otto Frei stood upon the dining-room table, which had been pushed against the wall. Used plates and dirty cutlery had been stacked at one end of the table; at the other a big terrine of soup still presided amongst several towers of bowls. The space in between served Otto as his stage.

The room was dark, lit only by a desk lamp that a pimply youth in an ill-fitting suit held angled at Otto's painted face. The mime's body, dressed entirely in black, was visible only as an outline, all apart from the white cotton gloves that emerged from the surrounding darkness with a curious intensity. One of these gloves – the right – was holding a rolled-up newspaper. Just now there was no movement to Otto's body or his face. He stood stock still, chin out, legs spread, the paper raised like a club above his head, in the aspect of a man who is listening intently for some faint and far-off noise. The audience was quiet, hushed: it, too, was straining its ears. Beer looked around himself but in the near darkness it was impossible to make out anything but shadows; the glow of cigarettes hung scattered in the dark.

And then a strange, soft buzzing rose within the room, as of a fly caught against a windowpane, struggling to get out. The sound was so vivid, and the mime's reaction so immediate and natural, that Beer did not think to search for its origin in anything but the air in front of Otto's scrunched-up face. The mime's head and eyes were following

383

the fly's trajectory. Disgust, anger, then cunning flashed across his whitened features as he watched it dart in front of him before settling on the rim of a champagne flute that balanced precariously at the top of a pile of dirty crockery. The mime took aim with infinite deliberation. Twice he raised the newspaper as a conductor raises his baton, wrist first, preparing the *fortissimo*, then, dissatisfied by his approach, cut short the down-swing and started the motion all over again. Each of his movements was accompanied by a subtle variation of the fly's buzzing. It was as though it too were watching him and preparing its evasive manoeuvres. At long last he swung, his face lit up by such a blissful sense of triumph that half the audience burst out laughing, then stopped themselves lest they shoo the fly. The tip of the newspaper caught the champagne glass at the side of its stem and lobbed it with surprising softness high into the air above the audience's heads, from where it was plucked by a brown-sleeved arm and hand. As for the fly: it escaped, buzzed furiously around its attacker, then settled on the mime's white and twitching nose. He stared at it, cross-eyed, began to slap at himself with wild abandon, gouging first one eye, then the other, slapping each cheek in repeated motions, then hitting his crotch on a mistimed back-swing, to the merriment of all. The fly sought the only shelter left to it and flew into his gaping mouth, then bounced half-crazed between his puffed-up cheeks, its constant

384

changes of direction closely mirrored by the bulging roll of Otto's eyes.

It was only now, during this invisible game of tennis, that Beer caught sight of Yuu and thus was able to pinpoint the origin of all the sounds: the buzzing, the whistle of displaced air when Otto swung his baton, the booming slaps when it collided with his cheeks. The fat Japanese sat on the windowsill at one side of the table, half hidden by the curtain that fell around his shoulders like a cape. Balanced on his meaty thighs there lay a variety of objects – a rattle, a cheese grater and spoon, a pan filled with rice – that he would manipulate with his left hand while his right pressed his trumpet to his lips. His eyes, meanwhile, were trained across and on the stage, taking in each little movement and translating it into sound. He matched it so closely that even once alerted to his presence it was hard to believe that it was Yuu and not the stage that was the source of his sly ruckus.

The act came to a close. Otto, shaking his head from side to side, had finally managed to knock the fly unconscious. Dizzy himself, stumbling from one end of the table to the other, he plucked the fly from his lips, then tore out each of its wings (two scraps of confetti came loose between his fingers and fluttered down into the crowd). He smiled, bent low to find a soup bowl perching in the dark, and with a magnificent little plop, dropped in his emasculated enemy before taking hold of a spoon and returning to the pleasure of his dinner. A fanfare sounded, the lights were turned on, the artist showered with thunderous applause. Soon after the audience began to disperse. Otto retired from his table, accepted the bottle of beer proffered to him, and was lost in the crowd. Beer, amused despite himself, turned away from the stage, and availed himself of the opportunity to look around, scanning the crowd for familiar faces.

Virtually the first person Beer saw was Teuben. The detective was leaning casually against the windowsill and laughing at somebody's joke; when he caught sight of Beer he cocked an eyebrow in a lazy greeting. Turning away from him, his merriment gone, Beer lit a cigarette and pushed deeper into the room. His eyes found Zuzka, sitting near the wall opposite the impromptu stage, her hands and eyes on her lap and seemingly heedless of the bustle that surrounded her. Just now one of the guests approached her and addressed a few words to her hunched back, then shrugged and left when he was unable to draw a reaction. Speckstein himself was sitting in an armchair not far from her, looked grave and sweaty, and more than a little drunk. Unsure where else to go, Beer pushed over to their side of the room, knocking over an open bottle of schnapps that had been placed carelessly on the ground. He stooped to righten it, then, their eyes now level, caught Zuzka's glance from a few feet away. She blanched, looked away, her legs re-crossing in front of her. Her face looked as though she had been crying, and her blouse gaped at the stomach, exposing a half-inch of skin. She was the only woman in the room.

More determined now, Beer worked his way over to her. There were people everywhere, flushed and talking, more than thirty in this room alone. The carpet was speckled with cigarette butts and ash, bits of dropped food. A man near the window had thrown it open and was yelling something at the street below. Not far from him, another had switched on the wireless and was dialling his way through the stations: static crackling and mixing with the other noises, before he settled on a rendering of Wagner, blaring tinnily from the wooden box. Beer reached the wall, shouldered past a pug-nosed drunk in a chauffeur's uniform who was holding two shot glasses to his eyes like goggles, to the loud laughter of his friends, and arrived at Zuzka's side. In the absence of another chair, Beer lowered himself to one of his knees and muttered a stiff, formal greeting. She pretended she hadn't heard and he had to repeat it before she looked up and answered him curtly with the conventional response.

'This is not quite the party I had pictured,' he told her, trying to make light of the chaos surrounding them.

She flashed him a cold, absent look.

'Yes,' she answered stiffly. 'Uncle is put out.'

'I haven't seen you in the past two days. I thought you would look in and check on Lieschen.'

He paused, hoping Zuzka would pick up the

thread. She didn't. Unsettled, urged by a vague sense that he owed it to her – and to Eva – to explain himself, he leaned closer to Zuzka's ear.

'The man you saw,' he told her quietly. 'He visits me sometimes. Or I visit him.'

He paused again, looked for a way to couch the nature of his predilection.

'Two nights ago he came around. In the middle of the night. It was reckless of me to let him in, and more reckless yet to fall asleep. I have been feeling awfully reckless of late.' He tried a smile, felt a vein twitch at his temple.

'The thing is, you mustn't tell anyone, Fräulein Speckstein. Zuzka. Please.'

At this, she stood up and ran off. She never even turned her head to look at him. Her hands, he had noticed, had been bunching up the cloth of her skirt above the knees, and as she ran away now it fell awkwardly, its symmetry disrupted, the hemline rumpled at the front. As she left the room, some of the men looked after her. Beer saw Teuben peel himself out of his group by the window and follow her, smoothing down his hair as he crossed the room. It might have been best to follow them himself, but the doctor did not have the strength. Depressed, exhausted, Beer raised himself far enough to sit down on the chair Zuzka had just vacated. He was welcomed by the heat left by her buttocks. It triggered a sadness in him and he sat, hunched over, head bowed, in much the same aspect she had just abandoned.

CHAPTER 6

Frau Vesalius was standing in front of the kitchen window, taking a break. She had not had a moment to herself since early that morning and was enjoying a cigarette. The party had exhausted her. All evening she had been bringing out more food only to watch it disappear within minutes. Things got even worse when the lout from across the yard showed up with the Chinaman in tow: the fat Oriental had come straight into the kitchen and scoffed everything in sight, all the while complimenting her profusely on her culinary skill. All by himself he had eaten the better part of one of the strudels, and much of the second pot of tripe soup. It was only with the start of the performance that she had managed to get rid of him and some peace returned to her kitchen. Frau Vesalius felt that her cigarette was well deserved.

Behind her, in the corridor outside the kitchen, some guests were loudly discussing the course of the war. The English were massing in France, and the Finns and the Soviets were fast sliding towards war. There was an urgent note of bravado in their drunken discussion, as of men who needed to impress upon themselves their heedless courage in the face of a future enemy. She had heard this type of talk before. It had been a little over twenty years ago that her son had had his legs shot off on the eastern front, three weeks before the peace of Brest-Litovsk.

Vesalius looked down into the yard. There were more guests there, officers by the look of them, standing near the tree and engaged in a game in which two of them were exchanging blows to the stomach while the others took bets on who would vomit first. Another man had taken off both his jacket and his shirt and was using the iron frame of the carpet-beating rack to perform gymnastic feats: presently he catapulted himself into the air, attempted a somersault, hit some tree branches and fell hard on to the ground. His friends' laughter was soon joined by his own high giggle as he stood up beside them and wiped the blood from his face.

Frau Vesalius cast a glance at the kitchen clock. It was gone ten o'clock. The way everyone was drinking, the party would be over pretty soon; the Professor would run out of booze and those who were still standing would push off to find some girls. The men's boisterousness did not disgust her. After all, they were young. The only thing she resented was that she would be asked to clean up their mess, and put up with Speckstein's grumpy complaints.

A movement caught Vesalius's attention, and she turned around to see Zuzka come running into the kitchen. She was moving too fast for the clutter of the room, her head bowed low, the features hidden behind the flow of her hair, and before she had taken three steps she crashed into the little table and chair. The noise startled the girl. She looked up and was evidently surprised that she had ended up there; turned to leave again, then stopped, her body racked by a sob. Vesalius watched her, mockery mingling with compassion. Zuzka noticed her look: she held it for a breath or two, and found enough warmth in it to join her by the window.

'Here,' the housekeeper offered. 'Have one.' She held out the packet.

Zuzka shook her head, took one anyway.

'I don't smoke,' she said.

She watched Vesalius take a drag, then picked up the box of matches from the windowsill and lit her own, took a careful little puff. It seemed to calm her. There were no tears now in her eyes.

'You should go,' the old woman said.

Zuzka nodded, embarrassed, looked to one side in the vague direction of her room.

'In a moment.'

'I mean home. To your family.'

Zuzka did not protest. They stood quietly for some minutes, blew smoke at the window, the girl working her way through her cigarette with rapid, shallow drags. She managed not to cough.

'I was writing to my sister earlier,' she muttered

in a tender, quiet voice, then coloured when she saw derision in Vesalius's face.

'I know myself it's stupid. Writing to the dead.'

She tried to smile but it froze on her face. Unhappiness did not become her. There were women, Vesalius thought, who looked fetching after they had cried: purified. Not Zuzka.

'You were twins?' she asked, breaking the silence. 'The Professor mentioned it.'

'Yes,' Zuzka nodded. 'Two peas in a pod. When we were small, father used to say that it was she who'd become the doctor. And I would settle down and marry rich.'

'How did she die?'

'Polio. When we were twelve. A long time ago.'

'You should go home.'

Again the girl nodded, screwed the cigarette into the window's glass, then started when she noticed a man standing in the kitchen just a few steps away. It was impossible to say how long he had been there. Vesalius, too, had not noticed him enter and stared sour-faced at the intruder. He was tall, fat in the hips, held himself remarkably still. A smell of mints and of some type of musky cologne streamed from his awkward figure; the dark, sunken eyes were flat like a doll's. But what struck her most, and most unfavourably, was the shape and colour of his lips. They looked painted on with a two-groschen brush, thin and fraying at the edges. Zuzka saw him, winced, and immediately ran to the door, keeping as much distance between herself and the man as possible. Vesalius looked after her, then back to the man. He was holding a brandy glass, was taking steady, quiet sips. After a few moments he turned and left without a word. In the doorway he nearly crashed into the fat Chinaman who had come to forage for more food. The two men tried to squeeze through the doorway at the same moment, their bellies touching at its centre. Vesalius barked out a laugh, turned back to the window, and lit another cigarette.

CHAPTER 7

He followed her. Like a good hunting dog he sniffed out her room even though she'd closed the door behind herself when he was still out of sight. Perhaps there was no trick to it; perhaps he'd simply opened all the doors until he found her. He was a police detective after all. Who was to tell him that it wasn't allowed?

He stepped in as naturally as though it were the cloakroom; closed the door again with the softest of touches. She'd switched on the light when she'd come in, two minutes earlier, had sat down on the bed. Teuben stood under the tasselled lampshade as though it were a shower head. His dense mop of hair seemed to absorb its light: a deep and inky black. It had to be a wig. He was still holding his brandy glass, a sliver of liquor was left at its bottom. Zuzka wondered whether he was drunk.

She made a movement to get up from the bed, but a gesture from his hairy hand bid her to remain seated. He moved calmly, without haste.

'You were there the other night. When I met Eva. Hiding in the doctor's flat. You heard us talk.'

He drained the dregs of his glass.

'How much did you hear?'

'Nothing.'

Teuben smiled. He looked around, stepped over to where the chair stood near the window, wrapped his hand around its backrest, but did not sit down.

'Nothing. Or everything. What does it matter? A funny man, this Dr Beer. Difficult to figure out. You were talking to him just now. Looked like you were running away from him. Did he say something you didn't like?'

The detective gave her a chance to respond, but she merely shook her head and drew her knees up in front of her body, hiding her chest. The heels of her shoes made dimples on her coverlet.

'A strange man, this Beer,' Teuben repeated, his dark eyes following her movement. 'I thought for a while he fucked her himself. But I suppose he's fucking you.'

'I will scream for my uncle.'

'Don't bother,' he said, turning away from her and opening the window. 'I'm only here to take in the view.' He pushed his face out into the night.

Almost immediately he broke into a laugh.

'Now will you look at that,' he said, grinning, and waved her over to the window.

She obeyed despite herself, keeping her distance, and squinted cautiously to where his hand was pointing into the darkness. When she said she could not see, Teuben withdrew from the window and watched her take his place. Above them, a floor and a half up, and at a steep angle to their right, two men in uniform had heaved the big stairwell window from its hinges and stood jostling, shoulder to shoulder, balancing within its frame, their trousers open, and pissing into the darkness of the yard. All she could make out with full clarity was the tips of their boots, jutting out from the window frame, and the twin cascades of urine raining down into the yard. Down there, on the muddy ground, emerged the Oriental, Yuu; he stopped, looked up, then carried on towards the door of the back wing. Teuben stood next to her, quietly laughing.

'Like children at a birthday party. And tomorrow they'll be sent off to war. For the greater glory of the Reich. It all seems a little silly, doesn't it?' He burped, drew a watch from his trouser pocket, checked the time.

'But anyway, I'd better be off. There's another lady waiting for my visit. Not a word, you. Your uncle is an influential man, connected. But nobody's out of reach.'

The detective's hand snapped forward as he said this, grabbed her by the wrist, finger and thumb connecting across her bones.

'These are volatile times.'

It surprised him that she did not flinch from his grasp. Instead she bent closer, so that he would be able to see her face. Up close she struck him as near hysterical, her mouth twitching, her cow eyes filling up with tears. Something gave inside her. All at once she was speaking, shouting, shaking head to toe.

'You are going to see Eva, aren't you?' she shouted. 'Did you know that my uncle raped her? She was only a child. Her name was Evelyn then. Evelyn Wenger. It was all in the papers. And tonight, I thought that Otto would –' She raised her free hand and rolled it in a fist in a gesture meant to denote punishment, or revenge. 'In his performance, you see. But all he did was chase a fly. Everybody laughed.'

She opened her mouth and let out a giggle. Her breathing was laboured, whistled in the depths of her. Puzzled, Teuben let go of her wrist.

'What the hell are you talking about?'

'He killed Uncle's dog.'

'Who?'

'Otto. Because of his sister. Because of what he did to her.'

Teuben heard it and laughed, his thin lips parting around teeth and gums.

'You've been writing a novel, I see. Cute. But Eva's always been Eva, and I'd bet good money that Speckstein's never seen her in his life. As for the dog, I have the killer in a cell at the police station. He has all but signed his confession.'

He shrugged, dismissed her with a wave of his arm.

'What you are,' he said, 'is a little cuckoo. But that's all for the better. Just go on crying wolf.'

He left a moment later, having watched the disappointment spread across her face. His boy looked like that, when he got a present he didn't like: flushed and sulky, anger giving way to tears. Zuzka threw herself on to her pillow. From the back, legs spread, the skirt riding up to the top of her knees, her hips awriggle with her sobs, she didn't look half bad. Teuben left without bothering to close the door.

CHAPTER 8

The clock struck ten-thirty. It was a six-foot grandfather clock of Danish origin, in white lacquered wood with gold-leaf trimmings around the face, and stood, somewhat awkwardly, between two of Speckstein's bookshelves where it was in danger of getting lost amongst their bulk. On another occasion Beer might have gone up to it and studied it more closely; opened up its case and watched the pendulum in its rhythmic movements and the near imperceptible descent of its twin weights. As a boy he had owned a John Alker longcase that had been bequeathed to him by a paternal uncle and had spent many happy hours taking it apart, cleaning it, and then reassembling it with infinite care. Now he listened to the tall clock's chime with a mixture of trepidation and hope. Teuben had disappeared. He did not dare hope he had left the house altogether; nor did he wish to assume that by some policeman's trick he had let himself into the doctor's flat without waiting for permission. It would have been easy enough for Beer to run up and see if such worries were misplaced, but the doctor did not stir. All he had done was shift from the chair in Speckstein's living room to one in his study, where there had been fewer people at the time. Beer's mouth was dry and he thought he should get up and find a drink of something, but the lethargy that had taken hold of him was impossible to shift.

The clock struck ten-thirty and he looked around. Beer was surprised to find himself alone in the room. Through the open door he could see that the living room, too, had begun to empty out. The men had eaten and drunk their fill, and many seemed to have left in search of new entertainments. In another half-hour or so, only the dead-drunks would be left, passed out in some corner and impossible to shift.

Speckstein entered. He had been sitting in his armchair in the living room ever since Beer had arrived at the party, but now Beer watched him get up rather heavily and walk into his study. He, too, it seemed, had had too much to drink, and was swaying on his short march between the doorway and his desk. When he reached it he seemed to have forgotten why he'd come; looked up lost and puzzled and found Beer sitting with his back against the wall. The Professor was wearing an old-fashioned dinner jacket and a beautiful white ruffled shirt. Only the pin he had threaded through his lapel announced his membership of the Party that many of his guests had literally worn upon their sleeves. When he saw

Beer, he nodded to himself and began to stagger towards him. Halfway there, his eyes began to water and he stopped to dig a handkerchief from out his pocket; blew his nose, then wiped the corners of his eyes. Even in his inebriated state there was a certain gentlemanly elegance to his movements. Beer stood up to greet him. The leather upholstery of the chair he had been sitting in creaked as he lifted out his weight, a sound so animate and plaintive that both men involuntarily turned to stare at the chair, as though expecting it to move. It took an act of will for them to shift their eyes from chair to one another.

'Herr Professor,' Beer said in greeting, then found himself at a loss as to how to continue. 'My congratulations on your party.'

Speckstein waved away his words with his handkerchief, then raised it once more to his teary eyes. A slight shiver seemed to shake his figure.

'Are you unwell?'

'It's nothing, Dr Beer. I was just thinking about Walter. My dog. I miss him tonight.'

'Why yes,' Beer answered, embarrassed, mentally sifting through the conventional remarks one made to those who were recently bereaved. But none of them would seem to fit.

'I am very sorry for you,' he said at last.

'The Chief of Police tells me Detective Teuben is holding a suspect.'

'So I understand.'

'He killed my dog?'

'I suppose.'

'You don't know?'

'I am assisting purely on the medical side of things. Though even there I'm out of my depth.'

'Nonsense, Beer. You are a luminary in your field. And this Teuben fellow – he's nothing but trash. A vile, coarse, brutish piece of trash. You know what he did to me? He –

'But here he is himself,' he finished, embarrassed, becoming aware of Teuben's arrival a fraction too late. 'We were discussing the case, Detective.'

Teuben smiled, gave the ghost of a bow.

'I've just come from the washroom, Herr *Zellenwart*. Some of the lads have made rather a mess of things, I'm afraid. You might do well to tell your housekeeper.'

The two men stood looking at each other for a moment, Speckstein erect, weepy, drunk; the detective slovenly and brazen.

'I will see to it,' the Professor said stiffly.

'Good. It will give the doctor and me a chance to catch up on the case.'

They walked a few steps behind Speckstein, the detective holding on first to Beer's elbow, then to his wrist. When their host swung left towards the kitchen, Teuben manoeuvred them onwards, to the front door. The SS man was still standing in the doorway on his self-appointed vigil, and let them pass without a word. Halfway up the stairs, a cold draught blew into the building where somebody had ripped a window off its hinges. It lay, shattered, on the steps. A young man lay not far from it, the same flaxen-haired youth who had previously held his head and been comforted by the soothing whispers of his friend. He was alone now, passed out amongst the shards; a splinter of glass had evidently cut the side of his nose, which bled lightly past his mouth and cheek. They stepped over him without comment and continued on their way to Beer's door. Once they had arrived, Teuben watched Beer struggle with the lock and reached out at one point to steady the doctor's hand. Inside, Beer took two quick steps and tried to usher Teuben into his kitchen.

'I have the new autopsy report,' he said hastily. 'Perhaps we should go over it together, see whether it's what you had in mind.' His hand went to the inner pocket of his jacket and withdrew some carefully folded typed sheets of paper. 'Why don't you sit down?'

'Later,' Teuben laughed, amused, looking past the doctor's shoulder to the bottles of beer standing on the kitchen table.

'Were you planning on getting drunk, Herr Doktor? Keep some for me. Afterwards, we can sit down and have a beer together.'

Even as he spoke, he seemed to change his mind and reached past the doctor to grab one of the bottles, sunk it in his jacket pocket.

'In case I get thirsty.'

He turned around, started walking down the

corridor, the doctor running after him, hard at his heels.

'About that, Detective. The infection, it is bad today. I had to reapply some maggots. Maybe if you wait just a few days –'

Teuben stopped dead in his tracks, seemed to enjoy the fact that Beer ran into him, bumping his chin on the detective's shoulder.

'And if she were crawling with them.' Teuben laughed. 'You know, I think I'm in love.'

Again he started walking, and again Beer ran alongside, talking at him, giddy now with agitation.

'There's something else. I'm . . . an invert. That is to say, I sleep with men. It's why my wife left me.'

He succeeded in bringing Teuben to another halt.

'Oh my,' he answered, still grinning, then spat. 'Is this true?'

'Yes.'

'I had no idea.' He looked the doctor up and down as though he saw him for the first time. No disgust or irritation showed on his face, just wonder mixed with calculation.

'You must stop it at once, of course. Until after the trial. I need a credible expert witness.'

He took another step towards the bedroom door; laid a hand upon the handle, opened it, then turned around.

'But why are you telling me this now? Surely you are not planning anything stupid. Look here' – he leaned into the doctor, placed a big hand on his neck and cheek – 'this is not the time for games. There's no point punishing yourself, Dr Beer, if that's what's going through your head. And don't think for a moment that what is about to happen is the worst there can be. If she ends up in a hospital, it will happen a hundredfold and worse. I just want this once. And then your statement, sworn in court. That's all. You can live with that, I assure you. If you couldn't, why, you would have moved her by now and put a bullet through your brain.'

He studied Beer another second, then dropped his arm, turned and stepped through the door.

'But enough talk.'

Shaking, his eyes on the bottle of beer sticking out of Teuben's jacket pocket, Beer followed him into the bedroom. Eva lay as he had left her, her eyelids closed, the bed-sheet neatly folded underneath her chin. She looked pristine, calm, composed. Teuben kneeled down at her bedside, a smile splitting his features, and began to peel back the sheet.

'Good God, but she's pretty,' he muttered, unbuttoning the top of his shirt. 'Ghastly gown you put on her.'

Beer wanted to leave but was rooted to the spot. The detective reached for her neck with both hands as though he was planning on strangling her.

The moment he touched her – at neck, cheek

and collarbone, squeezing her skin with fingers that were as greedy as they were tender, his bluff face still split by a smile – Eva started sweating, unaccountably sweating, soaking her linen night-dress in a matter of moments until her body emerged as though from under yards of water, ivory pale, her ribs showing like the bones of a corset. Alarmed, Teuben withdrew his hands and stared in fury and wonder at the outline of the breasts that had emerged beneath the damp cloth.

'It's the fever,' Beer muttered and started forward.

With sudden violence, Teuben jumped up and pushed him back and out the room.

'Leave us!' he shouted, slammed the door in Beer's face.

The doctor took five steps, fell to the floor, and clapped his hands over his ears so he would not have to hear a thing.

CHAPTER 9

Zuzka did not cry for long. Soon after Detective Teuben had left her room, the sobs lost some of their intensity and she made an effort to wipe the tears and snot from her face. When she tried to stand up, she noticed that she had lost sensation in one of her legs. She sat down again, and began massaging her calf and ankle. Very gradually the numbness was replaced by the pain of pins and needles running through her skin. Her breathing was ragged; she seemed to have to gasp for air. Even so, she hobbled out into the corridor and on towards the front door, where she searched frantically to locate her coat. She found it at last, locked away in a cupboard, along with her uncle's hat and umbrella and Vesalius's thirty-year-old *Loden* coat. In her haste to search its pockets she lost her balance and fell into the cupboard, then had to pull herself out by the strength of her arms; her legs were giving way under her.

At length she located what she had been looking for, took a step towards the front door (a man in a black uniform was standing there, watching all her movements with close interest but making no move to help her), then decided otherwise and headed into the living room instead. There were very few people left there now: a drunk sitting in an armchair, mouth wide open and sleeping with a dirty china plate cradled in his lap; and a group of four men who were talking to Otto in one corner of the room, while the latter was spooning custard out of a dessert bowl with his fingers, then licking them off with childish glee. He had taken off most of his make-up, though some paint still clung to the creases of his face. Drawing closer she realised that the men were complimenting Otto on his performance and making suggestions for future acts. One of them – a muscular man in his forties, with a messy fencing scar beneath one eye – seemed to be a senior figure in the Party's youth movement, and was painting a picture of an open-air performance in the Augarten, in front of an audience of 'five thousand German lads', and was offering his help in putting together material with a 'suitable, pedagogic content'. Otto smiled, licked his fingers, and nodded his thanks when one of the others held out a bottle of schnapps.

It took Zuzka a few minutes to attract Otto's attention. She tried to catch his eye, but he seemed to look right through her, was focused on the food, the booze, the fawning, loud-mouthed men. In the end it was the youth leader with the duelling scar who pointed her out to him.

'Looks like you have another admirer,' he said

rather loudly, turning around and scrutinising her from top to toe. 'Fräulein Speckstein, I believe. You two know each other?'

Zuzka shook her head and was relieved to see Otto do the same. The mime seemed to be angry with her for intruding on his moment of triumph; he knitted his brows and stared at her with a peculiar coldness. The man with the scar did not seem to notice.

'Well, Fräulein,' he said. 'Did you enjoy the show?'

She coloured and did not know how to answer; panted rapid, shallow breaths, her eyes fixed on Otto, pleading with him to please hear her out. All four of his admirers were staring at her now while she stood sweating into her blouse.

'Speechless, are you? Oh my, my dear Herr Frei – you must have made quite the impression! I believe the lady is going to swoon.'

The men started laughing. She pushed through them and staggered towards Otto. It must have looked to them as though she were drunk and had decided to throw herself around his neck. For a moment his ear was very close, and she aimed for it, came close enough to kiss.

'You lied to me,' she said.

And: 'Eva is in danger.'

Her hand found his, and tucked into his palm the jagged edge of Anton Beer's key. He pushed her away as though she had embarrassed him; listened angrily to the hooting of the men. Only then did it seem to dawn on him what he was holding. He excused himself and walked briskly out the room. Zuzka looked after him, shaking, while the youth leader next to her offered to escort her to a chair and, in the process, slipped a hand on to her inner thigh.

She let him do it. In the confusion that raged in her there were things that were soothed, not angered, by his clumsy touch.

CHAPTER 10

Beer did not notice Otto's entry until he marched past him down the corridor. It would not be accurate to say he ran: it wasn't the gait of a man trying to catch the train before it pulls out of the station. He might have walked ten miles like this to good effect, the long, steady stride of a man who knew his destination. His tread fell at the centre of Beer's sprawled-out legs. The doctor was sitting on the ground, covering both his ears: saw a shadow fall, followed by a much-worn leather sole. When Otto passed him, Beer looked after him as he might stare after a passing omnibus that had almost run him over. It took him far too long to get to his feet.

Otto walked into the bedroom. Beer wasted a moment looking back down the length of the corridor. He wanted to see whether the front door was closed. It was. When he finally stumbled after Otto, he was ten seconds off his pace. He expected the shouts of an argument, or the laboured breathing of two men engaged in struggle. Instead he heard nothing – the rush of his own blood – and was confused to find in his bedroom a scene of total calm. Eva lay there, uncovered and naked, her body frozen in her condition's false composure. At the foot of the bed stood her brother, big hands dangling from his wrists. Teuben lay splayed in front of him, his feet towards the doctor, the upper part of his body hidden by the corner of the bed. His leg moved a little – the right, his foot scraping for a toehold – and Otto bent down to him without any haste, picked him up by his shirt collar and smashed his head into the radiator underneath the window. The leg's movement ceased. It hardly took a second.

Confused, disorientated by how something so momentous could have happened so fast, Beer ran forward and fell to his knees right next to the detective. The man lay slumped on one side. His shirt was unbuttoned, as were his trousers, and he was no longer wearing his jacket or boots. At the top of his head two narrow furrows ran through the skull where he had hit the sharp-edged piping of the radiator's front. A separate collision, also with the radiator (each impact had left a smudge on its white paint), had cut open the cartilage that connected his left ear to the side of his face: it had come loose and dangled darkly against his jaw. It was from this wound that most of the blood was flowing, staining his hair, his neck and the shoulder of his white shirt a vivid red. Beer bent down to search his throat for a pulse, but found none. As he turned the detective from his side on to his back, the blood-wet shirt gaped across the chest, revealing those large lopsided nipples that Beer remembered from his initial examination of the man.

'You've killed him,' he said flatly, and stared over to where Otto was tugging Teuben's boots back on to his feet. He moved up the body, tucked the penis back into the trousers and stuffed the shirt inside the waistband, then did up its buttons one by one.

'Did you hear me, Otto? He's dead.'

The mime nodded absently, stepped to the window, opened the curtains and looked out. Whatever he saw seemed to displease him, but even so he hardly hesitated: turned back to the corpse, scooped hat and uniform jacket from off the floor and began threading first one arm, then the other through its sleeves. A bottle of beer fell out of the dead man's coat pocket and rolled under the bed. Otto ignored it. He seemed to expect no help from the doctor. Otto's features were absorbed by the most intense anger; and yet his body moved with peculiar precision and purpose, like that of an experienced soldier under fire. Beer, who had little experience of physical courage – he had never sat in a trench or faced a man intent on hurting him in earnest – recognised it now for what it was: not the laboured grappling of the soul with an act from which the body shrank, but action pure and simple, the doing of what needed to be done. In the same manner – wearing the same aspect, his face shaking, the movements calm –

Otto might have led a bayonet charge, or carried a dying comrade out of trouble. Beer watched how he put the hat on Teuben's head, then pulled it down to cover the mangled ear, which he tucked under. In the next instant he had dug his hands into the dead man's armpits and begun turning him around so that the head faced the doorway rather than the window.

'Take his feet,' he ordered.

When Beer didn't, Otto began to drag Teuben down the corridor on his own. He was halfway to the door before Beer found the composure to run after him and plead with him to stop.

'We mustn't move him,' he said. 'The police—'

Otto never even broke stride. 'What are you, crazy?' Only when he reached the front door did he set Teuben down.

'And where are you taking him?' Beer tried again. 'The staircase is full of people.'

But Otto was already opening the door. He turned off the light and slipped out, leaning the door to behind him. Beer heard him run down the stairs. A minute later, he returned. As he stepped back into Beer's hallway, he seemed to remember something, turned on his heel and ran to the door across the landing, pressing his eye to the neighbour's spyhole.

'Nobody there,' he grunted on his return. 'Take his feet.'

It did not occur to Beer now to disobey.

And so they walked out into the stairwell. The

414

lights were off, the space alive with far-off noises. Teuben's big, ungainly body hung between them like a slackly rolled carpet: on the stairs, his backside kept brushing against the ground. From the first, it was clear that Otto knew where they were heading. Beer froze when their boots crunched upon the broken glass that lay scattered across the stairs. The flaxen-haired youth was still lying there rolled up into his stupor: blood on his nose, the knees tucked up underneath his chin, wedged into the corner of the foot-wide step. Otto seemed untroubled by the man's presence. He gestured to Beer to set Teuben down in front of the empty window frame, then readjusted the detective's hat, which had threatened to come loose.

It was hard work to haul him up and push his head and upper body over the window's inch-wide ledge. Otto, it turned out, was as strong as a bear. Before them loomed the yard, looking dark and abandoned from this height. The chestnut branches shielded much from their view. At the last moment, when they were already bending down to take hold of Teuben's ankles, the mime reached around to unbutton the detective's fly again; tugged his penis through the Y-front of his underpants. They picked up his feet and calves until they were level with the window, then pushed. The dead man fell: silent, ungainly, head over heels. 'We'll never get away with it,' the doctor whispered, but he pushed Teuben out the window all the same, then stood in the window frame, watching him fall. The body hit a tree branch, then the crossbar of the iron frame that stood in the yard to assist the beating out of carpets: grazed it, left a chunk of face in the care of its cold metal, bounced and rolled. It came to rest half-buried in the piles of dead leaves that had gathered underneath the chestnut tree. Nobody shouted, nobody screamed; magpies rustling in the branches. Beer looked across the courtyard at the rows of windows blinkered by their curtains: his white, ironed shirt gleaming like a flag hung out into the night.

He stood there half a moment before Otto yanked him back inside. He yanked him hard and by the collar: two mother-of-pearl buttons popped near the throat and fell, lightly clicking on the ground to scatter amongst shards of glass. Cursing, but moving calmly nonetheless, Otto bent to retrieve them, then marched Beer back towards his flat. They entered, locked the door, stood staring at one another without uttering a word. Wordless still, they spilled into the kitchen. The mime saw the bottles of beer grouped loosely on the table and reached for one, only to watch the doctor snatch them up in a sudden panic, and upend them in the sink. His movements were so hasty, his hands so unsure of themselves, that he broke first one, then a second bottle, and cut his finger open on its jagged neck. Otto watched him with dark wonder; turned to his left to search the larder, found a bottle of brandy, which he uncorked and then set quickly to his lips. He swallowed and swallowed, breathing deeply through the nose, until half the contents were gone. His eyes grew glassy, the angry flush that had marked his face began to clear. Without a word he stepped up to the sink where Beer was still rinsing out the bottles, pushed him aside and washed some blood off his now trembling hands. Then he turned, stepped into the corridor, and ran out the door, quietly, not turning on the light, leaving behind the brandy, and a crumpled tea towel that he had thrown on to the ground.

THREE

When Elvira Hempel was a girl of three or four there lived near her parents' house a scrap-metal merchant who owned a clapped-out circus horse called Lotte. Lotte had very large and frightening teeth. On command the horse would throw itself down on to the ground and play dead. Then it would jump back to its feet. Elvira and her elder brother picked through the rubbish at the local tip, then sold it to the merchant. It seems he overpaid: he gave them soup to go with the pennies, in exchange for rusty tins and wire hangers; bent, broken spokes of worn-out umbrellas. There are some other childhood memories, from before the hospitals, asylums, orphanages, but not very many: how her father stole a goat and chickens, and a coffin for his deceased son; how her mother tied the youngest siblings to the legs of the kitchen table when she left them at home unsupervised. One day her father caught a dog in a wash basket. They ate it for supper. It was a sheepdog, that; he slaughtered it himself. It might have been 1935. In the 1990s, some fifty years after her sister was gassed, Elvira published these memories, along with those others: the years of eczema

421

and bed-wetting, the cold showers and the beatings, the day she stood naked next to a pile of shoes and clothes, and waited for her turn to pass the metal door ahead. She writes how she dreamed of owning a doll. She was six then, maybe seven, and needed something to beat up. In the end she made do with her little sister, Lisa, who, too, had been diagnosed and apprehended. There were other children on the ward: one was one-eyed, another had a pinhead; some were epileptics, and some had fathers who were vagabonds or thieves. There is a document that attests to Elvira's 'debility and psychopathology', signed by a Professor Fuenfgeld on the 6th of September 1938. In a separate document her parents, too, were declared feeble-minded though neither was examined nor threatened with incarceration. In the early 1940s, after several years spent in a borstal, her middle brother was inducted into the Waffen SS. Examination of his family tree had revealed him as a pure-bred Aryan; he served guarding prisoners in Magdeburg. Lisa was killed on the day before her fifth birthday. Elvira walked free after six years of institutionalisation. She was eleven. She does not know why she survived. She wasn't even sterilised. After the war, in the first year of occupation, she lived for some time with her father. They ate dog meat again. So did many others. She wrote it all down, a document of anger. There is a photo at the front of her book of Lisa looking at the camera. The child is two. She does not smile.

CHAPTER 1

On the night of the 4th of November, at 11.03 p.m., a body fell from the stairway window between the second and third floor of the apartment building at – *gasse* 19. It hit a number of branches of a chestnut tree, which – without themselves taking much damage – contrived to turn the falling body and redirect its face into the path of the carpet-beating frame's iron bar. The impact shattered parts of the left frontal, parietal, and malar bones; it ripped open one cheek and knocked off the falling man's hat, which came to rest, crown down, not far from his right hand. The man himself ended face down, arms outstretched, one knee raised in a near-ninety-degree angle, that is to say, in an aspect reminiscent of a crawling toddler who has lost his balance and has fallen flat on his face. The man's thick hair and the inch-deep heap of fallen leaves that surrounded his head served to mask the severity of the injury from casual observation.

For a good few hours yet, there was to be little such observation, casual or other. At the moment of the man's fall, the yard had but a single occupant, a burly, forty-seven-year-old Japanese male with a pockmarked exterior whom his neighbours routinely, if not maliciously, identified by a racial epithet pertaining to the Chinese. We know him as Herr Yuu. He had stepped into the yard from the narrow door leading to the apartment building's side wing (of which he was a resident) with the express purpose of recovering a bow tie that he had removed – and subsequently forgotten – during his performance at a festive gathering hosted by Professor Josef H. Speckstein on the first floor of the building's front wing. Yuu entered the yard at eleven sharp. It was not yet raining, despite the dense cloud cover that had gathered in the city's skies in the hours after dusk, and he, surprised to find no other guests of said festivity out in the yard, had lingered a moment to smoke a cigarette. His stomach was full, and he was dyspeptic, the result of consuming too hastily too great a variety of rich and sugary foods. The noise he heard was slight. The branches gave a rustle, some twigs were snapped off, and the metal bar sang out a ringing note that his musician's ear registered as a B flat. Of the man himself, Yuu saw nothing apart from his prone shadow. Confused by the noise, slight as it was, and the lumpen outline of the man, Yuu looked up and attempted to trace the trajectory and origin of what his ears had witnessed. What he saw was the white breast of a dress shirt leaning out the empty window frame above. It lingered for a breath or two, then withdrew with considerable haste. In the face of this event, Yuu, trumpeter, did

424

not persevere in his intention of retrieving the missing bow tie, but turned on his heel instead, and retreated into the side wing, at the top of which he was renting a garret room decorated with an unusual number of mirrors. There were no other witnesses.

At 11.19 that night, driven out by an urgent call of nature, a young, handsome *Rottenführer SS* emerged into the yard and parted with his water not two feet from the corpse. He was in an advanced state of inebriation. As he struggled with his trousers' fly, a bout of nausea overcame him. He fell to his knees and vomited up a mixture of tripe soup, roast beef in cream sauce, and apple strudel in custard; then, unable to keep his balance, he fell face down into the leaves and was soon overcome by sleep. Within minutes, two magpies swooped down from the higher branches of the tree and began pecking through his sick. A third magpie found a separate source of food clinging to the metal bar some yards away from them. Several other birds would join their efforts in the course of the night.

At 5.07 a.m., with no sign of dawn yet in the eastern skies, a sudden and intense rainstorm hailed down upon the scene, dispersing what was left of the vomit and washing off a good part of the organic matter that remained sticking to the iron bar. It roused the SS man, who, disorientated, turned on to his back, completed the buttoning of his fly which he had commenced six hours previously, and then staggered off without giving his surroundings a second look. He was pleased to find that the tram service was already up and running and would deliver him home in a matter of minutes.

At 5.39, the building's janitor entered the yard from the direction of his front-wing, ground-floor flat. Despite the prevailing gloom he saw the prone body almost at once and, walking over to shake it awake with the tip of his boot, realised that the man was dead rather than drunk. For a moment he stood over him and looked up at the windows surrounding him. All the curtains remained drawn. He shrugged, moved away from the corpse and unlocked the metal door leading to his cellar workshop, where he planned on eating some slices of sausage and drinking the day's first bottle of beer.

By 6.55 three further persons had passed the dead man. Two of these – Hermann Berger and Petr Novak – had not only noticed the body but quickly ascertained that it was dead. Neither raised the alarm. After a quick inspection of the windows above him, Hermann Berger continued on his way to join a friend whom he had promised to assist in the early-morning repair of his privately owned motorcycle, which had got mangled in a collision earlier that week. Afterwards the two friends planned on spending their Sunday in the Prater, away from their wives, drinking beer and partaking in its many amusements. Petr Novak had entered the yard because, having been woken by his wife's cold-induced snore, he had looked out the window and made out a boot through the latticework of branches of the slowly balding chestnut tree. Curiosity drove him down. When he found the boot belonged to a dead policeman in his dress uniform, he judged it best to return to his apartment and remain by the window until some other person had discovered the corpse.

It wasn't until half past seven that a neighbour, conscious of the various pairs of eyes that might be looking on, gave vent to her upset at finding a 'dead copper with a bashed-in head' out in the yard, and made enough noise to oblige Herr Novak (who owned a telephone) to dial for the police. Two young policemen presently showed up. Amongst the first of their actions, as several neighbours would subsequently confirm in pubs across the city district, was to tug at the dead man's thick mop of hair. They wished to ascertain whether or not it was a wig. It wasn't. By nine o'clock Teuben's body had been slipped on to a stretcher and carried off, and two detectives were making the rounds, questioning first the neighbours, then tracking down the guests who had attended Speckstein's party. But it was as so often in such cases.

Nobody had seen a thing.

CHAPTER 2

Lieschen woke a little after five. It was the rain that had woken her, a sudden storm that beat against the windowpane at the far end of Beer's study and raised her startled from a dream. The girl had slept on the floor, on the little nest she had made from two of Beer's blankets. She had fallen asleep shortly after being locked in by the doctor, her colouring pencil still in her hand; had woken once, an hour or so later, needing to use the chamber pot that Beer had provided, and then been unable to sleep as several shadows had passed the locked door. Frightened, suspicious, she had walked over to the keyhole and looked out. She had seen a pair of legs and polished boots being dragged past the door, closely followed by the doctor. A little later he had returned and begun to crawl on his hands and knees up and down the corridor, a tea towel in his hand, his face close to the ground. A bucket of water had been by his side. He'd pushed it along as he had crawled forward inch by inch, on his way to Eva's room. Somewhat shaken by this odd behaviour, the girl had retreated to her nest

428

and once again fallen asleep, burying herself deeper and deeper in the blankets, then kicking them off altogether later in the night.

It was cold when she woke, and the patter of raindrops confused her. Around her, half crumpled, lay the pictures she had drawn the previous day, a collection of animals that rustled as she stepped over them with naked feet. There was very little light. The curtains leaked a little of the city's luminescence. It sufficed for the girl to make her way from blankets to window. Rather than pushing the curtain aside, she crawled under it and emerged on the other side: stared at the raindrops streaking down the pane. The yard was dark beneath her, though there was in this darkness the suggestion of shadows: of the tree whose crown spread out before the window; and of something moving down below. Curious, Lieschen opened the window and leaned out enough to see straight down. Somebody switched on the light in the hallway that connected the courtyard to the building's front door: his shadow was thrown into the yard. The light was soon switched off again. And yet, in this brief interval of illumination, staring through the swaying branches of the tree, the girl thought to have made out the shape of someone lying in the yard, and held on to the impression of a pair of boots, black and polished, the heel of one gently wedged into the shaft of the other, and the toes pointed out.

In the darkness that resumed it would have been

429

easy to dismiss the vision as a flight of fancy: it was cold and rain kept blowing in; there was a warm and cosy nest of blankets not five steps away. But the girl decided to stay where she was and even leaned further out on occasion, exposing more of herself to the elements. For the next three hours she stayed at the window, leaving only twice: once to fetch some blankets and wrap them around her frame, and a second time to scoop up the hedgehog, which she could hear scrambling around near the table behind her, and lift it up on to the windowsill, where it sat, unmoving, twitching its nose at the rain.

The downpour passed, and very gradually some light began to permeate the yard. With every minute she became more convinced there was a body stretched out in the leaves beneath the tree, though at any given moment she could see only a part of it through the ever-changing constellation of its swaying branches. She watched the janitor come into the yard and walk over to what she thought to be a boot; watched Herr Berger and Herr Novak crouch down next to the prone form. They all looked up but not one of them saw her, standing between the curtain and the windowsill, the twitching hedgehog by her side. By the time the police arrived, a group of neighbours had formed a ring around the man and stood talking, smoking, shuffling their feet.

At this point Lieschen's attention wandered elsewhere. The hedgehog, having grown confident after hours of dormancy, had begun to explore the dimensions of the wet windowsill and was inching ever closer to its edge. She watched its slow, grasping movements with peculiar fascination: rested her chin on the window frame, and clasped her hands behind her back as though to prevent herself from making any move to save it. The hedgehog reached the edge and teetered; one of its feet had stepped into emptiness and the others were scrambling for balance, a movement that only brought the animal closer to its doom. In the last instant, when the hedgehog had already begun to curl itself into a ball to avert this unknown danger, Lieschen suddenly cried out and snatched it up. She did it so clumsily that her left hand batted the animal rather than grasping it, and it was only by clapping together both hands with great force that she managed to gather it up. A good dozen of the spikes buried themselves in her palms and wrists. The punctures did not bleed but immediately started to itch. Lieschen turned away from the window, pushing aside the curtain as she did so, and dropped the hedgehog on to the floor. There it remained motionless, rolled up into its ball. The girl stared at it, head bowed, and for the first time in many days she felt like crying.

When Lieschen looked up, Beer was standing in the door watching her. He walked over to her, drew aside the curtain that still clung to her narrow, crooked shoulders and looked out.

'So you already know,' he murmured, and

crouched down beside her. He seemed to want to say more, but kept stumbling over his words. His hands rose, tried to touch her, but Lieschen dodged them, stepped away. One of Beer's fingers was bandaged. The girl sat down on the blankets and massaged her itching hands.

'It's like this. I might have to go away for some weeks. On business, you see. If – if I am not back by tonight, find Zuzka. You will, won't you? You like her.'

The girl did not respond or even look up, and when he inched closer and tried to touch her hair she once again evaded him. His cheeks, she noticed, were pale and as though shaking, and he had not yet shaved. After some minutes, he stood up and began to walk out. She caught him up in the corridor, pulled at his coat-tails with finger and thumb.

'I'm hungry,' she said.

It was a surprise to see how happy this made him: his whole face lit up.

'Come then,' he said, ran ahead to the kitchen and cut her some slices of their two-day-old bread.

CHAPTER 3

Beer sat and watched the girl have breakfast. She was quiet, her hands were red and swollen, but she was eating one slice of buttered bread after the other, piling on strawberry preserve with a spoon. Sometimes, when she thought he wouldn't notice, she looked up and searched his face. It took him some minutes to name the emotion that spread across her features during these furtive looks. Pity. And yet she kept her distance, and flinched every time he moved too fast.

Beer was tired. He had been up much of the night, crawling along his floorboards and cleaning up every speck of blood he could discover. There hadn't been much. Teuben's hat and uniform had served as effective bandages. Three times he had ventured out on to the landing to see if there was any obvious trail leading back towards the flat, but had seen nothing at all, just the muddy dirt of a stairwell that had not been cleaned for days. In the end he had fallen asleep in the living room. By the time he woke up, the police were in the house.

It was Sunday, the day of rest. After breakfast, Beer spent an hour drawing the remaining letters of the alphabet on to the cards he had prepared for the purpose. When he was done, he put them away in his desk and went to tend to Eva. Ever since leaving for Speckstein's party he had barely been able to look at her. Her eyes seemed to bore into him, an unfaltering stare, the sclera yellow and inflamed. Beer had no words to counter this stare. He fed and hydrated Eva as one did a plant. When he turned his back on her, some aural illusion suggested to him that she was doing likewise: he heard the rustle of her cotton sheet. It made him pick up the pace. Later, when he stood in the bathroom, trying to shave, the blade kept catching on a mole upon his cheek. He left the door open so he would hear when the police came knocking.

As the hours of the morning passed and the police still had not come for him, Beer found his thoughts drifting above all to the morgue, that dank and smelly room in which one rifled through the dead, as he had done with Grotter, Teuben watching, sucking on his mints. It seemed inconceivable to him that the pathologist on duty would not notice the twin grooves in the detective's skull and conclude that they did not match up with the trauma received during his fall into the yard.

When the police finally arrived on his doorstep, he felt relieved. It was three o'clock in the afternoon. It was an old detective, fifty-five going on sixty, a short man with narrow shoulders who had the appearance of having recently lost a lot of weight. His cheeks hung pale and lifeless in his clean-shaven face, the balding head looked careworn and wrinkled. Only the eyes were sympathetic, blue, round and sleepy, embedded in a web of lines.

'Detective Boltzmann,' he introduced himself, reaching out a little hand in greeting. 'Like the physicist. Could I have a minute of your time?'

Beer nodded and stepped aside to let the man into his flat, having checked first that the bedroom door was closed. But the detective made no move to come inside and motioned Beer into the hallway instead.

'If you don't mind, I would like to talk to you at the station.'

Beer agreed, fetched his hat and coat, and followed the man down the stairs. Outside, Detective Boltzmann opened the door of a Mercedes and closed it gently once Beer had settled himself in the passenger seat. There was no driver. Boltzmann took the wheel himself.

'If you don't mind, let's not talk until we get there. I'm a terrible driver. Better keep my mind on the road.'

Despite this announcement, they made their way across the city quickly and efficiently. Inside the police station, the detective gestured for Beer to lead the way, occasionally offering a soft-spoken word of direction. Boltzmann's office was three doors down from Teuben's. It was a much smaller

435

room, and much better appointed: held a desk, two upholstered chairs, several bookshelves and a large, hand-coloured map of Vienna. At the detective's invitation, Beer took a seat. He was half inclined to make a clean breast of things. The thought of lying to this man exhausted him. In the end it was little but habit that stayed his tongue. Tired, thanking the man for his kindness, he accepted the detective's offer of a cup of coffee and a cigarette.

The interview began. There was a frank directness to Boltzmann's manner that Beer found pleasant. He answered all questions as simply and accurately as he thought safe.

'You know, of course, that Detective Teuben is dead.'

'Yes. I saw it from the window. This morning, I mean. Some policemen were carrying him off.'

'But you did not feel you should go down and offer your services?'

'No.'

'Why not?'

'I hardly knew the man. And I supposed a doctor was no longer needed.'

'He consulted you on a string of murders he was investigating, did he not? And he asked you to perform an autopsy for him, circumventing normal procedure. I found the report among his papers.'

'Yes.'

The detective pursed his lips, perhaps to indicate that his was an unpleasant duty.

'You were both at Herr Professor Speckstein's party. I have two witnesses who saw you go up the stairs with him some time after ten o'clock.'

'He asked me for a word. I took him to my surgery, so we could talk in peace. He said that he had solved the case.'

'And?'

Beer paused, opted for the truth.

'He wanted me to rewrite the autopsy report.'

'To what purpose?'

'To suggest that there were possibilities other than self-harm.'

Boltzmann nodded, as though this tallied with his assumptions.

'And did you?' he asked, then bent across the table to offer Beer a second cigarette.

'I said I would take another look at my notes,' Beer answered, colouring. 'See whether I made a mistake.'

The detective waved his hand to indicate he understood the doctor's predicament. 'How long did he stay?' he asked.

'Not much more than ten minutes. I offered him some brandy. He knocked back two or three quick glasses.'

'He was drunk.'

'I suppose. Did he fall out that window or—?'

'Or was he pushed? It seems you are a natural policeman, Dr Beer. Perhaps it is not so odd he consulted you after all.'

Boltzmann leaned back in his chair and folded

his hands behind his back. Once again Beer was struck by how emaciated the man looked. It was clear that he was suffering – or had only very recently recovered – from a serious illness. His shirt collar looked two sizes too big.

'I think we can dismiss foul play,' the detective continued. 'He was a big man, and there is no evidence of violence on the stairs. The window was shattered much earlier, and there was a drunken youth sleeping underneath who tells us he didn't leave until dawn. Who'd be crazy enough to take the risk?'

He paused, shook his head again, settled forward in his chair.

'No, he fell out while pissing, like an idiot. And I am left with all his notes.'

He reached into his desk and pulled out several thin folders.

'They used to be my cases, you know. The dog, that is, and two of the other killings. But then I had to take a leave of absence. May I ask what you told him when he asked you for your opinion about the murders?'

'I told him they were in all probability unrelated. That there was a chance that the women had been attacked by the same assailant, no more. That the rest was just rumour and coincidence caused by anxiety about the war.'

'And what did he say to that?'

'He told me he had a suspect who would clear all his files.'

Boltzmann nodded, scratched his throat. None of this seemed to surprise him, but he seemed glad about the corroboration Beer was providing.

'Yes. He was cooking his own soup. Had a young man in custody downstairs, and a confession typed out for him ready to sign. I talked to the boy earlier today. Two broken fingers, happy to accuse himself of anything I suggested.'

He snorted, a hint of anger creeping into his sleepy blue eyes.

'He picked him well, Teuben did. Semi-literate degenerate getting by on a menial job. Teuben even found some women who know the boy and are willing to testify that he's been acting queer. Nothing concrete, of course, odd looks and phrases, but enough to spin a story in court. Groomed the boy, and got him ready for the stand. Teuben even told him that he'd become famous. Bigger than Kürten, Haarmann, the lot – that's what he promised him.'

'He is innocent then?'

Boltzmann shrugged, tugged at his tired cheek.

'The funny thing about people is that, if you tell them they are intelligent, or beautiful, or important, they believe you. Not at once, of course. The first time you say it, they protest and tell you they are nothing of the sort, and that all these others who have spent years telling them they are stupid, and ugly, and inconsequential had it right all along. But if you repeat it long enough, the thought occurs to them that you are telling the truth, because in the depths of them, tucked away somewhere, they have always considered themselves intelligent, beautiful and so on. And conversely, if you tell a man he is a scoundrel, or better: a louse (it's good to put a picture to this sort of thing), and keep telling him, all the while treating him just so (that is to say as a louse and nothing but a louse), well, he'll soon discover in his heart that this is what he is and knew himself all along to be, precisely, a louse. Some people' – here he made an expansive gesture, as though buttering a large slice of bread, first on one side, than on the other – 'they are more easily moved in one direction, and some in the other, depending on how they are knit, but in the end' – he finished the buttering and held up the invisible slice – 'it comes to the same. And guilt, let me tell you, guilt is the easiest lie of all. After all, in his heart, who has not murdered?'

He finished, exhausted, pleased with himself. 'But anyway, look who I am preaching to.'

He paused just long enough for Beer to misinterpret the phrase.

'You are a psychiatrist. You have no need for my policeman's theories.'

They sat in silence until a noise distracted them. It came from outside the room, a woman's high-pitched shout. Boltzmann rose from his chair, rounded his desk, and opened the door. The shouts grew louder, but no more distinct. Whoever the woman was, she was clearly in a state of deep distress. Disturbed by the sound, thinking that his services might be required, Beer rose and stood behind Boltzmann in the half-open door. At the far end of the corridor – where it opened into the front reception area – there stood a woman dressed in black. Her son was by her side. The boy was anaemic-looking, nine, maybe ten years of age, had dark hair and rings around his eyes. The woman was shouting at two uniformed policemen who were holding her by the arms and trying to calm her down. She was clutching the boy's wrist with obvious violence. The child did not complain but simply stood there, staring up at his mother.

'Teuben's wife,' Boltzmann murmured over one narrow shoulder. 'She has been three times already.'

The policemen were dragging her over to a chair, then leaned on her shoulders to force her to sit down. The boy staggered after her, dragged along by her white-knuckled grip. He was wearing a little velvet jacket. The collar was askew. Beer could not take his eyes off him.

'It's hard to make sense of,' Boltzmann went on. 'He was a real swine, Teuben was. And yet she loved him.'

Gently, as though not to startle anyone, the detective closed the door and returned to his chair. Beer remained where he was, standing in front of the closed door, though he turned around to face Boltzmann when the detective resumed their conversation.

'Well I suppose that settles it, Dr Beer. All there remains to do is for me to call the Chief and tell him the good news. That we are stuck with five unsolved murders, and not a suspect to our name.'

Beer tried to focus on the detective, his mind still busy with the boy. 'Won't he be upset?' he asked. 'Teuben hinted that the people in charge would prefer a clean solution.'

The detective smiled – sadly, it seemed to Beer – straightened some papers on his desk.

'I have cancer of the bowel, Dr Beer. It's unpleasant, but it releases me of any need to be politic in my dealings with power.'

He stood, smoothed down his shirt, held a hand out to Beer. They shook across his desk.

'Thank you for your time.'

Beer turned, drifted towards the door, then stopped himself short.

'Morphine,' he said quietly. 'Find someone who will sell you morphine. Take lots of it. It won't cure anything, but—'

'Thank you, Dr Beer.'

On the way out, Beer was afraid he would run into the woman and her boy, but it seemed they had been ushered out of sight. From behind one of the many doors there issued the sound of her shouting, quieter now, her voice trembling under the strain. Beer fought the instinct to break into a run.

It wasn't until he was back at the front of his own building and stood staring up at its familiar façade that a sense of relief began to displace the thought of Teuben's son. The police had dismissed Teuben's death as an accident. Otto's brazen action was to have no consequence; Eva was safe. As he climbed the stairs and passed the first-floor landing he bumped into Yuu. The trumpeter was closing the door to Speckstein's flat behind himself and looked flustered when he recognised Beer. The ground beneath their feet remained littered with cigarette butts and broken glass; it crunched when they moved.

'I for-got my bow tie,' said the Oriental in his high, lilting voice.

Beer shrugged, muttered a greeting, brushed quickly past. Upstairs in his room, he sat down in his armchair and poured himself a drink. All his problems were solved. All he needed to do now was to find a home for Lieschen. He took a sip and wondered whether his wife could be convinced to take an interest in the crippled girl.

CHAPTER 4

While Beer was speaking to Boltzmann at the police station, Zuzka went to see Otto. It was the middle of the afternoon. The police had quit the building some hours ago and a sense of Sunday quiet had settled in, despite the events of the morning; the smell of baking was spreading through the yard. Her uncle had been questioned extensively, of course, but had forestalled any interrogation of his niece. All day then, she had spent in bed, getting up on occasion to stand by the window and watch the scene down below. There was no doubt in her mind as to what had occurred. Her symptoms were better, though there remained an awkward limp.

When she walked over to Otto's rooms, she did so in plain view, defying the gaze of Frau Berger, who was leaning out the window, staring at her. The mime opened his door at once, and asked her in. He seemed unchanged: laughter, anger, suspicion running through his features in constant succession. He flopped down on the bed and gestured for her to join him, but she remained standing, studying its dirty sheets. Otto shrugged, picked up a beer bottle, drank from it, then wedged it insolently between the tops of his thighs. Zuzka blushed and looked away. Her eyes found the sink and splattered mirror. It was easier to speak to him like this, looking only at herself.

'You lied to me,' she said. 'The girl in the article. The medium, or whatever she was. She isn't Eva.'

He gave her no answer, sat breathing behind her, quiet on his bed.

'Why did you kill Uncle's dog?'

'Who says I did?'

His voice was mocking, playful. He had spoken like that when he'd told her to step out of her skirt. It had made her bashful then; aroused. It made her angry now.

'I know you killed the detective,' she hissed, turning around to face him in her anger. 'You threw him out the window. I will tell them everything. Everything.'

She took two steps towards the bed. On it sat Otto and stared back at her, first fearful, then predatory, the muscles bunching in his face.

'What do you want?'

She thought about this, bit her lip. When she replied it was to stall for time.

'Tell me what happened to Eva. How did she get to be the way she is?'

So he told her, his body moving with the story, frowns and gestures filling in the gaps. 'When we were thirteen,' he said. 'She was laying cards, telling the future. Mother had taught her, and she was making good money, attracting big crowds. She worked on a stage, telling people what was in their pockets, or on their minds. Afterwards, you could come to her tent. Get a proper reading. Women asking who'd they marry, were they with child. A lot of people came. She never got it wrong.

'One night, after the show, a man went in to hear his fortune. He was a gentleman, a doctor, a lawyer, I don't know. I never even saw him. He came out the tent very pale and told us that Eva had some sort of seizure. Mother rushed in and right away there was a lot of shouting. She kept yelling it was rape. The man ran away. Father went looking for him. Late that night he came home, and his fists and shirt were all bloody. Maybe he found him, or maybe he got drunk and into a fight. As for Eva, she stopped speaking, moving, bit by bit. Would stare at us with those eyes she has. We took her to the doctor, but it was no use.'

He shrugged, swung himself up from the bed, knocking over the beer that had nestled against his crotch. The liquid poured out and soaked into his mattress and sheet. She saw it, slipped past him, reached for the bottle with shaking hands.

'You love her,' she said, struck by the thought. 'I always thought you wanted rid of her.'

He grunted, took the bottle away from her, dropped it on the floor. His hands, when they reached for her, seemed enormous to her: two calloused shovels folding over her shoulders and

446

back. Up close he stank. His cotton vest was stiff with old sweat.

'I'm going away,' she said, then kissed him on his mouth. All her fear poured into that kiss, and all that yearning she thought of as love. But when she opened her eyes halfway through, she caught him watching her with calculation, not tenderness. She let go of him then, and ran out the room, her heels very noisy as though she were punishing the stairs.

CHAPTER 5

Frau Vesalius came to fetch Beer a good hour after he had finished his dinner. He assumed it was to tend to Zuzka's hypochondria and accepted with good humour, then was surprised when the housekeeper led him into Speckstein's living room instead. Other than the faint smell of cigarette smoke that clung to the walls, there remained little sign of the mess made by the party. The Professor stood in the door to his study and bid him come in. He seemed nervous, was dressed in the elaborate type of hip-length dressing gown that the English called a smoking jacket; his stockinged feet were stuck in a pair of embroidered slippers. Sitting down behind his desk and picking a cigar from a wooden box, he struck Beer as out of place, a social remnant from a different era trying hard to cope with the new mores. His uniform, Beer noticed, was no longer hanging from its habitual hook on the back of the door.

'Are you under the weather, Professor?' Beer enquired politely as he took a seat in the chair indicated by his host. 'Anything I can do for you?'

Speckstein stared at the doctor as though the

448

answer to his question required a great act of thought. It took him a moment to locate the cigar cutter and remove the cigar's tip, then light it with a match. When the cigar was fully lit, and he had puffed two or three plumes of aromatic blue smoke into the air above their heads, the Professor seemed to have collected himself sufficiently to speak. He started very quietly, his melodious Viennese strangely at odds with his words.

'You loathe me,' he said, not looking at Beer. 'You think it should be beneath me, playing spy for the Party. Do you know what the common people call us, the *Blockwarte* and *Zellenwarte* of this world? *Treppenterrier.* Terriers of the stairwell. Always barking up some leg. And quite right they are. It *is* rather shameful. But what am I to do, Dr Beer? Accustom myself to my own obscurity? It chafes, let me tell you, and over the years, the heart breaks out in a rash. I can see you smirking. You do not approve of metaphors, it seems. Not from a man of science. Smirk away, Dr Beer. I know you have been smirking all along.

'Do you know how I lost my position at the university? I suppose you were a student then. All I did was agree to a friendly request. There was to be a scientific observation of a so-called medium. Politicians, physicists, writers – half the city had already been invited and many a sceptic confessed himself impressed. I was asked to examine the girl and watch her as she changed into a specially prepared suit. She was fourteen, pubescent, pimples on her chin. They led me to a back room. I performed the examination, then watched her strip naked, climb into the suit. The girl, I remember, was unperturbed. She stripped off like a seasoned *grisette*; grinned at me while I stood at the sink washing my hands. She performed and conjured up, I don't know how, the ghostly image of a bearded man that some held to be Rasputin and others identified as a murderer who was to be executed later that week. We had dinner, congratulated the girl's parents on her talents, and discussed theories of how her trick might be achieved. I went home, had another drink, and went to bed.

'Two days later a policeman showed up on my doorstep informing me that the girl's father was charging me with rape and molestation. A medical report left little doubt that she had been violated. My defence counsel dared to suggest that the girl's own father made a more likely suspect – he'd been a simple innkeeper before his daughter brought him fame, with a history of skirt-chasing – and the public rose in uproar. When the girl was called into the witness stand, she refused to speak but pointed to me repeatedly when asked to identify the perpetrator. Through some miracle I was acquitted, but my reputation was shot. I felt I had no choice but to resign. I even moved house, into this shabby building full of proles. And for ten years, everywhere I went, people pointed their fingers at me and called me a monster while addressing me as "Herr Professor" to my face.'

450

He paused, exhausted. As he spoke he had mangled his cigar between his fingers. He noticed it now, extinguished it, and threw it in the waste basket. Beer had listened without making a sound, acutely embarrassed by the whole situation.

'But I can see by the look on your face that you don't believe me, Dr Beer. I was acquitted, I resigned like a gentleman, and yet nobody has ever believed me.'

The Professor reached forward for another cigar, then abandoned the thought no sooner had he opened the wooden box. His eyes were pleading with Beer to break his silence. The doctor stood, began walking towards the door.

'I'm very sorry, Professor. I really cannot see why you summoned me here. If you'll excuse me.'

'Dr Beer. I have been told you pushed the detective out the window after the party last night. There is a credible witness who says he saw you do it. I feel it is my duty to pass it on to the police.'

Beer stopped dead in his tracks.

'Do you deny it?'

'May I –' he said. 'Pardon me, Professor, but may I use your bathroom? I am feeling a little sick.'

He ran out of the room before Speckstein was able to grant him his request.

When Beer returned, he looked pale but composed. Frau Vesalius was there, pouring out two cups of tea. The Professor waited until she had left before he resumed their conversation.

'I take it then,' he said, 'that you do not deny the charge.'

'It's more complicated than that,' Beer told him simply, and sipped his tea.

'Well, you can explain it to the police. I will call them first thing tomorrow.'

'Tomorrow?'

'Yes. It occurred to me that you might like the night to put your affairs in order.'

'Thank you, Professor.'

'Don't mention it. It is a small courtesy. From one physician to another.' He gave a quaint little bow. 'Just one more thing, Dr Beer. Do you know who killed my dog?'

Beer thought for a long time before he answered.

'Some hooligan,' he said at last. 'Because of your position, I suppose. It has no connection to the murders.'

The Professor nodded sadly, and turned his attention over to his tea. Beer was dismissed.

Before leaving the Professor's flat, Beer stopped off in the kitchen, ostensibly to return the cup he was still holding. Vesalius was there. He could not tell how much of their conversation she had over-heard. It did not matter either way.

'Frau Vesalius,' he said.

'Herr Doktor?'

'Could I ask you to tell Fräulein Speckstein that I'm in the house and would like to check on her health?'

'Of course.'

The housekeeper walked out and returned momentarily.

'I'm afraid she does not want to see you,' she said.

The doctor nodded. His voice betrayed his impatience. 'Tell her it's about Lieschen.'

Vesalius shrugged, and went back to Zuzka's room a second time. Again she returned shaking her head.

'I am to tell you she does not care who it is about.'

Beer frowned, puffed out his cheeks, then marched out of the flat without another word. Vesalius looked after him for several moments. She had not been quite honest with the man. Zuzka had cried herself asleep hours ago. The housekeeper had not bothered her with either of the doctor's queries. It was time, she had decided, that the girl climbed on a train and was on her way back home.

CHAPTER 6

When Beer closed the Professor's door behind himself, he did not climb the stairs back up to his own flat but instead headed downwards and out into the street. He had no destination in his mind: he simply wished for air, and to stretch his legs; avoid the scrutiny of the two cripples whom fate had stranded in his life. It was past ten at night, and the street was near deserted. Beer had no overcoat and soon began to shiver. For the first time that autumn he thought he could smell the impending winter. Perhaps it would snow.

For the length of a cigarette Beer paced the pavement in front of the building and found himself somehow peculiarly charmed by the changes of light as he stepped in and out of the lamp post's yellow glare. With every step his shadow wavered, breathing an odd sense of animation into trees and trash cans, the broken bottles lolling in the gutter. Ever since he'd been a boy, Beer had thought that there was a strange sort of magic to the night, when the material things – dirty, ordinary things, the debris of the everyday – took on a significance at once sinister and beguiling. Every broken cobble turned into a sign. He reached for the wall to steady himself, then dug a fingernail into the muck that clung to its old plaster.

A cat called. There were puddles on the ground, muddy and shallow, their edges caked with rotting leaves and cigarette ends. He stepped in one, watched the water part around his sole, felt it soak into the leather. A cat called, the same or some other, announcing its availability for all to hear. Beer lit a new cigarette and followed her call. He found her at last, sitting on a blown-out tyre behind the metal gate that led to the Pollaks' abandoned yard. She called again, hopped down, then sniffed the ground, an orange tabby, slight of frame. Perhaps she could smell the old dog's blood. Her tail was raised along with her rump, the shoulders lowered into a submissive crouch. When she became aware of the doctor's presence (he must have shifted in his stance, his head bent low before the grille that surrounded the gate's lock), she shivered and leapt, was lost amongst the junk. Beer watched her disappear, then turned to his left and made his way into the building. More boldly than he had some weeks ago, not caring when his jacket elbow snagged on a broken nail, the doctor negotiated the soot-stained corridors and boarded-up doorway and carried on towards the workshop and yard. The smell of urine hit him as he stepped into the workshop's little kitchen; its shelves had been robbed of their rows of penny cups. Outside, he stumbled amongst the heaps of trash until he thought he had found the place where Walter had lain and been discovered. He crouched and thought of Lieschen, throwing herself down amongst the dirt: the bend of her misshapen body, the little dress pushed up to reveal her knickers and her thighs. Not far from him, the cat called again, needy, driven, soliciting a tom. She fell silent when Beer straightened and headed back towards the building; he saw her swishing her red tail. For some yards she followed him, then leapt into the sink in the abandoned kitchen and sat there licking her own paws. The doctor smiled and bid her farewell.

When Beer stepped back out into the tunnel that led from metal gate to street, he was startled to see a man leaning against the wall diagonally across, his hips and back arched forward so that only the shoulder blades made contact with the brick. His left hand was buried deep within his trouser pocket and seemed to be rummaging for some unknown thing. His right hand hung motionless by his side and looked bulky, as though encased in a bandage, or a cast. There was very little light in the gateway, but the doctor thought he made out the horsey outline of the laundry boy's chin. His eyes had been closed, but just then they snapped open, and a low moan escaped his mouth. A moment later, the laundry boy realised Beer was standing not four feet away.

He reacted at once. The left hand stopped its

rhythmic movement, the right hanging heavy, like a club. He peeled himself off the wall, and began to walk away from the doctor, heading for the street ahead. Perhaps he was but an apparition: within two steps he had turned into a shadow moving amongst shadows, his footsteps' patter a quiet drumbeat in the dark. When Beer spoke it was directed at the building itself, the peeling walls and broken windows; the clods of rat shit smeared into its cracks.

'I'm a coward,' Beer called into the darkness. 'A coward, a coward. Though it was brave of me to take her in.'

It was impossible to tell whether the laundry boy understood or was simply frightened by the voice that was shouting at him in the dark. Picking up his pace, his right shoulder slumping from the weight of the cast, he took three more steps and reached the end of the short tunnel; turned to his right and was lost from sight.

'You're a louse!' Beer yelled after him. 'A louse. And I – I am an intelligent man.'

He smoked one last cigarette, threw it in a puddle, then pulled out his wallet to see how much money it held. A moment later he had left the gateway, headed back towards his house, then crossed the yard and mounted the stairs in the building's side wing.

Anton Beer had made up his mind how to proceed.

CHAPTER 7

The first thing Beer did, when Otto let him in, was switch off the lights. Later, during the days of his interrogation, it might help if no witness had seen them talk. Otto grunted, shrugged, but did not object. They sat down together, thigh to thigh, upon the dirty bed. Beer reached for his wallet. For a giddy moment it was as though he'd engaged Otto to become his lover: the strange and solemn moment when money exchanged hands. Beer liked them cleaner, not this rough. He wondered what Otto would have done, had he known his thought. As it was, he received the banknotes without murmur. It was too dark to say whether he was surprised.

'There is something I need to know first,' Beer said to him. 'Before I can tell you what the money is for. You killed someone some weeks ago. A law student. The same night the dog got killed. He was found near the Gürtel, the face smashed in, multiple stab wounds in his neck and chest. You really must have hated the man. A white smudge from your face paint was found on his sleeve. And afterwards you came home to wash your bloody hands.'

Beer paused, turned his face to the mime. Now that his eyes had adjusted to the gloom, he could make out Otto's eyes. They were sitting so close, Otto's breath was falling on his face, the bitter smell of beer.

'I need to know, Otto. Why did you kill him?'

'I didn't.'

'I know you did, Otto. And I don't much care. I just need to know why. There is a lot of money in it for you, if you give me a satisfactory answer.'

Otto hesitated, stood up. The motion was seamless: he did not rock back to gather momentum, or push off with his hands. He simply pulled himself up by the strength of his legs.

'He was my landlady's son,' Otto said. 'The last place I lived. Before moving here. I told them Eva was sick. An accident. The landlady sat with her sometimes, fed her her food, turned her over in her bed. But there was always her son, sniffing around.'

'Did he threaten you?'

'He talked about those movies. *Erbkrank*, the lot. Left me pamphlets on the dinner table. But that wasn't what he wanted. He—'

Otto paused, lashed out at the mirror. It wasn't so much a punch as a swipe, palm open, clawing at the reflection of his face.

'Same as Teuben,' he went on, his voice shaking with anger. 'One evening, when I was away.'

Beer understood. 'He raped her. How did you know? Did he injure her?'

Otto shook his head. 'No. But I knew all the same. So I moved house. It took me days to find a flat, there's nothing going, even with the Jews all skipping town. Three days it took me, and him grinning at me across the breakfast table. At last I found this hole; paid through the nose, I did, and tried to forget about that swine. Until I saw him come to watch my show. For a laugh, I suppose, to rub it in. When the show was over, I followed him out. I was worried he'd notice my face. The paint, I mean; I didn't have time to go clean up. So I did what I always do when I go home: put on a cap, tied the scarf all the way up to the eyes. He never even turned around. On the Gürtel he stopped off at a whore's. I got him when he came out. He wasn't grinning when I was done.'

Overcome once more by his old anger, Otto kicked over the chair, then took position in front of Beer, both fists rammed into the sides of his hips. Even more so than during their conversation on the bed, his proximity felt out of place. Beer sat staring straight at his crotch.

'So why are you here, Dr Beer?'

Beer rose, stepped past the mime; bent down and righted the chair Otto had knocked over, then stood holding on to its back.

'It's like this, Otto. Somebody saw us. Saw me. At the window. Speckstein knows and he will tell the police. Tomorrow morning I will be arrested. And a few days later, so will you. Unless you run away.'

460

Halfway through Beer's explanation, Otto had started to shake his head.

'I'm not running away! Not now. I met people at the party. Important people. They liked my show. Things are looking good for me.'

'You are not listening. I will be arrested. It might take a day or a week, but sooner or later I will tell them the truth. Then they'll come after you.'

Otto stared at him, stepped over, put a big hand on Beer's chest.

'You're threatening me.'

'I'm telling you what will happen. But there's a way you can go free. And make some money at the same time. I just needed to know you had a good reason to kill that man.'

Otto thought about it. The light of the moon came in through the window and caught his face full on. It was as though he had reapplied his paint. Beer looked at him, his heart beating against Otto's palm. He counted twenty beats until the mime made up his mind.

'How?' he asked at last.

'I will give you a letter, some more cash. The letter will be addressed to my wife. She lives in Switzerland. You take a train to Vorarlberg or the Tyrol – don't tell me which, the less I know the better. You can buy a day visa at the border, if you think your papers can stand the scrutiny. Or else you have to bribe a local to lead you across the mountains. The letter will instruct my wife to sign

461

over to you a thousand reichsmarks. In whatever currency you please. As simple as that.'

Otto listened to these instructions, let go of Beer's chest. Every time he moved the moon cut new shapes out of his face.

'Why help me? I killed him. Why not just give me up to the police?'

'Because there is something else you have to do, Otto. You have to take the little girl along. Anneliese. There won't be any money if you don't bring the girl. That's what the letter will say. If it's only you – then there won't be a penny.'

Beer had thought that Otto would be insulted by these terms, or ridicule the thought of dragging a ten-year-old girl across mountains in November, but he simply nodded as though he thought their bargain was fair. Slowly, giving himself a few more seconds to think it through, he raised his palm, spat in it, then offered it to Beer. Somewhat awkwardly, Beer repeated the gesture: he too spat in his palm, then accepted the handshake. Once in his grasp, Otto held on to him.

'And Eva?'

'She'll be safe. I have a plan.'

A lightning struggle ran through Otto's features: concern, suspicion, fear for his sister wrestling with the wish to hand her over for good.

Beer made it easy for him.

'It's better you don't know the details. Do you need to see her? Say goodbye?'

He answered without hesitation. Relief shone in his eyes, so obvious as to be indecent.

'No.'

'Then I'll meet you outside the front door, at a quarter past four. You can catch the first tram to the station.'

Beer wished to leave, but still Otto held on to his hand. The mime's left dipped into his shirt pocket, picked out a cigarette, stuck it in his mouth. He pulled out a second, looked at the doctor, saw him nod. Only then did he break the seal between their hands and pat down his trousers in search of some matches.

They smoked, each lost in his own thoughts. Halfway through his cigarette, Otto opened a bottle of beer. They passed it back and forth. When Beer finally turned to leave, it must have been past midnight. There remained precious little time.

'One last thing,' said Otto, as he watched the doctor step through the door. 'Last night, when I reached for the beer. After we'd thrown him out the window.'

He mimed the event, lifting Teuben's body against the pivot of the invisible window frame. Even in so casual a gesture he was able to recall the event in all its details. His body told stories when he wasn't even trying.

'All the beer was poisoned, wasn't it? You were hoping that the detective would drink one. But he never opened his bottle. It fell out of his coat pocket.'

Beer gave a barely perceptible nod. One could hardly count it an admission. 'What does it matter now?' he asked.

'What did you plan on doing with the body?'

The doctor flashed a tired smile. 'I don't know.'

'You don't know?'

'Goodnight, Otto. See you at a quarter past four. Here, take my watch.'

He took it out of his pocket and passed it over.

Five minutes later he was back in his own flat. He wrote the letter first, leaving it unsigned, then gathered up whatever money was in the house. Lieschen was sleeping on her blankets. Her clothes were dirty, she had not changed them in days. They would have to do. Coming into Eva's room, he found himself hoping she was asleep. She was, but her sheet and clothes were wet with urine and he had no choice but to change her and wake her in the process. The green eyes stared at him as he bedded her head back into the pillow. Then he bent close to her, until their noses nearly touched.

'I lied to your brother just now,' he whispered to her. 'I told him there was a plan.'

They were so close, his smoke-and-beer breath reflected back on him. Perhaps it reminded her of Otto.

'There is no plan,' he whispered. 'I will ask Speckstein to look out for you. He's a doctor, after all. He, too, swore an oath.'

'All I can do now,' he whispered, 'is help the little girl. Make sure she gets away from here.

'It's a shame,' he whispered. 'I was going to teach you how to speak.'

He stayed there with Eva until it was time to wake Lieschen and get her ready for her journey to the Alps.

CHAPTER 8

Zuzka woke at four-thirty in the morning. She was still wearing her clothes. No sooner was she fully conscious of her surroundings than she started to pack. Her suitcase was on top of the wardrobe. She fetched it down, opened it, found the return ticket for the train that her father had bought her before she had set off for Vienna. Back then she had protested that she might not be back for years. Now she quickly stuffed it in her handbag. She packed her underwear and stockings, two of the blouses that she liked; the winter skirt and the fur-lined hat. Everything else could be sent after her, or replaced. Not once did she step to the window and look out. The yard was quiet. Other than that, she did not want to know.

By a quarter to five she was ready to go. All that remained was to say her farewells. Her first instinct was to write a note. She found a pen and paper, put together two or three lines, and left them on the seat of her wooden chair. Then it came to her that she was being rude. Her uncle was an early riser. There was a chance, at least, he would already be awake. She left the suitcase by the front door, slipped into her coat, then walked back through the flat to the big door that separated her uncle's apartment from the rest of the rooms. Her uncle's bedroom was to the right of the living room, opposite the study. She stepped up to the door (it was open a crack) hoping to see the light of his bedside lamp, but the room remained in total darkness. Through the gap came the noise of Speckstein's snore: not the regular, throaty breathing of a happy sleeper, but a desperate, gagging battle for air accompanied by an odd whinny. For a second it occurred to her that he was not alone in the room: that there was a man there, with his hands around her uncle's throat. She dismissed the thought as too fantastic. Some minutes later she had left the flat and was walking to Alserstrasse with her half-empty suitcase in her hand, hoping she would find a taxi that would drive her to the Westbahnhof.

CHAPTER 9

Otto and Lieschen arrived at the train station a little before five.

Over his back there was slung a dirty canvas bag. It held all his belongings. They had met Beer in the dark of the building's doorway, then rode the tram. At the entrance to the station a man with a handcart was selling hot rolls. Otto bought a half-dozen, and passed one on to the girl. They ate hastily, in silence.

Lieschen was holding on to the back of Otto's jacket. It was the doctor's doing. He had crouched down to throw a blanket around her shoulders like a shawl, then had taken her hand and clamped it firmly around the hem of Otto's coat. From that moment on, she hadn't let go. All through the tram ride she had stood behind him, sullen and watchful, clutching his coat. When he'd got off he had moved too fast for her, and she'd stumbled on the steps that led from tram to pavement. He had caught her by the elbow, put her back on her feet. And again she'd followed him in her crablike walk, one shoulder leading, her chin drawn low into her narrow chest.

468

All the while he was eating the rolls, Otto was weighing his options – weighing them not with the head, it was true, but weighing options nonetheless, his body mulling over the next step. Time and again, he stuck a hand in his pocket: touched the money Beer had given him, and the letter promising a fortune far beyond his ken. The girl clung to him, stifled his movements. When he lit up a cigarette, he almost caught her with the back of the hand that struck the match. She flinched, but she held on. They walked together, took a look at the platforms, the station abustle with passengers, porters, the bark of frightened dogs.

On platform number three there sat a woman on her little suitcase, stooped-over and miserable, a fur-lined hat covering her hair. She was young and well built, careless of posture; the skirt had caught upon the suitcase, revealed two shapely inches of calf. It wasn't until his eyes had rested on her for some moments that he recognised her as Zuzka. He stood and stared at her, then quickly turned around. An unaccustomed lump had risen to his throat that he knew to fight only with anger. He marched off, quickly, back into the station building, the girl running after him, trying to keep pace. Once inside the building, lost in the bustle of the crowd, he found an empty bench and sat down. The action forced Lieschen to let go. She looked at him in dismay, then clambered up next to him, kneeling on the bench's painted slats of wood. For the first time they were face to face. Otto wondered whether she had seen Zuzka. Perhaps he should run to the platform and pass the girl over, Beer's instructions be damned. He was surprised when she spoke to him, her fingers pulling at the dirty slats. She spoke quietly; breadcrumbs were sticking to one corner of her mouth. Otto had to lean forward to hear.

'The Herr Doktor told me that you took care of Eva,' Lieschen said. 'For a great many years, he said. Ever since she was a girl.'

He shrugged, then nodded, blew some snot past his thigh on to the ground.

'Yes.'

Gravely, not looking at him, the little brow creased, she offered him her hand, perhaps to thank him for the service rendered to his sister. He shook it, held it, stared in wonder at this little hunch-backed girl.

He was still holding Lieschen's hand when they boarded the six o'clock to Innsbruck. They sat in silence, his buttocks shaking with the engine's tremor, waiting for the station master's whistle to send them on their way.

CHAPTER 10

It was Frau Vesalius, not the police, who came for him the next morning. Almost despite himself, Beer had fallen asleep: had seen off the girl, then lain down next to Eva, eyes closed, holding her hand, and fallen asleep. When the bell rang and he ran to the door, there clung to him still a snatch of his dream: his wife in a smoking jacket, beating Teuben in a game of chess. Two painted fingernails, swooping down upon his queen. Beer opened the door, smiling a little, then turned around to check his kitchen clock.

It was a little after nine.

Beer had expected someone earlier; he thought it good of the Professor to give him warning before sending for the police. There was an odd agitation in the housekeeper's features that he had never observed in them before, but Beer was too preoccupied to pay it much heed. She gave him no time to wash his hands and face. 'You must come at once, at once,' she kept repeating, and ran ahead down the broad flight of stairs. When they reached the flat, he was surprised to see that she had left the door wide open. Nor did Vesalius bother to close it after them: she simply ran on, through the entrance to Speckstein's living room, and turned right into his bedroom without pausing to knock. The curtains were drawn and the room was lit only by the bedside lamp. Speckstein was in bed, half buried under blankets, the legs sprawled out at awkward angles. His eyes were open, frothy spit was dangling from his chin. In his struggle he had knocked over a glass of water on the nightstand; it had soaked through the pages of a leather-bound volume of Klopstock's verse.

'He usually rises early. I came in to look five minutes ago. Is he—?'

Beer jumped forward, found a pulse.

'He's had a stroke. Call an ambulance.'

Vesalius left the room, and Beer began talking to Speckstein, the reassuring, sober queries of his office. He was answered only by a moan.

The ambulance arrived after ten or twelve minutes. Beer was granted permission to ride along. At the hospital, he sat for an hour in the waiting room, then went outside to breakfast on a coffee and a salted bun. On his return, the chief physician agreed to see him. Gruffly, in the blunt shorthand used among colleagues, he confirmed that Speckstein had suffered a severe stroke. The right side was paralysed, he had lost the power of speech, and there was a possibility of brain damage. For now, he was to remain under observation. When asked whether he would contact the next of kin, Beer replied that he would entrust the task to Speckstein's housekeeper. The man nodded his agreement, then shook Beer's hand.

'Speckstein,' he said as he was leading the doctor out the door. 'Not the same Speckstein who raped that little girl some years ago?'

'He was acquitted,' Beer replied stiffly.

'Got away with it, eh? Well, now the chickens have come home to roost.'

He closed the door after Beer.

Outside, in the hospital gardens, the sun was shining. Beer bought a piece of pastry in the bakery across the street, then sat down upon one of the park benches, and stared up into the sky. At one point he started laughing and laughed so violently that he spat pastry crumbs all over his chest. He was thinking of a pair of painted fingernails, slowly converging upon the ivory features of a chiselled queen.

PART IV

WHISPERS, ECHOES

A sound wave is a longitudinal wave whose speed of diffusion through air at twenty degrees Celsius is approximately three hundred and forty-three metres per second. As it passes through air, molecular friction and related effects begin to absorb the sound until it leaves the range audible to human ears. If initiated within an enclosed space, the wave will be both reflected and absorbed by the enclosing walls, in proportions that depend on the walls' physical properties. Absorbent materials such as glass wool will convert the sound wave's energy into heat and have a dampening effect; polished concrete, by contrast, will bounce back the wave with minimal absorption and can, in specially designed spaces, be utilised to direct and focus the sound towards a specific place within the room. Individual objects whose natural frequency of vibration matches the frequency of the sound wave (or one of the wave frequencies belonging to its harmonic series) will absorb the wave's energy and register a corresponding increase of vibration in a process known as 'material resonance'; in specific cases this may lead to an amplification of the sound and/or to the destruction of said object. If the enclosed space within which the sound wave is released is connected to other enclosed spaces through a system of open pipes such as those found in ventilation and heating systems, the pipes' diameter is likely to match the amplitude of specific pitches of sound, and thus allow for their easy entry and transmission. In the case of cylindrical tubes this may result in their undistorted transmission across surprising distances.

CHAPTER 1

Professor Josef Hieronymus Speckstein did not recover his powers of speech. The right half of his body remained paralysed. After two days of near-total immobility, he summoned sufficient strength to reach for a pencil and a piece of paper left on his bedside table for that purpose, but his left hand was so shaky, and so unaccustomed to writing, that nobody could make any sense of his wild squiggles. Perhaps they were nothing but squiggles: it was possible he had lost a substantial part of his mental faculties. Faced with the nurse's incomprehension, he closed his eyes and whimpered like a dog.

Six days after his initial attack, Speckstein suffered a second, more violent stroke. Resuscitation was attempted but proved futile. The physician on duty did not reprimand the nurse when he overheard her telling her colleague that it was 'just as well the old pervert is dead'. He signed the death certificate at 4.57 in the morning. He had three more hours on his shift.

★   ★   ★

The funeral was splendid, if small. The *Gauleiter* and Mayor both sent flowers. Of the guests who had attended his party ten days previously, only Dr Anton Beer was present. The Professor's brother, Ernst, came by himself and left no sooner had he settled all formalities. He explained to the priest that his daughter was very sick; otherwise he would have come to sit with his brother during his final moments on this earth. They shook hands by the side of the fresh grave. In the air between them hung the winter's first snow.

Frau Vesalius was also present at the funeral. She is not reported to have cried. Some weeks after the ceremony, she was pleased to receive a letter from Speckstein's executor informing her that the deceased had left her a sizeable inheritance in his will. She opened the first bank account she had ever had, rented lodgings of her own, and indulged her taste for pastries to the full. Within three months she had put on fifteen pounds. They suited her. Her face filled out and lost some of its habitual sourness of demeanour.

CHAPTER 2

Zuzka arrived home to the news of her uncle's stroke. No sooner had he greeted his daughter than her father announced he must leave for Vienna the next morning. Zuzka's lungs had cleared up the hour she had left the city behind, but that very night the numbness in her lower body spread to such a degree that, by the early hours of the morning, she was no longer able to move either of her legs. Her father postponed the journey, then postponed it again when her health deteriorated further. A specialist was called in from Graz, who diagnosed a neurological disorder caused by an untreated infection. He was liberal in his abuse of 'whatever quack' had looked after her in Vienna, and gave detailed instructions to the young doctor who had recently opened a general practice in their neighbourhood. As for Zuzka's erstwhile shortness of breath, the specialist blamed an allergy, perhaps to mildew. When questioned, Zuzka remembered a patch of blackened wallpaper by the side of her bed.

★   ★   ★

Two months into Zuzka's treatment, the young doctor who looked after her suggested that her recent bouts of nausea had a cause other than her disease. Zuzka burst into tears when she received this item of news, and the young man sat by her bedside and held her hand in sympathy and consolation. When he went home that evening he carried with him the memory of her smile and the many glimpses of her naked flesh he had caught throughout the period of treatment. These confused him and he spent a sleepless night. In the morning, he spilled the hot cup of coffee his landlady had brought him and suffered an unpleasant burn on his inner thigh.

The next time the young doctor visited Zuzka, she confessed to him some details of the rape she had endured. He believed her. He wanted to believe: the doctor was not a handsome man. It took him all of three days to declare himself. They married in haste. Once her condition had become obvious, some wagging tongues in town claimed that the doctor had screwed her while she was too sick to object. Bride and groom stayed up late on their wedding night, playfully haggling over the unborn's future name.

CHAPTER 3

Otto and Lieschen made their way to Innsbruck, then on to Bregenz and Dornbirn. From there, the former mime boldly approached the border, but turned tail when he caught sight of the border guards, their holstered guns hanging from their belts. Unconvinced that his papers would pass muster, and unsure what story to tell them concerning the little girl, Otto moved south to Hohenems, where he made cautious enquiries about crossing the border by some other means. After a day of nervous questions, Otto found a farmer who agreed to smuggle them across in the back of his van. The man took his money and shook his hand. They ate well that night, pork sausage and mash, the girl smiling, chewing, one fist buried in the fabric of his coat.

On the night before their journey, they slept in the farmer's barn. Otto heard the police while they were still out in the yard. It was snowing outside. He sat up, pulled all the money from his pocket, and slipped it down the side of one sock. Next he tore up Beer's letter and stuffed the fragments in his mouth. He was still chewing paper when the farmer led the inspector up the ladder to the loft. Lieschen woke only when the policeman shook her by the leg. Otto bent to kiss her hair before being led off.

They were separated at once. Otto was questioned, his papers scrutinised. They wired to Innsbruck, then to Vienna, but neither his description nor his fingerprints matched anyone on their wanted list. Faced with the inspector's questions and threats, he stuck to silence. The only time he spoke was to deny that he had wished to go across the border. The farmer had quite simply misunderstood.

They put him in a cell and charged him with vagrancy. A policeman, posing as a fellow bum, was placed in the cell with him and instructed to pump Otto for information. The man's hands were dirty, but when he took off his shoes to sleep, Otto noticed that there was not a shred of dirt underneath his toenails. The next day, annoyed by the man's clumsy attempts to ingratiate himself, Otto broke his nose and shoulder by throwing him into the wall of their cell.

The regional court tried him for vagrancy, assault, and the carrying of forged identification papers. A biometric examination revealed him to be hereditarily tainted; legal records unearthed a prior conviction for assault. He went to a labour camp rather than prison. After nineteen months of incarceration, he was given the option of joining a penal military unit. By October that year, he was sitting in a trench outside Leningrad, a minute cog in the machinery of Operation Barbarossa.

Lieschen, meanwhile, had remained obstinately silent and was transferred to a Bregenz orphanage. On the night of her arrival, the train was delayed due to a derailing further up the line. Lieschen arrived too late to join the other children for their dinner, and was brought straight to the dormitory. The big room held about thirty cots. Each had a number. The blanket she was given scratched, and when she woke the next morning, a ring of girls had collected around her and were laughing and pointing at her hunchback.

In accordance with institutional policy Lieschen was tested for idiocy at the end of that week. The test was administered by a slim woman of fifty, her hair half hidden under a nurse's cap. Her face was wrinkled and drawn, but she had the most remarkable eyes, green and lively and kind. Lieschen was asked to answer a list of questions. The first of these read: 'Can you name the twelve months of the year?' The nurse cautioned her that it was of the utmost importance that she answer all the questions to the best of her abilities. But Lieschen just sat there, staring up into those eyes, and a shy, fleeting smile brushed over her lips.

CHAPTER 4

On the day of Speckstein's funeral, Dr Anton Beer ran into Yuu, the trumpeter, as the latter came walking into the building. Beer asked Yuu for a word. Their conversation was brief.

'You gave me up,' Beer complained.

'I'm a-fraid so.'

'Will you do it again?'

'I do-not like to med-dle.'

'You didn't seem to mind the first time.'

'I did-mind, Dr Beer. But I-was hung-ry and I nee-ded to find work.'

'Did Speckstein help you with that?'

'He gave-me a letter of intro-duc-tion. It-has proved use-ful.'

'For what it's worth, I did not kill him.'

Yuu bowed and brushed past him without another word.

That afternoon, Beer decided to teach Eva how to speak. One at a time, he held up the letters of the alphabet he had drawn on to pieces of cardboard, and instructed her to blink when he reached the one she wished to use. The idea had come to him several weeks previously, but he had put it into practice only with reluctance. Now he embarked on it methodically, going through the cards with great patience and then a second time, thinking that she might have missed a cue. But Eva just stared at him, big solemn eyes. After he had worked his way through the alphabet a third time, Beer gathered up the cards and left the room.

The next day Beer threw the hand-drawn letters in the bin. He did not mention them again.

Beer called his wife. Because he was afraid that all foreign calls were being monitored, he used a public telephone and called collect. A man answered and told him she was out. When he enquired whether a little girl had arrived along with his letter, the stranger told him she had not. He wrote to his wife that evening, and two weeks later received his wife's answer informing him that neither Otto nor Lieschen had made it through.

On the 3rd of January 1940, Eva died. It was a time of dark nights: a total blackout had been ordered for the city in anticipation of bombs that would not fall for another four years. Eva had caught the flu Beer had contracted over Christmas. She succumbed in a matter of days. He had never much cared for the phrase, but now he felt its comfort: 'She had lost all will to live.'

Getting rid of her body proved surprisingly easy. Beer claimed she was a vagrant whom he had found on his doorstep the previous night; by the time he had examined her, it was clear that there was no more need for an ambulance. There had been no identity card and nobody came to claim the body; one assumed she may have been a Jew. Many a colleague commended Beer's charity when he agreed to cover the funeral expenses.

Eva was buried on the 5th of January. Afterwards, stripping the bed, and flipping the mattress, Beer discovered underneath the iron bed-frame a bottle of beer that had rolled there on the night of Teuben's death. He sat on the floor, clutching the bottle in both his hands. It was only then that he allowed himself to weep.

All week he lay awake at night and listened to the sound of Eva walking up and down the flat. She never spoke to him. He spent many hours wishing that one day she would.

Beer took to drinking in a bar. Even so, he rarely got drunk. In November of 1940 he was sitting there, clutching a letter. He was joined at his table by a veteran of the Great War whose split-open skull had been mended with the help of a steel plate. They exchanged greetings, then drank their beers in silence. After a while, Beer started to cry. The man looked at him with interest.

'It's nothing,' Beer told him. 'I'm suffering from reminiscences.'

'What's that?'

'Nothing. Something I read. In a book that's now forbidden.'

The letter he was holding was his notice of conscription. He was to report to the barracks in Krems the next day at noon. When he locked up the door to his apartment early the next morning, he felt a weight shift from his shoulders. Behind the door a pair of naked feet walked steadily from bedroom to waiting room and back, a somnambulist's step, careless and light.

CHAPTER 5

Four months after the laundry boy's cast had come off, he was arrested for the attempted rape of a fifteen-year-old girl who was taking a walk in the Volksgarten at dusk. After a week spent in investigative custody he was let go again. The girl's account contained serious contradictions; it was discovered she was sexually active and had expected to meet a lover in the park. Police records indicated that the laundry boy had been investigated before but did not specify the charge. The two detectives who had dealt with his case were both dead. One had fallen out of a window, the other had died of cancer of the bowel.

In November of 1940, on the same day Dr Beer received his conscription notice, the laundry boy, too, was asked to present himself at the barracks in Krems. They met in the exercise yard. Neither of them acknowledged their acquaintance. Despite being described as belonging to 'inferior stock', the laundry boy soon distinguished himself as a soldier and was awarded the Iron Cross. He was

491

active in the eastern campaign and transferred to a special commando. His precise duties remain unknown.

CHAPTER 6

In the months from September 1939 to May 1940, the janitor spent an average of one night a week making sausages. Neurath supplied the meat, blood and intestines. The factory he was watching at night was adjacent to a knacker's yard. He was able to steal a few buckets' worth of meat a week. The janitor supplied the workspace. Theirs was a cottage industry, small-scale and inefficient. But the economics were simple. Meat had been rationed virtually from the beginning of the war. With increasing demand on the various fronts, and an increasing number of farm workers conscripted into the *Wehrmacht,* domestic supply would shrink. The janitor had seen it happen before: during the Great War, considerable profits had been made on the black market. The two men agreed to hoard their sausage until prices were at their peak. Only occasionally would they sell off a few pounds. Anton Beer received a kilo of pepper salami on Christmas Eve, in grateful acknowledgement of his discretion: he accepted the parcel while feverish with flu. Frau Vesalius bought ten marks' worth in November 1939 in order to supply her employer's party with sufficient food. Neurath took a pound or two along whenever he went whoring. The janitor traded sausages for schnapps. He had a nephew who had set up a still in his garden shed, and had contacts with a farmer who supplied him with potatoes and a little grain.

In the May of 1940, Neurath succumbed to pneumonia and died after protracted hospitalisation. With his death, the janitor's supply of animal matter dried up for good. By this time the two men had produced some four hundred kilos of horsemeat salami. They had stored them by suspending them from the beams of the janitor's workroom ceiling: a forest of sausages hanging like wind chimes across the expanse of the room. The janitor liked to walk among them, his shoulders brushing the waxed pieces of string they had used to tie off each length of gut, and savour the smell. In one corner stood the old bathtub they had used to mix the meat. In wistful moments, deep in his cups, he would sit in it and talk to the dog.

He dreamed of it sometimes. In his dreams the dog was always licking his hands. It had licked them when he'd given it the piece of liver he had spiked with arsenic, unperturbed by the strange taste. First though, he had fetched the knife; had cut the dog loose from where Speckstein had tied it up in the yard; had held on to the rope and led it down into his cellar; the old dog panting, struggling

494

to keep pace. On the stairs it had lost control of its bladder: crouched and pissed, joints so stiff it whimpered when it moved. Downstairs, in his workshop, on the old newspapers he had spread out upon the floor, it'd accepted the liver and licked his hands; shivered, fell over, the blind eye cloudy, rolling once between its red, infected lids. He had thought it dead, or dazed, and thought it best to cut its throat. He pricked it, fumbled, found the dog come back to life, its gap-toothed mouth clamping round the jacket he then wore. They fought like two men in a bar brawl, each struggling to pin the other with his weight. Only one of them had a knife. He thrust and slashed and then he hacked, found the soft side of the belly, dog guts spilling near his face. In his dream there rose the smell of dog shit, oozing, spreading, fresh from the tap. He wrapped the beast in an old blanket and carried it out like a bag of trash. A heave and a push sent it sailing over the gate into the Pollaks' abandoned yard. On the way back into the building, he ran into the trumpeter: his jacket torn and bloody from the fight. They passed each other without speaking. In his dreams, sometimes, the fat man smiled and put a cornet to his firm and puckered lips. A single note, high and bleating, it always whistled him awake. He would sit up then, raise his hand to his nose, and sniff it for the telltale smell of Walter.

★　★　★

In the spring of 1944, Frau Vesalius dropped by for a visit. She and the janitor had seen each other on and off, enough so as to remain friendly, and she wished to trade an old pocket watch for however much sausage the janitor would think it worth. When she came to call at his ground-floor flat – huffing a little, having grown stouter with the years – he received her in his undershirt and thrown-on trousers. He smelled of cigarettes and idleness; the rotten fumes of half-fermented wine. His workshop had long been converted into a bomb shelter. The remaining sausage was stored under his bed. They sat down at his kitchen table and he poured out two glasses from a clay bottle. It wasn't long before he complained of not being able to sleep.

'Why not?' she asked.

'I dream,' he answered, and told her about the dog.

She never even flinched. 'Why did you do it?' was all she wanted to know.

The janitor waved one hand in a gesture meant to encompass many things: the dog's rheumatic, painful stumbles; the telltale trail of urine that would follow its passage up and down the building's flights of stairs.

'It was old,' he said, 'and I was sick of cleaning.'

She shrugged, poured herself another glass of wine.

'You got away with it.'

He nodded. 'Yuu knew. And Beer. They never talked.'

'The doctor?'

'Yes. He came down here one morning and he knew everything. How I'd gone looking for Lieschen and found Grotter's body in his bedroom; left the front door open for someone else to call it in. First thing he says to me is this: "I know you killed the dog," he says. "Down here. In this very room." He said you heard it through your pipes.'

'My pipes?'

'Your radiator pipes. They lead back here. He said they carried up the sound.'

'Yes,' she smiled. 'I remember telling him that. But I had no idea. What else did he say?'

'Not much. All he wanted to know was did I have a bathtub full of blood? I showed him the workshop and he stood there, shaking his head. "Well," he said, "you scared the little girl." And then he left without another word.'

They drank some more, and the janitor sold Vesalius four pounds of sausage. On the way out, he held on to her hand and would not let her go.

'I still don't know what all that fuss was about,' he said, drunk and tired and defeated. 'After all – it was only a dog.'

'Yes,' she answered. 'It was only a dog.'

She pulled herself loose from his hand and stumbled drunkenly back into the street. Night was falling, and in the distance she heard the first of the air-raid sirens raise its howl at the moon.

She quickened her pace, hoping to arrive home before she'd have to take refuge in an unknown shelter, her feet slipping on the rain-slick cobbles, rushing, cursing, stumbling to be safe.

AUTHOR'S NOTE

Writing a book of fiction that is set in the past means entering into an awkward and often rather dysfunctional dialogue: between what was and what might have been; between the demands of veracity and the lure of drama; between the representative and the remarkable; between the grind of research and frenzied inspiration. For all the inaccuracies that litter the book, it was motivated by an earnest attempt to understand what it meant to live in the period and place I was writing about, and it is to this, the experience of my cast of 'ordinary Austrians', rather than to any specific body of facts that I attempted to be faithful. I can make no claim that I understand National Socialism. That would mean that I understand how a society could have produced camps designed to exterminate those who used to be neighbours, colleagues, teachers, doctors, plumbers, violinists. It seems important, however, to struggle towards understanding, which for me began with picturing a block of flats, filled with neighbours, colleagues, teachers, doctors, plumbers, violinists.

The story of *The Quiet Twin* is set in October and early November 1939. The book does not attempt to provide a precise account of these weeks and months. I have taken certain liberties with the weather, have ignored some key events such as the commencement of deportations of Jewish men, and introduced a spree of killings that has no precise equivalent in fact (even though a number of sensational murders did take place between April and September of that year). There are inaccuracies and slight anachronisms in my allusions to the procedures and pace of Austrian mobilisation. Thomas Mann's attendance of a 'spiritistic' seance took place some six or seven years prior to the point indicated in the novel (and not in Vienna), though other details are correct. The italicised sections that separate the various chapters are, with minor exceptions, accurate in their details. Some things, as the saying goes, are too strange to have been made up.

The secret murder of psychiatric patients and the physically handicapped known under the Nazi cypher 'T4' did not commence in earnest until the spring of 1940. It might be argued, therefore, that some of Anton Beer's and Otto Frei's worries are not only premature but anachronistic. The chief point, however, is that nothing was known for certain, least of all the timetable of mass murder. Beer, working in a psychiatric ward where the spirit of 'National Socialist medicine' was gaining ground, and Otto, witnessing the aggressive circulation of propaganda that sought to prejudice the population against the sick, might be forgiven for anticipating the implementation of the regime's homicidal policies. Forced sterilisations had long been taking place throughout the Reich.

The part of Vienna where the book is set has undergone significant architectural changes since the Second World War; the group of buildings I describe does not exist in this precise constellation. Even in the 1930s, courtyard workshops like Pollak's auto-repair shop were more typical of the second district, where they can be found to this day. The inhabitants of Vienna's apartment buildings often did display a startling sociological diversity; rich and (working) poor often lived in a proximity that would be highly unusual in modern-day Britain, the USA, or Canada, though somewhat less so in the cities of Central Europe. Windows that opened to the main street rather than the yard typically indicated more desirable living spaces.

One aspect of the specifically Austrian experience of National Socialism that the book fails to explore is the 'Austrofascist' regime that ruled the country in the years immediately prior to Austria's annexation by the German Reich. Some oblique reference to this fact is made by Teuben who indicates that some of Speckstein's authority derives from the fact that his membership of the Party dates from the years when it was declared illegal by the Austrofascist regime. I am hoping to address this theme in a future book.

All characters in this book are free inventions, which is to say an amalgam of figures I have met in my research and in real life, reimagined into the context of the story I was telling. Many of them are perfectly ordinary figures, though I have tried to resist the temptation to make them so ordinary as to reduce them to types: neither Beer, nor Zuzka, nor the drunken, nameless janitor are meant to represent anyone but themselves. If I have eschewed depicting the spiritual life of a dyed-in-the-wool Nazi ideologue, this should not be taken to imply that such people did not exist in 1930s Austria. My primary interest in this book belonged with the army of opportunists whose crimes were at times as grave in their consequences as those perpetrated by the true believers. Sixty-five years after the Second World War it is easy for most of us to convince ourselves that we could never have belonged amongst those who would have held wrong-headed beliefs; it is a more nagging question to wonder what one might have done in order to secure some modicum of social and material success.

As both Beer and Teuben remark, Speckstein is an unusual figure, and bears a somewhat unusual name. The question of how he, the disgraced Professor with aristocratic pretensions and Hapsburg nostalgia, a person, in short, who might as easily have been found amongst the (conservative, Christian, Austrofascist or Monarchistic) enemies of National Socialism as amongst its

502

ranks, ended up as a low-level functionary within the Party, will have to remain the subject of a separate narrative; it is not, however, a story that is any less plausible than any number of biographies of actual Party members who achieved a much higher rank than my fictional *Zellenwart*. It remains unclear to me whether the past is better explored through 'representative' figures or through those whose choices and fate surprise.

Physicians, a number of whom I count amongst my friends and family, will complain that Beer's mode of examination and therapeutic approach are unorthodox in some regards, and be dismayed at certain professional oversights (though they may allow me to remind them that surprising, at times inexplicable, oversights on the side of – tired, overworked, out-of-their-depth – physicians are a common enough occurrence). Anton Beer's understanding of the physics of sound is also not without flaws; like many others he has learned in school an inaccurate explanation for why the rhythm of soldiers' boots may destroy a bridge. In short, not all mistakes and inaccuracies that are to be found in this book are the direct result of my ignorance. For those that are, I am heartily sorry.